SOMETHING FOR NOTHING

Something for Nothing

A NOVEL BY

David Anthony

ALGONQUIN BOOKS OF CHAPEL HILL   2011

Published by
ALGONQUIN BOOKS OF CHAPEL HILL
Post Office Box 2225
Chapel Hill, North Carolina 27515-2225

a division of
WORKMAN PUBLISHING
225 Varick Street
New York, New York 10014

This is a work of fiction. While, as in all fiction, the literary perceptions
and insights are based on experience, all names, characters, places, and incidents
either are products of the author's imagination or are used fictitiously.

Library of Congress Cataloging-in-Publication Data
Anthony, David, [date]
Something for nothing : a novel / by David Anthony. — 1st ed.
p. cm.
ISBN 978-1-61620-022-0
1. Businessmen — Fiction.   2. Husbands — Fiction.   3. Business failures —
Fiction.   4. Thieves — Fiction.   5. Drug traffic — Fiction.   6. Social status —
Fiction.   7. Wealth — Fiction.   8. Murder — Fiction.   I. Title.
PS3601.N55583S66 2011

813'.6 — dc22   2010052419

10 9 8 7 6 5 4 3 2 1
First Edition

For Erin and Aidan

I had been getting something for nothing.
That only delayed the presentation of the bill. The bill always came.
That was one of the swell things you could count on.

—ERNEST HEMINGWAY, *The Sun Also Rises*

SOMETHING FOR NOTHING

ONE

CHAPTER ONE

Anton Radkovitch was a Jew, but Martin had hired him anyway—had hired him, in fact, for precisely this reason. Or at least this is what he'd been telling people for the past six months, ever since he'd offered him the job and fired one of his two full-time employees, along with a part-time secretary, to pay for the move.

"You know," he'd say, affecting what he thought was just the right sort of jokey, ironic tone. "He's got the thing with the money, and the bankers, and all that stuff."

Plus, he said to his wife and anyone else who'd listen, the guy had a degree from Stanford University. To Martin, this was nothing short of amazing. Martin had a two-year degree from Armstrong College, a shit business school in Berkeley, and it was hard for him to imagine breathing the rarefied air of the Stanford campus for four full years. He'd been there for the end-of-season football games between Cal and Stanford, and had always been impressed by the lush landscaping, the red mission-style tiled rooftops, and the curved, whitewashed stucco archways. You could always tell who the Stanford students were in the crowd, even when they weren't sitting in the student section. It wasn't the money—Martin knew plenty of people with money. It was that they really did seem smarter, keener, more aware than the people Martin knew.

Driving now through town, Monday morning, late, hurrying to get the kids to school, Martin thought about Ron Beaton, the full-time guy he'd fired in order to hire Radkovitch. They'd been good friends since second grade, and it hadn't been easy.

"You're *firing* me?" Beaton had asked. His voice had actually quavered, and when he stood up from his desk, fists clenched, Martin had thought for a second that Beaton was going to hit him. "For what? For being your best salesman? Jesus, Martin, I thought we were friends. There's something wrong with you, you know that?"

Later, when Martin told his wife Linda that Beaton had punched a hole in the wall and stormed out, maybe crying, he'd expected her to back him up—maybe even sympathize with him. But in fact she'd been just as disgusted with him as Beaton had been.

"You really are pathetic," she'd said, not looking at him, which was what she always did when she was genuinely mad at him. "Seriously. I mean it."

Martin had explained that he didn't have a choice, that business was bottoming out, and that this new guy was commissions only, so it was a huge savings. The second half of this wasn't true, of course. In fact Radkovitch was getting all of Beaton's salary and then some. That was the only way he could afford him. The guy had worked for Merrill Lynch—he had experience and connections. Plus, he was good-looking, and he had that jocklike way about him that people liked (he'd even played varsity tennis at Stanford). Guys like that cost money.

But the first half of what Martin said was definitely true. Anderson Aircrafts was in free-fall. He was the only dealer of used aircraft in the entire Bay Area, and for years things had been great. There were weeks when it seemed everyone wanted to come out to his little office at the Hayward airport and plunk down three or four thousand dollars for a used Cessna or maybe a Piper Cherokee. Sometimes they were the sort of rich guys you'd expect. The assholes who'd gone to Berkeley or USC twenty-five years ago, and who had the money and time to seek out a new hobby, one that seemed romantic but maybe a little less physically demanding now that they were middle-aged. There were plenty of buyers, though, who didn't fit that profile, who might wander in on a whim, asking to trade a car for part of the payment (which Martin was happy to do).

But then about six months ago the Arabs said no more oil, and now no one wanted to buy a plane that cost a million dollars a month for gas. Or maybe it was just that no one had any money anymore. Certainly the banks weren't signing off on loans the way they had even a year ago. Martin had read something in the *Chronicle* about how for years all the U.S. cash reserves had been pulled out of the country to pay for Vietnam and now for oil, and how even though Nixon was printing more and more money, it was basically disappearing. The details were lost on him, but he got the point. And he'd seen the pieces on the news about the Arabs and their palaces—he knew where the money was. It was buried in a big secret chamber somewhere in the desert, under the sand and the heat and the oil derricks, far away from desperate Americans like Martin Anderson.

Martin chuckled. What a fucking mess. Could things possibly get any worse?

"What's so funny?" his son Peter asked from the backseat of Martin's Cadillac (a sharp-looking 1972 Coup De Ville—he'd traded straight-up for a 1968 Cessna 210H Centurion). Peter was nine, but he acted both older and younger. He was writing in the notebook he'd been carrying around for a while now. It was some sort of diary he used for taking notes about everyone around him. He'd gotten the idea from a book about a kid who's a spy of some sort, and now he was driving everyone crazy with his snooping and scribbling.

"Nothing," Martin said.

"He's laughing at the people in the gas lines," his daughter Sarah said. "We've got gas in our tank and they don't."

Her voice was flat, but Martin heard the irony behind it, recognized it as her new way of talking. You're an ass, and I know it, the tone said. Thirteen years old. Eighth grade. Trouble. She was wearing a yellow shirt held on by straps that tied behind her neck, so that her shoulders and her arms were bare. A halter top, Linda had called it. She was also wearing a too short skirt made out of denim that was frayed at the bottom. She was in the front seat, with him, but was turned away, looking out the window. This was the most he'd heard her speak in weeks, practically, except when she was on the phone, talking to her girlfriends—or, sometimes, to the boys who were starting to call (he could tell by the set of her voice). He remembered how, not long ago, she'd been obsessed with saving gas stamps for the set of tinted drinking glasses the Gulf station was giving away. Now she couldn't be less interested in something like that, and now the Gulf station didn't give anything away, anyway.

But she was right—it was a Friday, and so the lines were huge. It was the thirtieth, so only people with even-numbered plates could pump gas. And they could only pump five gallons or ten dollars' worth, whichever came first. All through town, lines snaked out of gas stations and onto the road, with the cars in line pulled over to the side. Some of the lines were really long. Most people had their engines running, probably because they still had half a tank, and you couldn't fill up if you had half a tank or more—you had to burn up gas to get gas. Everyone looked stressed out.

He saw a couple of people he recognized and was tempted to give them a quick honk, maybe a sympathetic wave. But he knew Sarah would suspect him of gloating—she'd interpret his wave as one that really said "you're screwed." And of course she'd be right, or at least half right. Because the truth was that he could pump his own gas, out at the airport; he didn't need to put up with the misery of the cattle lines. At first he'd kept a low profile about this, but lately he'd been dropping hints about it here and there. He knew he'd regret it—already he'd gotten a few weekend phone calls from people offering to pay double or take him to dinner—but he couldn't help himself.

He pulled into the drop-off circle at Sarah's junior high school. Lots of tall, shady oak trees and a big happy rainbow painted on a wall in front. But it didn't take an expert to figure out that the school was dysfunctional. A couple of the classrooms faced outward toward the parking lot, and in each window there were tangled, broken blinds hanging at skewed angles. Martin was pretty sure that the blinds matched the chaos of the classes. Kids walking in and out, stoned and giggling, ignoring the teacher. And he knew what the teachers were like—either some tired old lady, or some young guy trying to be pals with the kids to make up for having been a lonely outcast when he was a teenager.

It had been Martin's idea to move out to the suburbs from Oakland. That was about three years ago. He'd pushed for the move mainly for "the schools"—the code for the race issue in places like Oakland. But this wasn't cutting it. Yes, the elementary school seemed pretty solid (and as a bonus, a couple of the female teachers were fantastic looking; several times Martin had popped into Peter's fourth-grade class just to check out this year's perky twenty-seven-year-old and her short dresses). And yes, they'd heard that the high school was supposed to be wonderful. That was the word: "wonderful." But everyone seemed to agree that success in the high school required surviving the junior high. It was as if the junior high were a ship that sank a few hundred yards off shore every year, buffeted by gale force winds and huge waves. The goal was to swim to shore or, better, get into one of the few life rafts. But inevitably, some didn't make it. Martin pictured Sarah flailing against the storm surge, buoyed by a life jacket but for the most part helpless against an angry ocean. She might survive and make it to shore, but, he felt, she was going to be too weak to make it any further.

"Okay, bye," Sarah said, slipping out of the car.

"Hey," Martin yelled to her before she could slam the door shut.

She stopped and looked at him, but everything about her was leaning away from the car—her knees, her shoulders, even her feet.

"Have a good day," he said. He offered up a smile, but she just nodded and closed the car door.

Martin took a quick look back at Peter, but he had his head in his notebook. He was about to turn the wheel and drive off when someone slapped the roof of his car and leaned in.

Fuck. It was Gary Roberts.

"Hey there, Martin," he said with a little chuckle. He looked back toward the rear of the car. "You're even-numbered. Looks like today's your fill-up day."

Roberts had been a local swimming legend—Olympic caliber, apparently. But now he and his wife owned a couple of the local Baskin-Robbinses. The ice cream was pretty good, but Martin couldn't stand talking to either Gary or his wife, especially as it was inevitable that they'd start yakking at him about their kids. Martin knew that their daughter was class secretary for Sarah's grade, or something like that, and got excellent grades. Their son, who was about Peter's age, was also an *A* student, and he was already a star swimmer (or so Roberts had told Martin). Both of Martin's kids got lousy grades. *C*'s and *D*'s, even in P.E. They were smart enough, but they couldn't be bothered, apparently. Sarah cut class all the time—probably, he knew, to smoke pot. Peter had a different set of problems. He was strange, fat, and didn't have any friends (though Martin wasn't ruling out drug problems for Peter in the near future). The saving grace was that both of Roberts's kids were homely. They had their dad's piggish little snout.

Martin looked at Roberts for a second, thinking. He had to lean away from him, both because he was wearing strong cologne and because he had a faint smell of rot on his breath.

"Actually, Gary, I don't need to do the gas lines," he said. "I've got a pump out at the airport. I just fill up out there."

He gave Roberts a pursed-lip smile, fake but amicable, gauging his expression. He knew he shouldn't have said anything, that Roberts was the town gossip, but it was worth it. Screw you, Martin thought. He glanced at Peter in the rearview mirror. He could tell he was listening.

Martin watched Sarah walk toward the far side of the main building, toward some bike racks. Where was she going? The bell had just sounded as they drove up, and he knew for a fact that her class wasn't over there, in the bike racks. There was a group of boys standing there, though, and they looked up and smiled as Sarah walked up to them.

Martin looked back at Roberts and saw that he was smiling appreciatively.

"So," he said to Martin. "Your own gas station. Nice."

Roberts had blond, receding hair and reddish-blond eyebrows. He didn't look like a swimming hero now. Fleshy, balding. And Martin saw, suddenly, that his lips were thick and splotchy. He wasn't just a creep, Martin decided. He was also disgusting.

"Hey," Roberts said, leaning in a tiny bit closer. More bad breath. "When're we gonna hook up for some salmon fishing? I know Brian would be thrilled. I think he'd love to spend some time with Peter. You bring the kids out with you sometimes, right?"

Roberts was referring to Martin's boat, a six-year-old, forty-six-foot Viking. Wood-hulled, a big below-deck cabin space, with a little living room area, a kitchenette, and a couple of beds up in the prow. He'd named it *By a Nose,* in reference to the racehorse he'd had at the time and that horse's penchant for close finishes (now he had a different horse, and this one seemed to like close races, too). The boat had cost him almost as much as his house—more than a thousand dollars a foot, Linda had pointed out. In fact, she'd been horrified when he'd bought it about two years ago.

"You've got a lot of toys, Martin," she'd said. "Let's see: racehorses, cabin up at Tahoe, and now a deep-sea fishing boat. Are you sure we can really afford all this?"

The honest answer (which he hadn't given her) was no. But he'd bought it anyway. He kept it in Jack London Square Marina, in Oakland, and when the salmon were running, he'd head out under the Golden Gate Bridge and past the Farallon Islands and catch the limit. Sometimes he'd bring back more, but more than once he'd been stopped by a game warden at the dock, and so he had to be careful, hide the extras down in the cabin, in a separate cooler. Sarah wasn't interested, but Peter loved it. He'd started baiting his own hook, and he wasn't squeamish about handling the fish once they reeled them in. Those were good days out there, even in crappy weather and even when they didn't catch anything. Martin wasn't sure, but he thought that the boat was starting to become a refuge for Peter—an escape from getting teased and bullied (or just plain ignored) at school. So even if Gary Roberts brought twenty gallons of Baskin-Robbins to the marina, there was no way in hell he and his jerk-off son would ever set foot on his boat.

"Listen," Martin said to Roberts, nodding. "The fish aren't running yet, but when they do . . . let's do it." Martin glanced in the rearview mirror; Peter made momentary eye contact with him, then looked back down at his notebook.

Roberts gave the top of Martin's car a slap and took a step back. "Gotta go," he said. "Delivery coming in from Berkeley at nine, if the traffic isn't too bad."

Martin nodded and gave Roberts a half wave. He wanted to say that there wouldn't be any traffic because no one had any gas, but he didn't want to extend the conversation even that far.

He turned forward one last time to watch Sarah. The sun was shining at an angle through his windshield, and it was hard to see her clearly. He certainly saw—again—that her skirt was too short. Even from this distance he could see that her tanned legs looked long and appealing, and he had a feeling that the junior high boys and even the male teachers would be checking her out all day long.

He also had a feeling she'd be getting high at some point during the day. Maybe more than once. For all he knew, she might not even make it to class. He and Linda had suspected this for a long time. Then, a couple of months ago, Linda had found a bag of pot in a hidden compartment in Sarah's purse. It was one of those things made out of an old pair of jeans; you undid the zipper to get to the secret compartment.

"Martin," Linda had said to him, holding the bag out toward him. "Look at this." From her expression, Martin had thought that it was going to be something genuinely awful—a bunch of pills, or a cut-off finger, even. But when he saw the little bundle of dried up, greenish-brown plant material, he'd been relieved. It was a problem, he knew that. But not an emergency.

Linda had felt differently, though, and soon Sarah was in drug-counseling class two nights a week at a high school a few towns over.

It was a family thing, and so they had to go with her; they even had to take Peter. There were films of heroin junkies retching in stairways; tough-love talks by cops and detectives and ex-addicts; counselors talking about opening the channels of communication in your family. It was a little crazy.

"So how do we know they're not using actors in those films?" he'd finally asked at one point. They were in the car, driving home, all four of them staring silently out the windows into the darkness.

Peter had laughed, and Martin could tell he'd scored points with Sarah. But Linda hadn't been amused.

"That's right, Martin," she'd said. "It's all a big joke. You're a comedian."

Martin apologized, but what he really felt was relief—he'd almost made the same joke right there in the classroom, in front of all the kids and parents. And he would have done it, except that a couple of the cops were a little intimidating. This was especially true of one of them. He was a detective—one of those plain-clothes guys, like on TV—and he'd shown them his bullet wounds from two separate shootings during drug raids in Oakland. Martin remembered him, because during a break the guy had stopped Peter and asked what he was reading. (It was *Baseball Stars of 1973*.) They were just out of earshot, and Martin saw that they talked for a couple of minutes.

Later, when he asked what they'd talked about, Peter just shrugged and said "The A's."

"What about them?"

"Just, you know, the playoffs and stuff."

"Did you tell him we went to a playoff game last year?" Martin asked.

"I don't know," Peter had said, his voice flat and hard to read. "I don't think so."

"Did you tell him we live right near Sal Bando?" Martin persisted. "That you've trick-or-treated at his house?"

Sal Bando was the third baseman and team captain for the A's. Martin's realtor had told him that Bando lived nearby when they were first looking at houses. He'd also mentioned that the A's catcher, Gene Tenace, lived somewhere in town as well. Bando's house was nice, but not incredibly nice. Like some other houses in the neighborhood, it had a Japanese theme. Sand pits and ponds and decorative wooden extensions on the arches of the roof. It even had one of those sit-on-the-floor dining-room-table things (or at least that's what the realtor had said).

Martin was pleased to realize that he was in the same income bracket as a guy like Sal Bando (though he was pretty sure Bando wasn't up to his eyeballs in debt like he was). Peter, though, was thrilled. He was obsessed with Bando and with the A's more generally. Walked the dog past Bando's house every day, wrote reports about the A's for school, listened to all their games on his little orange transistor radio.

Martin had never spoken with Bando, of course, and in fact he'd only caught a glimpse of him a few times. The first time he was by himself. It was as Martin was driving past, and Bando had just walked out his front door. Martin had seen him plenty of times on TV, and had even seen him a handful of times live, in games at the Oakland Coliseum. Here, though, because he didn't have his uniform on, he seemed bigger, somehow, than Martin realized. He really filled out his street clothes, that was for sure.

"He's a big motherfucker!" he'd said later on to Linda, giving over to his excitement. "I'll bet he's got a huge cock."

Linda had shushed him, motioning to indicate that the kids were in the house somewhere. But then, after a pause, she'd also laughed, which Martin liked—Linda could roll with the crude humor once in a while, even give a little back.

"He had nice shoes, too," Martin had also told her. "Alligator, I think. He was wearing light-brown slacks and some sort of short-sleeved shirt. He's got big arms. He's a big guy."

Martin's only regret about this sighting was that he'd made the mistake of slowing down a little too much to check him out. This made Bando turn to look at him, and when he did it was obvious what Martin was doing. But Martin didn't panic. He just gave him a little wave—"Hello, neighbor!"—and Bando did the same, his thick forearm and meaty hand raised in response.

More than once after this, Martin had fantasized about building on this encounter somehow. He'd read about the Brooklyn Dodgers—the way stars like Pee Wee Reese, Gil Hodges, and Duke Snider were just regular guys in the neighborhood near Ebbets Field, and he wondered if Bando was up for something like that. This wasn't Reggie Jackson, after all, who was a genuine superstar, and far too rich and flashy for Martin's neighborhood. Guys like Bando and Tenace, they were all right. He'd heard somewhere that they were the real enforcers in the dugout and the locker room, and it made sense. You didn't win the World Series, as the A's had done two years in a row, without a few guys keeping things in order. And look, Bando wasn't the team captain for nothing, right?

The scenario he thought about most often revolved around a fishing trip with Bando. Martin and Peter would swing by early, before it was even light, and they'd drive out to the marina, talking about Charlie Finley, the A's owner, and why he was an asshole. Martin would show Bando the ins and outs of deep-sea fishing, and then later, someone would snap a photo of the three of them—Martin and Peter and Sal Bando—once they were back on the dock, all of them sunburned and tired but their faces flushed with excitement because they'd caught their limit and had a great time. Peter would take the photo to school, watch the other kids shit their pants with jealousy. And Martin would frame it and put it up in his office—though he'd act like it was no big deal. The customers would eat it up, and even Radkovitch would be impressed.

MARTIN HURRIED TO DROP Peter off at school (no sign of his teacher today, unfortunately), and then hit the freeway. He was going to be late, he knew, but he tried to give over to it. He sighed audibly—heard himself do it and wondered if he did it more than he realized (Linda said he did it all the time).

Had they made a mistake in moving to the suburbs? Walnut Station and the other little suburban enclaves nestled east of Oakland and Berkeley were in a beautiful area, no doubt about it. All along the freeway it was open foothills, large stretches of tall grass, and patches of old oak trees. From what Martin had been told (by Sarah, as part of a seemingly endless series of reports on the Gold Rush era), Walnut Station had been a Pony Express stop for San Francisco and Sacramento; the word *station* was the giveaway, apparently. That was why the town council still maintained some of the original mid-nineteenth-century buildings at the center of town. Or at least the facades of the buildings. Wooden exteriors, swinging saloon doors, rail fences. The main building was The Miner's Hotel. Now, though, it was a restaurant and a bunch of antique shops. The council hired a blacksmith to heat up his forge on weekends and say "Howdy, folks!" when you walked past, and to show kids how to hammer something on his anvil.

Martin thought it ridiculous—embarrassing. Not to mention boring. And that was the real problem, wasn't it? Walnut Station had turned out to be hot, isolated, and boring. He hated to admit it (and he certainly wouldn't admit it to Linda), but the move was a bit of a bust.

Living in Oakland, he'd had a quick commute. Better, he was close to the track, and most of their friends lived nearby. Now it took forty-five minutes to get to work, and he spent half his time driving back and forth to see their old friends—mainly because they hadn't made any friends out here in the suburbs. He'd thought for a while that a couple down the street, the Weavers, might become friends. Hal Weaver had inherited a big steel plant in Antioch, or Pittsburg, or one of those crummy cities by the delta, and he and his absurdly good-looking wife Miriam liked to throw a lot of cocktail parties. But the friendship had fizzled out. Martin would see cars in the Weavers' driveway and in the street, maybe a few people on the stoop, and know that he and Linda had been blown off. Once, Hal had even given him a friendly wave as he drove past, as if it hadn't even occurred to him to feel guilty for not inviting them. Maybe next time! the wave seemed to say.

Hal was a pompous, drunken lout, and so missing out on a friendship with him was no loss. But Martin was genuinely disappointed that Miriam had backed away—was mortified, in fact, to think that it might have been his fault. And probably had been. He'd have a few drinks, and the next thing he knew he'd be fawning over her, staring at her dark hair and deep blue eyes or her breasts. Or, worse, he'd make suggestive jokes and then laugh too hard, grind the conversation to a halt.

Even Linda had noticed it. "You're making an ass of yourself," she'd said to him the last time they'd been over there. That was six or seven months ago. He still saw Miriam in her yard once in a while. He'd spot her on his way home from work and slow the car to a stop, roll down the window and say hello, chat her up a bit. He knew he seemed overeager, but he couldn't help himself. And it wasn't just that she was so attractive. No, the real issue was that she seemed so contained and so confident. She'd look at him, smiling in a vague sort of way, as if it amused her to know he was that interested, or that curious. It drove him crazy.

He'd found himself thinking about her more and more the past few months—ever since that last party, in fact. Or a specific two-minute slice of the party, that is. He'd asked to use the bathroom, and Miriam had walked him into the living room and pointed down the hall. When he came back out she was gone (it had taken him a little extra time—he'd been worried about the splashing sound his urine would make, and that had frozen him up, made him have to take a deep breath and relax). And so when he emerged from the bathroom, he was suddenly gripped with the sensation of being alone in Miriam Weaver's house. Or if not alone, then unobserved.

So he'd lingered. The party was going on outside, but from the hallway the voices and bursts of laughter (forced Walnut Station laughter, Martin thought) were muffled. There were some photos along the hallway, and he'd paused to glance at them. They were mostly of the kids, who were nice enough, actually (which was a triumph, given what a dickhead their dad was). These were all in color. Shots of them out hunting at their duck club, getting their first Communions at church, stuff like that. There were also some older, black-and-white photos, mostly of Miriam and Hal when they were younger, maybe when they were first married, or before that, even. There weren't any kids in the pictures, anyway. Martin had to admit that Hal looked kind of handsome; he was certainly thinner, and he had more hair. And of course Miriam looked really incredible. She was one of those people who looked right at the camera. Jesus, she really was good-looking. Could someone please explain how Hal Weaver had managed to land someone like this?

Looking at the pictures in the hallway had made Martin think about Miriam Weaver and her private world. What she sounded like when she talked to a close friend on the phone, or maybe the letters she'd written but never sent. Or what she thought about when no one was around and the house was quiet for a change—her fantasies, her fears, her secrets. Down the hallway was the master bedroom; he could see the edge of their bed, and a bunch of ties on a clothing rack. And a couple of pairs of Hal's shoes on the floor next to the rack. That was about it, though. And there wasn't any time to peek in and see the rest of the room—it was time to get back out onto the patio (he didn't want Miriam thinking he'd used the bathroom to take a dump, after all).

But his brief foray to the bathroom had made him curious. He wanted a chance to wander around, feel the atmosphere, and touch the things that made it her house. He hadn't asked himself why this was the case, and he didn't intend to—not if he could avoid it. He just knew it was something he had a surprisingly strong urge to do. Ever since then, he'd thought about it off and on—thought about Miriam, her house, how he could get back in there. He thought about stopping by when he knew no one was around except Miriam, say hello, just checking in. But he knew he didn't have the guts for that. And it wasn't what he wanted, not really. No, he just wanted to walk around in there when no one else was around. Okay, it was a little strange. But it had become a daydream place to which he'd sneak off, even while he was sitting talking to Linda and the kids at dinner, or when he was calling the banks and telling them payment was on the way (which it wasn't). He'd be talking, engaged and animated, but really he was imagining being in Miriam's house.

Martin flicked on the radio and willed himself not to think about Miriam Weaver. Within fifteen minutes he was driving through the Caldecott Tunnel, watching the lights flicker past. The kids always tried to hold their breath the whole way through. It was about a mile long, and even without traffic it took a minute or maybe a little more to get through it. Peter still hadn't managed it (the kid definitely needed to get some exercise).

He braked for a traffic backup, and turned off the radio (there wasn't any reception, only static). A middle-aged woman next to him in a white Mustang was fixing her hair in her rearview mirror. It looked like a wig. She probably had five or six of them in her bathroom at home, he thought, all lined up on Styrofoam heads and waiting—hoping—that they'd be chosen. "Let's see," she'd say. "I'm going to wear you to work, because my boss likes this look, and you later on tonight, for cocktails."

Martin could envision this because he himself had a toupee (that was what he called it, though Linda liked to tease him and call it a wig). In fact, he had his own line-up of three of those Styrofoam heads in his bedroom. They were on his bureau, each one crowned by a toupee with a slightly different style: shaggy, wavy, and clean-cut.

Shit, he thought. Was there an accident up ahead? He had a lot to deal with at work. A lot to worry about, that is. Radkovitch had stopped by the office on Thursday, which had surprised Martin. He was supposed to be out all week, pounding the pavement, working on loan possibilities. He hadn't met yet with the guys from the Wells Fargo loan office (one of them was a contact from Merrill, apparently), but he wanted to talk about a backup plan.

"A backup plan?" Martin had asked. "What the fuck are you talking about? I thought the Wells Fargo guy was your pal."

"I know, I know," Radkovitch said to him. "He is. But just listen." Martin heard the irritation in Radkovitch's voice, and it occurred to him that Radkovitch was getting a little tired of him. He'd been surprised by this realization.

"Fine," Martin said. "Fire away . . . I'm all ears."

Radkovitch nodded, and Martin was struck yet again by his looks. Lots of thick, dark, wavy hair, green eyes. And of course he was really built. Tall and lean. He looked like an athlete, is what it was, right down to the nice tan, and the telltale band of white skin that showed where he put a sweat band on his right wrist when he played tennis.

"Well," Radkovitch said. "I've been talking to the people who own the Buick dealership in Oakland. You know, the big place on Shattuck, near Fortieth Street?"

"Yeah," Martin said, looking out the big front window at Michael Ludwig as he washed down a plane. "Go on."

"Okay," Radkovitch said. "Well, the thing is, I heard through some contacts that they've been looking for a way to diversify. And I think Anderson Aircrafts is exactly the sort of business they'd be interested in right now. In fact, they are interested, Martin. I talked to them last week. It went well, all things considered."

It was a way to land on his feet, Radkovitch had explained. Essentially, it would be a kind of buyout. Martin could still run things, but in point of fact Anderson Aircrafts would be owned by the Buick guys. They'd been in business forever, and even though times were bad, their pockets were deep. They'd be fine, and so Martin would be fine, too.

Of course, things would be different. It wouldn't be like owning the place. He wouldn't get the big bucks or be able to do the creative tax write-offs. He'd get commissions on sales, maybe a salary for managing the office. And they, in turn, would cover Martin's debts. Which were considerable, Radkovitch reminded him. He'd have to sell the place at Tahoe, the boat, and probably the horse—definitely the horse. But his place in Walnut Station would be safe.

"It could be worse," he'd told Martin. "I think you should give it some thought."

Martin had thought about it, all right. He'd sat there, projecting forward to his new life as a thinly disguised car salesman—a job he'd actually had a long time ago, before starting Anderson Aircrafts. He knew the drill: lots of hours, kissing up to customers, scraping for commissions, working your ass off. Get up, drive to work, drive home. Maybe have a good week here and there. And no time off—or probably not. And what would he have to do, anyway? No race horse, no boat, no membership at the club. Jesus fucking Christ, he thought. Maybe, if he was lucky, he'd be able to save up and take the kids to Baskin-Robbins and see fucking Gary Roberts once in a while.

Traffic in the tunnel started moving again, and soon enough Martin was driving through Hayward, almost at the airport and work. It was still overcast on the bay side of the hills, and much cooler. There were lots of gas lines here, as well. A couple of signs even read NO GAS.

He pulled over at Nelda's, the local diner near the airport, and bought a cup of coffee and some donuts—scarfed a couple down right there, put the rest in a bag for later. He'd give a couple to Ludwig. Then he walked over to the news shop next door to get the *Daily Racing Form*. He wanted to try for a few of the later races today at Golden Gate Fields, especially to see this one horse he'd been hearing about, Big Bad Wolf. Adrian Carmine, a hotshot jockey from L.A., was riding him, and he wanted to put some money on him. If there weren't any potential buyers coming by, why hang around? On Wednesday a guy in a white 240Z had stopped in and asked to set up a test flight for Monday morning—today. He'd even talked about trade-in value on the Z, which was usually a good sign. But something about the guy had made Martin think he was full of shit.

The other reason for going to the track—let's face it, *the* reason—was that he knew he needed to check in with Val Desmond, the trainer for his current horse, Temperature's Rising. He was running in the big stakes race out at the county fair on the Fourth of July. It was the main event of the year, and Martin was excited—thrilled—that a horse of his had made it into the race. Temperature's Rising was the third horse Martin had owned, and Val had trained all of them. The first two had been only okay, but Temperature's Rising was the real deal (for a local horse, at least).

Martin was also worried, though, because he'd been avoiding the messages Val had been leaving for him the past month or so. And, he knew, these weren't calls about the billing statements Val had been sending. (Martin didn't even know how much he owed anymore, couldn't bear to open the envelopes.) No, they were calls about the money Martin had borrowed from him. It was a lot of money. But what choice had he had? Penalties for back taxes; behind on the business loan; late on the bills for the Viking (he'd actually slept on the boat for a week to make sure some repo guy didn't snatch it before the check cleared); and of course there were the gambling debts. Too many calls to the bookie, too many trips to the track, and too many day flights up to Reno. This had all scared the shit out of him, and he'd turned to Val out of desperation.

Val and Martin had gotten close in the five years or so since Martin had hired him as the trainer for Gunpowder, his first horse. But he wasn't quite what you'd call a friend . . . or not a good friend, anyway. He was a little too intense, maybe even a little scary. And now Martin had proof of this scariness. Val hadn't threatened him—not unless you considered his recent offer to Martin a threat of some sort. He had a plan, he'd told Martin, something to "pull you out of the fucking hole you're in."

It was a straightforward proposition: fly down to Mexico, pick up shipments of heroin, and fly them back up to the Bay Area. Val said he'd give him five thousand dollars per flight. About one per month, he said. "For about a year. And then we're done. The guys who stay in it for too long, they're the ones who get caught."

As a start-up bonus, he'd forgive Martin half his debt, which now was well over eighty thousand dollars.

"You gotta admit, Martin," he said. "That's a pretty good deal."

Martin had thought he was joking, that this was Val's way of letting him know that he'd better figure out a way to pay him back, and fast. But Val wasn't really the sort of guy who joked around much. And when he kept looking at Martin and didn't smile, just raised his eyebrows, serious, waiting for a reaction, Martin realized that it wasn't a joke at all. Instead (and this was something Martin had thought later on, as he was driving home, reeling, trying not to steer right off the freeway), Val's calm expression was one that said "Now you know."

He'd only done it a few times so far, he said to Martin. Five or six. And it had been a while.

"It was when we were in Tijuana for some races," he said. "We drove it up in the trailers. It was mixed in with the hay. Besides, my connection down there had some contacts at the border, so we really just got waved through."

But Val went on to tell him about how in the past six months Nixon had issued orders for stepped-up border security, and that now it was too fucking risky to drive. People were getting caught left and right.

"It doesn't matter how many bribes you pay, or if you hide the shit in your car door or in a fake gas tank or wherever." They had dogs that would sniff it out, he said. Or they'd just randomly stop you and search your car, take it apart, find your dope, and lock you up.

But a plane was perfect. You could fly at night; you'd be invisible. You could haul lots of it. And there was nice money to be made.

Val had given him a vague account of how he'd gotten into it, something about some horse clients who were from Mexico, an old family with connections. Ramirez, or something like that. He was a horse breeder—he and Val had been working together for years. But Martin didn't press it. In fact, once he realized that Val was serious, and that some of Val's money was in fact drug money (that was the term, *drug money*), Martin had gotten quieter, thinking about the various questions Val had been asking him for the past few months about small craft planes. How far can you fly on a tank of gas in one of those things? How much weight does a light aircraft hold? And how regulated is small plane flight, anyway?

Yep, Martin thought as he walked toward his car, sipping from his coffee. Now I know.

But he also knew that it had been two weeks since Val had approached him, and that it was time to make a decision. In fact, Val had given this week as a deadline: no later than Monday or Tuesday.

"Just tell him I need an answer," he'd said to Ludwig when he called the office on Friday. "Yes or no. Tell him to use one of those skywriting planes if he doesn't want to talk to me."

Ludwig had asked what Val was talking about. "He sounded kind of pissed off," he said. Martin had told him that it was about whether or not to enter Temperature's Rising in a race down in Southern California, but he could tell that Ludwig wasn't really buying it.

Martin set his coffee, the *Racing Form,* and the donuts on a news box (as usual, the *Chronicle* had headlines about Nixon, gas lines, and Patty Hearst). He fished his car keys out of his pants pocket. He heard the sound of a plane engine and looked up. It looked like a Cessna 177, and it was gaining altitude as it moved off inland, to the east. Even from where he was, Martin could tell it wasn't one of his planes, but he wondered where it was going.

Huh, Martin thought. Maybe it's a sign.

But a sign of what? He wished he knew, because he still hadn't decided what he was going to say to Val.

CHAPTER TWO

By two-thirty Martin and Ludwig were in Martin's Cadillac, zipping north along the freeway toward Golden Gate Fields. The clouds hadn't cleared and you could feel the fog closing in, but it was still a nice day. The high couldn't have been more than sixty-five degrees, which to Martin was amazing, because he knew that just over the hills it was probably eighty.

The guy with the 240Z had been a no-show, and Martin had worked all morning to contain his frustration.

"Fucking guy," he'd said, over and over, sometimes to Ludwig, sometimes just to himself in a mumbled mantra. He remembered the feeling from his days at the car dealership, and he didn't like it. Some people just got off on acting as if they really were interested in making a big-ticket purchase, as if they really had that kind of money. Not for the first time, Martin wondered if these pretend buyers knew when they woke up in the morning what they were going to do.

"I'll be back in a while," a guy might say to his wife in the morning. "I'm going into town to act like I can buy something expensive."

"Okay, honey," she might say. "Make sure and get their hopes up."

"Oh, don't worry," the guy would answer with a laugh. "I will."

Martin had wanted to bail out before lunch, but he and Ludwig had ended up washing a few planes, playing cards, and then working through the listings in the *Racing Form* for Golden Gate Fields. Finally, though, Martin couldn't stand it anymore, and he'd talked Ludwig into closing up and going to the track with him.

"Hey," Ludwig said as they drove along the freeway. "Guess what I saw over the weekend? What movie, I mean." He had the passenger window down, and his shaggy hair was blowing in the wind. That was his new look—longish hair, sneakers, and jeans with a dress shirt. It was driving Martin crazy. Who was going to buy something from a slob? Martin always wore slacks, jacket, and nice shoes. You had to look sharp.

"I don't know," Martin said, shrugging. "*The Exorcist*."

"No," Ludwig said, shaking his head. "I did see that a while ago, though. It scared the shit out of me."

"Yeah, well," Martin said. "I saw it last weekend. And the weekend before that. Because I live with my daughter. She's possessed by the devil, just like the girl in the movie. She spins her head around and everything." Martin wished he could surprise Ludwig and actually spin his head 360 degrees for effect, but he settled for 90, moving his head right and then left in a simulation of a complete rotation.

Ludwig laughed and nodded. "You need to hire a priest and do the exorcism thing."

Martin shook his head, letting him know the weight of his burden. "No shit I do," he said.

Ludwig had listened to Martin complain about Sarah for the past year or so, about the drugs, the sullen anger, the older boyfriends with driver's licenses. Ludwig was thirty-eight and twice divorced, but he didn't have any kids. He seemed pretty much thrilled with this fact. He was an okay-looking guy, always had a girlfriend. Martin was glad he had his kids, but he did envy Ludwig's freedom. Get up in the morning, no one to worry about but yourself. He didn't necessarily want it, but it sounded all right sometimes. Especially lately.

"Anyway, no," Ludwig said. "Not *The Exorcist*. I saw *Westworld*. You know . . . the one with Yul Brynner as a robot cowboy? It came out last year, but it was playing in Oakland, at the Grand Lake. It was pretty good. It was great, actually."

"Sure," Martin said. He signaled, then switched lanes and pulled around some guy creeping along at sixty in his station wagon. "Yul Brynner gets his face blown off, but keeps coming after the main guy anyway, right? I remember that."

In fact, he remembered the night he'd seen it. He'd been under the impression that it was going to be a straightforward western. Probably not quite like *The Searchers* or *Red River* (good films, though a little dated), but maybe sort of like *Butch Cassidy and the Sundance Kid* (a great film). So he'd taken both kids—a night out with dad. But of course it turned out to be a crazy sci-fi thing, with tourists visiting a futuristic theme park. There were different "worlds" that you could go to: MedievalWorld, WesternWorld, and so on. They were utterly authentic, down to the last detail. And most important, each world was inhabited by robots that played the part of the citizens of that particular place and time. So in MedievalWorld you could have sword fights with robot knights and barbarians, and in WesternWorld you could have gunfights with robot gunslingers. But because it was a fantasy thing, you always won. You always drew your gun or swung your sword a little faster. And, better, as the customer you got to have sex with the female robots of the "world" you were in. He remembered sitting there in the movie theater, imagining himself in a fantasy world like the one in the film. It sounded pretty good—except for the end, where the Yul Brynner robot turned on the humans and started gunning them down. That was a problem.

"So you've seen it," Ludwig said, clearly pleased. "Good. Except Yul Brynner doesn't get his face blown off. What happens is that the main guy throws acid in his face. But yeah, it's the guy versus the robot. Man confronting his technological hubris. You know—the whole Frankenstein thing. It's actually a critique of the guys that go to Westworld. Our whole society, our belief that we can do or have anything we want. That we can play God."

Martin nodded, not really following. He checked his rearview mirror, looking to see if a cop might be sneaking up on them. He couldn't afford another ticket. Then he glanced at Ludwig. He suspected that his comment about Frankenstein and hubris were basically quotations from his girlfriend, Jenny. She'd studied movies over at UC Berkeley (where you could get a degree in anything, it seemed). Now she was a secretary or an advisor or something on campus. She was constantly making references to films and books, and always talking about how capitalism was undermining the human condition, political oppression, blah, blah, blah. Is this what they talked about over there? No wonder that school was so crazy, with the protests and the rest of that shit. Martin and Linda had gone out to dinner with them a few times, and it was always the same thing. It was incredibly tedious. He wondered how Ludwig could put up with it. She wasn't bad-looking, but still.

Just a few weeks ago they'd been roped into meeting in San Francisco, at Vanessi's, the old Italian place on Broadway with big, high-back booths and photos all over the walls of Italian celebrities who'd been there. They'd gotten into a discussion about Martin's daughter and her drug bust. Martin tried to blow it off, didn't want to get into it, but Jenny had been like a dog with a bone, wouldn't let it go.

"It's a cry for help," she'd said. "That purse, that secret compartment . . . you know what that is, don't you?" She'd looked around at them, incredulous. "It's a projected vaginal space," she'd said, as if it were the most obvious thing in the world. "She's putting drugs there, hiding them, but really she's saying that her sexuality is like a contraband substance. That it's something she feels is illegal. Or illicit. I'm not kidding."

Martin hadn't known what the fuck she was talking about (something he repeated over and over to Linda as they drove home across the Bay Bridge), but he'd managed to resist the urge to throw his drink in her face. He knew it was some women's lib shit, and that she felt pretty good about herself. And that she was drunk, as usual. He and Linda had exchanged glances (and Martin had sent a few glances Ludwig's way as well), but he let it go. Why bother?

"Hey," Ludwig said, breaking the momentary silence. They were about halfway to the track. "I know how we can make some money."

"Okay," Martin said. "Now you're talking. Let's hear it."

"Well," Ludwig said. "What about something like the *Westworld* thing? But something where people can get money? Or steal it? You know, a pretend thing. We set it up, and they pay us lots of money. But not with robots. I mean something more realistic, like with actors. The actors play along, let you call the shots, but it feels really real, you know what I mean?"

Martin looked over at him, then back at the road. "Like what?" he asked.

"Well," Ludwig said. "I don't know. What about a fantasy thing, like in *Westworld,* but where you rob a bank? Or where you pull off a jewelry-store heist? Maybe even a liquor store. It doesn't matter. It's just, you know, a robbery camp. You get to plan it out, do the robbery, the whole thing. The camp takes like three days. Or maybe it's a week. I don't know. But you sign up, pay your money and everything, and you get to plan and do a robbery of some sort. With some other people. But the catch is that it might not work. You've gotta do it right or the cops'll get you. And maybe, if you do a really good job, if you don't get caught or whatever, you get some kind of prize, or some actual money."

Martin nodded. It was silly, of course, but funny and interesting just the same. He knew—or was pretty sure, anyway—that Ludwig wasn't serious. Not seriously serious, anyway.

"Like Patty Hearst," he said.

"Yes!" Ludwig said, hitting the dashboard with his palm. "That's it! Patty Hearst meets Yul Brynner. Think about it! It's brilliant."

Martin pictured himself charging into a bank, clutching a machine gun, jumping up on a table, maybe shooting off a few rounds to get people's attention.

"Everybody down on the ground!" he'd yell. Loud—really loud. "Keep your fucking hands where I can see them!"

He'd always wanted to do something like that. Scare the shit out of everyone, send them sprawling, cowering. Maybe Ludwig was onto something. He thought about the security-camera pictures of Patty Hearst on the news and in the papers (which was ironic, because her father owned the *Examiner*). They were the images of her in the Hibernia Bank she and her nut-job SLA crew had robbed in San Francisco. She was holding a machine gun and it looked like she was shouting orders at the customers and employees (the gun was an M-1 carbine, he'd read, though he wasn't sure why he remembered this random detail).

"Do you think that's why she joined the SLA?" Martin asked. He switched lanes again. Why did people drive so slowly?

"What?' Ludwig asked, clearly not following him.

"Patty Hearst," Martin said. "Do you think she joined the SLA for that kind of thing? For the excitement? You know, to show everyone she was in charge, and they'd better listen and do what she says."

"I don't know," Ludwig said. "But I think I'm onto something. It could work. You might be surprised. All we need is some start-up money."

"Yep," Martin said, his mood changing. "All we need is a little bit of money."

They were quiet for a while after that, lost in thought as they sped down the highway. Martin thought about money and how he didn't have any. He assumed that's what Ludwig was thinking about, too. But maybe not. Maybe he was thinking about his BankRobberyWorld. Or Patty Hearst. Maybe he was imagining meeting her in secret. She'd be in disguise, sick of the SLA freaks and desperate for help. Martin could see the two of them, huddled in some restaurant and plotting how to steal a plane from Martin and fly away to Canada or some other safe country, one beyond the reach of U.S. law. Eventually (because now of course it was Martin's fantasy), she'd make contact with her father. In turn her father the newspaper tycoon would pay Martin for his airplane, and then, knowing a good thing when he saw it, he'd invest in Martin's business. Martin, for his part, would forgive Ludwig for his rash move—mainly, he would tell him, because he understood the impulse. And because he understood Patty Hearst's own motives a few months ago, when she pulled her gun out and yelled for everyone to do as she told them, that it was a bank robbery. Because this wasn't something that had happened in a fantasy world. She'd really done it, and that was a different matter altogether.

Yes, he thought as he parked the car. That was worth thinking about.

ONCE THEY'D PASSED THROUGH the big front entrance, they were greeted by the familiar smell of cigarettes and spilled beer. The guy on the P.A. system was making his prerace announcement ("Ten minutes till post time"), and the usual crowd was milling around. It was kind of an older crowd—middle-aged and up. Later on in the evening, some younger types would filter in, a couple of guys out for some fun, maybe with their dates. But for the most part the twenty-somethings weren't coming to the track these days, and certainly not the way they had when Martin was that age. Now, especially in Berkeley (or Albany, which was where the track was located, at least technically), horseracing was dated. That's all there was to it. The younger set that did come to the track were probably doing it on a lark—frat guys from the university, that kind of thing. Maybe they'd seen Secretariat winning the Triple Crown last year, had seen the highlights on the news, or had read about it in *Time* or *Sports Illustrated*. Or maybe they'd just seen that amazing photo of him coming down the stretch in the Belmont Stakes, the last race in the Triple Crown. Martin had cut it out of the *Chronicle* and taped it up by his desk for a while. Secretariat is in the foreground of the photo, and he's just off the rail, coming down the stretch. He's headed right for the camera, practically. But he's so far ahead—thirty-one lengths, it turns out—that Ron Turcotte, the jockey, is actually turning to glance over his shoulder at the rest of the pack. Looking at that photo, you get the sense that even Turcotte can't believe what he's seeing or what he's involved in. Martin remembered that after the Belmont win, Secretariat ran at Arlington with 1–20 odds. You had to bet twenty dollars to make one. But he won, of course, by nine lengths or something like that.

They recognized a few of the regulars—old guys shuffling around, a little lost, maybe a little too much to drink. Probably lonely. Ludwig made a point of saying hello to a couple of them, but Martin hung back and avoided looking them in the eye—mainly, he knew, because he was worried that this was the fate awaiting him. It might come sooner rather than later, he thought. Then the tables would be turned, and the younger guys he knew would pretend not to see him as he sat there mumbling to himself, writing shit down about odds and races on a scrap of paper with one of those little yellow pencils you got at the betting counter.

"Hey," Ludwig said. "I'm gonna place a couple of bets on the seventh and then grab a beer. Do you want anything?"

Martin shook his head. "No, thanks," he said. "And listen. I've gotta go downstairs and talk to Val, so how about if I track you down for the eighth race? That's the one I want to see. Down in the G section, where we usually sit."

Ludwig nodded and Martin watched him walk away. Ludwig was a sorry bettor, no doubt about it. But the good news was that he didn't seem to care. Like most people, he pretty much just read the odds listed in the *Racing Form* or on a Past Performance Sheet, and maybe glanced at the "expert" picks at the bottom of the page. He didn't think about weight carried, who the jockey and trainer were, distance, or (Martin's personal favorite) recent quarter-mile splits. (Secretariat had run the final quarter mile of the Derby in twenty-three seconds, which was really, genuinely phenomenal.) Occasionally Ludwig would go on a winning streak, and then he'd strut around like a peacock, acting like an expert. But more often than not he'd leave the track with empty pockets, usually having borrowed money to place a last bet. If they went out for drinks and dinner, Martin had to cover him.

Ludwig loved the track, though, you had to give him that. And it was this, more than anything, that had convinced Martin to keep Ludwig on instead of Beaton. Beaton was the better salesman, for sure; that, Martin knew, was why Beaton had been so angry when Martin had fired him and not Ludwig. But unlike Beaton, Ludwig shared Martin's passion for the track. It wasn't the horses themselves so much as the feeling you got just before and then during a race. He'd never been able to articulate it very precisely, but it had to do with the sense that so much effort and planning had all been boiled down and crystallized into a minute and a half or so of raw energy. Everything else dropped away, and you felt something completely different from what you experienced in your regular workaday world. Maybe that was it—the sense that when you were betting on a horse race, you were betting that the stars would align, and that you'd get to step inside a little pocket of time in which, for a minute or two, you were part of something that had come together in just the way you hoped it would. And if you owned the horse when that happened . . . well, that was something really special.

It was getting late in the day, and the floor was blanketed with discarded tickets. Golden Gate Fields printed tickets in a range of different colors—purple, yellow, green, blue—so by the end of the day, the floor was a big splash of color. Peter loved this. He'd crawl around on the floor, gathering them up by the dozens—by the hundreds, sometimes. Martin had mentioned the possibility that someone might mistakenly throw away a winning ticket, and the next thing he knew Peter was down on all fours, burrowing around, gathering all the tickets he could hold or shove into his pockets. He'd get filthy; aside from the tickets, the floor was covered with dirt and food and spilled drinks and cigarette butts. He'd never found a winner (though every so often Martin would pretend Peter had found one—would walk up to the betting window and act like he was cashing it in for a couple of bucks). But eventually Martin realized that Peter really just liked the tickets and the fact that they were so colorful.

"He's like a magpie," Martin always said. And though he thought it was a little weird, he didn't stop him, even when he got irritated looks from people who tripped over that strange kid on the floor. His son was having a good time, so those people could go fuck themselves.

Martin looked out at the big green-and-white board in the center of the infield, and saw that the seventh race was about to start. He was thinking about slapping down a hundred bucks on Big Bad Wolf in the eighth. Actually, he wanted to bet more. He was listed as 8–1 in the *Racing Form,* but Martin guessed it would go down as low as 6–1 or 5–1. Maybe lower. He'd run third his last time out, at Santa Anita, in a Grade 2 race, and he'd been second the time before that, at Bay Meadows. But both races had been longer than today's race—a mile instead of today's six furlongs. And in both races he'd been in the lead pack until the final turn, when he faded. Martin was sure that six furlongs was the ideal distance for him—that he'd be crossing the finish line in first place, just as he ran out of gas. And he'd heard that with Carmine handling him, his morning splits had been fantastic. It was obvious that this horse was due.

He jogged over to the betting area and found the shortest line. Charlene was at the window. She was at least sixty, but she tried to look thirty. She had tall, jet black hair, bright blue eye shadow, and heavily caked red lipstick. He'd placed bets with her before, but he usually did his best to avoid her window. She gave him the creeps.

"Hi there," Martin said. "A couple of bets for the eighth," he said.

She gave him a crinkly-eyed smile, then took a big drag on her cigarette and blew the smoke off to the side. He had a feeling she wanted to blow it right into his face.

"Okay," she said. "I'm ready when you are, big spender."

Martin took a deep breath and peeled off four crisp fifties. "Two hundred on the two horse to win," he said. It felt good. Yes, he'd planned on only betting a hundred dollars, but what the hell. He was going to win, and he knew it. Sometimes you could just feel it.

Next he put Big Bad Wolf into an exacta with High and Mighty, who was drawing 9–1 odds (down from 12–1, but that was all right). He put fifty dollars on this, and boxed it, so he paid a hundred dollars. Two more fifties—boom, boom. So any combo of Big Bad Wolf and High and Mighty at one–two would be a winner. If he got both the win and the exacta, he'd make some serious money.

THE STABLES WERE IN a separate building. You could only get from the grandstand to the horses through a tunnel that ran underground. But Martin knew the way, and the big security guy with the Golden Gate Fields jacket waved him through the double doors. Martin liked that. He didn't have an official track pass, but he liked being able to move around freely, to get access to the insider places. He ought to get something for all the money he'd plunked down here over the years, right?

The stable smell hit him the second he walked through the door— horse manure and hay. He could tell that the horses were alert, tensed up, maybe excited. They knew they were going to race. A few neighed or made that blowing sound with their lips as he walked past. He tried to remember what that was called. Chuffing? Did horses chuff? He wasn't sure.

A couple of jockeys were milling around, lithe and colorful and maybe a little goofy in their racing gear. He was struck as always by how small they were—120 pounds at the most. Peter was heavier than that (though he was fat, of course). The first time Martin took him down to the stables, a few years ago now, Peter got scared. He saw that he was about the same size as the jockeys, and thought he was going to have to ride their horse in an actual race.

Off in the distance he heard the seventh race start up. Val was over in the paddocks area, standing with a guy Martin had met a couple of times. A big shot. He had a bunch of horses—three or four, at least. The guy was about Martin's age, but he was loaded. Some sort of commercial real estate thing.

Martin could hear the announcer rattling off names during the race, and he could hear the crowd cheering, but he couldn't make anything out clearly.

Val looked over and gave him a quick nod. Martin hesitated—didn't want to interrupt—but then Val broke away from the guy and walked over. He put a hand out to shake Martin's and put the other hand on his shoulder. He was a good-size guy, with thick hands and a big nose. Slightly receding black hair, kind of bad teeth, not great skin. A few pockmarks. But also handsome in a rugged kind of way. He was wearing khaki pants and a maroon sweater, with a yellow collared shirt underneath. Not a great look. In fact, Val Desmond was a pretty lousy dresser. Maybe it was a requirement when you were a trainer. Maybe if your trainer looked too sharp, it was a problem.

"Martin Anderson," he said. "My long-lost client. Good to see you."

Martin nodded. He told himself to maintain eye contact with Val (which, he realized, was exactly what he told Peter to do when he was talking to his supposedly scary P.E. teacher, Mr. Richards).

"So Val," he said. He talked carefully—just like he'd rehearsed to himself earlier at work. "I've been thinking things over. About the plane runs and everything." He glanced around, to make sure no one was eavesdropping. "And so, yeah. I'm definitely interested."

Val raised his eyebrows, and folded his arms. His forearms were tanned and hairy.

"Definitely interested?" Val asked. "What does that mean? That doesn't sound like a yes."

Martin sighed. "For Christ's sake," he said. "What do you want me to say? One minute you're a horse trainer, and the next you're a fucking dope dealer. It's a little confusing."

"Look," Val said. He glanced around, then looked right at Martin, his eyes hard and serious. "I know what you mean. But I'm not a dope dealer. And who cares if I am? Because believe me, this is small time. I'm small time. I'm just out to make a few bucks—pay for the horses, pay off the house. You should see some of these guys. There's real money in this, you know. And besides, I'm just the guy who picks it up and delivers it to the real dealers. They pay me, and then they're the ones that get their hands dirty with all the shitbags that buy the stuff. But yeah, if you're gonna pay me to deliver it, I'll do it."

As he talked, Val began to exude that quiet, calm assurance of his. Previously this had been something Martin had liked and admired. It meant Val was a good horse trainer (or suggested it, anyway). Now, though, it seemed like it might mean something different. Martin wasn't sure what was different, exactly, but it was there. It was as if Val had been wearing a mask, one that was an exact replica of his face, down to the last detail, but a mask just the same. And now that the mask was off, his face (though it looked exactly the same in every detail) . . . well, now it was different somehow.

"So look," Val said, finally. "You've been ducking me for a while now, which is fine. It's a big decision."

He smiled, but then it faded.

"I think it's time to decide, Martin," he said. "What do you say?"

Martin felt a second slide by, and then two. But then he nodded, feeling suddenly impatient. "Look," he said. "I'm here, aren't I? I've thought about it. I'm all set. Count me in. Absolutely."

Val looked at him for a second, and Martin could tell that he was trying to read him.

"Are you sure?" he asked. "Because once you're in, it's like losing your virginity. You can't go back."

"Val," Martin said. "I'm sure. Really. I'm sure."

Val stood there for another long moment, then clapped him on the side of the shoulder with his fat right hand. Martin resisted the urge to wince. Val really was a strong guy.

They talked for a while. Or Val talked and Martin listened. But Martin's mind kept wandering. He posed questions to himself, and answered them just as quickly as they became thoughts. Do I really have the balls to do something like this? (Probably not). What's it like on the other side of the border? (Scary. Terrifying.). What will I say to Linda if she finds out? (I did it for you—a lie she'd throw back in his face so fast he'd have to duck.) And of course he asked the most basic question of all: What if I get caught? (I'm fucked.)

And that was that. They talked for another minute or so, with Val saying they'd make a run as soon as two weeks from now—that he'd have to make some calls and then phone Martin with details, have him come out to the house and pick up the money for the buy. And then Martin was retracing his steps through the underground hallway and back up to the main area.

As he walked he felt a strange elation. A burden had been lifted. He knew this feeling might change, and that he'd probably start to regret what he'd just done. But for now he was just glad the conversation with Val was over, and that he had a plan. He'd been drifting, rudderless, for months. For more than a year, in fact. He'd hoped Radkovitch would be his ace in the hole (and despite his shit-bird idea about the Buick dealership, Martin was still hoping Radkovitch would come through with the Wells Fargo loan). But time was running out, and he needed to try something else. If someone had told him a few months ago that that something else would involve running drugs up from Mexico for Val Desmond, he'd have laughed out loud. But he was desperate. Debt was chasing him around like the Headless Horseman in that old cartoon that came on every year around Halloween. It was closing in on him, in fact—he could hear the horse's ghost hooves pounding close behind him. And so really, what choice did he have? He'd worry about the repercussions later.

When he got back to the grandstand, he stood looking out at the big board in the infield, checking out the odds on Big Bad Wolf. They were still at 8–1. Okay, he thought. Good.

He also noticed that there was a ripple on the water of the big ponds they had out there in the infield, and that the geese and seagulls looked cold and unhappy. The fog was starting to drift in.

Martin made his way over to the G section. He was in a bit of a daze, but he felt pretty good.

"So," Ludwig said. "I put down fifty bucks to win. How about you?"

Martin looked at him and smiled. "Let's just say I'll be buying the drinks."

They stood there and listened to the guy in the white pants and red jacket play the tune for the start of the race on his trumpet. The kids always liked this part. Sometimes between races he'd play a real song. Nothing elaborate, just some little jazz tune, or a Sinatra song, maybe. Martin had heard him play "The Girl from Ipanema" a few weeks ago and had thought it was pretty cool.

Big Bad Wolf broke from the two position and shot right to the front of the pack. He and Carmine were in red, and, using his binoculars, Martin kept his eyes locked on them as they drove forward. Martin was surprised by the quick start, but he figured Carmine was worried about getting boxed in on the rail. He'd probably keep him in hand after the first turn, Martin thought. But he was a little worried.

"He's out pretty fast," he yelled to Ludwig, lowering his binoculars for a second. He had to lean close to be heard over the gathering noise of the crowd. The grandstands were only about half full, but there weren't many empty seats in the area immediately around them, and people were yelling and shouting as the horses sped down the track.

Ludwig nodded but didn't answer. He had his own pair of binoculars, and he was focused on the race.

Martin watched, waiting for Carmine to slow the pace. But Big Bad Wolf didn't let up, and pretty soon he'd dragged another horse with him into a solid lead. It was the four horse; Martin wasn't sure what his name was. Behind Big Bad Wolf and this other horse, there was a chase group of three about three lengths back. The others were already out of it.

What was Carmine doing? Sure, the race was only six furlongs, but from what Martin could tell, Carmine had him just about flat out. Did he really think he could steal the race like that?

The horse running with Big Bad Wolf fell off the pace along the back stretch, and fell in with the chase pack, so now it was Big Bad Wolf, and a group of four horses trailing about three lengths back. The chase group began to separate out a little bit and form a single-file line along the inside rail.

Huh, Martin thought. He felt a leap of excitement.

"That's right, big boy," Ludwig yelled, lowering his binoculars for a second and hopping up and down a couple of times. "Keep it up."

"Come on, Big Bad Wolf!" Martin yelled, his voice joining in with the rising din of the crowd. "Come on, now!"

But as soon as they started cheering, the gap between Big Bad Wolf and the chase pack started narrowing. Martin shifted his binoculars and saw that one of the horses in this group was High and Mighty. He was about half a length off the other three horses running with him, but he'd moved to outside, and he was looking pretty good. Strong and smooth. Shit, Martin thought.

Martin swung his glance back to Big Bad Wolf. Carmine was crouched low over his back and neck, and it almost looked like he was whispering to him. What would he say? Something encouraging— "Just a little farther. You can do it"? Or something panicky—"Don't look back. They're gaining on you"?

As they hit the final turn, the horses leaning almost imperceptibly to the left and digging hard into the soft soil, the lead had collapsed to two lengths. Big Bad Wolf was trying to hold them off, but it didn't look good. You could practically see the lactic acid building up in his legs.

Come on, you motherfucker, Martin thought—yelled out loud.

By the time the horses hit the eighth pole and started down the final stretch, the lead was one length. Carmine had his whip out and he was working Big Bad Wolf's flank, but it didn't matter. The other horses were reeling him in.

"Oh my God," Martin said as one horse (it looked like it might be High and Mighty) shot past Big Bad Wolf with about forty yards to go. The announcer yelled over the loudspeaker, confirming Martin's guess. The people around them were yelling and screaming and cheering. Jeez, he thought. Did everyone bet on this horse except me?

And then the other three horses from the chase pack caught Big Bad Wolf, and the whole group crossed the finish line in a clump. From Martin's vantage point it looked like at least one of them had passed Big Bad Wolf, maybe more. Martin watched as the jockeys stood in their saddles and slowed the horses. Carmine reached over and patted Big Bad Wolf on the neck—maybe a gesture that said sorry for whacking the shit out of you with my whip.

"What the fuck was *that*?" Ludwig yelled. He lowered his binoculars and looked at Martin. Then he sat down. He looked stunned. Incredulous. It was obvious that he'd been convinced that Big Bad Wolf was going to win—that he hadn't even considered the possibility that he might lose.

"I don't know," Martin said, shaking his head.

He closed his eyes. Three hundred dollars, down the drain. Just like that. Poof. What a fucking idiot.

"Jesus *Christ*!" Ludwig yelled—screamed. "I thought you said this guy Carmine knew what he was doing!"

Here it comes, Martin thought. Not that he felt like defending himself. I should've known, he thought. Big Bad Wolf isn't a finisher. The problem isn't the length of the race—it's what he does when he sees the finish line. He doesn't have the stuff.

The announcer was reading off the names of the horses that had placed, but Martin wasn't paying attention. Why did I bet two hundred dollars to win? he asked himself. Wasn't one hundred stupid enough?

He looked out at the board. He saw that the seven horse had won. That was High and Mighty. The payout wasn't posted yet, but he'd won all right.

Then he looked at the Place slot, at the number of the horse that had finished second. And there it was. It was the two horse—Big Bad Wolf. Hey, he thought. Look at that. He hung on after all—he must have just made it.

He sat there for a second, thinking. He was tempted to check his ticket, but he resisted the urge—he didn't need to. Because he knew what it said. He'd double-checked it after Charlene gave it to him. He'd bet the 2–7 exacta—Big Bad Wolf and High and Mighty. But he'd boxed it, and so it didn't matter what order the horses finished in. He had the first- and second-place horses, and so he'd won. Yes.

He was about to tell Ludwig about his win, but when he looked over at him, he decided against it. Ludwig was slumped back in his seat and staring outward, maybe at the geese flapping around out in the ponds, or maybe at the coastal hills just on the other side of Highway 101. Martin watched him pull his ticket out of his pocket, look at it, and then crumple it up and throw it away.

The payoff for the exacta still wasn't posted, so he wasn't able to calculate how much he was going to clear. But he knew it would be a lot—over five hundred dollars, for sure. Definitely more than he'd lost on his other bet.

This, he thought, was a good sign. First the handshake with Val Desmond, then the winner on the exacta box. It was all about having a backup plan. That was how you beat the system. Because these days you couldn't count on anything to work out, could you? You either gave your money to the cranky lady in the betting booth or you handed it over to the guy at the bank, and then you just crossed your fingers. Sure, you tried to be smart about it, but things could happen—your horse could stumble out of the gate or even break down, or the fucking Arabs could choke off the oil supply. So why not have a plan B? At the track today it was the exacta box. In Martin's life—his real life—it was the deal with Val. Now his business could tank, but it wouldn't matter (or it wouldn't matter as much, anyway). Because he was going to start bringing some money in through the back door. He'd covered himself, and if things went well, he might win big (or he might avoid losing—which to his mind, at least lately, was another version of the same thing).

Martin looked over at Ludwig. He was still sitting there, but he wasn't scowling anymore. He was looking down at a *Racing Form* and mumbling to himself—he was getting ready for the next race. Good, Martin thought. Martin was tempted to tell him to try boxing some bets, but he knew better. Instead he stood up. He wanted to cash in his ticket and then give Linda a call. He knew he was going to be late and that this would piss her off. But he also knew she'd be pleased to hear the good news—the news about the race, that is. He didn't even consider saying anything about Val Desmond and their new agreement.

CHAPTER THREE

Martin slept like a baby Monday and Tuesday nights. He felt relieved—at least he'd made a decision. Better, Val was off his back. No more scary messages, no more wondering how to deal with the money he owed him. He had a plan, and that was more than most people could say. He'd even been in a good mood at home, patient with the kids, frisky with Linda. She'd been wary but eventually receptive.

"What's with you?" she'd asked, but even in the darkness of their bedroom he could tell she was smiling. It was like old times—or like things had been until a few years ago, when suddenly they were only having sex once a month (if that), and he could sense a latent resentment in her.

But by Wednesday he'd realized what he'd actually signed on for with Val, and by the time Thursday morning rolled around he was a wreck. Flying to Mexico? For drugs—for *heroin*? Are you fucking kidding me?

He stood in his underwear, looking at himself in the bathroom mirror, trying to picture himself making the deal. He'd land the plane in some field, leave it running, and just hop down, a suitcase of money in one hand and a sawed-off shotgun in the other.

"Not so fast," he said into the mirror, imagining some Mexican guy reaching out for the cash. "Let me see the drugs first. Then you'll get your dinero."

He looked at his fleshy belly, pale white skin, and bald head. He used to have bigger arms and strong shoulders, but now he looked older and weaker. Even his face had lost its sharpness. When had that happened? Down the hall he could hear Sarah screaming at Peter about something. He took a big gulp of air.

Not a chance, he thought. I can't do it.

Linda was getting ready for work (she'd started back at her job as a secretary in the insurance office in November, after the first shock waves from the oil embargo). So he made breakfast for the kids, scrambled eggs and toast. Sarah ate like a bird, but Peter shoved the food into his face. It was as if he hadn't eaten in weeks.

"Jesus, Peter, slow down," Martin said. "What're you, part of the Donner Party?" He and Sarah exchanged a glance.

Peter shrugged. "Everybody thinks it's so horrible that the Donner Party ate each other, but it wasn't," he said. "I'd have done it, too. For sure. I mean, the people they ate were already dead. It's not like they were saying, 'No, no, please don't eat me.' And their bodies were frozen in the snow. It's the same thing as the hamburger we have in the freezer. It's not that big a deal, when you really think about it."

"Okay," Sarah said. "But I don't really *want* to think about it right now. I'm eating. It's disgusting. *You're* disgusting."

Peter shrugged. "Hey," he said. "I'm just trying to survive."

Martin rolled his eyes. It was as though they were plotting to annoy him—had practiced their parts, even. He looked out the window and watched their dog Arrow sniff around and muse about the ideal spot for his morning dump. He reminded himself to send Peter out to pick up the dog poop from the yard before the end of the week. He also reminded himself that he didn't have to go in to the office if he didn't want to. He was still the boss, right? It wasn't like he was punching a time card, for Christ's sake.

So still without his toupee, he took the kids to school, then went back home and called Ludwig.

"I'm sick," he said. "You're on your own today. Sorry."

"You mean you're playing golf?" Ludwig asked. "Is that it?"

"Fuck you, Ludwig," he said. "I'm really sick." He slammed down the phone. Why did everyone always assume he was lying?

He sat by the pool for a while, drinking coffee and thinking. It was early May and nice out, warm.

If he backed out of the drug deal with Val (not that this was really an option anymore), he'd sink like a stone, financially. Sure, the Wells Fargo guys might loan him some money, especially if Radkovitch pulled some strings. But how long would that actually last, anyway? Would the Arabs ever open up the spigots again? Maybe oil was going to a hundred dollars a barrel—not just for a while, but for good. Maybe the party was over, America.

On the other hand, if he flew to Mexico—did it for a year like Val said—he might actually turn the corner. It just might work. He might just be able to keep on being the Martin Anderson he'd managed to create in the past ten years or so. Not the drifting loser who'd stumbled through his twenties and was headed for a bleak life as a middle-manager sales guy. No, this was the guy who'd started a business, had been successful, and had then moved with his family out to the suburbs. Sure, the suburbs had been a disappointment, but still, did any of his friends from high school live near Sal Bando? No, they didn't. And yeah, Martin's brothers liked to mock him, calling him "the banker," but that didn't stop them from asking him for loans all the time. It wasn't easy to get by as a photographer or a musician, was it?

Martin watched the Pool Sweeper make its circuit around the pool. It was like a space ship patrolling the mini solar system of Martin's pool. Its hoses swept around the pool's bottom, blasting away at the algae. In some ways, Martin realized, the little machine was a real task master: it circled the pool all day and night, bringing order and cleanliness to this important part of Martin's backyard. If you were an errant leaf or piece of walnut skin, you were in trouble.

He sipped his coffee. It was cold. If he didn't take the job (could you call drug smuggling a job?), he'd have to tell Linda that he was broke—that *they* were broke. And that would be very nearly as bad as giving up the Viking and the horse. Not because she'd be angry. She'd probably understand that it was the oil crisis that had done him in, rather than his own bungling (she didn't know about the gambling debts, of course, but she didn't know about the back taxes and the interest on them, either). No, telling her was out of the question because she'd see him differently—look at him differently. She wouldn't say anything, but he'd know. He'd be right back to being the guy who'd lied to her fifteen or sixteen years ago at a fraternity party in Berkeley. He'd been at Armstrong, and she was visiting from Boston for the summer, staying with her cousin. He crashed the party with a couple of friends, and when they met he told her he was a business student at Berkeley. He kept up the charade all summer, but then suddenly Linda was pregnant with Sarah. And that was that. She was Irish Catholic, and they had to get married. But he also had to tell her the truth—that he wasn't a student at Berkeley, that the fancy house they were staying in didn't really belong to his family (he was house-sitting for some friend of his boss's at the car dealership where he was working), and that, yes, he'd swapped out the photos on the wall and the mantel for pictures of himself and his family.

He'd never forget the way she'd looked at him . . . not at him, but into him. And what she saw was the person he'd tried to hide—not just from her, but from pretty much everyone. Including himself. And, he knew, if Anderson Aircrafts went bust, then the wall he'd built up brick by brick between himself and the outside world (Linda included) would come crashing down all over again. It wasn't that he had something horrible to conceal. In fact, it was almost the opposite. His real fear was that, when exposed, the real Martin Anderson didn't add up to much of anything at all.

"Fuck," Martin said out loud, and with enough irritation that the dog's ears went back.

He stood up, threw the dregs of his coffee into the bushes, and within five minutes he was pulling out of his driveway and driving slowly down Miwok Drive. The realtor said that Miwok was the name of an Indian tribe that had lived in the area a hundred or so years ago. He'd pointed out that a lot of the neighborhood streets in Walnut Station had Indian names. Martin thought it was a little odd to name your streets after the people you'd exterminated to make room for you, but he certainly wasn't on a crusade. He wasn't some anthropologist out from UC Berkeley looking to start protests, or put some ads on TV like the one with the Indian crying about roadside trash. Peter loved to make fun of that one. He'd recite it whenever Sarah left her socks or dirty dishes or whatever lying around the house.

"Some people have a deep abiding respect for the natural beauty that was once this country," he'd say, affecting his most serious look. "And some people don't."

When he drove past the Weavers' house, he saw that the driveway was empty. Hal's Mercedes was gone, and so was Miriam's station wagon. Martin knew where Miriam was. Tuesdays and Thursdays she taught art at the high school. He wondered what the kids thought of her. Especially the boys. She probably put up with a lot of shit in there. When he was that age he died for good-looking teachers. Couldn't stand it. He'd act out, make an ass of himself—anything to get their attention.

He also wondered what the other teachers thought of her. The men probably hovered around her classroom door, acted surprised to see her when she came out in her smock or whatever she wore, her hair up, her expression a little mysterious.

"Oh, hi," they'd say. "I didn't know you were teaching today. How'd it go? I hope those kids aren't giving you too much trouble. Some of them think art is just free time."

She'd see right through it, he knew, but it bothered him just the same. Not that he'd be any different. He'd tried the same crap with Peter's fourth-grade teacher—some horseshit he'd stolen from Linda about how the kids weren't quite adolescents but weren't really little boys anymore, either. On the other hand, she'd engaged him, told him about how crazy a couple of the boys could be. So there was that.

At the intersection not far past the Weavers', about eight or nine houses down, he didn't keep going straight ahead, like he usually did. Instead, he took a right, and then another right a few hundred yards after that, onto the frontage road that ran along the outside of their neighborhood. On his right was the walnut orchard that bordered the

neighborhood and acted as a kind of buffer between it and the frontage road. The neighborhood kids played back there all the time. Some
of the older boys had put up tree forts, probably smoked cigarettes and
looked at *Playboy*. They had battles with the green walnuts that were
all over the ground. Peter said they used garbage-can lids as shields and
pelted the shit out of each other with the walnuts. Sometimes, on a
quiet evening when they were really going at it, Martin could hear the
shouts and screams from his yard. He liked hearing it, but he got annoyed that Peter wasn't out there with them.

"That sounds like fun, doesn't it?" he'd asked once or twice, but
Peter said that the older kids threw the walnuts too hard.

Martin slowed for the opening he wanted. He pulled onto the dirt
and then forward until he was shielded from view by the rows of trees.
You'd have to really be looking to notice him back there. He turned off
the ignition and sat there, not really thinking, just sitting. His window
was rolled down, and he listened for any unusual sounds, maybe someone tending the trees. But he didn't hear anything. He sat for another
minute or so, feeling the tingling in his body.

He got out of the car and cut into the orchard, toward his neighborhood. Whoever owned the orchard came through once in a while and
plowed the soil into big loosened chunks of dirt, and so he wasn't able
to walk steadily in his alligator shoes. He slipped and stumbled a little,
holding his right hand out for balance now and then. But he didn't fall.
He had to stop once or twice to get his bearings, figure out which house
was in front of him. Then he saw where he wanted to be, and headed
toward the gap in the Weavers' fence. It was one their kids had made for
easy access to the orchard—just a couple of slats that had been kicked
out. Martin had noticed it during one of the cocktail parties. He'd
been out on the patio, yakking with some neighbors and tossing back
drinks and stealing glances at Miriam. Standing now on the orchard
side, he peeked through the gap. He would have been surprised to see
anyone, but he wanted to give it one last glance. There weren't any signs
of life, and so he squeezed himself through.

Martin walked quickly across the yard toward the house—didn't look right or left, just walked through the tall grass (sure, the landscaping was plush and expensive, but Hal needed to get his shit together and mow the lawn—either that or have one of the kids do it, for Christ's sake). In a couple of seconds he was up on the patio, his hard-soled shoes crunching and scraping a little bit on the brick. And then he was inside, right on in through the sliding glass door that led into the living room. No one locked their doors in the suburbs. Yes, there was the occasional robbery here and there, and for a while people would be more careful. A few people might put stickers on the windows or signs on the lawn that said something like HOME PROTECTION SYSTEM. And then next to it there might be a sign about not letting your dog shit on the grass. But people let their dogs take a crap wherever they wanted, and they didn't pick it up. Martin certainly let his dog pick his spot, and there was no fucking way he was going to stoop over with a plastic bag and pick up dog shit. It was the same with alarm signs—they were bullshit, too.

He didn't have a specific plan. He hadn't even planned to sneak into their house this morning. But his worrying out by the pool had given him too much free-floating energy. And then when it had occurred to him that Miriam was out working, he couldn't not do it. It seemed as if one minute he was sitting in his backyard, and the next he was squeezing himself through the Weavers' back fence.

Martin went through the living room to Hal and Miriam's bedroom and stood in the doorway, looking around, taking it in. He walked over to the bed and ran his hand along the sheets—nice and soft, a high thread count. They were white, which Martin was relieved to see—no cheesy red or gold or anything like that. And no absurd mirrors on the ceiling, or Hawaiian sunset wallpaper. Though he did notice that the bureau located across from the foot of the bed had a nice big mirror.

He climbed onto the bed and sat down, swinging his feet up, crossing his legs at the ankles and resting his back against the headboard, which had a bamboo weave. He looked at himself in the bureau mirror.

He didn't smile at himself. He just sat there staring—staring at himself staring. Then he raised his right hand in a feeble, uncertain wave. It was proof: he really was sitting on Miriam's bed like this, and the person he saw in the mirror was actually him, rather than some ghost self who'd followed him here and who was seeking to make the leap from the two-dimensional space of the mirror into the three-dimensional reality of his world.

Martin swung his feet back down to the floor, and began to look around, pulling open drawers, stepping into the walk-in closet, looking on the shelves in there. He didn't know what he was looking for. Once he located her underwear drawer he made the obligatory search through its contents, but really only so that later he wouldn't regret not having done it. The next time he talked to her, he'd know he'd run his hands over the bra and panties she was wearing—and that was worth something, he thought. But he was actually more interested in finding out if she'd hidden something beneath her underwear. Sex toys, certainly—that would be very interesting. But he'd settle for an old photo that was important to her, or a note of some sort. Or a diary. That would be a gold mine.

The idea of the diary set him on a new round of searching. He reopened drawers and looked under sweaters and T-shirts; he stood on a stool and peeked on the top shelves in the walk-in closet. And he got down on his hands and knees and ran his arms between the mattress and the box spring. Nothing.

Under the bed, though, it was a different story: there were at least half a dozen guns. He plopped belly down onto the carpet (it was an ugly olive green, but recently vacuumed) for a closer look. There were a range of shotguns, from a little .28 gauge up to a couple of .12-gauge guns. The rifle was a .30-06, he was pretty sure. There was a medium-size pistol that said Colt on the side and that he thought was a .38—he was almost positive. There was another gun that was in a little yellow-and-black box labeled TP-70. It also said ".22 CAL." Martin took it out of the box. It was flat and light and small. The handle was black, and the barrel was a gray metal. He liked it. He saw that there was a little clip that you inserted into the handle, and that there were bullets in it. They were small, like baby bullets.

Jeez, he thought. He knew that Hal Weaver was a big hunter—did the whole duck-hunting thing out in the delta, got in some deer hunting on his property on Mount Diablo. Martin had even traded with Hal, salmon for duck. But it was pretty weird to put your guns under your bed. Not to mention stupid and unsafe—especially loaded guns. What were the odds that the kids didn't know they were here, within easy reach? Martin thought he wouldn't be surprised to hear someday that one of the Weaver kids had been killed in a home shooting, or at least in a hunting accident. It happened all the time. He was about to put the pistol back into the box, but then he thought better of it. Instead, after checking to make sure the safety was on (it was), he put the pistol into the front pocket of his pants. Then he put the lid back onto the box and set it back in the spot where he'd found it, up against the wall and in between two of the shotguns. Yes, it was stealing, but that's what you got for having a loaded gun in your house, Hal.

He was just climbing to his feet when he heard the front door open. Open, then close. Then he heard the rapid click-click of shoes on the entry hallway tile (women's shoes) and then coming down the hall, toward the bedroom, toward him. No hesitation, no trip to the kitchen for a glass of water or a Coke (he was suddenly thirsty). Did Miriam somehow know he was here? Was she marching back to confront him? He looked at himself in the mirror of the bureau as he stood there, still stooped over. He looked like a cartoon version of himself, eyes bulging and white with terror.

He had just enough time to crouch behind the bed and then lie down on his right side. If she came to her side of the bed, which was on the far side of the room, the farthest from the doorway, she'd see him. He wasn't sure, but she might even be able to see him in the mirror. That, he thought, would be doubly terrifying. But of course it didn't matter if she saw him in the mirror or straight on. Either way, she'd be completely horrified. He could imagine her scream, and her terror-stricken look when he sat up and faced her, sheepish, hands up and telling her it was all right, he could explain ("I lost something," he'd say). He could also imagine himself from her perspective, lying there next to her bed, panicked-looking—not a robber or a rapist (the obvious first choices), but a freak. What the fuck are you doing in my house? she'd be justified in asking. He wouldn't have an answer for her, though, because he didn't have one for himself.

But she didn't come around to his side of the bed (or her side, depending on how you thought about it—it was more hers than his, after all). Instead, he heard her walk right into the bathroom, adjust her clothing somehow, sit down, and then pee. He could hear the urine stream down and hit the water, and then he heard her sigh. She kept peeing for a long stretch of seconds, and he realized that she'd been rushing to get inside and use the toilet. Had barely made it from the car, from the sound of it. Linda complained about this; there were times when she almost didn't make it to a bathroom. In fact, he'd been out places with her when she'd simply had to run behind some bushes and pee right there on the ground while he kept watch for her.

Of course, Martin wasn't keeping watch for Miriam while she peed in her own bathroom and in her own house. He was an intruder, and if she saw him, he'd go to jail. He'd miss his trip to Mexico. He'd miss the big horse race at the fair. And he'd miss what was left of his children's youth. They might come and visit him at whatever jail he was in, but it wouldn't be much. Peter would look down at his feet and mumble, and Sarah would roll her eyes, eager to get out of there and back home so that she could make some phone calls.

His first instinct was to simply jump up and sprint right the fuck out the house—just blast out of there, hit the fence, jump into his car and drive off, the car fishtailing through the big dirt clods of the orchard, and then righting itself once he hit the frontage road and the freeway after that. He could even call from Mexico, and if it seemed as if Miriam had spotted him, knew it was him, he'd just never come home.

But she *would* be able to identify him, he was pretty sure. There just wasn't enough space to make a clean break. And besides, he was so terrified, he wasn't sure his legs would carry him out of the room, much less across the yard and all the way to his car. And so, as she unrolled the toilet paper and wadded it up and wiped, he rolled onto his back and tried to inch himself under the bed. But he didn't fit. It was a pretty tall bed, but he just couldn't do it, just couldn't wedge himself under there. So, as she came walking out of the bathroom, he held his breath, willing himself to be small and noiseless. He willed himself to cease existing—tried to transform the scenario into the dream (the nightmare) when you were in an impossible situation (one exactly like this, in fact), and somehow you became invisible at the very moment you were about to be caught by your enemy, or flew away just as you were about to be hit by an oncoming car.

Martin heard Miriam stand in the space between the bathroom doorway and Hal's side of the bed. She was talking to herself, but quietly, whispering, almost. He could tell that she was thinking about things she had to do. He could also tell that she was in a hurry. For him, though, things had slowed down, and he was able in the stretched-out pocket of time he'd entered to think with surprising clarity about his situation, and the options that remained open to him. For starters, he knew he had the option of killing her. He certainly didn't want to do that. But he also knew he didn't want to go down the path that getting caught (because he hadn't killed her) would entail. He wasn't sure how to do it. He could shoot her with the .22, of course; it was right there in his pocket. But that would be loud and risky. And could you actually kill someone with that gun? It was awfully small. He could also knock her down, strangle her, or maybe use one of the pillows to smother her. Then he'd tear the house apart, make it look like it was a robbery gone wrong. Stranger things had happened.

He thought, as well, about kidnapping her, forcing her to come with him to Mexico. But he wasn't able to sustain the absurd notion of actually getting her into his car and then into a plane. Nor, therefore, could he muster the necessary energy for the related, extended fantasy of her eventual decision to love him and their new life in Mexico.

But of course he wasn't able to sustain the fantasy of killing Miriam, either. He was pretty sure that he could have killed Hal Weaver in this situation—might have already done so, in fact, especially if he'd grabbed one of the shotguns from under the bed. Eliminating the Hal Weavers of the world wasn't a moral dilemma as far as Martin was concerned. In fact, the brutal but mysterious murder of Hal Weaver might present advantages to Martin. He could become the caring friend and neighbor to Miriam, the one person to whom she could confide her secret fears and fantasies, the things she hadn't been able to communicate to Hal because in fact their marriage had been over years before the murder. And maybe—inevitably—Martin and Miriam would have sex right here in this bedroom, in the very bed separating him from Miriam.

Martin heard a ringing sound, and suddenly time resumed its normal speed. Was it a home alarm, he wondered, finally kicking into gear and warning Miriam there was an intruder in her home? The bell sounded again, and he heard Miriam mutter, "All right, all right already." And then he heard her walk out of the room and down the hall.

Someone was at the door. In fact, he realized, this was probably why she was home: she'd come to meet someone here. Seconds later, as she opened the door and greeted the person, he was able to glean that it was a repair guy of some sort. Something about the dishwasher or the garbage disposal, he thought he heard them say. Something in the kitchen, anyway. But at that point he wasn't really listening. By that time he was on his feet. He felt for the .22 in his pants pocket, then scanned the top of Miriam's bureau for something—anything—to grab.

And then he was pushing open the French doors that led out onto the back patio. He slipped out of the house and onto the crunchy-sounding brick, and then as quickly as possible down to the lawn and along the fence. Finally, and without looking back (in case he'd been spotted from the house, which he doubted: the kitchen didn't look onto the backyard), he pushed himself through the gap in the fence and out to the orchard and then to his car, stumbling again through the big, frustrating chunks of dirt.

He was soaked with sweat. His heart was beating so furiously that it actually hurt. He caught his faint reflection in the driver's-side window, but he ignored it. Instead, he opened the car door and sat down. He pulled the door shut and scanned the orchard. He didn't see anyone. No one was chasing after him, apparently. After another couple of seconds he realized that he was giving off a sickly odor of fear—any cop stopping him now would drag him in on that basis alone.

Another minute or so later, still feeling the heavy beating of his heart, he looked down at his left hand, and saw that he was carrying a small jewelry box. A tiny jewelry box: it was about six inches long and maybe three inches wide, he guessed. He must have grabbed it from Miriam's bureau. He didn't even remember reaching out and taking hold of it, but he must have, because here it was, in his hand. It looked old, like a keepsake of some sort, he thought. It was pewter or silver or something like that, and it had intricate, swirling designs on the lid. The metal was black and oxidized in the crevices of the swirls.

He sat there for a second, looking down at it, and then he opened the lid. Inside, it was lined with a reddish felt, and nestled into the material were several small items, each of them probably important to Miriam in some way, and valuable looking. There was a pair of diamond earrings, a silver locket on a silver chain, and two rings. One of the rings had a large stone that looked like an emerald, and the other one had a lot of tiny diamonds set into it. The one with the diamonds looked like an old engagement ring; Martin figured it was her mother's, or maybe her grandmother's. She was probably planning to give it to her daughter someday—had been planning, that is, because it wasn't going to happen now. There was no picture in the locket, which he found disappointing. He'd been hoping to see one of those old photos of someone from the 1920s, with the person stiff and formal but in a way that spoke to the greater seriousness and maturity of earlier generations.

Under the jewelry lay three coins. They were gold. One was a ten-dollar coin dated 1908. It had a picture of an Indian on it. There was also a twenty-dollar piece dated 1900, with some sort of Lady Liberty image on it. She was surrounded by a halo of stars. Last, there was a one-dollar coin from 1854. Like the one from 1900, it had a Lady Liberty image on it, and she, too, was surrounded by this semicircle of stars. Martin held them in his hand, as if assessing them. They were hefty, he thought. And pretty valuable—probably a couple of hundred dollars apiece.

He looked up again, scanning the orchard, and then twisted around to make sure no one was sneaking up on him, or that there wasn't a cop slowing down, trying to figure out why that car was back there in the orchard. No one.

Martin put the coins back into the box, and put the box under his seat. Then, remembering the gun in his pocket, he took it out and slipped it under the seat, setting it next to the jewelry box. He started the car, swung it around, and started to drive slowly out of the orchard—no need to peel out fast, fleeing in a panic. He slowed to a stop at the edge of the road, waited for a pickup truck to drive past, and then pulled out.

As he drove toward the highway, it occurred to him that those coins were probably even more valuable than he'd thought. Gold prices had skyrocketed in the past year as oil prices shot up, and so these would fetch a nice little bit of cash. Not that he was stupid enough to try it—if Miriam noticed the jewelry box was missing, the first thing she and Hal would do is call the local coin dealers and pawn shops. Plus, it wasn't like three gold coins would set you up for life (or pay off someone like Val Desmond). Still, it was exciting . . . and almost exactly what he'd hoped for when he decided to actually break into her house and snoop around. It was as if he'd stumbled onto a little bit of treasure back there in Miriam's bedroom. And the best part was that now it was his.

CHAPTER FOUR

Val called a little over a week later and said he was ready to set up a run to Mexico. Ramirez was about to get another shipment, and, as planned, he'd offered to cut Val in. Martin didn't know how much Val was making off these exchanges, but it had to be a fair amount if he could afford to forgive half of Martin's debt, and then pay him five thousand dollars every time he flew down there.

Val wanted Martin to drive out to his house in Pleasanton and pick up the cash. "You should come and see Temperature's Rising, anyway," he said. "His morning splits have been great. I think he's got a real shot at the fair."

Martin said okay, fine, and half an hour later he was on the way. It was a Saturday, and he wasn't up to much. He wondered if he should have acted busy, said it would be a few hours, but the talk about Temperature's Rising had made him too excited to bother. Being on the main card was a big deal, at least for the local racing community. No, it wasn't going to get written up in the *Daily Racing Form,* but the area trainers and jockeys would know whose horses had gotten into the race and which ones had done well. Martin was more than a little pleased to think that he might become an owner the local people in the business might know and talk about.

"Oh, sure," he imagined people saying as they sat at the track looking through a race program. "That's Martin Anderson's horse. He's hooked up with Val Desmond, but he seems to be the brains of the outfit. His horses always run strong."

In fact, of course, it was Val who suggested horses to Martin— Martin wouldn't have known where to look, much less what to look for. And Val's inclination was toward tall and lanky horses, rather than those that got by on raw power. A horse like Secretariat had both height and power, and certainly that was ideal. But that sort of horse was out of Martin's league (out of Val's, too). And so Val tended toward horses with the long stride, which could gobble up yards and yards of track with each gallop. They were better at longer distances—a mile and up, basically. None of this six furlongs stuff. Cloudy River and Uncle Jack had been in this general mold, and both had been pretty solid horses, each of them winning a handful of races in the couple of years that Martin had owned them. Martin wasn't sure, but he thought he might've actually turned a profit with them. At the least he'd come close to breaking even—boarding and training included. Most people couldn't say that about their racehorses.

As for Temperature's Rising, he was like an exaggeration of the type. He was 16.2 hands tall and noticeably lean—skinny, almost. Only just over a thousand pounds. And as Val had explained to him, he had nicely formed withers. They were a little high, but not too high—not a problem for a saddle, but it seemed as if the vertebrae of his withers were quite long front to back, which meant (again according to Val) that he could really rotate his shoulders backward and increase his stride length.

Once or twice Martin had heard people make a passing joke about how thin Temperature's Rising was. But they stopped talking when they saw him run. He wasn't going to be a Grade 1, nationally recognized horse. He was definitely kicking some serious ass at the local tracks, though. And to Martin, it was as if he'd managed a date with the prom queen. If his horse actually won at the fairgrounds, it was going to be as if he'd managed to go all the way.

As he drove, Martin felt his spirits begin to lift a little bit. He was starting to imagine himself as a boxer, one who'd been cruising through the early rounds, jabbing and pretty much scoring at will. Those were rounds one through six, say (the early years with Anderson Aircrafts). But he'd walked into a left hook in about the seventh (with the oil embargo). He'd been knocked on his ass, in fact, and he'd been in trouble for the next two rounds after that (no business, mounting debt). But now it was the tenth round, and it seemed as if he might be getting his legs back, and his jab was starting to work again. Yes, he was cheating, if you wanted to look at it that way (because drug smuggling was the very definition of cheating—he knew that). It was like his trainer had given him a piece of metal to put into his right glove. But cheating was better than getting the shit kicked out of you, wasn't it?

He laughed—laughed out loud right there in the car. He glanced around, but there weren't any other drivers next to him. He was relieved. Not that it would have mattered, really, but still, he didn't want to seem like a nut—some wacko driving along and talking and laughing to himself. Though he could just have been listening to the radio and heard something funny. Like the *Comedy Hour* on KSFO. Peter listened to that at night sometimes; he'd take notes and then do the whole routine for Martin in the morning. Bill Cosby, Bob Newhart, Hudson and Landry, the Smothers Brothers. Most of it was pretty funny, though of course it was a little weird coming from a nine-year-old.

In truth, Martin liked the harsher humor better, Don Rickles especially. He loved it when Rickles picked out people in the audience and abused them. He and Linda had gone to see him in Reno a year or so ago. The guy was a genius. Imagine making money off of ridiculing people like that. Martin remembered one line in particular. Rickles had picked out a guy and started in on him: "Who picks out your clothes? Stevie Wonder?" It was a line he'd heard before, either on one of his comedy albums, or maybe on Johnny Carson. It didn't matter—it was better hearing it live. He hadn't been able to see the guy Rickles had targeted, but he could just imagine the look on his face. Martin had practiced the look he'd have on his own face if Rickles chose him. It wasn't one of those big, stupid smiles. No, he'd just sort of fold his arms and chuckle, nodding, as if saying "Okay, okay, you got me." Rickles would like that better, he thought. A little more self-contained—that was always better.

Val's house was in the foothills. It was built into a steep part of the hillside on three different levels—very modern and Frank Lloyd Wrightish. Sunken rooms, big windows, high ceilings—the works. The view from the living room was really nice, especially at night, when you could see the lights of Pleasanton (and the fair when it was under way in the summer). Linda loved the place. She really went for the "nice lines," as she put it, and the slick furniture.

Martin liked Val's house, too, though he'd predicted more than once that the whole thing was going to come sliding down the hill someday, after the next big earthquake hit the Bay Area.

"Before the year 2000," he'd say to Linda. "Mark my words."

"Okay, Martin," she'd say. "If you say so."

He knew she thought he was jealous of Val and his house . . . and maybe he was. But he really did think that someday a huge quake was going to show up people like Val, who had their houses perched in im- possible places, hanging there as if in defiance of gravity (to say nothing of the San Andreas Fault).

However cool and modern Val's house was, Martin was actually most taken by the eucalyptus trees. They surrounded the house and ran throughout the whole of his property. He had about twenty acres. It was split into two parcels, one at street level, where he kept most of the horses that he worked with, and then another section up higher, on a sort of plateau that was either natural or that had undergone some serious grading at some point. This was where his house was, and where he did a lot of training work with the horses. All of it had a forestlike feel, but not the kind you got up at Tahoe, surrounded by pine trees, or maybe in Muir Woods, surrounded by 200-plus-foot redwoods. This was different. Val had explained to Martin the way eucalyptus trees had been imported to California from Australia as a possible substitute for pine trees and redwoods, and whenever he went to Val's, Martin felt as if he were stepping into a kind of exotic forest. The long, thin eucalyp- tus leaves were all over the ground, some in piles one or two feet high, and they smelled incredibly sweet, almost like some sort of spice.

Martin drove up and parked just past the carport and next to the big wire fence that ran along the house—around the pool and lawn area, reaching back to a couple of work sheds just shy of the stables. Val had put the fence in a few years ago to keep his scary 190-pound Great Dane from attacking unsuspecting guests. Its name was Rex. It was one of those tiger-striped things. And it was huge—easily the biggest dog Martin had ever seen. He'd seen it stand and put its paws on Val's shoulders, and when it did, it was taller than Val.

The dog was also vicious. Martin had heard over and over that Great Danes were gentle, but that was a bunch of bullshit, at least when it came to this dog. When Martin or anyone else came to the house, it barked and slathered and generally made it clear that it wanted to bite your face off. Val had told Martin about the time the dog had actually gone through a sliding glass door after some landscaper who'd been teasing it. According to Val (who heard it from the landscaper's boss, who'd heard it from another worker who'd been right there), the guy thought the dog couldn't get to him, and so he'd really been teasing him. The dog had barked like crazy, and then it had run right through the door. It plowed into the guy, glass flying everywhere, and tore into his arm like a big leg of lamb.

That's how Val put it. "Like a leg of lamb." That was the punch line when Val told the story, and Martin had laughed on cue. It was a good story, and it was believable, because the dog seemed genuinely unhinged. Martin's own opinion was that the dog should have been put down after the attack, regardless of whether or not it had been provoked. Wasn't it just a matter of time before Rex decided he wanted to show someone else how badass he was, or before he decided he was sick of dry food and wanted a chunk of human flesh again?

"Martin Anderson," Val said when he came to the door. "The man with the plan." He squeezed the shit out of his hand and smiled, showing off his not-very-good teeth, and Martin smiled as well. Val was a little scary, but his smile was usually genuine, and it was sort of hard to resist—infectious, even.

"That's me," Martin said. He regretted the line the second it came out of his mouth. It seemed a little off . . . maybe even a little weak. Somewhere toward the back of the house the dog was barking. *Woof, woof. Woof, woof, woof.*

"Listen," Val said. "I think that horse of yours has got the stuff. He's been having some great workouts."

Then half an hour zipped by as they talked about Temperature's Rising and the upcoming race at the fair. They walked outside, and then ambled (that was the word that popped into Martin's mind) down the long, wide path that led to the stables on the upper lot. It was lined with walnut trees on either side and banked with big juniper bushes. Higher overhead were the eucalyptus trees, and so this was a little tunnel under the broader canopy. Martin had seen Val and his guys walking horses along this path, and it always made him think of the film clips he'd seen on TV of horses at their stables in upstate New York or Maryland or wherever as they prepped for the big races—the Travers Stakes or the Belmont or maybe the Preakness.

He thought for a second about walking along here with Val and Temperature's Rising, and chatting with Jim McKay for a segment on *Wide World of Sports.*

"You know, Jim," Martin would say. "I'm not gonna lie—the money's great. But really, I'm more interested in the sport of it. I know it sounds hokey, but it's almost a spiritual thing for me. Being there at the track, watching him run. . . . I don't know if I can put it into words."

"What about it, Val," McKay would ask. "What's next for Temperature's Rising?"

"The sky's the limit, Jim," Val would say. "There's just no stopping this horse."

Of course, most of this would be total bullshit—which was okay, because guys like Jim McKay were full of shit, anyway. But Martin actually did want to tell someone how he felt about horse racing. About what it was like when you were standing right next to the track, leaning on the rails, and you could feel the power and energy of the horses as they pounded past. It was amazing, and knowing that one of those horses was yours . . . Martin wasn't sure if he'd be able to convey how that felt, but he thought it might be worth trying.

Val was in a chatty mood, which was unusual. He talked the whole time they were in the stables looking at Temperature's Rising. He told Martin that his weight was just right, that the problem with his foot was all better (Val had even pulled him out of a race four or five months ago because of it), that his splits were fantastic, and on and on.

"He's really on right now. He knows there's a big race coming up. You know what it is? He's confident. Cocky, even. You can just tell. He can't wait to get out there. On Monday we took him out to the track at the fairgrounds, and when he walked out there you could tell he was really into it. Jose said he had to pull back on him a little, make sure he didn't overdo it."

Val was stroking the horse's mane as he talked, and holding his face up to his own, nuzzling him. In between comments to Martin he muttered little baby-talk sentences to Temperature's Rising. The horse jerked his head back a little bit, but he didn't seem nervous or put off. You could tell that he was used to this with Val, that there was a connection there. Plus, Val had an apple in his hand, and Martin knew Temperature's Rising was waiting for Val to give it to him.

"I'm telling you, Martin," Val said, patting the horse on the shoulder. "If he keeps up this way, forget the Pleasanton Fair. That'll be a breeze. I'm talking about taking him down to Santa Anita, getting him into a couple of serious races down there. And I mean Grade One."

"Really?" Martin said. "You think?"

Val patted the horse again and rubbed his cheek against his muzzle. Temperature's Rising jerked back again, but only a little.

"Sure," Val said, still looking at Temperature's Rising. "Absolutely. His times are right there. And he's tough. This is a lot of horse, Martin."

Val leaned close to the horse and changed the tone of his voice, like someone talking to a two-year-old. "Aren't you tough, TR?" he said. "You can handle a little jostling, can't you? Those jockeys down there

play rough, but you can handle it, right?" The horse took a step backward, but Val had his harness, so he didn't try to move any farther. Val
laughed, and then, still holding onto the harness, he stepped back and
held out the apple to Martin.

"Here," he said to Martin. "Give him this. He knows he's about to
get it, and he really wants it."

Martin hesitated for a second, but then stepped forward and took
the apple out of Val's hand. Val always had him do something like
this—feed him something, or hose him off or brush him down. Maybe
even put a little hay in his feed box. It was Val's way of having him connect with the horse, make him feel like he was investing in something
he knew more intimately. But Martin also knew he was being tested—
that he had to show Val he wasn't afraid to be close to a racehorse.

The problem, though, was that actually he *was* afraid. In fact, horses
scared the shit out of him. He just wanted to own them and watch
them. No intimacy required. And he could tell they didn't like him.
Gunpowder, Uncle Jack, and now Temperature's Rising. He was convinced they wanted to bite his hand off or kick him, maybe knock him
out and then stomp him to death. "This is what you get for making me
race around a dirt circle with some crazy guy on my back, thrashing me
with a whip." That's what they'd say just before finishing him off with
a hoof to the head.

Martin stepped forward, holding out the apple to Temperature's
Rising. He reached his head toward Martin's hand, bumping it with
the top of his nose. Martin pulled his hand back a little bit, and this
made the horse jerk his head back and neigh, sending spit all over
Martin's hand.

"Come on, Martin," Val said. He was still holding on to the harness.
"Don't be shy. Just step up and hand it to him. He won't bite you. He's
only nervous if you are."

Martin glanced at Val and then at Temperature's Rising. The
horse was leaning forward again, intent upon getting the apple out of
Martin's hand. Martin took a step forward and held the apple right

under the horse's mouth. He felt the big sloppy gums on his hand as he bit into the apple—felt him bite through about half of it, swallow, and then suck the rest of it up into his mouth.

Martin looked at Val and smiled, and then wiped his hand on the back of his pant leg. It was disgusting, and he thought immediately of taking his pants to the dry cleaners.

Val laughed, showing off his bad teeth again. "I always knew you were an animal person."

Martin nodded. He was trying now to contain his irritation. "Okay," he said. "So it turns out I'm not Marlin fucking Perkins. Jesus. I just want to own them, not be best friends with them." He wiped his hand on his pant leg again and gave Val an exasperated look. "So are you going to offer me a beer, or what?"

On the patio, sitting by the pool, Martin watched Val's wife Angela as she handed them two beers and walked away. She and Val were both in their early fifties, but he'd have believed it if she said she was ten years younger. She had thick dark hair and a full figure—she looked great. He remembered for some reason that her father was right off the boat from somewhere in southern Italy. Maybe that's what it was: her Italian blood.

Val was still talkative, but he'd shifted tone. He was more serious now, really looking at Martin and making sure he was listening, taking in what he was saying.

"It's totally corrupt down there, you know," he said. "These peasants grow the opium up in the Sierra Madre, which are a couple hundred miles away, and then they use mules to carry it to the villages. I mean, imagine—that's how primitive this shit is when it starts out."

Val shook his head, looking at Martin, incredulous. Martin wasn't sure how he was supposed to respond. He fiddled with his bottle.

"And *that's* when the big drug guys come in," Val went on, taking another sip of his beer. "They come in to the villages and buy it up, and then take it to some other place where they process it. The police and the military are all on the take, and so the drug guys—Alvia Perez, that's the main guy—they just run these local villages all over Baja and the northern part of the country. Everyone works for them. One of them just snaps his fingers and suddenly twenty people are running around, moving shit, keeping watch, whatever. Women and little kids, even. It's fucking crazy, but it works, I guess. I mean, they're super poor, these Mexicans. And this is money for them, right?"

Martin shrugged. He couldn't tell if Val was arguing that the drug trade was bad for these Mexican peasants and villagers, or good. Maybe he was saying both. Or maybe he didn't know—didn't even know what the hell he was talking about.

"Anyway," Val said, wiping his mouth. "Apparently Mexico is the main place for producing heroin these days. They call it 'Mexican brown,' or 'Mexican mud.' It used to be Turkey, but not anymore. They grew shitloads of opium there, and it would get processed and then sent to France. And then from France, they'd send it to New York. That's the French Connection. You know, like the movie. But then about a year or two ago, the Turkish government outlawed opium poppies. You can't grow them anymore. It was like the Arabs and their oil—fuck you, no more opium. And so no more heroin. And no more French Connection, of course. And now, because of that, Mexico supplies most of the heroin in the U.S. They just stepped right into the market, and now the shit is just flowing over the border."

"Huh," Martin said. "The French Connection."

He was amazed that the Gene Hackman movie from a couple of years ago had actually revolved around the same heroin trade that he was entering into here in California. It hadn't occurred to him to think about it that way. He'd liked the movie all right, and he remembered getting caught up in the atmosphere and the drama of the film, especially the chase scenes. But it was ridiculous that Gene Hackman had won an Academy Award for his role as the cop in the movie. What was his name? . . . Of course, that was it. Popeye Doyle. He was supposed to be a real tough guy—broke the rules, beat the shit out of the crooks, and the rest of it. But the problem was that you could tell that Gene Hackman wasn't athletic or strong at all. He was a skinny guy who would've gotten his ass kicked by any self-respecting street thug. And so you really could feel him pretending to be a tough guy. He overdid it, is what it came down to. Steve McQueen would have been better. Even Paul Newman, although he was too handsome, probably.

"But look," Val said, breaking the momentary silence. "You don't need to worry about all that stuff. Like I said, my man Ramirez and his guys are all right. They're cool. He's connected somehow to this Perez big shot—he's his brother-in-law or cousin or something like that—and he breeds and trains horses for Perez and some of his pals. And so because I'm pals with Ramirez—we go way back—I'm getting a kind of insider deal. Plus, this isn't a big operation, really. It's just a little side job he's kind of tossing our way."

Val explained how Martin would fly to the little airport in Santa Barbara and meet up with Derek Hano, a horse guy that Val worked with in the L.A. area. Then, when it was dark, the two of them would fly past San Diego, over the border and down to Ensenada, the touristy port town not far beyond Tijuana. Or just south of Ensenada, to Ramirez's ranch. He'd have a landing strip lit up for him, Val said. He quizzed Martin about flying at night, whether he could locate a specific location without much to go on, and so on. Martin assured him that it wasn't a problem, that he'd done a lot of this sort of thing. Which was true. Before starting Anderson Aircrafts, he'd done side work for the Forest Service, dropping guys in behind fire lines, landing in crazy spots in the middle of nowhere, way up in the Sierras, or in Oregon and Washington. It wasn't a big deal.

"Good," Val said. His expression was relaxed, and he gave Martin one of his big Val Desmond smiles. Then he reached over and patted him on the shoulder. "That's good. I knew I could count on you."

Martin thought that he detected a brief flash of something in Val's eyes—a latent wariness, maybe—but then it was gone, and Val was standing up and finishing off his beer.

"Listen," he said. "Let me get that money, and then you can take off. I've gotta be somewhere in a while. So just hang on a second—I'll be right back."

Martin watched as Val walked away, down a short path that led off the patio area, away from the stables and toward a big shed that backed up to a fenced area. Val opened a gate in the fence, and then disappeared into the shed. Martin realized that it was the dog's kennel. He'd seen Val walk him down there before, and had listened to Rex bark from behind the chain-link fence—had seen him throw himself against it with his big fat paws. He was scary even when he was locked up. Martin remembered that Val had converted the shed into a kennel after Rex had ripped up that guy's arm. But he didn't know why Val was there now. He wondered for a quick, worried moment if Val was planning to let the thing out of the cage—maybe menace him a little bit, let him know what would happen if he screwed things up or chickened out. He looked around for the dog, but didn't see him.

The ground around him was littered with fluffy little yellow flowers and long green seed pods. They must have dropped from the big acacia tree that shaded the patio area. It reminded him of that Dr. Seuss book. He imagined thousands of civilizations crying out to him from their individual little acacia flower worlds. "We are here! We are here! We are here!" He felt as if he could understand their basic complaint, which to his mind was a feeling of utter helplessness. He looked at his beer and wondered if he might be a little drunk. But he'd only had two beers. It was the stress. Too much time being anxious and trying to hide it.

And then he found himself thinking about Linda. What would she say to all this? She'd tell him to get the fuck out of there before Val came back with the money, that's what she'd say. But even if he did leave Val's without the money, she'd tell him that it was over, that she wanted out, right now. Because he'd gone from being a bungling liar to a dangerous fool.

"Don't you know what happens when drugs are involved?" she'd ask him. "People get hurt. You'll get hurt. Or arrested. And then what happens to us—to me—to *my* life?"

He'd tell her that it was all for her, for her and the kids, but she wouldn't buy it, not for a second. "No," she'd say. "It's all for *you*. And do you know how I know that, Martin? Because everything you do is for you. Even when you think you're doing it for me or for the kids or for someone else, it's always for you. For Martin. And you know what? It always has been."

A minute or two later, Val emerged from the shed. He opened the gate and started back up the path toward Martin, carrying a green trash bag. Even from where he was sitting, thirty or forty yards away, Martin could tell that it was filled with bundles of money. Huh, he thought. So Val keeps his cash in the dog's kennel. Not a bad idea. Who would go in there to look for it? It would be like going into a grizzly bear's cave. Even if you knew the money was in there, would you really want to hunt around for it, knowing that the grizzly might come home at any moment?

Val plopped the bag onto the metal patio table. "Here you go," he said. He didn't sit down again, and Martin knew it was time to get going. "All you have to do is land the plane and hand it over to the guys down at Ramirez's place. Hano knows all the people involved. There's nothing to it."

"Okay, so this coming Friday, right?" Martin asked, standing up. "May seventeenth?"

"Yeah," Val said, smiling again. "That's right. Mark it on your calendar."

Martin nodded, acknowledging Val's sarcasm.

"All right," he said. "I'll be there."

He reached out and picked up the trash bag. He couldn't wait to get into his car, drive off and park somewhere, so that he could look through it all. He didn't know why, exactly—it certainly wasn't his money. And in some respects it didn't much matter how much money was actually in the bag. Ten thousand dollars, a million—he was going to hand over all of it to the drug guys, and in return they were going to load up his plane with heroin, so that he could fly back to Hayward and get five thousand dollars for his efforts. But still, it was a lot of money.

Val gave Martin a pat on the back, and turned to walk into his house. "Be safe," he said.

Martin started to say something in reply, but he realized that Val wasn't listening. The conversation was over, and it was time to go. Val stepped into his house through the sliding glass door, and when he opened it Martin he could hear Rex barking. *Woof, woof. Woof, woof, woof.* Then the door closed, and he couldn't hear the dog anymore. Or maybe just faintly—he wasn't sure.

He held the bag out for a second, as if weighing it (it seemed to be at least ten pounds, maybe more), and then he folded the loose part of the bag over the top of the bulky part. He tucked it under his arm, let himself out through the gate, and headed for his car. He put the bag into his trunk, and then got into his car and sat there for a minute, looking out at Val's yard and thinking. He had a lot to do before the trip.

He was about to start the car when he heard—or thought he heard—Rex's barking again. Then he started the car and backed up so that he could swing around and head down the hill, wondering as he did if maybe he was going to hear that faint barking sound all the way to Mexico.

CHAPTER FIVE

Martin was still thinking about the money and the hiding place he'd chosen for it on Monday morning. He'd put it into a leather satchel Linda had given him a few years ago, and shoved it to the back of the upper shelf of his closet. But knowing that it was sitting there just a few feet away from him while he lay in bed or got dressed was driving him crazy. He had to keep resisting the urge to take it out and look at it and count it—or just plain touch it.

Which is exactly what he'd done after leaving Val's house on Saturday. He'd driven straight home and dumped the money onto his desk in the spare room. (They called it Martin's office, but it was really just a junk room cluttered with toys the kids had outgrown.) Linda had taken Peter somewhere, and Sarah was at a friend's, and so he had the house to himself. Val had said to just leave the money in the bag—in fact, he'd made a big deal out of it, and Martin had wondered briefly if Val had some way of knowing if he removed it. But he knew this was ridiculous, and so he'd dumped it out onto his desk.

It was more money than Martin had ever seen (except on TV shows and in films—though he'd heard that it was illegal to use real money for movies, that it had to be fake). He'd been involved in a larger transaction when he was setting up the initial loan for Anderson Aircrafts, but he'd never actually seen that money, let alone touched it.

The money was divided up into lots of bundles that were bound with rubber bands. It was a little like Peter's baseball cards. Peter kept his best cards separate, the Hank Aarons and Reggie Jacksons and Sal Bandos, but most of them were sorted into teams, rubber-banded, and stacked neatly into shoe boxes and cigar boxes.

Now, Martin thought, he knew where all of America's missing

cash had gone. Yes, the sultans over in the Middle East had a lot of it, and the bankers in New York had their slice as well (and no doubt Radkovitch slept on a mattress full of money). But, he realized, a big chunk of his and everyone else's money was sitting in leather bags just like this one. All over the country they were being filled, handed over, and zipped off to places like Mexico to buy drugs. No wonder Nixon had to keep printing all those greenbacks.

He counted. There were one hundred and ten bundles, and each bundle held one thousand dollars. Who'd done all this arranging and counting? He considered the possibility that it had been Angela, but then he realized that this was absurd—the idea that she'd involve herself in any aspect of drug smuggling was laughable (and in fact Martin doubted she knew anything about what Val was up to). Maybe it was one of the Mexican jockeys, or one of the young guys who helped out in the stables. Or maybe it was just Val. It wasn't hard for Martin to picture Val sitting there alone in one of the stables late at night, the money spread out on a blanket he'd draped over a hay bale, and sorting it out by flashlight.

At one point, he held a packet in his hand and thumbed the edge. It made a kind of flicking sound, like someone with a deck of cards. The numbers in the upper left-hand corners of the bills whizzed by. It occurred to him that if he drew a stick figure on the corner of each bill, each one with legs or arms slightly higher or lower, it would seem as if the stick person were moving when you flicked through the packet of bills. He wondered what the drug dealers in Mexico would think if one of them noticed a stack of bills with an animated sequence built into it. Would they gather around the person who had discovered the unex- pected little moving cartoon, pointing and laughing and perhaps shed- ding for a minute their identities as bad-ass drug guys? Would their faces crease into smiles—youthful again for a brief moment? Would they say "Hey, those Americans sure are goofy"?

Martin must have sat there at his desk, looking at the bills, touching them, musing in his own abstracted way, for at least half an hour. It was as if they were trying to cast a spell on him, whispering their siren song and urging him to keep on touching them. He'd read books and seen movies where people were transfixed and suddenly changed by the sight of money, or by an unexpected windfall. Like the woman in *Psycho*. She was a workaday secretary, and then, suddenly, she got her hands on a big stack of bills, and she didn't look back. It was Janet Leigh; she was really good in it. Sexy, but also just believable. She told herself she was stealing the money so that she could get married, pay off her lover's debts, and give them a fresh start, but you weren't supposed to buy that, not really. She took the money because it was there, because it had whispered to her, and then she headed out into the night, driving like a maniac.

MARTIN'S ORIGINAL PLAN FOR Monday morning had been to head to the office. He and Ludwig had talked about generating some ideas for a couple of ads in the *Oakland Tribune*. Plus, Martin thought he might invest some of the money he was going to get from Val in a TV spot, and he wanted to bounce the idea off of Ludwig—in part because he wanted Ludwig to know that he was still trying and still had some juice. (The actual idea had been Sarah's: she'd been watching some clown in San Jose trying to peddle his used cars on one of the local channels, and she'd asked Martin why he never did that. He'd told her that those ads never worked, but in fact he'd been dumbfounded by the commonsensical brilliance of the suggestion.)

But instead of driving to Hayward, Martin was with Peter at the marina in Jack London Square, loading the Viking up for a day of fishing and an overnight on the boat. Maybe they'd fish the next day, too. They had some time, because Peter had been suspended from school for the week. They could contest it, Mrs. Bishop had said when she was leaving their house Sunday night—a high-drama visit that had left Peter looking shell-shocked. But this would mean meeting with the principal, and she'd made it clear he wasn't the sort who messed around.

"I don't think we should put him through that," Mrs. Bishop had said. "Let's just let things cool off."

Martin suspected the real issue was that she just wanted a break from Peter (and he didn't blame her). But he didn't say this out loud. Instead, he came up with the fishing idea.

At first Linda had looked at him like he was out of his mind.

"Let me get this straight," she'd said. "Your son gets suspended from school—from fourth fucking grade, Martin—for a whole week. And you . . . your idea is to reward him for it? Take him out fishing? Shouldn't we be *punishing* him? How about making him do some chores? Make him think about what he did."

Martin had nodded, conceding that she might be right. "I know, I know," he said.

He also knew what his own father's response would have been: the belt, total lockdown, the works. But, he said, he had a gut feeling that this was the wrong time to come down hard on him.

"It's like she said," he told her. "I think we should just let things cool off. Something's wrong. I can try to talk to him on the boat. Maybe he'll open up a little bit."

And that, he went on to say, was probably better—more useful—than slamming the door and throwing away the key. He was a sensitive kid. And he was smart. This wasn't some freaky pet-killer thing, where they'd found a cache of cat carcasses in the basement, for Christ's sake. He wasn't the next Charlie Manson.

Martin was pretty sure that Linda understood this as a reference to the thing with Sarah and the drug classes, a suggestion that it had all been a big waste of time and money (which it most definitely had been). But she didn't say anything, and in fact she seemed persuaded by his reasoning. This surprised him, but he was just as surprised to realize that he probably *was* right. The kid had gotten a little nutty, and although a fishing expedition might not solve anything, it probably couldn't hurt, either. Plus, Martin realized, getting away for some fishing might help him steel himself for his upcoming trip to Mexico. He needed to get out of the house for a day or two, clear his head, and stop thinking about things. Val, Mexico, and the money. The money, the money, the money.

IT WAS ANOTHER COOL DAY on the bay, with low clouds promising protection from the sun for most of the afternoon. The early rush of serious fisherman had long since gone, and now there was a quiet, lazy feeling hovering over the docks. Someone's voice carried across the water, past the sound of running engines and the slow *slap, slap* of the water against the dock. The air smelled of that mixture of salt and gasoline that Martin loved.

He walked along the floating pier, holding an ice chest and on top of it a big tackle box. A big cruiser, forty-five feet at least, chugged by and created a wake, and he widened his stance to help keep his balance. Martin looked over at Peter as they trundled along, side by side. He was wearing jeans and a big hooded sweatshirt that said BERKELEY across the front, and carrying their fishing rods and a sleeping bag. He was sucking a big red sour ball as he walked along. A strand of red saliva was dripping down his chin, and, because his hands were full, he wiped it off with his shoulder.

"How're you doing?" Martin asked him. Peter nodded, indicating that he was fine. Martin saw that he was looking at the schools of little fish that were darting back and forth just below the surface of the water.

"We're too late to go out into the ocean today," Martin said. "It's too far. I was thinking we'd go up to Suisun Bay, and try to hit some sturgeon out by the mothball fleet. Harold told me that it's a good spot right now. He said some guys caught a four-footer out there a week or two ago. It was over a hundred pounds."

Peter nodded again, raised his eyebrows, and mumbled in approval.

"Plus," Martin said, "the A's have a day game today, in Boston. It starts at about three, East Coast time, so it'll be on about noon here. How does that sound? Catch some sturgeon and listen to the game. I think Vida Blue might be pitching, but I'm not positive."

They got to the berth for *By a Nose,* and Peter set his load onto the dock with a clatter. He took the sour ball out of his mouth and nodded, wiping his mouth with the back of his hand.

"I think you're right," he said. "I think Vida Blue *is* pitching today."

Martin had taken Peter to a game last year when Blue was pitching. They'd had good seats, not too far from the first-base dugout: close enough that you could hear the ball pop loudly into the catcher's mitt. People said that both Gene Tenace and Ray Fosse, the A's other catcher, put extra foam in their mitts when Blue was pitching. That told you how hard he was throwing.

Peter climbed onto the boat. "Did you know that Gaylord Perry uses a spitball?" he asked Martin. "It's an illegal pitch. No one can hit it. But he doesn't use spit—he uses Vaseline he hides on his hat, or on his uniform. And no one can catch him. The umpires always try, but they can never find anything."

Peter went into a mock windup, and then followed through as if throwing a pitch. He looked awkward, both because the boat was rocking a little bit and because he was uncoordinated and didn't really know what he was doing. He'd go out in the backyard and throw tennis balls against the side of the house—he'd drawn a target with chalk—but it didn't seem to have helped his form very much. Martin knew he should get out there with him, try to help before the other kids were too far ahead, but Peter was no athlete. And Martin was always too busy. Or too tired out from worrying.

Martin nodded, smiling, and climbed onto the boat. "Perry's been around for a while," he said. "He used to pitch for the Giants. Did you know that? He and Willie Mays played together for a long time. But, yeah, he's really good. Maybe he'll pitch against the A's when they play here later in the season."

"You're right," Peter said, staring at Martin. "They probably will play here. I bet he *will* pitch. Oh my God. Do you think we could get tickets? Could I invite someone?"

They talked like this off and on for a couple of hours, first as Martin got the boat ready and maneuvered it out of the marina and up the Oakland Estuary, and then as they sped up and headed north toward Suisun Bay, the tributary bay that pushed out from the northern half of San Francisco Bay. Martin was enjoying himself. He liked listening to Peter yak at him like this. He'd been increasingly quiet and withdrawn lately, and it killed Martin to think that he might be unhappy, and that for the most part he himself was powerless to do anything about it. There was plenty of time to be miserable when you were older— when insecurity and disappointment came knocking, and you discovered that happiness was something you chased but couldn't ever quite catch up to. Couldn't there be a rule of some sort about childhood? Couldn't someone mandate a carefree existence at least until you were, say, ten years old, one in which there were no fears or worries and no crippling self-consciousness? This was why he decided against quizzing Peter about what had happened at school. If it came up, so be it. They'd certainly grilled him pretty hard when Mrs. Bishop was at the house. Martin had done everything but tie him to a chair and put a desk lamp in his face. And where had it gotten them?

The gist of the issue, Mrs. Bishop had explained after pulling up in her crappy Volkswagen Bug (Martin had watched through the living room window, and seen with disappointment that she was wearing jeans, not one of her short dresses), was that Peter was suspected of sending a nasty note to a student in class. Martin had scoffed when he heard this—had felt relieved, even. But Mrs. Bishop had put him straight pretty quickly. The note, she'd explained, was strange. Or disturbing—that's how she'd put it. "It's a disturbing note," she'd said, sitting there on the couch in the living room, looking back at Martin and Linda as they looked at her. Martin hadn't been able to wrap his brain around the fact that she was actually there, in their house. He felt strange, and anxious, sort of like when he was visiting a doctor, whether it was for him or the kids. He'd suddenly start larding his sentences with big words, misusing half of them, probably, making a fool of himself, unable to stop.

"Disturbing how?" Linda had asked. "What did it say?"

"It said, 'Jesus hates you,'" Mrs. Bishop said. She said it quietly and succinctly, and Martin could tell immediately that she'd been practicing her delivery, that she'd been going over it on the way to their house, in her car. "It was typed. And written with all capital letters."

Martin stared at her for a second, trying to process what she'd said, but feeling the words slide away from him.

"'Jesus hates you'?" he asked. "What do you mean, 'Jesus hates you'? In capital letters? Are you certain about this? That sounds vaguely implausible. Or indeterminate, anyway."

"There are some other notes," she said in response, giving Martin a quizzical look and then directing her attention toward Linda. "All of them were typed. And they all play mean psychological games. They really are kind of nasty. One says, 'Everyone thinks you're ugly. Do you?' That kind of thing. But the bad one—the worst one—was the one about Jesus hating someone."

"There are other notes?" Martin asked. "That Peter sent? Where did he send them? To their houses?"

"*Martin,*" Linda said, giving Mrs. Bishop what he knew was an apologetic glance. "They get them at *school.* Where do you think they get them? They just get them. Don't you get it? Our son is sending weird notes to people."

Linda and Mrs. Bishop had taken over after this, talking and talking. It was as if he were a car wreck that they'd finally been able to move off the road, so that traffic could start flowing again. And eventually, after they called Peter in and questioned him for half an hour or so, he'd given them this much: that the idea for the notes, and in particular the Jesus note, must have been lifted from the book he'd been reading, the one about the spy and the notebook. It was the sequel to *Harriet the Spy,* Peter said (of course, Martin thought, the thing with the notebook). But Peter also said he'd talked to lots of other kids about what happens in the books—including the secret note-leaving. So, he concluded, it could have been anyone. Maybe someone he'd talked to, or maybe someone who'd heard about it from one of these people.

"But it wasn't me," he said, his face a study of blank confusion.

And then they were standing again at the front door, with Mrs. Bishop exiting instead of entering.

Martin remembered that he'd insisted on shaking her hand, and that she had surprisingly rough skin. "Thank you for coming over, Mrs. Bishop . . . or Allison. Or whatever we're supposed to call you."

She'd smiled at him, but it was a confused smile, one that indicated that she wanted to get the hell out of there (or get the hell away from him, he realized, even before they were done shaking hands). He also remembered watching her as she walked toward her car, and knowing as he was doing it that he was letting his gaze go a couple of seconds too long. And then he'd looked over and seen Linda looking right at him. Her arms were folded across her chest. Martin had thought at that moment—he remembered it clearly, standing there with Peter on the deck of the Viking, the wind blowing in his face—that his wife was very attractive, and that he was actually a pretty lucky guy. But before he could say this (or before he could reach over and hug her, which is what he was about to do) she'd turned and walked inside.

THEY MADE IT OUT to the mothball fleet by about one. It was a big group of older ships, most of them from World War II. There were hundreds of them, floating patiently out in Suisun Bay, waiting for someone to remember that they were still around. Some of the ships had seen serious action during the war. The one they were heading for, the SS *O'Brien,* had been some serious action—had taken part in D-Day and served in the South Pacific (and now, Martin knew, it was a good spot for sturgeon fishing).

The official line was that the ships were kept in reserve in case of an emergency of some sort: to carry military supplies, or even grain or coal. But according to Hal Weaver, the truth was that it was too expensive to even scrap them. It was, he told Martin, cheaper to buy Japanese steel.

"Pretty ironic, huh?" Hal had said. "We build the ships and win the war, but now they're kicking our asses in business. I mean, we can't even afford to get rid of the ships! I've actually contracted to scrap a few of them, but I lost money on it. Unbelievable."

Martin looked up at the ships as they drew near to them and slipped in and out of the long shadows they cast on the greenish-gray water of the bay.

"Wow," Peter said. "I forgot how big they are."

Martin nodded—he knew what Peter meant. Looking down at them as you drove past (the Martinez Bridge gave you the best vantage point), the ships looked like little toys that some kid had set down on a pond. But from where they were now, on the water and only a couple hundred yards away, you saw them for what they were: giant steel monoliths that towered silently overhead. And it was this combination of immensity and silence that made it feel eerie out there when you pulled close to them. This was especially true on a foggy day—sometimes you wouldn't see them until you'd practically run into them. Then it was as if a ghost fleet of pirate ships had suddenly emerged out of the fog.

There was no fog today, just a light breeze from the north. They could smell the stink of the oil refineries in Benicia and Martinez and Vallejo.

Those old towns actually had some character—more than the made-up character of Walnut Station, that's for sure. Benicia had even been the state capital for a year or two at one point. But they'd been bought out and overrun by the oil companies. Standard, Shell, Gulf, Exxon, and the rest of them. He couldn't even keep the names straight anymore. They'd plopped down their giant production facilities right on the edge of these towns. Crazy mazes of pipes winding hundreds of feet in the air, huge smoke stacks, big fat holding tanks the size of city blocks, practically. At night, when the facilities were lit up with different-colored lights, it looked like an amusement park, or the Emerald City in *The Wizard of Oz*. Nothing could have been further from the truth, of course. For one thing, it really did stink. Martin couldn't imagine how anyone could live there. Could you get used to something like that? Martin didn't think so. But you never knew, maybe if you'd grown up there you wouldn't notice. In fact, maybe if you were from Martinez or Benicia or one of the other little towns up there—maybe towns like Walnut Station smelled bad to you, or smelled wrong, somehow.

In the first two hours of fishing they caught an ocean trout, a few bullheads, and a stingray. The stingray was big—almost two feet across from wingtip to wingtip. They laid it out on the deck on its back, so they could see its whitish-gray underbelly. Its mouth looked strangely human. It opened and closed as they stood there looking at it.

"It's like it's trying to tell us something," Peter said, looking at the ray and then at Martin.

"You think?" Martin asked.

"Yeah," Peter said. "Maybe it's some kind of warning."

Martin smiled, but he wasn't sure if Peter was joking or not. It was hard to tell with him these days. He was tempted to ask, but he decided against it. He picked up the ray and threw it off the side of the boat, back into the water. They watched it float there for a second, hard to see in the brackish green of the bay, and then it glided away.

After an hour of no action (not even a bite), and after they listened to the game for a while, Martin told Peter stories about ghost pirates looking down at them from the ships, rattling their sabers and warning them off, maybe shooting a few ghost muskets and cannonballs at them. A while after that, Peter got up in the prow, shooting his pretend gun at the pirates, ducking and firing in some sort of pitched battle with Captain Kidd or whoever it was he was imagining out there. It was a nice game, nice to watch him play. Eventually, Martin joined in, and then they started battling each other. They climbed all over the boat—up onto the bridge, along the narrow side ledges, into the cabin. Finally, Martin used his favorite maneuver: he slipped down through the forward hatch, snuck through the bedroom and cabin, and then came up behind Peter and scared the shit out of him. Maybe, he said to Peter, the ghost pirates on the battleships had been helping him.

"Yeah, right," Peter said. "You wish." But Martin could see him thinking about it, glancing up at the boats and wondering.

Martin looked upward along the steel side of the *O'Brien*. It was like standing next to a building. A ship like this would be a great place to hide, he thought, if you really needed a getaway. Fill the Viking with provisions, take it out there, sink it, and then climb up the big ladder that was still affixed to the side of the *O'Brien*. You could last a year or more up there, Martin thought, especially if you caught some fish. You could capture rainwater in buckets. Shit off the side of the boat—whatever. And the beauty of it was that they'd think you'd been lost at sea. When they did finally track you down (because in the end they always did), you could go out fighting, shooting at the police and whoever else it was that was after you until you were out of ammunition and too tired to care, anyway.

After the stingray, they couldn't catch anything. Finally, Martin suggested that they both jump off the boat and into the water.

"Come on," he said. "It'll be great. We'll jump at the same time. I dare you."

"No way," Peter said.

"Why not?" Martin asked. "What's wrong? It's not that cold."

"Aren't there sharks?"

But Martin persisted, and then he started in with the bribes. "I'll give you a box of baseball cards," he said. "How many packs are in a box? Twenty? Thirty? Come on—you can't turn *that* down. And think how impressed Mom will be. Plus, you can tell your friends about it when you get back to school. They'll wish they'd gotten suspended, too."

It was Martin's first reference to what had happened, and he knew he was taking a chance.

Peter stared at the water, and Martin felt as if he could hear him thinking. He looked at Martin, then shrugged. "All right," he said. "But we're both doing it, right?"

"Absolutely," Martin said. "But we've gotta take our clothes off. Once you're wet, your clothes will be too heavy. You'll get tired out right away. You'd drown if you had to swim very far like that."

So they stripped and on the count of three they jumped in. The water was cold—really cold, Martin realized after about a second or two. His head started to hurt even before he surfaced after his dive. He came up splashing and a little panicked, gasping and turning immediately to look for Peter. If he was this cold, how did Peter feel?

But just a second later he spotted Peter. He was whooping and smiling at Martin and giving him a thumbs-up sign. Martin laughed, and they started back to the boat. The water was pretty calm, but even the slight swell of the bay made it a little harder to swim than Martin had expected. Peter wasn't much of a swimmer, and Martin saw that he had to kick and stroke with real energy to move the ten or fifteen yards to the boat (it had begun to drift away from them the second they dove).

They climbed up the little ladder on the stern. "Jesus," Martin said. He was breathing hard and shivering. He wrapped a towel around himself. "I feel like we just swam a mile—at least a mile. How do those guys who swim out to Alcatraz do it? My head hurts, it's so cold."

"I know," Peter said, adjusting the towel that Martin had given him. "It's fucking freezing."

This caught Martin off guard, and he laughed.

"Hey," he said. "Watch the language."

He watched Peter hop up and down, trying to pull his pants on. Martin saw that he was smiling. It was the first time he'd seen that in a while.

THEY HADN'T CAUGHT A sturgeon—not even one that was under the limit (which, Martin knew, he would have kept). And Peter hadn't offered up a sudden confession about his notes, his eyes brimming with tears, repentant, suddenly, for his actions (and Martin tearful as well, grateful for Peter's honesty). But that night, back in the marina, neither of these things seemed very important. The plan had been to go out to a fish place like the Sea Wolf, but Martin was tired, and he was able to talk Peter into settling for dinner on hot plates down in the cabin—canned Chef Boyardee raviolis and Campbell's chicken soup and toast. Martin had a few beers, and Peter had hot chocolate. Peter read a book with a knight on the cover (Martin had a feeling the notebook days were over), and Martin read a couple of semirecent issues of *Sports Illustrated*.

Peter was asleep by eight-thirty. Martin didn't fall asleep right away, though. He was uncomfortable, tucked with Peter into the V-shaped bunks up in the prow. He tried listening to the calm lapping of the water against the hull and to Peter's deep, regular breathing, but hovering at the edge of his thinking was what lay ahead. Very soon, Martin knew, things were going to change. He wasn't sure how, exactly, but he knew it would be different. Lying there in the Viking, Martin hadn't stepped over the line yet, at least not officially, and so he tried to relax and focus on the present moment—being there with Peter, listening to the sound of the water. But he knew that it was like Val had said back at the track: once you were in, you couldn't go back again.

||||||||||||

TWO

||||||||||||

CHAPTER SIX

Val's instructions had been simple and succinct. First, fly down to the tiny airport in Santa Barbara and meet up with Derek Hano. Then, once it was dark, fly with him down to Ensenada. Or just outside of Ensenada, to Ramirez's ranch. Once they got the dope, they'd pack it into the plane, and then retrace their steps. Hano would get out in Santa Barbara with half of the heroin. Martin would gas up the plane and then fly up to Hayward and give the rest of the shipment to one of Val's guys.

And so now—finally—he was on his way. He was really doing it. From the air, five thousand feet up and moving along at about 120 mph, the coastal hills looked to Martin like the little papier-mâché hills you might see in the garage of one of those people who built miniature railroad sets. Alan Guthrie, the guy who lived across the street from Martin, had one of these crazy setups. He was a sales guy for IBM in San Francisco—which was a little surprising, because in point of fact he was basically a redneck from somewhere in Georgia. He had a whole little world out in his garage, built on a bunch of big sheets of ¾-inch plywood: toy tracks snaking through a landscape of hills and plants, with little bridges and buildings, and signs with actual corporate logos, even mini people in frozen postures of activity. What a fucking waste of time, Martin thought whenever he saw Guthrie in his garage, hunched over and gluing some little piece into place, or watching his HO scale trains zip past and disappear into a fake tunnel. Guthrie loved to call them over to see some new bridge or grain silo he'd put in—he'd stand there sucking on his bourbon, yakking about his train dealer out in Detroit, how he had the best and most realistic stuff.

Martin guided his Cessna 182P Skylane along past San Luis Obispo, bobbing on the prevailing trade winds that swept along the West Coast. Down below, Highway 101 was like a little string that some kid had set down as a pretend road, and the cars were like busy ants, hurrying along the string, happy that it was there but knowing it might not last—that soon they might have to make their way off-road again, through the grass and trees and over the hills.

Near Pismo Beach, the coastline jutted in to the east. Martin swung right, out over the water. It was a clear day, and down below he could see a few sailboats, as well as a few larger commercial boats. It was an open expanse of white-capped water, deep blue and endless. If he wanted, he could simply veer off to the west and keep flying, out and out and out until he ran out of gas and plunged into the Pacific. No one would know where he was or what had happened to him. Fifteen or twenty minutes from now he could disappear into the ocean, drifting down to the sandy coastal bottom and lie there for years, maybe forever.

He landed in Santa Barbara at about three o'clock, and by four he was sitting in a little bar on State Street with Derek Hano. They were out on an open-air patio, surrounded by palm trees and seated just beyond a big stucco arch that had lots of colorful tile set into it. The floor was also tile; it was a muddy red, and the tiles were really big squares, with smaller and more colorful tiles set between them at regular intervals. The patio itself was bordered by thick stucco walls that were about waist high. People were leaning against the walls, drinks in hand, chatting.

The whole town was like this: white-washed stucco and red-tiled roofs and flowery bougainvillea vines and lots of palm trees. It was a lot like the Stanford campus, actually. This made Martin wonder if they'd see Radkovitch walking around the streets with a stack of books in his hand—maybe even a young, college-age version of him. The sighting would let them know that they'd entered a warp in the space-time continuum: one minute you're in Santa Barbara in 1974, sick with fear about flying down to Mexico and making a drug deal. Then the next minute you're up in Palo Alto in the 1960s, pretty much worry free and watching Radkovitch trotting around Stanford as he works on his fancy business degree. If he had to choose, Martin would opt for option number two, even though it meant watching Radkovitch live a life that Martin could only dream about.

"So what do I need to know?" Martin asked Hano. He was big—Hawaiian or Samoan or something. Thick arms and muscular shoulders, but also kind of lean, with narrow hips. He had straight, black hair, which was noticeably shiny, and green eyes. His hair made him look young, as did the fact that he had a sort of chubby, youthful face, like he still had some baby fat but only in his face. Martin knew he was thirty-four, because he'd mentioned it for some reason. He was actually a little funny-looking, but Martin could tell he was one of those guys who did pretty well with women, anyway.

Hano shrugged, and fiddled with his drink. It was a margarita, which Martin thought was a little absurd, given the setting and the circumstances. "Not a lot," he said. "I've dealt with these guys a few times now. They're cool—they're all right. We'll give them the money, they'll help us load up the dope, and we'll be outta there."

Martin nodded and sipped from his own drink, which was a beer.

"But this is a new set up, right?" he asked. "I mean, you haven't done it this way, have you—flying, I mean?"

Hano shrugged again, looking over at a table with a couple of secretary types. They were both blond and tanned, probably in their late twenties. Hano leaned back in his chair, stretching, showing off his muscles in his tight short-sleeved shirt. Martin felt a little jealous; he'd like to have arms like that. The guy had probably been a quarterback in high school, he thought, and had probably had sex with all the cheerleaders. Probably the bad girls, too, the ones who hung out behind the school or in the parking lot, smoking cigarettes. Martin had had minimal sexual experience in high school—a couple of quick drunken encounters, that was it.

"Well," Hano said. "Mostly it's been by car. We did have a guy who did a flight for us a few months ago, though. But then he backed out. Or something happened, anyway. I'm not sure. But that's why Val was so glad you were up for it. 'Cause driving isn't cutting it anymore."

He took a big swallow of his margarita, and glanced again at the secretaries.

Martin nodded, drinking from his beer. He looked out at the street. Everyone walking along the sidewalk was attractive. Or that's how it seemed. Martin had heard that a lot of Hollywood stars actually lived up here in Santa Barbara, and he wondered if he might see one of them strolling by. Paul Newman, or Jane Fonda. That would be something.

"So you're all set, right?" Hano asked. "You've got the flight coordinates, or whatever you call it? "

"Yep," Martin said. "I'm all set."

"Okay," Hano said. "Good. And you know they're gonna have a landing strip all set up, right? I mean, they've got lights and everything. So you can see it from the air. But the last guy was a little skittish about it—about landing in a field at night and everything. He was nervous. I don't know what he expected, but he didn't seem to like it."

Martin shrugged, and forced out a little laugh. "I'm all right," he said. "Honest. You don't have to worry about me." And it was the truth: nothing about flying made him nervous. As for how he felt about what they were going to do once they'd landed, that was a different story. That scared the shit out of him, in fact. But flying and landing? Not a problem.

"Okay," Hano said. "Great." He motioned to the waiter, who was standing with his back against a stucco archway, watching people on the street. Maybe the waiter was looking for movie stars, too. Martin wanted to ask him if he'd ever served a drink to a famous star.

Martin looked at the two women at the far table, thinking they were a little too skinny and probably too tanned for his tastes. They were definitely Southern California rather than Northern California. He thought about some of his daughter's friends, the older ones who sat out by the pool with her sometimes (a couple of them had seriously nice bodies; it was no joke). They'd sit out in the sun all day long. The tans looked better on them than on these women, though these women looked all right. His daughter's friends looked better because they were younger—that's all there was to it.

Hano reached out for his glass and downed his margarita. If Martin had done that, he'd have gotten a blinding headache instantly.

Hano leaned toward Martin, a little more serious now. "Listen," he said. "If you can get us there and land the plane, it'll be fine. Think about it. All we have to do is land, say hello, *hola, cómo estás,* do the exchange, and then we're back in the air. We don't have to worry about some fucking cops or military guys pulling us over, maybe making us pay them a huge bribe, or hauling us in to some shithole Mexican jail and keeping us there until we come up with a million dollars. And we don't have to worry about running into trouble at the border. When you're flying," he said, leaning back now in his chair and smiling, "there is no border. You know what I mean?"

He raised his drink to Martin and then to the women at the other table. One of them, the older one, raised her glass in return. She had a sly smile on her face.

"I mean, Jesus," Hano said, turning back to Martin. "Flying—it couldn't be easier. This is gonna be a snap."

THEY FLEW OVER ENSENADA at about ten. It was easy to spot from the air: there were lots of lights from buildings and cars. After that, though, it was pitch dark, and it was hard to find Ramirez's ranch. But after fifteen minutes or so of flying and circling and checking his instruments, Martin finally spotted the two long rows of flaming, kerosene-soaked rags that Ramirez's guys had put out as makeshift nighttime landing markers. It was pretty dramatic, dropping the plane down toward the two lines of light, seeing the glare and smoke and then feeling the bumpy unevenness of the packed dirt as they bounced and skidded along. Once beyond the flaming lights of the landing strip, it was absolute blackness, but he managed to taxi for about a hundred yards and then steer the plane back around and bring it to a stop somewhere in the middle of the rows of burning rags.

Sitting next to the eerie glow, Martin wondered if they were just waiting for some Mexican drug thug to come and start blasting away at them in the cockpit. He fought off the image in his head of the two of them riddled with bullets and slumped over in their seats. The windshield would be shattered and sprayed with blood, and blood would be draining out of them and covering the cockpit floor. If you got close enough, you'd be able to hear the droplets of blood dripping onto the soaked floor of the plane. *Drip, drop, plop.* It would be a mess, and maybe Ramirez's head honcho would get angry about it—the plane was valuable, and who wanted an airplane that had been shot up and sprayed with blood? Couldn't they have been killed outside the plane?

Part of his fear stemmed from what Hano had told him about the first couple of minutes after landing the plane—about what the drug guys would do to check them out. "They'll shine lights on us so that we can't see," he said. "And some guys will be out there pointing guns at us. Rifles and shotguns, probably. So just be cool. Once they're sure we're not some DEA assholes trying to trick them, they'll be fine. Everything will be fine. But just sit tight until they know it's okay. Don't spook the natives."

And Hano was right. A few seconds after he brought the plane to a stop, a blinding search light blasted through the windshield. And then two more lights, smaller, probably from big flashlights, were shined onto them through the side windows. It was incredibly disorienting, enough so that Martin barely noticed it when his cockpit door was yanked open and someone put the barrel of a rifle—or some kind of gun, anyway—against his head. He didn't look over, but he was aware that Hano's door had been pulled open as well, and that light was streaming in from that side of the plane.

"Come on out," someone said to him. "Hands up high." It was English, but definitely spoken by a native Spanish-speaker. Or, Martin wondered in his confusion and fear, was it a native Mexican-speaker? "Come on," the voice said again. "Move."

Martin stepped down, and someone guided him by the arm, turning him back toward the plane. The light was still shining in his face, and he was almost completely blinded. "Put your hands out on the plane," the same voice said. The gun was now poking him in the back.

He put out his hands and stretched forward, and then felt the cool metal of the Cessna on his two palms. He heard a brief exchange behind him, but it was in Spanish, and he didn't understand any of it. He wondered suddenly if Radkovitch spoke Spanish. Probably. Or maybe just French, and a little German. But he'd probably studied Spanish at some point, too, in the off chance that South American banking (or was it Central American banking?) ever took off in a meaningful way.

A couple of rough hands began to search him, probably for a weapon—and suddenly Martin realized that this might not be the start of a drug deal at all. This might, he thought, be the Mexican police, or even the military (was there a difference?). It occurred to him that Hano might be some sort of drug agent. Then, for the first time, he was genuinely scared. The hands ran along his legs, from his ankles up to his crotch and backside, and then all over his torso, his back, his armpits.

The air was cool and dry, but all around him it smelled of the kerosene lamps. As he stood there, his hands flat on the side of his plane and the man's hands brushing over him, insistent, he thought about Linda at home. She'd have the kids in bed, probably—or at least Peter would be in bed. Since Martin was gone, Sarah had probably negotiated with Linda to stay up late. Either that or she'd pretended to go to sleep, but was whispering into the phone she'd pulled from the study. She'd be hiding under her blankets, as if the darkness made her less audible, somehow, and the phone cord less visible as it stretched down the hallway. Martin knew that if the drug dealers told him he had one quick phone call before they shot him, his frantic attempts to phone home would be in vain. Standing out there in the weirdly lit smoky redness of the dirt runway outside of Ensenada, a long phone line stretching from Ramirez's house, he'd dial, his finger trembling and his breath coming in quick, short gasps, but all he'd get would be a busy signal.

"Okay," the voice behind him finally said. "Turn around."

Martin let his hands slide off the plane. Turning to face his possible execution, all he wanted to do was close his eyes. But when he swung around to see who was there behind him, no one was pointing a gun at him. Instead, he saw a stocky man with horribly bad skin. He was wearing a nice maroon leather coat and shaking hands with Hano. They began talking to each other in Spanish. Huh. Hano really was fluent. Martin had never seen a nonnative speaker talk to someone in another language. It was kind of amazing. It was almost as if he were faking it, just letting a bunch of random sounds pour out of his mouth, the way a kid might if he were speaking a made-up language. Blah, blah, blah, blah, blah. But here, of course, it was a real language, and this guy Hano was actually speaking it. How about that?

Martin noticed that a guy standing off to his left was holding a rifle of some sort, one with a handle on the bottom. He thought it was one of those lever-action jobs that he'd seen in various westerns. He wasn't sure. But he *was* sure that this was the gun that had been pointed at his head—held right up against his head, in fact.

"*Bueno,*" Hano said, finally. "*Podemos esperar. Ningún problema. Cualquier necesitas hacer.*"

The Mexican man nodded. And then, turning toward Martin, he stepped to the side, and with his left arm held out (like a matador, Martin couldn't help thinking), gestured toward a car that was parked about ten feet away. It was a slightly older model Mercedes sedan; it was hard to tell in the strange light, but it looked yellow, and maybe a bit faded. Martin looked over at Hano, who nodded and tilted his head toward the car, as if to say "Yes, it's fine, hop in."

And so that's what Martin did. He started toward the car and got in after someone—not the guy with the cowboy rifle—opened the rear door for him. The interior light flicked on as the door opened, and Martin saw that the car was clean inside. The leather seats were shiny and new looking, even though Martin knew that the car was at least five years old. A big fat guy was sitting at the wheel. He didn't turn around, but Martin exchanged a quick glance with him in the rearview mirror. A second later, Hano leaned down and started to climb into the car, so Martin slid over to the seat directly behind the driver.

The driver started the car, and then they were rumbling along over what seemed like a long stretch of hard, packed dirt. He couldn't see much at all (it was dark again now that they were away from the reddish glow of the oil lamps), but he knew they were whizzing along somewhere between forty and fifty miles an hour.

"So what's going on?" he finally said to Hano. "When do we load up the plane?"

Hano leaned back in his seat, stretched, and then yawned. "Well," he said. "It sounds like . . . it turns out . . . they're waiting on their shipment. It's gonna be a day or two late." He looked over at Martin, shrugged, and then turned to face forward.

Martin sat there for a second, processing what Hano had just said. "'They're waiting on their shipment'?" he asked, echoing Hano. "What does that mean? We have to take off out of here pretty soon, don't we?"

Hano let out a little laugh. "We can't leave until we've got the dope," he said. "And since it's not here, we've gotta wait."

Martin stared over at the dark silhouette of Hano sitting there next to him. Then he glanced at the driver. But the guy was looking straight ahead, concentrating on the bumpy dirt road. Did he speak English— understand what they were saying? Probably.

Jesus Christ, Martin thought. He had assumed they were being taken over to Ramirez's main residence, where they'd sit in some sort of comfortable, distinctively Mexican living room. It would have a rustic, wood interior, with big beams overhead and Mexican rugs on the walls. They'd sit on a large, cushiony couch, and Ramirez's wife, or maybe a sexy young servant (that Ramirez slept with from time to time) would serve drinks. The servant might lock eyes with Martin for a quick second, letting him know she found him attractive and interesting. Her look would imply that if he were brave enough, he should fly back and rescue her from her life of service in Mexico.

But they weren't heading for the hacienda. Instead, the car plunged into the night, the suspension rattling on the dirt road and its washboard ripples.

"So where are we going?" Martin asked into the darkness of the car. But Hano didn't respond, and suddenly the car felt incredibly quiet. The driver coughed, and then glanced at them in the mirror.

"Ensenada," Hano said, finally. "It's only about half an hour away. We're going to stay the night there." He looked again at Martin. His round face was barely visible in the darkness—really only a shadow. "Don't worry," he said. "I had to do this once before. It's not a big deal. Their connect is just a little late coming up from the mountains. It's all the way from the Sierra Madre, you know."

Martin felt a rising sense of panic. It was a little like one of those bad dreams—not quite a nightmare—in which you know you've got a rental car and it's overdue, but now you can't find it; you parked it somewhere but you can't quite locate the street, and because you're on foot, every wrong turn just takes up more time and energy. And then, once you do find the car, the tires have been stolen. And although you try to drive it anyway, the bare metal of the wheels grinding on the road makes this impossible. And then you're in a neighborhood you've never seen and the phones aren't working, and you're increasingly (incredibly) frustrated and also vaguely, indefinably sad. Why is this happening to me? you think in the dream. Why am I alone, and why won't anyone help me?

That's how he felt now as he realized he was moving away from his plane. He wouldn't be sleeping in his own bed tonight, after all. Instead, he'd be going to bed in a foreign country "south of the border," listening to strange sounds and smelling strange smells and just generally feeling the texture of somewhere else—somewhere new and unknown.

FORTY MINUTES LATER THEY were on the outskirts of Ensenada. The lights of the city rose into the night sky as they drew near, making Martin think of a fair at night—the glow cast on empty fields and parking lots, and the promise of fun and excitement the light seemed to contain. With any luck, he'd make it home for the Pleasanton fair in July, where he'd take the family, watch the kids on the rides, give them some money for the carnival games, and then kiss Linda and head on over to the track. Later in the day they'd all meet him, and the four of them would watch Temperature's Rising run in the big race. Maybe he'd win, and it would be one of those days when they all went home happy and complete—no arguing, no latent resentment, no crap.

"So here's what's going to happen," Hano said. He had his head resting on the seatback, and he was leaning sideways toward Martin just a bit, talking a little closer to his ear. He looked pretty relaxed for a guy making a drug run. "We're gonna get dropped off at a hotel," he said. "Or a motel, I guess. It's one I stayed at before. It's fine—it's not bad. But don't drink the water, of course. You know that, right?"

He paused, waiting for a reaction, and so Martin nodded. Yes, he'd known that, but he would definitely have made that mistake, anyway.

"We'll get something to eat," Hano said, "and we can check out Ensenada if you want. I don't know about you, but I'm pretty hungry. And the food's really good—not the kind of fake Mexican shit you get in San Francisco or wherever. Plus, I could use a drink. Definitely we should have some tequila."

They were quiet for a minute as the driver laid on the horn and leaned out his side window to yell in rapid-fire Spanish at a truck that was changing lanes and cutting them off.

"And then in the morning," Hano said, continuing, "we get up, have some pastries and eggs or whatever, and wait. They also have a kind of hot chocolate that's really good for breakfast. It's better than coffee, almost. It's the sugar, I guess. It gives you a real rush, and it kills a hangover."

Martin looked out the window at what was now Ensenada proper. Most of the buildings were square two-story edifices with simple plaster exteriors. They looked like cheap motels from the U.S. that had been plopped down over the border. The only difference was the rooftops, most of which had the curved, clay tiles that were apparently a requirement south of the Bay Area. That and the colors of the buildings. Practically every building was a different pastel color—light blue, yellow, green, light green. Strings of lights hung along the eaves or along second-story balconies. The colors and the lights gave the town an almost festive look—a little like a fair, actually.

People were out in the streets, standing in doorways, or sitting at tables. It seemed like there were tables everywhere—in front of small restaurants, markets, and even what looked like residential buildings. There were a lot of Americans. They tended to have nicer clothes, and most of them looked drunk. Martin watched a group of college-age kids—white kids, Americans—laughing and staggering as they tried to prop up a girl who could barely walk.

Farther up the street a group of sailors, probably from the naval base in San Diego, looked equally sauced. They were all wearing their white uniforms, with blue stripes on the sleeves and the flap that folded over onto their backs. One guy had another in a headlock, but they were both laughing; another was yelling to a group of Mexican girls standing across the street. Martin didn't get a good look at the girls, but it occurred to him that they were prostitutes. They were wearing miniskirts and high heels, and they had the practiced, bored posture of having stood on the street for hours.

They drove past a nice town square with a church on one side of it, and a big cement fountain in the middle. The fountain had been painted a deep orange color, and the spraying water was lit up by lights at the base of the fountain. Lots of people were gathered there. A few kids ran around or rode their bikes (though it seemed awfully late for them to be out). But for the most part Martin saw young men, some of them a little rough-looking in their jeans and white T-shirts.

They checked into their hotel, but because they didn't have any luggage, it was really just a matter of paying and then standing there while they made sure that Martin's leather satchel was tucked safely into the large safe behind the clerk's counter. Martin looked over at Hano as the safe clicked shut, and Hano nodded, satisfied.

Out in the street it was warm and bustling. Every half block or so a different song streamed out from a radio or a record player. Most of them were in English. He heard a few that Sarah listened to in her bedroom. But he also heard Mexican music. At one point they walked past a band standing in front of a club and playing what Martin assumed was some sort of Mexican folk music. One guy was playing a big fat guitar, and another guy had a bass that was almost as tall as he was; there was also someone on saxophone, and another guy with an accordion. Martin and Hano stood there in the street watching them for a couple of minutes, part of a small group that had gathered. An American sailor was standing near Martin; he had a bottle of Mexican beer in one hand, and he had his other arm around a young Mexican woman. He smiled at Martin. "Pretty good, huh?" he said, and Martin nodded.

They sat down at an open-air cantina, on tall stools along a wooden bar that looked onto the street. It was really just a big, wide window sill that doubled as a long table. The table and the surrounding window frame were painted a bright aqua color, and it occurred to Martin that someone might take a nice photo of him and Hano from outside the cantina as they sat there, elbows propped on the bar, drinking beer. It would be the sort of photo he could put up in the office (next to the shot of Sal Bando standing with him and Peter at the marina). People would notice it, and he'd explain with feigned reluctance that he liked to fly down to Mexico once in a while, drink in the culture a bit, do some deep-sea fishing, that sort of thing.

But even as he thought this, he realized that the photo could be used as evidence against him. "As you can see, ladies and gentlemen of the jury, Mr. Anderson made frequent trips to Ensenada, and he was clearly quite comfortable there. The state will seek to prove that, along with Mr. Hano, he was part of an elaborate smuggling operation, one that involved large quantities of heroin, easily the most addictive and certainly the most pernicious drug now threatening our nation's youth."

The menu, which was old and stained and creased, was a mystery to Martin, and so Hano ordered for both of them. "I've been here a couple of times," Hano said. "I know what's good."

They had a spicy soup of some sort, and then fried cakes made of plantains and stuffed with cheese. And then they had a big plate of shrimp in a brown sauce that was thick and hot. While they ate they drank, and pretty soon the bar was filled with their small bottles of Mexican beer.

"Wow," Martin said to Hano. "This food is really good."

"I know," Hano said. "It's like I told you—this is real Mexican food."

There was something so obvious about this that Martin didn't know how to respond, and so he didn't say anything. He figured it was about eleven o'clock. The street was becoming more crowded. The road was jammed now with cars, windows down and radios blaring. There were more and more sailors, shouting and reeling around and generally being obnoxious, but there were also lots of locals. They were young and looked like they were heading out to the bars and clubs. It was really bustling.

He and Hano talked about race horses, and about the A's. Hano was a big fan, and he seemed genuinely impressed that Martin lived near Sal Bando. And he believed Martin—or he seemed to believe him—when Martin told him that they'd been to neighborhood barbecues together, and that Martin and Bando had gotten to know each other pretty well. Martin also told him that he'd sold planes to several members of the A's, Reggie Jackson included.

"He was a jerk about it, though," Martin said, describing Jackson's purchase of a Cessna. "We actually had to threaten a lawsuit to get some of our money."

Martin knew he was pushing it with this last set of lies, but the alcohol was starting to take over and he couldn't help himself.

Hano, for his part, told him he'd been born on the naval base in Pearl Harbor not long before it was attacked by the Japanese.

"My father was on the USS *Shaw,*" he said. "He was killed in the second wave of bombings. So I never really knew him."

He went on to tell Martin that his mother moved him and his brother to California. Hano wasn't even a year old yet, he said, and they'd almost been sent to an internment camp because his mother was Japanese (it was his father who was Hawaiian).

Martin was impressed by this story, but he also knew that, like his own, it might be a tissue of lies. For all he knew, Hano had grown up in Santa Monica or Redondo Beach, an adopted kid in an all-white family that dragged him to church on Sundays. Sure, this was cynical, but how much could you really expect from someone who was willing to fly down to Mexico and smuggle heroin back into the U.S.?

At some point—Martin couldn't have said when—Hano had started ordering tequila. It wasn't long after this that things began to blur around the edges. He'd been getting steadily drunk on the little Mexican beers, but after the first shot of tequila he shifted into a different state of being. They both did. Suddenly they were chatting with people on the street as they passed by—women, of course, but pretty much anyone. They had a round of tequila shots with a group of sailors who were wandering past, and Martin was pleased when he made them all laugh with a series of imitations of Hollywood actors: Jimmy Stewart and John Wayne got the best response. The sailors were so impressed (and so drunk) that they began stopping passersby just to watch Martin's imitations. Martin was only too happy to comply. He wasn't even drunk so much as high—the tequila was like some sort of drug. He was having a great time. He felt uninhibited and confident—his money woes and Val Desmond and Ramirez and the drugs were a million miles away. They were problems that belonged to someone else.

Later, a couple of the waiters agreed to have a shot of tequila with them. Martin had his arm around the shoulders of one of them, and, at the waiter's suggestion, they sang "Country Roads," the John Denver song. The waiter had the words written down on a piece of paper that he pulled out of his pants pocket and unfolded and held out so that Martin and Hano could see it. Martin realized that the waiter probably did this with a lot of customers, maybe as a way to angle for a big tip, but he didn't really care. Singing this song, looking down at the man's scrawled-out English lyric sheet when he forgot the words, Martin felt suddenly as if he were in the midst of something—as if, rather than being outside and looking in, as was so often the case for him, he was in it, somehow, and a part of it.

And then they were with a couple of Mexican women. Young Mexican women, that is. He couldn't have said when or how they had joined them, but there they were. One was wearing a light blue minidress getup; it was one of those halter-top, bare shouldered things, and the dress itself was very short. She had great breasts. She was wearing white sandals, and her legs were all there, brown and smooth. Martin figured she was about twenty-five, or maybe a little older. Her teeth were a little crooked, something she tried to hide when she smiled, but she was actually pretty cute. She was sitting next to Hano, with her chair pulled up close to his, so that he could put his arm around her. Her brown hair was feathered back and held in place in stiff curls that framed her face, and she was wearing blue eye shadow that matched her dress. Her name was Maria.

The other one, Lucille, was wearing leather shorts and a tight, sequined shirt that was shoulderless on one side. The shorts were brown, and the shirt was a reddish pink. She was wearing thick platform shoes and red lipstick. Her outfit was a little ridiculous, but she was even better looking than her friend. She had deep brown eyes and long brown hair, down to the middle of her back, almost. She was younger than Maria; she said she was twenty-one, but Martin figured probably eighteen or nineteen. Maybe even seventeen, though Martin didn't want to think about it, especially when after a while she sat on his lap. The four of them had some tequila shots, toasting one another. The girls spoke a smattering of English, mostly gleaned from American television—beamed in free from San Diego, Martin guessed. It was funny, listening to them refer to Scope mouthwash, *The Flintstones,* and *The Jetsons,* and nice to watch the two of them look at each other and giggle. It was like being in high school again.

But this didn't last very long, because pretty soon (like in high school, actually) they paired off. Hano seemed to be playing it cool, chatting with Maria and joking around. But Martin wasn't able to contain himself. He ran his hand along Lucille's bare legs. She squirmed and pushed his hand away a few times, but she was also laughing and nibbling on his ear, licking it, and whispering something to him in Spanish. He could barely stand it.

Pretty soon he was kissing the girl, eagerly and sloppily, and after a while she said in her broken English that they should go somewhere else. Did he have a room they could go to? Martin looked over to check this out with Hano, but he and Maria were gone. Lucille laughed when she saw Martin's confusion, and she told him, mostly through gesturing, that Hano had already paid for all of them.

But she also told him he'd have to pay her twenty-five dollars to leave with her and that she wanted it before they left. She wrote it on a napkin: $25. Then she indicated that he should give the money to the man who was standing out in the street next to another young woman, also Mexican. He had his arm around this other woman, talking into her ear, and he was pointing at someone or something down the street. She was wearing very short cut-off jean shorts, platform shoes, and a red tank top.

At first Martin was confused, but then he understood. Of course, he thought. The idea that this young woman found him attractive or interesting, even if those qualities were connected to his money or his status as an American, was laughable. He was just some ridiculous pig from the U.S., one who was completely oblivious to the realities of her life here in Mexico—her struggles, her feelings, her dreams. But still, he thought in his drunken state of lustfulness (a state he recognized even as it overtook him and clouded his thinking), here she was. When would he get a chance like this again? If he didn't take advantage now, what would he think later on? He'd think he was a fucking fool, that's what he'd think.

And so, reeling a little bit, he stood up and took some money out of his pocket. He really didn't know how much—more than fifty dollars, anyway. "For your muchacho over there," he said. "Keep whatever you want." His voice was slurred, he knew, and he felt as if he were on his boat, swaying in an ocean swell. She smiled and put the money into a tiny pocket in her shorts, and gave him her elbow. They went out to the street, and Martin saw her wave to the man, who walked into traffic and hailed a cab for them. The man opened the door of the cab for Martin, and smiled at him with teeth that were all covered with silver and gold caps.

"*Tienes suerte,*" he said to Martin. "*Ella es muy buena.*"

Martin nodded, not knowing what the man was saying, but eager to get away from him and his metal teeth. He climbed into the cab, stumbling a little bit. Lucille followed, tumbling on top of him. Now that they were alone and in the dark, he felt even more desperate to touch her. He pushed up against her with his hips, practically climbing on top of her. And she was responding in what felt like a real way. She scratched the back of his neck with her nails, pulled his hair. He didn't care if she was faking it or not. And he didn't care if she charged $250 or $25,000. The cab driver watched him in his rearview mirror, but Martin didn't care about that, either. Plus, he realized, he had to keep his eyes open even in the dark, because every time he closed them the world began to spin and he felt sick.

MARTIN WAS LYING FACEDOWN on his bed in the motel room. His mouth tasted of vomit, and he saw that he had in fact vomited over the side of the bed, and even onto the mattress right next to his face. He had a horrific, blinding headache, and he felt that if he moved, he would get sick again. He didn't know how much time had passed or whether the girl—whatever her name was—was still around. What had happened in the interval between riding in the cab and now?

Martin lifted his head and turned over. At the foot of the bed Lucille was pulling her shirt on, but not before Martin saw that her breasts were a smooth light brown, plump and round and perky.

But even as he noticed this he was overwhelmed by his headache and a feeling of nausea. He closed his eyes for a second, felt sick again, and so opened them and raised himself slightly on his elbows. He saw that his pants were down around his ankles and that his shoes were still on. He slumped back against his pillow and the wall, watching as Lucille turned and walked toward the door. She glanced at him—not eye-to-eye, but via a mirror that was attached to a dresser near the foot of the bed. They made eye contact for a second in the mirror, and then she looked away. Her expression was impossible to read: it was neutral, blank. Not angry, not disgusted, and certainly not romantic. Just nothing. She opened the door and shut it behind her with a quiet click.

He stared at the closed door for a minute, not really thinking anything. Then he looked back at himself in the mirror. It was just like in Miriam Weaver's bedroom—though it was also different, of course. But there he was again, watching himself stare out of a bedroom mirror at himself. He looked a little strange, as if it were him but not really him at all.

He couldn't remember anything. One minute they were in the cab, with him desperate to pull her shorts down, and the next minute he was lying in a puddle of his own puke. The fact that his pants were around his ankles was a clue, of course, as was the fact that she'd had her shirt off when he woke up. But had she pulled her shorts on and buckled her shoes just previous to putting her shirt on? Maybe he'd had sex with her with his pants around his ankles—he'd certainly been in a hurry, from what he could remember. But glancing down at his flaccid penis and fat belly, he had the feeling that nothing had happened at all. She'd taken her shirt off and he'd dropped his pants, but after that . . . nothing.

It wouldn't have been the first time. Once, a few years ago, Ludwig had hired a prostitute and brought her to the office for Martin's fortieth birthday. Martin had never had sex with a prostitute—he'd always been too scared. But he'd gone along with it. What could you do? Beaton and a few other guys had been there, too. It was peer pressure. Plus, he'd been pretty buzzed. She'd taken him into the back room to give him a blow job, but he couldn't get it up. She tried to help him along, but it was hopeless. She'd been cool about it, didn't say anything when they came back out and everyone cheered. But he'd felt humiliated nevertheless, and had often thought he should give it another try—hiring a prostitute, that is—just to prove to himself that he could do it.

Lying there, watching the fan spin slowly above him, he felt disgusted with himself—especially when he thought about how turned on he'd been, how lecherous. Jesus, he was a pig. And the worst part was that it was a lose-lose proposition. Either he'd failed at the very moment when his desires were within reach—sex with one of those incredible young bodies he lusted after—or, worse, he actually *had* managed to get it up and have sex with someone who was basically a teenager, a high school girl.

He stumbled to the bathroom and threw up into the toilet. He retched again and again, until his ribs ached. As he retched and coughed, he saw how the toilet was filthy up under the rim with black streaks that looked moldy, and that spoke of months, maybe years of sick Americans hunched miserably over it, paying the price of indulgence.

HE WOKE UP IN the bathroom, with Hano kicking him gently in the legs and butt. "Wake up, sleepyhead," he said to Martin. "Time for school."

"Okay," he said. "All right. I'm up." B t he was embarrassed, especially as his pants were still down around is ankles. He did his best to stand and pull them up. His throat felt ra and it hurt to talk.

"Christ, Martin," Hano said, looking at him and smiling. "You look like shit. And it stinks in here, man. It smells like you puked your guts out. Flush the fucking toilet and brush your teeth, and let's get out of here." He handed Martin a toothbrush and a tube of toothpaste, and walked out into the bedroom.

Hano looked like shit, too. His round face was puffy and his clothes were almost comically wrinkled. But he didn't look as bad as Martin did. Or at least that's what Martin thought as he stood, his head spinning, looking at himself in the little cabinet mirror in the bathroom. He looked pale, and he had dark circles under his eyes. He still felt nauseated. There were creases on his face from where he had slept with his cheek on his shirt-sleeve, and his toupee was stiff and matted down on one side—from vomit, he realized. He groaned and pushed his face close to the faucet and splashed water onto his face. He was going to have to pull his toupee off. What would Hano say to that?

Hano stood in the doorway. He grabbed the top of the door frame with both hands and leaned forward, his arms muscles flexing and a smile on his puffy face.

"So," he said. "Senorita Hot Pants. She was a nice little package. I hope you got inside those shorts before you started puking."

Martin nodded as he splashed his face with water. "Definitely," he said, his voice still hoarse. "She was definitely a nice little package." He struggled through a wave of nausea, putting his hands on the edges of the sink and closing his eyes.

"Yeah?" Hano said. "And?"

Martin took a deep breath, feeling the nausea close at hand. "And," he said, taking a deep breath and opening his eyes and looking over at Hano, "I definitely got inside those shorts before I started puking."

Hano smiled again, raising his thick eyebrows. The gesture with the eyebrows reminded Martin of Gary Roberts, back in Walnut Station. But Gary Roberts seemed like a figure from a life he had lived a long time ago.

Hano nodded. "Excellent," he said. "Mine was good, too. She knew what she was doing. They were pros. Did you see their pimp? That fucking guy with the teeth? Yikes." Hano imitated the smile, and Martin felt another wave of nausea.

Then Hano was quiet for a second. He put his hands back up onto the top of the door frame, and from Martin's bent-over perspective he looked like he was actually hanging there, straining in silent concentration.

Martin turned off the water and wiped his face with a towel. He wondered if brushing his teeth was going to make him throw up again.

"Listen," Hano said. "Let's go get some of that hot chocolate shit I told you about. It'll kill your hangover. Or it'll help, anyway. And then we've gotta meet Ramirez's guys. The heroin came in last night—or early this morning. It's already packed into the plane. We need to wait until it's dark, of course, but we can fly out tonight, at least—if you're not too sick, that is." He leaned over and slapped Martin on the back with one of his big Hawaiian hands. "Unless," he said, moving out of the bathroom now and talking over his shoulder, "you're thinking about staying down here, and moving in with your new girlfriend. Little Miss Mexican Girl, or whatever her name was."

CHAPTER SEVEN

It took almost three days for Martin to recover. He'd felt okay during the flight from Mexico to Santa Barbara—helped Hano unload his half of the heroin, shook his hand, and all that. But by the time he touched down in Hayward he knew he was really sick. He had to run into his office to use the toilet while Val's guys put the rest of the dope into their car (he had terrible diarrhea), and even an envelope with five thousand dollars in it didn't make him feel any better.

He made it home sometime around dawn Sunday morning, but after that he stayed in bed, with the lights off, moaning softly. He couldn't hold any food down, and he was on and off the toilet all day and into the night. He could hear the kids pattering around outside his room, but everything sounded far away. Even when Peter was playing basketball—the hoop was on the other side of the bedroom wall—it didn't really bother him. He just faded in and out of sleep.

At first Linda was furious, both because he'd stayed away an extra day and because he was so obviously hung over.

"What the hell, Martin?" she said. "What did you do down there?" She was disgusted—slept in the guest bedroom, left him to suffer alone in bed during the day. Eventually, though, he managed to convince her that it was the water, that he had bacterial poisoning.

"It's Montezuma's revenge," he said. And after about twenty-four hours of misery he realized that this was actually the case, which in fact made him feel a little better. He didn't want to think he was quite *that* hung over.

When he finally emerged it was Tuesday, about noon. Linda was home because she'd been cut back to three days a week at work. She was glad for the extra time, but Martin was worried about the loss of income.

"So," Linda said. "He is risen."

"Okay," he said. "I get it. Very funny."

He was hungry, so she opened a can of soup and warmed it up for him on the stove. The kids were at school; it was their last week of the year. Peter was back in class, and so far everything was okay. No notes or anything like that.

"I waited all day yesterday for the phone to ring," Linda said. "But I guess it was all right."

They talked for a while about Mexico and the things he'd supposedly been doing down there but hadn't (his lies were so elaborate that he had to really concentrate). Then they talked some more about the kids, her parents, his dad, the dog, and the other things that comprised their life. Eventually, after some coaxing, he managed to convince her to get back into bed with him for some "afternoon action," as he put it. She resisted, but she was as ready as he was. It had been a while, and he was reminded of why they were a good match—or had been a good match, anyway, and still could be, at least sometimes.

He was drifting into his usual postsex nap when she said something about someone stopping by the house.

"So your girlfriend came by here the other day looking for you," she said.

"Uh-huh," he said, thinking she could be referring to anyone—even the dog that their neighbor brought over to play with Arrow. He was one of those furry things that looked like a sawed-off little husky. "And who am I dating now?" he asked.

"She said they had a break-in. And she needed to borrow some gas."

Martin was startled into wakefulness at the mention of a break-in, but he kept himself from looking over at Linda right away. He paused, counted to three, then turned his head toward her.

"Wait . . . *who* are you talking about?" he asked.

She glanced over at him from her sitting-up position in bed. "Who do you think?" she asked. "Miriam."

"Miriam?" Martin asked. "Down-the-street Miriam?"

She sighed, clearly a little exasperated. The postsex sweetness was quickly fading. "Yes, Martin," she said. "Down-the-street Miriam. Is there another Miriam out there that I don't know about?"

"Miriam's my girlfriend?" he asked.

Linda got off the bed and walked into the bathroom. He heard her turn on the water at the sink, fill a glass, then take a sip. She always slurped a little when she drank water. Why was she always so thirsty?

She came back and stood in the bathroom doorway, naked and leaning against the door frame.

"Yes, Martin, she's your girlfriend," she said. Her tone was flat. "You guys are going steady. You wrote a note to her in class, and she said 'yes.' Don't you remember that?"

She tilted her head slightly, accentuating her exaggeration, and then took another sip of her water. She looked good standing there in the doorway. The shadows were just right—it was like a photo in a magazine.

He was negotiating a series of conflicting feelings. On the one hand, he was pleased—thrilled, even—to hear Miriam referred to as his "girlfriend." It was like in high school, when you just wanted to hear the name of the person you were interested in or had a crush on. "I ran into Miriam Weaver at the market today." Even this was enough to provide Martin with a brief tingle of pleasure, especially if it gave him an opening for further discussion. "Oh yeah? Was she with her asshole husband?" He could go on like this for a while, extending the conversation and teasing out references to her, carefully indulging in a sort of vicarious access to her.

But of course for Linda to refer to Miriam as his girlfriend could mean various things. It might mean that she was on to Martin—that she knew he found her attractive, and probably that he found her incredibly sexy. She herself had commented on Miriam's looks a bunch of times.

"Wow," she'd say. "She's got the skin of a twenty-year-old. And those breasts. What a rack."

"Yeah, definitely, she looks good for her age," he'd say, trying to sound casual—even a little oblivious. "How old is she? I can't believe she's been married to that clown Hal Weaver for so long."

But—and this was more interesting, a bit exciting, even—if she was calling Miriam his girlfriend, it suggested (possibly) a form of jealousy, one that could (possibly) stem from a sense that Miriam had given Martin a little extra attention, attention that Linda had noticed. Had Linda picked up on something in this regard? This was unlikely, but it was certainly titillating.

Still, you couldn't overlook the fact that Miriam had showed up at their house to talk about the break-in. He was surprised she knew something had been stolen. Wouldn't she just assume that one of the kids had taken it? Or a housekeeper? (Did they have a cleaning lady? Most of the people on Miwok seemed to have cleaning ladies. Linda had hired someone to come in once a week, but she did a lousy job, mostly just pushed the dirt around.)

Finally, though, there was the horrific possibility that this was a veiled accusation. Jesus, maybe she'd seen him. Not while he was lying on the floor in her room, of course. She'd have screamed and freaked out. No doubt about that. But maybe she'd seen him sneaking out of her yard, maybe as he was squeezing his fat-fuck stomach through the slats in the fence.

"Okay, okay," he said, trying to sound impatient. "So come on, what happened? What sort of break-in? And why did she need gas?"

"Well," Linda said. She picked her bra up off the floor and started putting it on, leaning forward a little bit and reaching around back to snap it. "She came over and said she was out of gas—or that she didn't have enough for a trip they were taking up to Donner Lake. They rented a cabin up there, or something. I don't know. But she needed gas, and she was freaking out because it was Saturday and there weren't any stations open. "

She leaned over again, picked up her shirt from the floor, and slipped it on. Then she looked around under the sheets for her underwear, found it, and stepped into it. After that she got back under the covers, sat with her back against the headboard, and looked over at Martin.

"Huh," Martin said. "So you gave her some of the gas from the tanks in the garage?"

He wasn't all that surprised. People had been stopping by asking about gas for a while now. In the closet in their carport, he had five big twenty-gallon tanks that he'd filled up one day at the airport. He'd only tapped into this supply once, but he liked knowing it was there. He liked the personal security it provided—he wasn't ever going to run out of gas. But he also liked knowing that he had it, and that he wasn't letting anyone else have any of it. It was this last component of the equation that made having the gas so pleasurable. He knew it was bad—terrible, in fact—but he couldn't help it.

"Yes, I did," Linda said. "I know you don't want people to know we have it, but she was really upset. She said she forgot to fill up Friday evening and forgot that she wouldn't be able to fill up on the weekend. But she said Hal was going to be furious. Plus, she said she just couldn't stand the thought of how the kids would react if they couldn't go. She had some gas in the tank still, and she was hoping to drive out to the airport with me . . . or with you, I guess. I don't know how she knew you have gas out there, but she did. Anyway, then I showed her the gas tanks. She was really relieved. She really appreciated it."

Martin nodded, thinking about Hal and what a dick he was. He was pleased to come to Miriam's rescue, no doubt about that. But he was disappointed at having missed the chance to drive all the way out to Hayward with Miriam—even in separate cars it would have been something they did together. Plus, he would have been able to show her his office. And maybe they could have had coffee or a bite to eat out there. Maybe at Nelda's, or maybe even over at Jack London Square, where he could show her his boat. She'd have been impressed by that, he was pretty sure.

"Hal Weaver is a prick," Martin said.

Linda gave a little chuckle, and nodded. "Yep," she said. "He is. And he's creepy. He's a drunk and a letch. And he's ugly. Disgusting, in fact."

Now it was Martin's turn to laugh. "Jeez," he said. "You don't have to beat around the bush, you know. Why don't you tell me how you really feel?"

They both laughed again, and then they were quiet for a minute. He liked it when Linda was straightforward like that, even a little tough sounding. None of this suburban sweetness all the women out here thought they had to perform. In fact, it was the thing that had attracted him to her in the first place—that and her looks. She wasn't quite at the level of Miriam Weaver, but still, she looked pretty damned good just the same. He took special pleasure in knowing when younger guys were checking her out—the bag boy at the supermarket, say, or the guys at the local gas stations (when they used to go to the gas stations).

"So okay," Martin said, breaking the short silence. He wanted to hear about the other issue, the break-in, but he knew he needed to tread carefully. "She came over and got some gas. What about there being a break-in? Do you mean their car, or their house?"

Linda yawned, and let her head rest on the wall behind her. "I'm tired," she said. She gave Martin a soft little backhanded slap on his right shoulder. "It's all your fault," she said, and then smiled.

She was being sweet, Martin knew, trying to connect with him a little bit, so he was careful to bide his time. If he asked again she might sense that something was a bit off—but maybe not. A neighborhood break-in was actually a big deal, when you thought about it. In fact, maybe it was time to call up one of those alarm companies and hook up the house with a system. You never knew who was going to come wandering into your house.

Linda yawned again. "I don't really know what happened," she said. "She told me she wasn't even sure there was a break-in. She said when she came home one day last week—I forget which day it was—the outside door to their bedroom was wide open. You know those French doors they have that lead out to the patio?"

Martin nodded. "Yeah," he said. "I guess so. I don't know."

"They were open," Linda said. "And she said that they never, ever leave them like that, especially when they're going to be gone during the day."

The dog came into the room, announcing himself with a leap onto the bed. He wasn't supposed to be up there, and he knew it, so he lay there looking guiltily at them. Linda reached out and scratched him behind the ear, and he relaxed.

"And so?" Martin said, unable to not ask. Was it just him, or was she moving too slowly through this story?

"And *so*," Linda said, "she started looking around. And it looked like someone had gone through their stuff. Through their walk-in closet, and their shelves, and drawers, and that kind of thing. And then she realized that she was missing a jewelry box. She said it had some really nice jewelry in it, and it also had some gold coins that were super valuable. Her dad had given them to her on really special occasions, she said. One was for her confirmation, another was for her wedding, and one was for when one of the kids was born. Anyway, she said it's gone. The jewelry box, I mean. She said she's upset about the jewelry, but that the coins are worth tons of money. Thousands of dollars. A couple of them are really rare, she said."

"Holy shit," Martin said, less to her than to himself.

"I know," Linda said. "I asked her if she thought maybe one of the kids had taken it. You know, just playing around or something."

"Yeah," Martin said. "That's what I was going to say."

Linda shrugged. "She talked to them, and she said there's no way they did it. Plus, like I said, the room was sort of ransacked. She said it was like someone had been looking for exactly that one thing. Like they knew it was there and couldn't find it at first."

Martin thought about this, about the blind way he'd grabbed the box off the top of Miriam's dresser. About how he hadn't even really known it was in his hand until he got out to his car and noticed he was clutching it. Maybe, he thought, he'd known all along what he was looking for in Miriam's bedroom. But he also knew that this was bullshit, and that the theory of the thief with one item in mind was off the mark.

He thought about the coins. They couldn't possibly equal the value of the stacks of bills he'd carried down to Mexico, but still, there was something about the solidity of them that made him feel as if he'd finally gotten his hands onto something of real value. It was like it was more real than regular money, somehow—the dollar bills and even the change he carried in his wallet or his pants. They were like the old coins you read about in a fairy tale, stored away in a dragon's cave or in the giant's house at the top of the beanstalk. And he was the fairy-tale character upon whom good fortune had smiled—who'd stumbled upon this money at the very moment he needed it most.

"Well," Martin said. "I guess that's possible. I mean, it's a little weird that nothing else was stolen." He caught himself with this last line, and then added, "That's what you said, right? That the jewelry case was the only thing missing?"

Linda nodded, but she had her eyes closed, and Martin could tell that she wasn't interested in talking about the Weavers any longer. She had her head back against the wall again, and he wondered if she might fall asleep like that. She could fall asleep anywhere, and in pretty much any position—standing up, practically.

"Hey," Linda said. Her eyes were still closed and her head was still leaning against the wall.

"Yeah?" Martin responded. She had startled him a little bit.

"Thanks for getting me into bed here today," she said. "I miss you sometimes when we don't do this for a while."

"Hey," he said, putting his hand on her shoulder. "I know. I miss you, too."

THE NEXT DAY, MARTIN was in San Francisco. He'd driven over to take his dad out for a birthday lunch. Or a prebirthday lunch. His actual birthday, his seventy-eighth, was the following Saturday. But he and Linda were taking the kids to Tahoe that weekend, and this was what Martin was calling the beforehand makeup visit. Plus, he'd reasoned, it was poker day for his stepmother Eleanor and so this would give his dad something to do while she was out.

"You'll love it," he'd told his dad on the phone. "It'll be better than on your actual birthday. No one likes their actual birthday, you know."

Martin wasn't sure what his dad thought about his birthday, but Martin had begun to feel that way lately about his own birthday. He was forty-four, and it was still supposed to be a big deal. But it was too much. "Are you having a good time?" Linda would say. "It's your special day, you know. If there's anything you want, just ask!" But, of course, she didn't mean it when she said he could have anything he wanted. What he really wanted was to go out fishing or to the track, maybe up to Reno to gamble. Was that really going to happen? Not a chance.

"The kids want to celebrate with you," Linda said when he'd actually told her his birthday wish a couple of years ago. She'd looked at him like he'd just admitted to some sort of odd sex fantasy. "Don't you want to be with your family on your birthday? What's wrong with you?"

He was thinking about this as he made his way across the lobby of his dad's building. It was down in the Embarcadero, just off North Beach. The apartment was just a little two-bedroom thing with a kitchenette, but it was in a great location. You could even see the Bay Bridge from the balcony. It would have been way out of his dad's league, moneywise, if he hadn't gotten remarried about ten years ago to Eleanor. She was the widow of a shipping magnate of some sort—some guy who'd run a lot of the import docks over in Oakland, and who'd left her a big chunk of change when his heart gave out.

Martin wasn't all that crazy about Eleanor, but meeting her had been a godsend for Martin's dad. Martin's mother had died about a year earlier (pancreatic cancer—random, out of the blue), and his dad had been completely lost. He just couldn't fend for himself. Everyone had been relieved when he found Eleanor, especially Martin. It had bothered him to see his father so lonely—mainly, he knew, because on some level he was exactly the same. He talked a big game, but he knew that if something ever happened to Linda, he'd dry up and blow away.

The head doorman waved to Martin.

"How are you today, Mr. Anderson? Hello to Mrs. Anderson and the kids."

He always remembered Martin when he came to visit, and when he said hello he made it seem like Martin was a part of the more upscale part of San Francisco—like he belonged.

As usual, his dad took forever to answer the door. Martin could see him peeping through the eyehole at him, and he listened as he undid the various locks: the upper bolt lock, the push-in lock on the handle, the chain lock. Finally, he opened the door and stood there looking at Martin, smiling.

"Here he is," he said. "My son, the big shot." Then he turned and shuffled back toward the living room. The sunlight streaming in through the sliding glass door silhouetted him as he walked away from Martin.

They sat for a while, shooting the shit. They talked about the kids for a minute or two, but his dad wasn't all that interested. Never had been. "Kids," he said, shaking his head. And that was it. He changed the subject to the A's, whom he disliked. "They don't have it this year," he said. "They just don't want it bad enough."

His indifference about the kids drove Linda crazy, and for a few years Martin had been put off by it as well. But lately Martin had begun to appreciate it. There were other things to talk about, for Christ's sake. And besides, his dad hadn't been all that interested in Martin and his brothers when they were growing up, so why start now? Wasn't it a little late for that?

Half an hour later they were in a place in Chinatown his dad liked.

It was just one room, and they only served the side orders they brought around on the carts. Martin liked this food okay, but he would have chosen something different, that's for sure. Italian at Vanessi's or Little Joe's, or a seafood place, maybe. At least those places had some atmosphere. This place just had a few little fountains with rocks and bubbling water, some hanging things that looked like calendars with Chinese writing on them, and the waitresses in the kimonos, or whatever they were called. But the place was popular, you had to admit that. Today, as was usually the case on a weekday, there were a lot of white-collar types grabbing a quick lunch, probably glad to get out of the office for a few minutes.

"So when is your boy Nixon gonna give it up?" his dad asked, slurping at his hot and sour soup.

Martin rolled his eyes and shrugged. Suddenly everyone was giving him a hard time about Nixon—even people who'd voted for him, like his dad.

"Hey," Martin said, looking at the pictures of the food on the menu. "I don't remember you campaigning for McGovern. Or Humphrey, for that matter. You're as much to blame as I am."

His dad shook his head. "The nerve," he said. " 'I'm not a crook, and I don't know anything about the missing part of the tape. Must've been someone else. Maybe my dog Checkers ate it.' "

Martin laughed. "Checkers," he said. "Jesus."

He took a few sips of his soup, but he didn't like it. The texture was weird. He put down his spoon.

"Okay," Martin said. "It's true. The guy's a crook, and we all know it. And he knows we know it. But seriously, what would happen if he resigned? I mean, you can't just switch presidents, can you? Wouldn't the markets bottom out? What would the Arabs do? And what about Vietnam? What would happen over there?"

His dad shook his head. "Martin," he said. "Don't you get it? It doesn't matter who's in charge. Not anymore. Both the Kennedys could come back from the dead and it wouldn't matter. All that stuff just has to play itself out. Especially in Vietnam. The North Vietnamese are gonna take over the South, and that's all there is to it. And you know why, don't you?" He pointed his spoon at Martin.

Martin shrugged. "I don't know," he said. "Tell me." Here we go, he thought. He went off to fight in WWI when he was twenty-one, and so he's the authority on everything involving world politics.

"Because they're tougher than we are," his dad said to him.

"Okay, Dad," Martin said. "Whatever you say." He signaled for the waitress.

"You know I'm right," his dad said. "I mean, look around you." He gestured around the little restaurant, at the businessmen hunched over their tables, sipping tea, reading the paper, chatting with colleagues. "Look at us—Americans, I mean. We can't handle it when we don't have a full tank of gas, for Christ's sake. That's all I hear about these days. 'My gas, my gas. What am I gonna do?'" He shook his head.

The waitress arrived at their table, pushing a cart filled with plates of little pastries and rolls. She waited for them to decide which ones they wanted. Martin watched his dad as he pointed to a couple of dishes.

"Don't you have the big gas lines out in that town you live in?" he asked Martin when the waitress was gone. "You've seen those people in the suburbs. Can you picture them crawling through the jungle, defending anything? Their country, or their family? Not a chance. They're too soft—we're all too soft."

Martin was quiet, thinking. His dad was right, of course. People in the suburbs were soft. They were all a bunch of big, swaddled-up babies. Gary Roberts, the ice cream scooper, living in a network of tunnels and setting booby traps? Forget it. But Martin didn't like his dad's infer-ence that Martin was soft, too. "That town you live in." What the fuck was that? His dad knew exactly where he lived.

He sighed. His dad was started now, and like a windup toy, he was going to go on for a while.

America had peaked, his dad said. And now it was only a matter of time before there was another Great Depression. "The gas lines will be bread lines pretty soon," he said. "Mark my words." But this time, he said to Martin, more serious now, we won't be ready. Because everyone was a crook now. Not just Nixon—everyone. And soft.

"It's all a big trap," his father said. "It's like we've all been hypnotized. Maybe they put something in the water, or in the radio waves. Or on our televisions, maybe that's it. But whatever it is, it's working. We think we're happy, when what we really are is lost. We're trying to get back to the place where we used to be happy, or where we think we were happy, but we can't find it. And do you know why we can't find it?" he asked.

He waited a second for Martin to respond, but Martin just shrugged again—rolled his eyes at the drama and shrugged.

"Because we're soft?" he asked.

"No," his dad said. "Not that." He picked up his tea, then put it down before taking a sip from it. "We can't find it," he said, leaning forward across the table, "because we're using the wrong map." And then he nodded, raising his thick eyebrows.

Martin nodded in return, but he was only half listening. He'd heard it before, and he was used to tuning out his dad's lectures. Or sermons, as he referred to them. It was fine for an old man to be an armchair philosopher, he thought. He'd worked hard, raised a family—and it's true, he did fight in a world war, for Christ's sake. Let him talk, right? But Martin knew that he'd always been like this, had always been a blowhard. No wonder his brothers had turned out the way they had: a dope-smoking photographer and a musician in Vegas. Hardly the kind of jobs that keep you from being soft.

But still, he was willing to bet that if his dad were sitting here with his brother Alan, the hippie photographer, the two of them would be falling all over themselves to agree with each other. Not just about Nixon—it was easy to pick on him now that he'd been busted red-handed. No, they'd talk about how the oil crisis was a conspiracy between the U.S. and the Arabs to make money for a few elite families, or how Patty Hearst was actually a hero (or heroine) for turning on her capitalist pig of a father. That kind of thing. And Martin was pretty sure they'd make some joking references to Martin the businessman and his misguided pursuit of happiness out in the suburbs.

Eventually the topic turned to sports, and how Charlie Finley was ruining both the A's and professional baseball. They didn't have any trouble agreeing about that. And then it was time to go.

On the cab ride home they went past the new Transamerica Pyramid, the skyscraper they'd finished building a couple of years ago. It was the corporate headquarters for Bank of America. Martin's dad had worked in the same office with William Pereira, the guy who'd designed it. It was just after World War II, in Los Angeles. His dad was just a draftsman and they'd only said hello a few times, but still, they'd worked together. Martin was impressed by that.

"There it is," Martin said, craning his neck to look up at its sloping side as it extended upward and out of his line of sight. "Everyone said it was going to be a big embarrassment, but I don't hear anyone complaining now."

His father nodded. "Yeah," he said, leaning over toward Martin and following his gaze out the window.

They were quiet for a minute as the cab made its way along the street. Then Martin's dad slapped him on the knee.

"But don't forget," he said, looking at Martin and chuckling. "The Transamerica Pyramid . . . it's really just a big bank."

A couple of minutes later Martin was helping his dad out of the cab and into his building. The doorman helped get him into the elevator, and Martin walked him to his apartment, helped him get the door open. But he didn't go inside. On the way back out of the building, he made sure to give the doorman a nice tip, and then he was out on the street. He had to walk a couple of blocks to his car, which he'd left somewhere along Washington Street.

Martin sighed. He'd felt pleased with himself for setting up the lunch with his dad, but now he had the feeling, not infrequent when it came to these get-togethers, that maybe it hadn't been such a great idea after all.

CHAPTER EIGHT

The guy looked familiar. Checking him out through the peephole of his front door, Martin saw that he was tall and lean, with wavy dark hair and a big nose. And a little scruffy—the kind of look that was popular nowadays. Ludwig had that same thing going on. The shaggy hair and the sideburns.

He was wearing faded jeans, a black T-shirt that said something about New Jersey, and black high-tops. He was also holding what looked like a denim jacket. Martin thought about not answering the door, but the guy had probably seen his shadow pass across the tall, frosted window next to the front door. Plus, Arrow was barking, and Martin knew he wouldn't stop until he sniffed the mystery person standing outside.

With the door open and looking at him face-to-face, the guy seemed even more familiar. Where had he seen him before? Martin thought that maybe he was looking for work—maybe wanted to wash the windows, or give a bid on a new roof. Had he worked for Martin before? He couldn't remember. The problem was that he looked kind of cocky, like he knew something but was trying to wait until the last moment before giving in and smiling.

"Mr. Anderson?" the guy said. He lifted his chin just a little bit when he said this and raised his eyebrows. He was definitely about to break into a smile.

"Uh . . . yep," Martin said. "That's me. I'm Martin Anderson." He thought about saying "Call me Martin," but he didn't. In fact, he hated it when people did that. And it would have been especially weird at a moment like this. Did he really want some roofer calling him by his first name? That was one good thing about the suburbs—you could be an impersonal dick and no one thought it was inappropriate. It was downright normal, in fact.

"Great," the guy said. He reached out and handed Martin a business card that he must have had in his hand before he even rang the bell. "I'm Detective Jim Slater," he said. "I'm with the Narcotics Division for the East Bay Police Department." He smiled, finally, showing Martin an almost full grin—one that, to Martin's mind, had more than a hint of irony. Martin didn't say anything, just looked down at the card. And there it was: DETECTIVE JIM SLATER, EBPD. NARCOTICS DIVISION. There were some phone numbers underneath his name and title, and then next to this information was a little embossed seal of the State of California: there was the Roman-looking woman with her shield and a helmet that had the thing that looked like a brush on top of it; the California grizzly bear; a Gold Rush miner (yet again); and some sailboats, maybe schooners or something like that, sailing around on what looked like San Francisco Bay. He stared at the card for a second, then willed himself to look back up at the guy as he stood there watching him look at the card.

"I apologize for just popping in like this, out of the blue," Slater said. "But do you think I could come inside and talk to you for a few minutes?" His eyes narrowed for a quick second. "I just have a few questions for you, and it's important. I'll be out of your hair in a few minutes—I promise. I'd really appreciate it."

Martin felt himself tense up and then go numb all over. He could feel his face beginning to tingle, and his arms suddenly felt heavy. He felt tired—that's what it was. How did they find him so fast? Someone must have said something. Maybe they'd busted Hano down in Santa Barbara, and he'd given up his name. He wanted to blurt out Hano's name, and Val's, and get it over with.

He looked out past this Slater guy as he stood there in the doorway, out to where he'd parked in his driveway. It wasn't a police car, he noticed (thank God: at the first sight of a police cruiser, Alan Guthrie would be sure to immediately drop work on his train set and wander over, making sure everything was all right). It wasn't even the sort of plain cop car they always drove on TV (or that Popeye Doyle drove in *The French Connection*). It was a black Chevy Camaro—1970, he thought. It looked like it was in good shape. It was certainly clean and shiny.

Martin didn't see anyone else out there, either in the car or standing next to it. The guy must have come alone. He wondered if this was unusual. On *Dragnet* the guys always worked in pairs. But it was definitely the kind of thing that happened on that new cop show he'd seen a few times. *Toma,* or something like that. The guy who played Toma would dress up in some sort of disguise and make the bust all by himself. Martin wondered for a second if this guy was in disguise, what with the jeans and the rest of it. But then he realized the guy had already said he was a cop, and that this didn't make any sense. Had his partner hurried around to the rear of the house to provide backup? Were they going to take turns beating the shit out of him?

Martin knew—or sensed, anyway—that he should assert himself here just a little bit. Right about now he should be screwing up his face and saying something like, "What the fuck is this all about?" But he didn't think he could pull off something like that. Maybe if the guy had called to give him a heads-up: "Do you mind if I drop by to talk over a few things with you . . . like why you think you can get away with smuggling heroin into the U.S. from Mexico?"

But of course this was exactly the reason the guy *hadn't* called ahead—he wanted to catch Martin off guard. Martin knew this, saw the setup and saw how he ought to respond, but it didn't matter. All he could do was tell this cocky detective guy to come on in, sure, no problem, whatever he needed.

The cop followed as Martin led the way into the kitchen area, which opened out onto the living room. His house looked different to him all of a sudden: the big indoor gas barbecue and overhead fan, and then past that the leather couch, the painting of the Golden Gate Bridge, the array of framed photos taken in the winner's circle at the area race tracks, the built-in bookshelves. He glanced at the titles: *Catch-22, The Day of the Jackal, King Rat* . . . It all looked expensive, he realized—too expensive. Did it smell of drug money? He knew this was ridiculous, that he'd actually purchased the house and everything in it legitimately (everything except Miriam's jewelry box, that is). But it didn't matter. Standing there and asking this narco guy if he wanted a beer (and he did want one, which surprised Martin), he felt that there was only one conclusion the cop would reach: that this house was paid for by the poor peasants Val had told him about, the ones who picked the opium. Martin imagined them harvesting the poppies, loading up their mules, and then making the long, perilous journey out of the mountains and into some backward village in order to sell their goods at a slim, subsistence-level profit. Martin was suddenly certain that this cop did know their story, and that he was connecting it to his house here at 1186 Miwok Drive in Walnut Station, California. Or maybe the cop might be thinking that the house and all of its fancy crap were built on the misery of the dozens of heroin addicts he dealt with every day, month after month, year after year.

Martin thought again of the films he'd seen at his daughter's drug classes, the ones showing heroin users going through withdrawal—the puking, the tremors, and the other stages of misery that they'd been forced to watch in that uncomfortable little classroom. And then he realized with a sudden clarity that the detective standing in his kitchen was in fact the selfsame narcotics detective who'd given the scare-you-straight pep talk to the kids. And in fact, he realized, the wheels turning now, that this was the guy who'd pulled up his shirt and shown them his bullet wounds. Martin wondered if the guy recognized him from the class, but discounted the possibility. Martin had been one of the invisible parents, the ones who paid the fee and then sat there, glad they were doing the right thing, but also bored and a little embarrassed by it all.

The kids were out in the backyard playing in the pool. Martin had just turned on the pool's heater a couple days before, and the water was finally getting warm enough to be comfortable. Maybe that was why the two of them had been out there for over an hour without arguing or screwing with one another. Sarah had the radio on. It was just weak AM radio noise dissipating into the afternoon heat, but something about the sound gave Martin a sudden sense of support.

"So what can I do for you?" Martin asked as he leaned back onto one of the tall stools arranged along the counter next to the barbecue grill. His voice came out in a sort of trilling, wavering falsetto, and he noticed that he was sweating. He had to resist the urge to reach up and wipe the perspiration from his forehead—though he wondered if a wet, glistening forehead was more of a giveaway than the act of reaching up and wiping it off.

Slater sat down on one of the other stools at the counter (leaving one between them, thank God), and took a long swig of his beer. Then he glanced out the window at the kids. Peter was lying on his back on a raft, waving his arms wildly as he tried to move backward in a sort of spastic backstroke (it was a difficult move on a raft, Martin knew, but he looked really uncoordinated). From what Martin could tell as he sat there, following Slater's gaze and looking out through the sliding glass door, Peter was trying to move because Sarah was standing on the diving board, about to jump in and swamp him off the raft. They were both screaming, and overall it was a usefully idyllic scene. How could a family like this be involved in drugs?

But with a sideways glance Martin saw—or thought he saw—that Slater was aware of Sarah's body as she stood there, preparing to jump. She was in a bikini, and though skinny and still girlish, she was tanned and wet and attractive. Martin could see it, and he knew that this cop did as well. Sarah jumped and did an awkward cannonball, sending water high in the air and causing Peter to squeal with joy.

"That looks like fun," the cop said, turning back to Martin. "Nothing like a sunny day and a pool." He smiled, and took another sip from his beer.

"Yeah," Martin said, nodding slightly. "But I'm gonna have to drag them inside pretty soon. They won't put any lotion on, and my wife will kill me if they're sunburned. She's not here right now," he added. "She's out. She drove out to Berkeley with a couple of friends to shop and have lunch."

Martin said this, and then wondered what the fuck he was talking about. Lotion? Berkeley? Linda was in town, in Walnut Station, grocery shopping. Why had he lied like that? But of course he knew exactly what was going on. He was scared to death and prattling on, hoping to stem the rising sense of panic he was feeling. He took a sip of beer, but he was barely able to swallow it. It wasn't like the guy had stormed in and arrested him, but clearly he hadn't driven to his house to talk about the great lunch places in Berkeley.

Slater nodded, sipped from his beer again, and then set it down on the counter. "Listen," he said. "I know you want to know why I'm here—and like I said, I'm sorry to bother you like this, on a weekend and everything." He held his hand up to his mouth and burped lightly. "Excuse me," he said.

Martin nodded, knowing as he did that it was an awkward gesture. "Yes," it seemed to say. "You're excused."

"The thing is," Slater said, "a plane went down a few hours north from here—up in Humboldt County. It crashed. A small-craft plane. It was a Cessna. And from what I've been told, the serial number has been traced back to your business out in Hayward. Which means, I guess, that you sold the plane to whoever it was that had it."

Martin thought briefly about Slater's grammar—it was "whomever," wasn't it? He wasn't sure. But he knew better than to say anything and make the guy overly aware that he was in a swanky house in the suburbs, one where grammar and other forms of etiquette might be at issue. Though maybe the guy didn't even care about that sort of thing. Whoever. Whomever. What did it matter?

But just as quickly it occurred to him that Slater wasn't here to arrest him. Or it didn't seem that way, not given the general tilt of the conversation. And with that realization came an immense sense of relief. He felt as if he'd been given a reprieve—as if he'd received a diagnosis of terminal cancer, only to be told a week later that it was a mistake, that it was the wrong set of X-rays, it's really Mr. Johnson who's dying, not you.

Still, though, he was confused.

"Someone crashed a plane I sold?" he said. "I haven't heard about that. Who was the owner? Which plane was it? Are you saying that it's my fault? That it was defective or something?"

Slater held up his hands in a sort of mock-defensive posture. "Nobody's saying this is your fault," he said. "Really. And even if that were the case, it wouldn't be anything I'd be here about." He put his hands back down, glanced out at the backyard again for a quick second, then looked back at Martin. "As for the plane, we don't know who the owner was—that's the problem. But it was a Cessna. I can't remember the specific make. Hold on."

He set his beer down and took his wallet out of his back pocket. He dug around for a second, and then pulled out one of his business cards. On the back he (or someone) had scrawled "Cessna Skyhawk." "White and blue." "N38251."

Martin stared at the card for a second, and then nodded. He remembered the plane. It was a pretty nice one, actually. He'd sold it about a year ago. But he was having trouble placing the guy who'd bought it. He tried to remember the guy's name. David Something? He wasn't sure. But he did remember that the guy had paid about three thousand dollars, plus a trade-in on a pickup truck of some sort. If he remembered right, it was a tall blond guy, with a mustache. One of those bushy, porno-guy mustaches. He and Ludwig and Beaton had joked about it when the guy left the office after his first visit.

"The guy's gonna make a porno in it," Ludwig had said. "It'll be called 'Flight Lessons,' and it'll be some gal who takes guys up and does them at ten thousand feet. She can't help it—she gets off on high-altitude sex."

"No," Beaton said. "He'll fly to some remote place, maybe get stranded, and then meet up with a lost civilization of Amazons. You know, the women who run their own society, and kill men after they have sex with them. He'll try to escape, but they'll stop him. 'Fuck us, mustache guy,' they'll say. 'Fuck us.'"

Martin missed having Beaton around. Not necessarily because he was such a great guy—he was actually a pain in the ass. Always whining, complaining about something. But Ludwig really lit up when he was with Beaton, and Martin liked it when Ludwig was in a good mood. Ludwig had been sort of flat lately—he seemed bored, basically—and Martin felt as if it was partly his fault. Though the real problem was the fact that there wasn't any business. How long could you go to work every day, trying to sell something, and not see any customers?

"Well," Martin said. "I'm pretty sure I remember the guy. But I don't have any information about him here. I must have his name and address and all that stuff at the office, though, out in Hayward. But what do you mean you don't know who he is? Is he dead?"

Slater yawned. He looked tired all of a sudden. Martin hadn't noticed, but he had bags under his eyes, and dark circles. He was clearly one of those thin, high-metabolism guys with incredible energy and focus, but he also seemed a little ground down.

"Look," he said to Martin. "Here's the deal. When the plane was found, it was full of marijuana. Lots of it—about a hundred kilos or so."

"A hundred kilos of marijuana?" Martin asked. He was genuinely surprised. "In one of my planes?"

Slater nodded, clearly pleased they'd gotten to the point. "Yep," he said. "But the problem is that no one was in it. No bodies, no one walking around injured. Just a smashed-up plane and a bunch of dope out in the forest in Humboldt County. We only know about it because a park ranger happened to be nearby. It was total luck. It's in a really remote area, and if he hadn't seen it, we'd never have known about it. The plane would have sat there for years, probably. But he saw it go down, and it didn't take him very long to find it. A couple of hours, he said. But by then whoever had been in the plane was gone."

"Wow," Martin said. "I'm not sure what to say." And he didn't, not really. He'd heard about this sort of thing before, of course, but this was a little too close to home.

"Yeah, well, now you get it," Slater said. "And you know why I'm here."

Martin was about to answer—tell him that of course he understood, or something like that—but he was thrown off by a sudden high-pitched scream from the backyard. Martin looked out over Slater's shoulder and saw that Peter was spraying Sarah in the face with one of the hoses from the Pool Sweeper. She was trying to hide behind a raft, but it wasn't working very well.

"Sorry," he said. "My son is tormenting my daughter." He was feeling more comfortable now, but he also knew that he needed to tread carefully. This was a narcotics detective, after all.

Slater chuckled, looking over his shoulder at the kids in the pool. "That's all right. I've got a couple of little ones of my own. In Martinez. We don't have a pool, though," he said. "I bet they'd love that. We've been talking about one of those above-ground things, but I've heard they can be a pain." He looked back at Martin. "And to tell you the truth," he said, "I can't really swim very well. Pools make me nervous."

Martin nodded, noting the information. Martinez was lower income, for the most part. That's where you bought a house when you couldn't afford one anywhere else in the Bay Area. You bought a house there and then commuted to your job in Richmond or Berkeley or wherever. And when you came home at night you put up with the stench of the oil refineries. No way, Martin thought. Forget it. As for above-ground pools, they were definitely low-brow, maybe upper working class. If you put an above-ground pool into your yard in Walnut Station, you'd be labeled a hopeless loser. No one would come over to swim in it. Martin wondered if Slater understood this basic difference. He wasn't sure, but he knew enough to change the subject—he didn't need to remind Slater that Walnut Station was a big step up from Martinez.

"So what happened to this guy?" Martin asked. He wanted to re-route the conversation, but he was also interested.

Slater shrugged. "Who knows?" he asked. "I think he probably crash-landed the plane and then radioed someone to come and get him. I don't know why they left the dope there. They must have been in a hurry. Or maybe they were planning to come back. There were some motorcycle tracks nearby, and we think maybe he got picked up on a motorcycle, and so he couldn't carry anything with him."

"Huh," Martin said.

"Yeah," Slater said, smiling now. "That about sums it up. 'Huh.' That's what I said when I heard about this, too."

"Really?" Martin asked.

Slater's smile lit up for a second. "Sure," he said. "I said 'huh,' and then I said, 'We need to find out who sold this plane to this asshole, and get a description of him.' Because it turns out that the person it was registered to doesn't exist. He died in San Diego about five years ago."

Slater paused for a second, apparently to let this new bit of information sink in. Then he continued. "Isn't that something?" he said. "A dead guy came to your office and bought a plane. Then he flew it up to Humboldt County, picked up some pot, and then crashed it. But now, apparently, he's not dead, because he got up and walked away."

Slater smiled again, raising his eyebrows a little bit. "So maybe he's a vampire," he said, his voice becoming more ironic. "Maybe he's undead—you know, he's not dead and he's not alive."

Martin stared at Slater, not quite sure how to respond. Was he yanking Martin's chain? Did he know more than he was letting on? Of course he did. That's how cops operated. Especially detectives. But this guy seemed to be a little off. Either that or he was just a cocky asshole.

"Anyway," Slater continued. "The point I was trying to make is that we don't know who this guy is. And so I came out here to see if you might be able to recognize him from some photos I've got with me.

I mean, I'm going to need to check your records, and see what sort of information he gave you. But my guess is that it's the same alias we have on the registration."

"Okay," Martin said. "I can do that—look at the pictures, I mean. No problem."

"Good," Slater said. "That's good." He took another long swig from his can of beer, finishing it. Then he stood up and pulled out a manila envelope from under the jean jacket he'd been carrying when he came to the door. Martin hadn't noticed the envelope until now, which made him wonder if there was anything else he hadn't noticed. Did the guy have a gun under the jacket, as well? Or tucked into the back of his pants?

After that it was just like one of those cop shows on TV. Martin looked through the sheets of photos, saying "Hmmm" after every fifth or sixth image. The people in the pictures were the sort of guys you'd expect to see in a photographic lineup of possible suspects. They were all bad guys, basically. You could just tell. Greasy hair, bad skin, menacing expressions. Some of them had a sharp expression in their eyes, as if they were probably fairly bright, but had just made some bad choices (like getting over their heads in debt and smuggling heroin up from Mexico). But some of them just looked stupid. Their eyes were blank, vacant. In a few images the guys had their mouths hanging open. One guy looked completely surprised, as if it was only with the click of the camera that he'd realized the predicament he was in. "Holy shit," his expression seemed to say. "I think I'm in trouble."

As he looked through the images, he glanced up every thirty seconds or so at Slater. At first Slater watched Martin, gauging his reaction to the pictures. But after a while he started wandering around the room. He looked out at the kids (the screaming had died down, Martin noticed, which was a surprise; he'd been sure things were about to unravel). Then he walked over to the photos of Martin's horses in the winner's circles at Golden Gate Fields and Bay Meadows. Martin saw him lean close, peering at the images of him and Val and whichever horse happened to be in the picture. He read the captions, muttered "Huh" and then "Mmm" a minute or so later. He said no thanks to Martin's offer of another beer.

"Just concentrate on what you're doing," he said to Martin, his voice level, even a bit reassuring. "Tell me if anyone looks familiar."

Martin had been through about a dozen or maybe fifteen sheets of photos, when he saw the blond guy who'd been in his office.

"Hey," he said. He put his finger on the image, as if to keep it from moving away now that he had spotted it. ("No you don't," he'd say to the guy if he tried to sneak away from the little box that framed him in his photo. "You're not going anywhere.") He looked up at Slater. "Here he is. This is the guy."

Slater turned quickly from his scrutiny of one of the racing photos, and started walking over to Martin. He looked serious—his brow was furrowed, almost like he was frowning.

"Really?" he said. "Are you sure? Which one? Show me."

Martin kept his finger on the spot just in front of the image, and turned it so that Slater could see it right-side up. "There he is," Martin said. "That's the guy."

He felt pleased to have found the guy's image. He knew as he sat there, finger pointing proudly, that he was being sycophantic, acting like a pet cat that had just left a dead bird on his owner's doorstep. But he couldn't help himself. He was scared, but he was also impressed by this guy. The self-assurance, the intensity—and the gunshot wounds, of course. The guy had been shot in the line of duty after all. And not once but twice. Either he was an idiot or he really cared about his job and really wanted to put the bad guys behind bars. And although Martin was himself one of the bad guys (at least technically), he was excited to be able to help nab this other shadowy figure from the criminal underworld. Get him off the streets and all that. For all Martin knew, this very guy had been involved in supplying the pot that Linda had found in Sarah's purse. Plus, if Slater was correct in assuming that the guy had used a fake identity when buying the plane, then he'd lied right to Martin's face, pulled a fast one on him. And he didn't like that. Martin lied all the time, of course, but that didn't mean that he had to put up with it when someone did it to him.

"Okay," Slater said, nodding and jotting something in a small notebook he'd pulled out of his back pocket (again he'd produced something that Martin hadn't noticed at first). "Okay," he said again. "Great. This is great."

Martin sat there, his finger still pointing to the guy. "He's got a kind of porno mustache," he said, realizing even as he said it that it wasn't the right comment. "Or that's what we joked about, anyway. After he left, I mean." He looked at Slater, and he felt his face turning red.

Slater looked at Martin for a second, studying him. Then he reached down and picked up the photo sheet, sliding it out from under Martin's finger. He looked at it for a second.

"Ha," he said. "You're right. He does look like the kind of guy you'd see in a porno movie." He smiled, looked at Martin, and then back down at the photo. "It's that fucking mustache. Jesus, look at that thing. I'm gonna tell him that when we get him—that you thought he looked like a porn star."

"Hey!" Martin said, starting up from his chair. "Leave me out of this. I'm just the guy that sold a plane to him. Come on."

Slater laughed, and right away Martin knew that he'd overreacted.

"Relax," Slater said. "I'm joking. No one's gonna mention you to this guy. I mean, we still need proof that you sold the plane to him and everything, but that's it. Really . . . honest."

Martin was about to tell him that he was only pretending to get upset when the sliding door opened, and Sarah and Peter stepped inside. They were both wrapped in big towels, but neither of them had done a good job drying off, so they were creating puddles of water on the linoleum. They'd been talking about something as they opened the door and stepped into the house, but now they were silent as they stood looking at Martin and Slater. Or looking at Slater, that is—staring openly at the sudden presence of a stranger in their house on a Saturday afternoon. Though he wasn't technically a stranger; he and Peter had actually had a conversation once.

And it was this fact—the possibility that the kids might recognize Slater—that made Martin suddenly nervous. If one of them said something, then Slater would know that Martin's family was part of the more general problem of drugs in the area. What would he make of that? Would it dovetail with his initial impression (or Martin's sense of his initial impression) that something wasn't quite right down at the southern end of Miwok Drive—that things were a little *too* cushy for a mere suburban existence? Is this what he'd been thinking when he was looking at the pictures of Martin and his racehorses? Who wouldn't?

"Hey, guys," Slater said.

"Hi," Sarah said, pulling her towel up a little bit and covering her chest. It seemed like an unconscious move, but Martin approved.

Peter didn't say anything—just stood there, staring open-mouthed. Jesus, Martin thought. What am I gonna do with this kid?

Martin cleared his throat. "Kids," he said. "This is Jim Slater. It's just work stuff. We'll be done in a few minutes."

Sarah was already on the move. "Okay," she said.

Martin could tell that she was a little bit embarrassed to be standing there in front of a stranger—a handsome, thirty-something stranger—in her bathing suit. He watched her disappear out into the entry hallway and then listened to her pad down toward her bedroom. She was probably going to get on the phone and tell a friend about it.

Peter kept standing there, looking at Slater and dripping onto the floor. Martin was about to say something to him—quit staring, quit dripping on the floor, be less strange—when Peter said, "You're that police detective from the drug class. The one we had to go to at the high school. Are you here for that?"

Martin opened his mouth, closed it, opened it again.

Slater looked at him for a second, squinting a little bit, but then he opened his eyes wider in an obvious expression of recognition.

"That's *right*," he said. "I *was* there. And I remember you. I didn't recognize you at first. You're the A's fan. And you had the baseball book. How're you doing? It's good to see you."

Martin watched as Slater took two steps forward and reached out to shake Peter's hand. Peter had been holding his wet towel around his waist with both hands, but he reached forward and shook Slater's hand. The towel slipped as he did this, revealing a roll of pale and cellulite-covered fat. But he didn't seem to notice. He was smiling shyly, and Martin could tell he was pleased. And impressed. Pleased to be remembered, and impressed that Slater was a police detective (who'd been shot not once but twice).

Martin knew he needed to say something, to make it clear that he hadn't recognized Slater as the detective guy from the drug class (although of course he *had* recognized him). "Why was that guy pretending he didn't recognize me?" Slater might ask as he drove away in his shiny Camaro. "I think he's hiding something from me."

"Oh, okay—right," Martin said as Peter and Slater turned to look at him. "Yes, absolutely. You gave the talk at the class. You're the detective that got shot during a drug raid. Or in two different raids. Right?"

Slater stared at Martin for a second, but then he nodded. "Yeah, that's right," he said. "That was me."

Martin was quiet, not sure what to say. He had assumed Slater would say more, but he just stood there looking back at him.

"Wow," Peter said. "Did it hurt?'

Slater looked down at Peter and laughed, and Martin laughed, too. It was, he knew, a useful tension-reliever, and once again he was reminded that he really did love his son.

Slater stepped back over to his stool and sat down, leaning on the stool more than actually sitting. He crossed his feet at the ankles and crossed his arms over his chest. He looked pretty relaxed, but he also looked serious all of a sudden.

"You know," he said, looking now at Peter. "Not like you'd think. Or not at first, anyway. Later on it did. It hurt a lot. But not right away."

"Why not?" Peter asked. Martin thought about telling him to stop with the personal questions, but he could see that Peter was fascinated. What nine-year-old wouldn't have been? He was standing in his own house, talking to a cop (a detective) about getting shot. This would go a long way on the playground. Not to mention around the house. Martin knew that Peter was going to be Jim Slater, the narco detective, in a lot of imaginary shoot-outs for the next few months.

Slater shrugged. "I was in shock, I think. Your body just sort of shuts down when something like that happens."

"Did you think you were going to die?" Peter asked.

At this question Slater took a deep breath, as if considering how to answer, when Martin broke in. "Okay, Peter," he said. "That's enough. That's a little too much. It's not a game, you know."

"But he did get shot," Peter said. "And—"

"Peter," Martin said, his voice a little sharper now. "I said that's *enough*."

Peter rolled his eyes in exasperation, and then plopped down angrily onto one of the chairs at the kitchen table.

"It's all right," Slater said, looking over at Martin. "It's fine. I don't care—really." Then he looked at Peter again. He uncrossed his legs and put his heels up on the rung of the bar stool. He folded his arms and leaned forward, putting his elbows on his thighs.

"Yes," he said, looking right into Peter's eyes. It was almost as if there was a little cartoon-style laser beam connecting his gaze to Peter's as they sat looking at each other from across the room. "Yes, I thought I might die. Not the first time I got shot; I knew it wasn't too bad that time. But the second time, yes, I really did think I might not make it."

Peter was quiet now, and Martin knew he was surprised to have gotten the answer he was looking for.

Martin cleared his throat—knew it was a little too theatrical, but didn't care. "So you don't work out in Oakland anymore?" he said. "Isn't that what you said in the class? That you work out in the suburbs now?"

Slater nodded. "I used to work for narcotics in Oakland," he said.

"But the second time I got shot, my wife said that I had to quit or she was going to take the kids and leave. And I could tell that she meant it. She was really freaked out. So was I, actually."

He stopped and looked back at Peter, who was still sitting there looking at him. Then he held up his thumb and forefinger, pointing it at Peter, and made a little shooting noise. It was the sort of sound that Peter made when he ran around the house pretending to fight as a soldier in some sort of imaginary war. It was just the right move to make at that moment, Martin knew. It took some of the tension out of the air, and made Peter smile.

My son is smitten by this detective guy, Martin thought. Not that he was surprised. It was like the guy had just stepped right out of some cop show. The jeans and the T-shirt and the sneakers. What the fuck was that, anyway? It was a little much, Martin thought. The guy thinks he's fucking Serpico. He was suddenly ready for Jim Slater to leave—to get the hell out of his house and go be a hero somewhere else.

"So anyway," Slater said, his tone indicating that he was done with his brief narrative. "I was just about to turn in my badge when a position opened up out here, in the suburbs, where it's just a little bit safer than in Oakland."

He looked at Martin and raised his eyebrows, as if to say that he understood why Martin was living in the suburbs. "They were starting up a new narcotics bureau," he said. "The drug trade has been booming out here for a while now. You know, suburban money—rich parents, kids with money. They buy drugs, and so people sell them. And so finally someone up in Sacramento decided to get serious about it, throw some cash at the problem, bring in some guys with some experience." He smiled at Martin. "And so here I am, bugging you on a Saturday. But I gotta tell you," he said. "It's a lot better than kicking doors down in Oakland."

Martin gave a little laugh—forced it out. "Well," he said. "I hope you're not planning to kick down our door anytime soon." He chuckled again, but he knew it sounded a little off. "Because of the class where we saw you and everything." He tilted his head toward the door to the entry hallway, where Sarah had disappeared a few minutes earlier. "It was my daughter," he said. "It was just a bag of pot. A few joints' worth. My wife found it, and we decided to sit down hard on her. I don't remember where we heard about the course, but it seemed like a good idea. And it was . . . it was great. I mean, you know—I think it was useful for her. For us too, actually. We learned a lot. And I think the problem's solved. Or I hope it is, anyway."

Slater looked at Martin, thoughtful for a second. Martin wondered if he bought all of this bullshit. Probably not. Jesus. Could he have sounded any more like a nervous ass-kisser?

"How old is your daughter?" Slater asked.

"She's thirteen," Martin said. "She's young. The problem is her friends. She's got some friends who are a few years older, and I think they're a bad influence. You know, older boyfriends, that sort of thing."

Slater nodded. "Listen, Mr. Anderson," he said. "Like I said, there are a lot of drugs out here in the suburbs. And not just pot, either. So you can't be too careful. I think you did the right thing, taking her to that class. She's probably just experimenting with the stuff. But you've gotta let her know that it's serious, and that you take it seriously."

Martin nodded. He'd never actually thought that the pot in his daughter's purse was a big deal. And he thought that the whole drug class had been a fucking joke—in part because of the unrelenting earnestness of guys like Slater. He was about to say something more—something about searching Sarah's room and curfews (both of which were lies)—when Peter spoke up.

"Is my sister in trouble again?" he asked. He looked over at Martin, and then back at Slater.

This whole scene was, Martin realized, a little too intense for Peter. He knew the signs: the slightly quavering voice, the hands fidgeting together, the eyes getting a little bit watery. It didn't help that they'd dragged him to those stupid drug classes, or that he'd had to listen to the endless shouting matches between Sarah and Linda over the bag of pot. (Martin had opted for a vaguely neutral good cop posture: joking with her on the side, doing the occasional eye roll behind Linda's back, as if to say he thought Mom was going a little overboard, too.)

"Peter," Martin said. "This doesn't have anything to do with your sister. Detective Slater is here about something totally different. It's just about one of my planes at work."

"That's right," Slater said. "I'm just here about someone who bought a plane from your dad. And," he said, standing up and stretching, "I'm on my way out the door."

Slater stretched his long, lean body and then sort of shook himself. Like a cat, Martin thought. No wonder he isn't dead. He's got the nine lives thing going for him.

"Listen," Slater said to Martin. "You've been a big help. I didn't really expect to get an ID on this guy so quickly, so this is great. But I've gotta ask you for one more favor. Do you think I could stop by your office on Monday and get a copy of his sales records from you?"

Martin's first instinct was to say "no—not a chance." The thought of having to go through more of the same out in Hayward made him want to weep. What was Slater going to think when he saw Martin's planes? What self-respecting narcotics detective wouldn't be able to connect the dots? But he knew he couldn't say no—that he had to be amenable. And so he just nodded. "Sure," he said. "Whenever you like. Not a problem."

After this Martin told himself to relax, and think like the version of himself he was a month ago. Like an innocent person, that is. That's how you got away with things, he knew. You convinced yourself you were innocent, so that when the police stopped you, you believed you hadn't done anything. But that was easier said than done, especially with some fucking hero detective guy lingering in your house on a Saturday afternoon.

Martin walked Slater out into the entry hallway, with Peter trailing close behind them.

"So, Peter," Slater said as Martin opened the front door. "It was nice to see you again. He reached out and patted him on his bare shoulder.

"It was nice to see you, too," Peter said. He stood there looking at Slater for a second, and then he said, "Have you been to any A's games this year?"

Slater smiled, looked at Martin, and then back at Peter. "No," he said. "I haven't. I went to a Giants game a while ago, but it was cold and foggy, and they lost. I had a lousy time. I hope I can get to an A's game before the end of the year, though."

Peter struggled a bit to gather his towel and wrap it around his belly more effectively. "Well," he said. "We're going to see Gaylord Perry pitch against them in July. It's going to be part of my birthday present. We don't know what day he's pitching yet, but when we find out, we're going to get tickets." He said this as if he was announcing the birth of a new child, and Martin felt a quick stab of anxiety at realizing that he'd forgotten about tracking down tickets for the game.

"Really?" Slater said. "Wow. That's pretty cool. I wish I could go to that game. I'd love to see him throw that spitter. You know that's what he does, right? He does it right in front of everyone, and no one can catch him. The umpires, the TV guys—forget it. He's just too good at it."

Peter was smiling now, ear to ear. "Yeah," he said. "I know. I don't even know who to root for. I mean, I don't want the A's to lose, but I really want him to win."

"I hear you," Slater said. "I always root for the bad guys—which is a problem, because I'm the guy that's supposed to catch them." He laughed, ruffled Peter's hair with his hand, and then looked at Martin.

"I'll be by on Monday," he said, and Martin nodded as Slater gave him a quick wave and walked toward his car. Martin wasn't sure, but he thought he might have detected a change of expression when Slater looked at him this last time—as if his mention of bad guys extended to him. But Martin doubted that Slater meant he'd be rooting for him. That didn't seem likely at all.

CHAPTER NINE

The meeting with Slater in Hayward went fine. When he showed up Monday morning, he didn't seem to have any sort of secret agenda. Martin knew that he might be just biding his time, playing good cop for a while. But Slater really had seemed fairly normal, as if the first encounter at Martin's house had broken the ice and they were now on friendly terms. He'd even mentioned Peter's birthday and the A's game.

"He's a cute kid," Slater said.

"Thanks," Martin said as he handed over the file on the pot smuggler. "I think he liked you, too."

Martin knew better than to think that his worries were over, but he was pretty sure that Slater wasn't on to anything yet.

His hope was that the rest of the day would go just as smoothly. The plan was to drive up to Berkeley for a late lunch (and drinks) at Spenger's, the fish place down by the bay, on Fourth Street. He and Ludwig were going to meet up with Radkovitch, and go over the meeting with the Wells Fargo guys that Radkovitch had finally been able to set up. Martin was dreading the meeting, but he was glad for the excuse to get out of the office and away from the increasing claustrophobia he was feeling there, bouncing around, waiting for buyers who didn't seem to exist anymore. And he didn't want to hear anything bad from Radkovitch while sitting in the office. He needed to be out, have a drink in his hand.

But just as they were locking up the office for the day—Martin was literally standing outside, with the key in the door—the guy with the white 240Z came driving up. Holy shit, Martin thought. That's him. Better, Martin saw that he was with a woman—younger, mid- to late twenties. Definitely not thirty, even. Not bad-looking, either. Long brown hair, tight jeans, boots.

How about that, Martin thought. Maybe he'll want to impress her, let her see that he knows how to make a deal.

"Hey," Ludwig said. "Is this your guy?"

"I think so," Martin said. He noticed that the guy was dressed in the same white sweater and jeans that he'd been wearing the day he stopped by the office. "Or else it's someone dressed up like him, and in his car."

"Wow," Ludwig said. "Great. Who's the girl?"

"I don't know," Martin said. He gave Ludwig a sideways look, and then walked down to say hello to the guy and his girlfriend (he wasn't sure why he was assuming she was his girlfriend . . . maybe she was just a friend with a passion for airplanes).

"Hey there!" Martin said, smiling and squinting in the afternoon sunlight. He wanted to seem animated, but he didn't want to overdo it, either.

"Hello!" the guy said, kind of shouted, actually, and then waved to Martin. He walked over and put out his hand for Martin to shake. He used one of those irritating overhand shakes, the one where the hand starts high, up around the shoulder, and then descends into yours. Kind of ridiculous—definitely a fraternity handshake.

The guy started talking right away. He was sorry he hadn't made it by the other day, and sorry he hadn't phoned. Everything had gotten crazy, he said, and then he'd lost Martin's card, and so on. But was there still time to check out the plane they talked about?

"Definitely," Martin said. "Absolutely."

Martin, the guy, and his girlfriend were in the air within half an hour. (Ludwig had offered to come along, but Martin said no.) They went up in the 1970 Cessna 177A Cardinal that Martin had had on the lot for a while now. Close to a year. But it was the plane the guy had been interested in, which was exciting. Martin explained that it was the model that Cessna had put out to replace the earlier Cessna 172.

The 172 was a good plane, he said, but it was a little bit underpowered (as was the original 177). The 177A had a 180-horsepower engine, so it could climb more quickly: the initial rate of climb was about 650 feet per minute. It also had a higher cruising speed: about 110 knots, or 125 mph, at least on a nice day. And it was a good plane for aerial photos, which was what the guy had said he wanted. This was because the Cardinal didn't have the old wing support strut that was always in the way when you wanted to take photos of anything directly below. (What Martin didn't say, of course, was that the guy should really be looking for a 177RG. That was the plane that provided the big improvements on the earlier models of the 172 and 177s, yet stayed within the ballpark, pricewise. Plus, the RG didn't have the handling problems—the pilot-induced oscillation—that plagued the first 177. But Martin didn't have an RG on the lot, so forget it.)

They cruised across the bay, over the Bay Bridge, Treasure Island, and Alcatraz, and then shot out across the Golden Gate Bridge. It was a nice day. The fog was starting to make its way in under the Golden Gate, but the air was still too warm on the bay side for it to be able to really stay thick and blanket the area. That would happen eventually—by midnight or early morning, maybe—but for now there were just wisps of fog streaking along the top of the water by the bridge. From their vantage point, about three thousand feet up, you could still see the rugged coastline through the fog, its gray rocks pounded by angry breakers. It looked wild, almost prehistoric.

"Isn't it amazing from up here?" he said to the couple. He had to shout a bit over the din of the engine. "Can you imagine what the first explorers must have thought when they sailed into the bay? Who was it? Sir Francis Drake?"

He'd posed these questions to potential buyers plenty of times before, and usually they were eager to respond, eager to look out the window and imagine a time when the bay and the surrounding hillsides were utterly pristine. But not this time. The couple nodded, but he could tell they weren't paying attention.

"That's where we go fishing on the weekends," he shouted to them a while later. "My kids love it. Especially my son. We even went out with Sal Bando last month. You know, from the A's? The team captain?"

His absurd lie had leapt forth from his mouth completely unbidden. It was like when someone startled you and you shouted involuntarily. That was it—it had been involuntary. He noted with some surprise that he'd been lying fairly regularly lately. There was the one he'd told Hano about selling a plane to Reggie Jackson; but he'd also told a guy at the track last month that in high school he'd been all-city in football, at linebacker, though in fact he'd never played a down of organized football; and he'd told yet another guy at the club that he'd gotten a business degree at Berkeley. It was a little unsettling.

But up above the San Francisco Bay and swinging back toward Hayward, he thought that if a few white lies helped make a sale, what difference did it make? Maybe they'd strike up a conversation about the A's, and that would be the clincher.

Of course that didn't happen, though. He tried yakking at the guy about the plane some more, the downward-tipped conical wingtips and a few other things, but something had happened. Every few minutes the guy tossed him a couple of questions about the plane (he did know what he was talking about, Martin had to admit that). But when Martin answered with real energy, the guy just nodded. He really wasn't paying attention. It was like when you asked your wife or kids about their day. Sometimes you stopped listening even before they started talking. Martin was pretty sure that was what was happening here.

Twenty minutes later they were back on the ground, and Martin was shaking hands with the guy.

"How'd it go?" Ludwig asked, smiling and looking right at the girl-friend. But she just looked at her boyfriend and gave him a "let's get out of here" nudge.

And that's what they did. No sooner had Martin let go of the guy's hand than they jumped into their Datsun, waving absently and speed-ing away. Watching the car turn out of the lot area, Martin knew he'd never see them again—that they had vanished into the busy mix of the Bay Area like figures gliding silently into the fog that would push its way across the water and onto the coastline within the next twenty-four hours.

"Huh," Martin said to Ludwig. "I thought when he came back that we had a chance. A good chance, actually."

"Yeah," Ludwig said. "Me, too. But you never know, do you?"

"No," Martin said. "I guess not."

They stood there for a few seconds at the bottom of the office steps. It was getting chilly.

"So do you think she'll call me?" Ludwig asked. "I mean, I gave her my card and everything. You know, just in case."

Martin looked over at him. "No," he said. "I really don't think she's going to call."

Ludwig was quiet for another second. "I think you're right," he said. "She's not going to call."

MARTIN HAD WANTED TO drive to Spenger's, but Ludwig insisted. Once they were under way, though, he was pleased to be speeding around in Ludwig's gray 1969 BMW 2002, the bay popping in and out of view as they zipped north along the freeway. The clouds hadn't cleared and you could feel the fog closing in, but it was still a nice day. It was almost two; they were both hungry, and Martin was desperate for a drink.

Spenger's was a regular routine for Martin, especially on Fridays. It was semi-regular for Ludwig. Sometimes they'd meet Jenny. But usually it was just Martin, Ludwig, and maybe one or two other guys. Linda never came. They drank too much, she said (Jenny included), and when they drank too much they were cruder and more obnoxious than usual (and here she included Jenny again). "And someone's gotta be there when the kids get home, you know," she'd said more than once, usually with a little edge to her voice.

Not long ago Martin could have counted on Beaton as well, but, of course, those days were over. Martin missed Beaton, but he was also plagued with guilt about firing him, and so it was a relief to think he probably wouldn't see him around. Beaton didn't seem to go to Spenger's anymore, at least not for lunch. Martin loved it there. He loved that it had been in business since the nineteenth century, when guys like Jack London were prowling around Berkeley and Oakland, writing books about sled dogs and wolves and Alaska. He loved the old-time nautical atmosphere: the brass instruments, the big stuffed marlin and tuna, the fishing nets. But even more he loved the hustle and bustle of the place. There was always a wait for one of the forty or fifty wooden dining tables, so there was sure to be a big crowd at the bar. Standing there waiting to eat, downing drinks, you had to yell to be heard. Martin felt that the noise made things more intimate: you had to lean close to someone's ear to really make a point, grabbing his arm or putting a hand on his back—or hers.

They saw Radkovitch on the sidewalk. He was wearing a navy blue blazer, light blue dress shirt, and charcoal-gray pants. It looked like he was wearing his nice Oxford shoes.

"Jesus," Ludwig said as he pulled the car into the lot across the street. "There he is. Look at the fucking guy." He put the car into park and yanked up hard on the emergency break.

Martin knew exactly what Ludwig meant. Radkovitch stood out in a crowd. That's all there was to it. It was the whole package—the looks, the general air of confidence and sophistication. And it was obvious that women ate it up. But he didn't walk around like some sort of alpha dog, rubbing it in your face. In fact, there were times when Martin wasn't sure if Radkovitch even knew he was so handsome or that women were dying for him. Even that was maddening. "I'm kind of amazing, but I don't really seem to know it." That kind of thing. Martin had been out with him at Spenger's before, talking about the business, and it was like being out with Cary Grant, for Christ's sake. A couple of months ago, a woman had bought him a drink, right out of the blue. Martin had wondered if Radkovitch was going to try to chat her up, or at least return the favor and buy her a drink. But he just waved to the woman, raised his glass, and mouthed "thank you." He hadn't even seemed fazed, which to Martin meant he was used to it. Martin remembered the feeling as he sat there: he was the other guy, the one who hadn't had a drink sent over to him. And the reason no one had sent one to him was that no one could see him. He was used to women preferring Ludwig over him, but this was different. With Radkovitch he felt invisible.

They sat in Ludwig's car and watched Radkovitch for another few seconds. Radkovitch hadn't seen them yet. He fidgeted, looking up and down the street, and then at his watch.

"He looks like he's waiting to catch a cab," Ludwig said. "Maybe he got tired of waiting for us. If we wait a few minutes, he might leave. He probably doesn't like Spenger's, anyway."

Martin sighed. "Okay, okay," he said. "I know. Look, he bugs me, too. Although I don't know—he's all right, I guess. He's just kind of uptight."

"All right," Ludwig said, looking over at Martin. "But he drives me fucking crazy. He's so smug. And so . . . I don't know. Just kind of pleased with himself. You know?"

Martin nodded. He knew Ludwig resented Radkovitch because Beaton had been fired to clear space for him. But he also knew that Radkovitch made Ludwig feel insecure. It was the Stanford degree, the work at Merrill Lynch and all that, but it was also his family money. Radkovitch's dad was a big Wall Street executive in New York City, one of the guys who really did have his hands on the country's purse strings. Ludwig's dad had been a construction guy of some sort for a big contractor in the Bay Area. Martin couldn't remember which one. But he'd never been more than a foreman, running around job sites with a clipboard. Working his ass off, basically. Not that Ludwig wasn't educated. Unlike Martin, he'd gone to an actual four-year college (San Jose State). But he'd dropped out just before graduating. His father had died, he had two younger brothers and a sister still in high school or maybe even junior high, and so he had to go get a full-time job. No more school. It was a sore spot for him, and a guy like Radkovitch was salt in the wound.

Martin pulled the handle on his passenger-side door, but paused to look over at Ludwig and make eye contact with him. "Look," he said. "This is work, all right? Don't get into it with him. It's not worth it, and especially not right now."

"Okay," Ludwig said. "But he's not going out with us later, is he? What if we go to the track?"

"I don't know," Martin said. "No. Maybe."

"Hey," Ludwig said as they stood waiting for a couple of cars to pass before crossing the street. "Do you know why Jews like to watch porno films in reverse?"

Martin looked at him as he buttoned up his coat. It was getting cold. Summer in the Bay Area. "What?" he said.

"It's a joke," Ludwig said, smiling. "Why do Jews like to watch pornos backward—in reverse?"

Martin smiled back at him. He'd never heard this one before.

"I don't know," he said. "Why?"

"Because," Ludwig said, "they like to watch the part where the hooker gives the money back."

Martin snorted and shook his head, and they half-jogged, half-walked across the street. Terrible, he thought. Terrible, but kind of funny.

Martin thought Radkovitch looked a little annoyed that they were late, but he didn't call them on it. You could hear the din of the lunch crowd even from the sidewalk.

"I'm sorry it took so long," Martin said. "I ended up having to take a guy up in a plane. One of the Cessnas, the 177A. He came by a while ago, and then stopped in again just as we were leaving. We flew around the bay. Him and his girlfriend."

"Great," Radkovitch said. "How'd it go? What do you think?"

Martin nodded. "I think it went pretty well," he said. He could feel Ludwig looking at him but didn't return his glance. "I think he's on the hook."

THEY HAD DRINKS IN the bar area while they waited for a table. Ludwig and Radkovitch had bourbon, and Martin had a gin and tonic. It was too loud to do much but look around at the other people. Ludwig saw some friends and wandered away, signaling that he'd be back.

A minute later Martin and Radkovitch were seated at a table, back in the far corner of the big dining room. It was actually best that Ludwig wasn't around. Maybe he'd known that, and that was why he'd drifted away—but probably not.

Martin knew he was supposed to chat with Radkovitch, break the ice a little bit, but he wasn't up for small talk. He was more nervous than he'd realized—if the Wells Fargo guys had said no, he was in a lot of trouble. Sure, Val's money helped, but it wasn't enough. He'd have to set up a daily shuttle to and from Mexico to get out of the hole he was in.

He looked across the table at Radkovitch, but he didn't know where to begin. He felt tired, suddenly—as if he'd reached the end of a long journey. He was returning to his home city, one he'd been told was under siege. It had been surrounded for weeks by an invading army of Huns, and reinforcements and supplies were badly needed. People were dying in the city—not just soldiers, but women and children. His wife and his children. They were looking at total annihilation. The problem was that he knew he might be arriving too late, after the city had been sacked, and after his family and friends had been slaughtered or maybe carried away into slavery and misery.

"Okay, so, Anton," Martin said. "How'd it go today? You know, with Wells Fargo and everything?"

Radkovitch shrugged and glanced away, off at the crowd at the bar. Martin followed his gaze (no sign of Ludwig), then looked back at Radkovitch.

"Well," Radkovitch said. He paused, and Martin could tell he was thinking about how to proceed. "Not great. It didn't go so well."

Radkovitch looked down at the table, then up at Martin. He tried to give Martin a reassuring look, a kind of half smile, but it looked more like a wince. Martin felt a little bit sick, suddenly.

"Not great?" Martin asked, echoing Radkovitch. "It didn't go so well?" It was quieter at the table than it had been at the bar, but it was still hard to hear perfectly well. "I thought you said that they liked the look of things. What the fuck, Anton? What happened?"

Radkovitch shrugged again. He coughed, took a sip of his drink. He wiped a little bit of sweat off of his forehead. Martin could see that this was making Radkovitch uncomfortable.

"If you'll recall," Radkovitch said, "what I actually told you was that I wasn't really sure—wasn't one hundred percent sure—what they'd say. That it wasn't a sure thing. I know I told you that."

Martin rolled his eyes. He knew he was being theatrical, but he couldn't help it. What right did he have to be surprised? His business was in the shit can. He was buried under mountains of debt. Of course they'd said no. But he felt indignant anyway. Outraged, even.

"What the hell am I paying you for?" he asked. Or yelled—it seemed as if the restaurant was getting louder by the minute. He should have chosen a better place to meet, but this was his safe zone. Or so he'd thought.

Radkovitch shook his head. He looked like he was about to respond to Martin when the waitress walked up to their table, and so he stopped himself, leaned back and waited. Martin recognized her, and thought she might recognize him as well, if only vaguely. He was pretty sure she was a student of some sort. Kind of attractive. Blond. A little on the thin side. Maybe an athlete. Martin felt the urge to reach out and hug her, pull her onto his lap—not in a sexual way, but to soak up some of her youth and potential.

The waitress took their orders for lunch and more drinks (or Martin's order for another drink; Radkovitch was holding steady with his first bourbon, which irritated Martin). Radkovitch took a big breath, but Martin cut him off.

"Look, Anton," he said. "I'm sorry. I shouldn't have jumped on you.

I apologize. It's just that I—I guess I'm a little freaked out right now. I thought this was going to work out. Not that it was a sure thing, but . . . you know."

"Martin," Radkovitch said. He spread his hands out on the table, looking down and concentrating. Martin knew he was trying to pick his words carefully. "I think you should have been more up front with me—and with them—about the lien on your inventory—on the planes."

Martin nodded. "Okay," he said. "What did they say? What do you mean?"

"They were upset that you listed them as assets." Radkovitch looked up, and made eye contact with Martin, raising his eyebrows. There was a hint of reprimand in the gesture, Martin realized.

"Well, aren't they?" Martin asked. "Or can't they be?"

"They aren't assets if they're already listed as collateral on another loan," Radkovitch said. "You know that, don't you? You don't really even own them."

Martin felt desperate. This wasn't the conversation he'd expected. He looked around the room and saw Ludwig, drink in hand. He was talking and joking with people Martin didn't know. A younger crowd, from the looks of it.

Martin looked back at Radkovitch. "Okay," he said. "Fine." He took a deep breath, and let it out, slowly. He wanted to get this conversation over with before Ludwig rejoined them. "So what are we talking about here? What's the bottom line? Are they giving us the money or not?"

Radkovitch shook his head, a series of tight, quick side-to-side movements. "No," he said, and then pursed his lips. "Definitely not." He picked up his glass but set it down without drinking from it. He rubbed his hand on the table, forward and backward a couple of times.

Martin sat there, feeling numb. As if he'd just been in a car accident. Not a bad one, but one in which you might be hurt, and you were sitting there, not sure yet if you were really injured—not sure what had just happened, in fact. One minute you're driving, the next minute—*wham*!

He took a deep breath, started to say something, then realized he didn't have anything to say.

"Oh," he said.

"Listen," Radkovitch said. "I know you're upset. But don't forget about the Buick dealership. That's still on the table. It's a good option, Martin. It's something we should consider."

Radkovitch kept talking, but Martin started to tune him out. He thought for a second that he knew now how Al Pacino's character felt in that scene in *The Godfather,* the one where he's at the restaurant with the Italian mobster and the big Irish cop. They're trying to take over the family business, they've tried to kill his father, Marlon Brando, and now Al Pacino is going to kill them. Only they don't know it, and he's trying to work up the courage to do it. He's sitting there listening to the mobster, who's speaking Italian, and you can tell Pacino isn't really paying attention to what the guy's saying to him—because he's about to shoot him.

That was how he felt sitting there with Radkovitch. He liked the reference, because it allowed him to think for a second about standing up and shooting Radkovitch. He'd stand up like Al Pacino had, with his surprise pistol, and pop him right in the throat, or in the forehead. *Blam, blam.* Fuck you, you spoiled brat. Everyone in the restaurant would spin around at the noise, would see him standing there over Radkovitch as he lay bleeding on the floor. And then (just as Al Pacino had been instructed in the movie) Martin would drop the pistol, and wouldn't make eye contact with anyone . . . except maybe Ludwig, who'd probably give him a look that suggested he was both horrified and impressed. Then he'd head out the door into a new life. Maybe to Hawaii. How much would a ticket to Hawaii cost if he just walked into San Francisco International an hour from now and said "I need a one-way to Honolulu"?

Radkovitch's voice drifted back in. It was more shit about the Buick guys, about landing on his feet. Across the room Martin saw Ludwig again. But to his surprise, Martin saw that Ludwig was now standing over there talking to Beaton. They were scanning the room now, and it was only a matter of seconds before they all made eye contact.

"Listen," Martin said. "I'm not feeling so hot. I've gotta get out of here."

He pushed his chair back and threw some money on the table. He didn't know how much, exactly, but it was more than enough to cover the tab.

"Okay," Radkovitch said. He looked surprised, but also a little embarrassed, either at having been rude or because Martin was unraveling. It was the latter, Martin knew. Definitely.

Martin was about to stand up when he saw that Ludwig was suddenly standing at their table.

"Hey, guys," he said. Beaton was with him. He was standing there next to Ludwig, staring down at Radkovitch with a frozen smile on his face. He looked a little drunk.

Shit, Martin thought. What the fuck was Ludwig thinking?

"Ron," Martin said. He stood up quickly, put his hand out to Beaton. Beaton hesitated for a quick second, but then he reached out and took Martin's hand. They looked at each other, and Martin felt a sudden rush of relief. It was good to see Beaton again. And, though he wasn't certain, Martin felt as if Beaton was glad to see him as well.

"Hiya, Martin," Beaton said. Then he glanced down again at Radkovitch, who was still sitting. It was obvious that Beaton knew who he was; either Ludwig had told him or it was just that easy to figure out.

"Oh, hey—yeah," Martin said. He gestured toward Radkovitch. "Ron, this is Anton Radkovitch. Anton, this is Ron Beaton. Ron used to work for us—for Anderson Aircrafts."

Radkovitch stood up quickly and put his hand out to shake hands with Beaton. "Sure," he said. "Right. Nice to meet you."

"That's right," Ludwig said, putting his arm around Beaton and gesturing toward Radkovitch. "This is our new finance guru, Ron. He's a fucking wonder boy. He's gonna save the business. In fact, he's gonna save the whole fucking economy. He's gonna call his pal Kissinger, and they're gonna get together and fix things up. Isn't that right, Raddy?"

There was a pause as everyone looked over at Ludwig. He was smiling, but he looked drunk and pissed off. Martin knew he should intervene, but he felt frozen.

Radkovitch let out a little chuckle and then shook his head. "No, Ludwig," he said. "You've got it all wrong. You don't want a Jew meddling with the economy. I mean, you know why money's green, don't you?"

There was a pause as everyone looked over to Radkovitch, and then back at Ludwig again. Ludwig shrugged. "I don't know, Raddy," he said. "Tell me."

"Because Jews pick it before it's ripe," he said.

There was another pause, and Martin could hear the wheels turning—in his own head, and in everyone else's (except Radkovitch's, of course). And then he started to laugh, along with Beaton, and even Ludwig. And then Radkovitch laughed, too.

"Ha," Martin said. "That's a good one, Anton." He clapped Radkovitch on the shoulder. It was a good move—kind of ballsy, he thought. Take Ludwig's comment and throw it right back in his face.

Beaton smiled and patted Ludwig on the back. Then he grabbed a chair and sat down.

"Come on, Ludwig," he said. "Sit down. Let's have a drink."

MARTIN GOT HOME EARLY. He was in a good mood—even took the kids out to the local A&W for root beer floats. He was glad to have made contact with Beaton again. He was a good guy. Maybe he should've fired Ludwig instead. Ludwig could be a real fuckhead, no doubt about it. Beaton was no prince, but he'd never pull the kind of stunt that Ludwig had at Spenger's. Imagine. He'd basically called the guy a Jew to his face.

He went to bed still feeling enthused, but he woke up a few hours later to the sound of Peter calling him.

Martin hopped out of bed, cursing quietly. Why tonight? Peter's nightmares had been less frequent than they had been a few years ago;

for a while he'd woken up almost every night. Martin, who was a much lighter sleeper than Linda, would get up, hustle into his room, and get into bed with him. It was a bad habit, but all he cared about was getting Peter back to sleep as quickly as possible. If he was awake for too long—anything more than a minute or two—he wouldn't go back to sleep for at least an hour. Maybe two, even.

Peter had had a dream about the story Martin had told them on the way home from the A&W. They'd been driving along with the windows rolled down and a pleasantly warm breeze moving through the car, when Peter had complained about the smell of road kill. It really did stink. But trying to be funny, Martin said it wasn't road kill that smelled so bad, but that the whole area was built on an ancient Indian burial ground. What Peter smelled were the corpses of those Indians as they were rising from the dead to enact revenge on modern society for its recklessness and bad behavior. Sarah had given him a roll of the eyes, and Peter had given him his standard, "Yeah, right, Dad." But clearly it had gotten to Peter.

Martin climbed in next to him and within minutes, Peter fell back asleep. Martin fell asleep, too. And then it was his turn to have a nightmare. He dreamed that his own body was rotting, and because it was summer and hot, his skin was starting to liquefy, and he was giving off a horrible stench. The only thing that would combat the smell was an expensive cologne from the men's department in I. Magnin's, in Union Square. Linda drove him across the Bay Bridge with the air-conditioning cranked up as high as it would go in an effort to keep him from melting and smelling. The kids turned their faces away and held their noses.

He woke up in the morning to the dog licking his face. Surely it was Arrow's breath that brought on the dream. But as he lay there, still trying to wake up, Martin was convinced that he smelled rot. It was as if the scent of his dream body was trapped in his nostrils. He felt to see if his flesh was staying in place, or if it was starting to slide off the bed. He couldn't figure out why the dream wouldn't go away. Jesus, he thought. I've gotta get my shit together.

He thought about the conversation he'd had with Radkovitch when they were leaving Spenger's. Martin had stopped him as he was getting into his car. It was a green 1972 Alpha Romeo. A 1300 GT. A nice car, Martin had thought more than a few times. And one that hit just the right note. It was stylish, even a little sporty, without seeming like he was trying too hard. It was a nice car.

"Listen, Raddy," Martin had said. "The Buick thing. I'll think about it. But I've got a few things I might be able to fall back on. I think I can come up with something, if you give me a chance. If you can call the dogs off for a while."

Radkovitch had looked at Martin for a second, then nodded, mouth set. It was his best earnest look, Martin knew. The problem was that, the more Martin saw it, the less certain he was whether it reflected real earnestness and interest or something feigned and maybe a little affected.

"Sure thing, Martin," Radkovitch had said. "It was just an idea. I think it's a good one, but it's just a suggestion. Don't worry, though. We'll work this thing out, one way or the other."

Martin stood there as Radkovitch got into his car and then rolled down the window.

"And besides," Radkovitch said, raising his voice over the sound of his engine and smiling. "If nothing else works, I'll call Kissinger and we'll cut a deal with the Arabs, get the oil flowing."

Martin laughed and waved as he drove off, but even as he'd hustled over to where Ludwig was waiting for him in his car, he'd known that no one was going to be calling Kissinger on his behalf. And even if that were to happen (and it wasn't), Kissinger wouldn't have known who he was, and wouldn't have cared.

"Martin who?" Kissinger would say. "Never heard of him. Is this really something we need to talk about?"

"Never mind," Radkovitch would say. "Forget it. He's no one."

CHAPTER TEN

About a week later, Martin was in the office in Hayward when the phone rang. Ludwig answered, and then struggled trying to figure out which button to push to transfer it over to Martin's desk.

"Martin," a familiar voice said when he picked up the phone. "Derek Hano. How're you doing?"

"I'm fine," Martin said. "Pretty good."

Martin's heart sped up a bit. He felt Ludwig's eyes on him, but he wanted to try to keep it cool—didn't want to turn away, cover the phone, and talk in a hushed voice, or anything like that. Ludwig knew Hano was a horse guy, and that Martin had flown down with him to Mexico to see some horses that Val knew about (or that was the story that Martin had told him). So probably Martin was worrying too much.

"What's up?" Martin asked.

"Well," Hano said. "I'd like to say I'm just calling to say hello—you know, to check in on my buddy Martin." He paused for a quick second, then laughed. "But actually this is a business call. I just talked to Val. And he asked me to get ahold of you. Looks like we're on for another trip down south."

Martin leaned back in his chair. "Really?" he said. He said it a little too forcefully—with a little bit of alarm in his voice, even—and so Ludwig glanced up at him. This meant that Martin had to give a little wave and let Ludwig know that everything was all right. But he was surprised. Blindsided, was more like it. He shouldn't have been—he knew that. But somehow he'd allowed himself to think that he was all done with his work for Val, that he was now retired from his career as a drug smuggler.

"Yeah," Hano said. "Really. Do you think I'm making this shit up?"

"No," Martin said. He forced out a chuckle. "I just . . . you know. You caught me off guard. I've got a lot going on up here, and I guess I'm surprised. I thought it would be a while, that's all."

Martin heard Hano let out a sarcastic snort. He wasn't buying it.

"Well, look," Hano said. "I'm busy, too. But not too busy to say no to a nice little paycheck. I mean, that's why we're doing this, right?"

"I know, I know," Martin said. He sighed. "So what's the plan? When do you want to go?"

He looked at Ludwig, who was pretending to read the newspaper while he listened.

"At the end of the week," Hano said. "Val said he wants us to head down Friday night. So it's not like we've gotta just drop everything and leave tomorrow, right?"

Martin was quiet for a second. "Yeah," he said. "You're right. It's fine." He looked out the window, at the empty parking lot. "But do you think it'll go a little smoother this time?" he asked.

"Sure," Hano said. "Probably. I think so, anyway. But if we do get delayed, at least you know you've got a friend down there that you can visit. I mean, you wouldn't mind a chance to sneak off and visit your little Mexican girlfriend, would you?"

Now Martin offered up a quick chuckle—tried to just laugh it off.

"Hey," he said. "What about you? *You're* the one who's hoping to get back out there."

Hano laughed. "Shit yes, I'd like to go back out to Ensenada again," he said. "Are you kidding me? That was some Grade-A pussy, my friend."

Martin rolled his eyes. He recognized the advantages of this posture—the one where you embrace the thing you're being teased about or accused of. Ludwig was good at this. "Hell yes, I jerked off last night," he'd say. "And I'm gonna go do it again right now, in the bathroom. Will you hand me my *Penthouse* magazine, please? Bottom drawer. The one with the blonde on the cover. October nineteen seventy-three."

Martin had never been good at it. He was too self-conscious for effective bantering, too worried about how he was being perceived. He knew it, and he'd tried to overcome it, but it was no good. Whenever he tried the bluster and bravado, he sounded fake. Plus, his friends had his number—Ludwig and Beaton and those guys were all over him whenever he tried to swagger a little bit. Maybe if he moved someday and took up with a new set of friends—maybe then he'd be able to become the person who doesn't give a shit what anyone else thinks.

A few minutes later Hano hung up the phone in Santa Barbara, and Martin did the same in Hayward.

"Looks like I'm heading down to Mexico again," Martin said to Ludwig. "Val's got another scouting trip he wants to make." He shook his head. He'd already given Ludwig a story about how he and Val were thinking of buying some horses down in Mexico. Not to race, he'd told him, but to resell or to breed. An investment. He'd even thought about asking if Ludwig wanted to get in on it, but he didn't, just in case Ludwig said yes.

"Uh-huh," Ludwig said. He didn't even look up from his work. "Horses and hookers, it sounds like."

"Yeah, well, that's an important part of the transaction," Martin said. "The seller wants to show you a good time. You really can't say no."

Ludwig looked up at Martin, and they smiled.

Then pretty soon they were talking about some movie Ludwig had seen. But even as they talked, Martin's mind kept drifting back to Hano . . . and the girl in Ensenada. Because Martin had in fact been thinking about what would happen if they had to go back. He'd avoid the tequila—that was for sure. But when he thought about the feel of Lucille's firm, bare legs, or the sight of her bare breasts in his hotel-room mirror, he was excited. And curious. Would he be able to experience the thing he'd missed out on? Because even if they'd had sex—which was doubtful—he couldn't remember it.

IT WAS CLOUDY ALL along the coast on the way down to Santa Barbara. They were the kind of low stratus clouds that hugged the coastline and only came up to about six thousand feet, and so it was easy to pop up above them and not have to fly blind. The extra bonus was that the low clouds meant a smooth flight—no turbulence. But flying above them was disorienting, because from above the clouds everything looked the same. It was a lot like driving the Viking, actually: just a big sea of gray. He was skimming along the top, reassuring himself every now and then that the instrument panel was reliable and that he wasn't actually lost. A couple of times he had to resist the urge to dip down through the clouds, just to see land and convince himself that he wasn't off course and maybe fifty miles out to sea. It was exciting to be up there, feeling as if you were weightless—feeling as if you were floating, defying gravity. But you had to be careful, because the truth was that you weren't weightless at all. Gravity hadn't forgotten you. It was just giving you a temporary pass while it waited for you to screw up.

He descended into Santa Barbara at about six o'clock. When he walked into the tiny terminal area, Hano was sitting there in a plastic chair, looking at him with a big shit-eating grin.

"There he is," he said to Martin. "Charles Lindberg, Jr."

"Hi, Derek," he said.

Hano looked like he'd been spending time in the sun—his dark skin was now a deep shade of brown. He was wearing jeans and a short-sleeved yellow shirt that made him look even darker than he already was. Martin had decided on khakis, a white T-shirt, and a blue v-neck sweater. He'd ditched his alligator shoes for some navy blue boat shoes. He had a feeling that neither of them had managed to effect the drug-smuggling look. He knew this was a good thing—dark leather jackets and mirrored sunglasses were probably a bad idea—but he was a little embarrassed just the same. What would the Mexicans think? Look at those two jackasses, they'd say. Can't we sell to someone with a little more style?

They had some time to kill, so they went to the same outdoor patio place as last time. It was busy, but not bustling—mostly pairs of people having drinks and chatting quietly. Martin had the feeling that Santa Barbara was one of those towns where no one worked, and where everyone hung out in cafés and looked good. Kind of like Berkeley. The only people who actually had to do anything were the waiters and waitresses, the cooks and bartenders. But even that was a job where you really didn't expend much effort—especially at this place, Martin thought as he looked over at their waiter. He wasn't the same guy they'd had before, but Martin noticed that he was standing right where the other waiter had, leaning up against one of the white stucco archways and looking out at the street. Maybe his plan was to just stand there and wait to be discovered by some Hollywood director who happened to be walking past. Then the waiter could become famous and not have to work anymore.

"So," Hano said as he sipped his beer. "I've been hearing about that horse of yours. That he's got a good chance at the Pleasanton Fair. A really good chance."

Martin felt a surge of excitement. He couldn't think of anything he'd have rather heard at that moment—aside from the sudden news that the trip to Mexico was cancelled but that they were going to get paid anyway.

"Really?" Martin said, trying to sound casual—casual and surprised. "Who said that? Val?"

Hano nodded. "Yeah," he said, drinking again from his bottle. "Val and a couple of other guys. Do you know Dale Jenkins?"

Martin shook his head, no.

"Well," Hano said. "He's one of the trainers with me at Barker Stables. He's got a client who might have a horse running in that race, a guy from somewhere in Orange County, and he was saying that you're the main competition. Or that your horse is, I mean. Temperature's Rising, right? Ricky said he's the horse to beat."

Martin sat there, absorbing the notion that he, Martin Anderson, was the owner of a horse that people he didn't even know were describing as the favorite in a championship horserace. And these were people who knew what they were talking about—not just some clowns at the local track. How about that?

"Huh," Martin said. He was trying to contain himself. "It does seem like he's running really well right now. And Pleasanton is a good distance for him—he likes the longer races. He's not a sprinter."

"Sure," Hano said. "Yeah, that's right. That race is a mile." Martin wasn't sure what to say; he didn't want to come across as too eager to talk about his horse, and so he took a long drink from his beer. Evening was setting in, and the air was actually a little chilly. The low clouds had hung in there all day, never clearing, and so the warm air hovered up above. Not that anyone seemed to mind. The sidewalk was busy with people. But you could see that no one was in a hurry; these people were ambling, strolling. They were making their way from one place to another, but they weren't really headed anywhere specific or important. They were fine with a chilly summer evening.

"Hey, listen," Hano said. He looked around, checking out the woman a few tables over who was laughing at something her date had said. "How long have you and Val been working together? With him as your trainer, I mean? A while, right?"

Martin shrugged. Now he was looking at the woman. "I don't know," he said. "Six years? Seven years? Something like that. He's trained three horses for me. Why?"

Hano raised his bottle with his left hand and motioned to the waiter.

"No reason," Hano said. "Well, actually, that's not right. I guess I'm just thinking about your options. I mean, with Temperature's Rising. Don't get me wrong, Val's a pretty good trainer. A really good trainer, in fact. He definitely produces good horses. But it's a small operation. And, you know, there you are, up there in Northern California, and the truth is that there isn't much of a racing scene up there. Not really. There are some good horses, but it's nothing like Southern California. And in L.A., or the L.A. area, you get a lot more exposure. Especially if you're looking to break into Grade One races—which, from what it sounds like, you should be doing with this horse."

The waiter walked up with two beers, one for Hano and one for Martin, then headed back toward his spot at the stucco column.

"Anyway," Hano said. He picked up his beer. "I'm just saying that if you're interested in making a move, you might think about working with Barker Stables. With us, I mean. With me. I think we can do a good job for you: get your horse into some good races, help him move up the chain a little bit. I mean, look, we're not talking about the Derby here, but he might qualify for some races with pretty nice purses. Really nice. And I just don't see that happening if you stay located up in the Bay Area. No offense to Val, of course. It's just that, well, I don't know if he's thinking outside of his little domain up there. You know?"

Martin sat, looking at Hano. He knew that there was a bigger racing circuit down south, but he'd never thought seriously about being a real, active part of it. Maybe a race or two, but that was about it. Locating down there? He didn't know if it was realistic. There was the money, for one thing. But also the horse. Deep down, he wasn't sure that Temperature's Rising was the real deal. Wasn't he just a big fish in a small pond—a tiny pond? But here was Hano, suggesting that he really did have the goods.

"Well," Martin said. "That sounds interesting. It sounds great, actually. But I don't know. Like I said, Val and I have been together for a long time. And it's really because of him that I've had some solid horses. I mean, it's not like I showed up at his stable with Temperature's Rising fully formed. He's the one who kind of brought him along."

"Look," Hano said. "I'm not trying to do anything behind Val's back. Really. I'm just thinking about the bigger picture. And besides, this kind of shit happens all the time. It's not a big deal. If you owned Secretariat, then yeah, that's a big deal. But that's not what's going on here. You've got a nice horse, and you're a good client, but Val and I won't be going to the mat over something like this. We've known each other for a long time, too. Five years, or something like that."

Hano stood up. He stretched and yawned, and Martin noticed that one of the women at another table snuck a quick glance his way.

"I gotta go to the bathroom," Hano said. "But then we should probably hit the road, okay? Or hit the skyways, or whatever you guys say."

Martin looked at his watch. It was about eight-thirty. They were supposed to make it to Ramirez's place sometime between twelve and one.

"Okay," Martin said. "Go ahead. I'll pick up the tab."

Hano nodded. "All right," he said. "And I'll pay for the drinks in Ensenada." Then he leaned over and gave Martin an open-handed whack on the shoulder.

"Listen," he said, looking right at Martin. "I wasn't trying to pressure you about your horse. Honest. It was just an idea. If you want to stick with Val, great. I was just talking, that's all. Just shooting the shit. You know?"

Martin forced out a smile. Hano was leaning in a little closer than he needed to, but Martin resisted the urge to lean away. He could smell the beer on Hano's breath.

"Sure," Martin said. "I know. I'll think it over. We can talk about it."

Hano looked at him for another second or two, then patted him again on the shoulder.

"Good," he said. "Great."

Then he straightened up and headed off toward the bathroom. Martin watched him walk up to their waiter and say something, and then point toward Martin. The waiter nodded. Martin knew that he'd told the guy to bring the tab, but he couldn't help feeling as if Hano had told the guy that he had a loser at table three. "See that guy?" Martin imagined him saying. "He doesn't know a good thing when he sees it."

THE LOW CLOUDS HUGGED the coastline all the way down to Ensenada. This made for a smooth flight, not to mention giving them a spectacular view when they pushed through the clouds above Santa Barbara—the sun had just set, and it was as if they'd been invited to a private viewing of nature's wonders up at six thousand feet.

But the clouds also made it hard to find Ramirez's ranch once they got as far as Ensenada. Martin had the coordinates, but they weren't *that* exact. He had to dip below the clouds and circle around, looking for the landing strip with the burning rags. And just as with the first trip, it was confusing, because once they were past Ensenada, it was utter darkness. It was like flying over the ocean at night.

"Do you know where you are?" Hano asked more than once. "Are we lost?"

"Yeah," Martin said, finally. "We've come back down into another time period, one from before there was electricity. If they don't kill us, they'll treat us like gods."

Hano snorted, but didn't give over to a real laugh. Martin could tell that Hano was nervous about the plane. At least I've got one edge over this guy, Martin thought.

A few minutes later Martin spotted the two parallel lines of lights, and a few minutes after that they were bumping down onto the dirt landing strip. Just like before, he taxied down and past the runway, and then he wheeled around in the sudden darkness and came back toward the lights. It was hard to see through the glare of the burning rags' smoke, but as they moved along Martin gradually made out a couple of dimly lit figures jogging along, guns in hand. It really was as if they'd descended into some sort of primitive civilization. Martin had thought he was going to feel better this time, but there was something about the men and the setting that scared the shit out of him all over again.

What am I doing? he thought.

He stopped the plane at the edge of the two rows of burning rags, and they went through the whole process of putting their hands up against the plane and being searched. There was a slight breeze, and Martin felt as if the smoke from the rags was blowing right into his face. It made his eyes burn and tear up, but he was afraid to move his hands to wipe his eyes. Instead, he leaned his face over and rubbed his eyes against his biceps, first the right arm, then the left. But as he did this it occurred to him that the Mexican guys would think he was crying. The men were talking to one another in Spanish, and he wondered for a second if that's what they were saying.

Eventually someone gave him a quick pat on the shoulder, indicating that he could turn around. And then Hano was talking to one of the guys in Spanish, and they were climbing into the backseat of a car. Or Martin was climbing into the car. Hano was about to get in, but then he started talking to someone in Spanish again. Martin sat there looking at Hano's legs and midsection as he stood there, leaning against the car door and talking. Martin tried to pick up a stray word here or there, but it was hopeless.

"Okay," Hano said, leaning in to look at Martin. His face was a weird reddish color, from the glow of the landing strip flames. "We're all set. They're just gonna load up the plane. But Ramirez is here, so give me the money, and I'll give it to him."

"What?" Martin said.

Hano shrugged. "I don't know," he said. "I guess he decided to come check things out. But we gotta pay him, right? So give me the bag, and I'll give it to him. I'm the one who speaks Spanish."

"But what about me?" Martin said. "Shouldn't I be there? I mean, to hand it over?"

Hano looked at him for a second, glanced out at whoever was standing there next to the car, then looked back at Martin.

"Martin," he said, more serious now. "This isn't the time to fuck around. Who gives a shit who gives him the money? I speak Spanish, and I've met the guy before. And they just told me to do it, for Christ's sake. Just give me the money, and I'll be right back."

Martin sat there for another second, thinking and staring at Hano. Was there a decision to make here? Should he just get out of the car and march around to the other side, and say "No, we're both doing this"? Would it matter? Did he really need to look Ramirez in the face?

"Martin," Hano said. Martin saw that he was talking through gritted teeth now, and looking right at him. It was similar to when he leaned over to look at him at the restaurant, but more serious . . . more intense. "Just give me the fucking bag. Please."

Martin sighed and handed the bag over to Hano. It was the word *please* that made him give in.

"All right," he said to Hano. "Sure. Here you go."

Hano reached out and grabbed the bag, and nodded at Martin. "Good," he said. "Thanks."

"So you're gonna be right back, right?" Martin said. But Hano had straightened up and was closing the car door. When the door clicked shut the interior light turned off, and so Martin was left alone in the darkness of the car.

For a few seconds he sat there feeling miffed. He watched as Hano walked over and shook hands with someone—with Ramirez, apparently—and then handed over the bag of money. Martin squinted and tried to get a look at Ramirez, but it was all just shadows and flickering light. He was just a guy, maybe vaguely Mexican-looking. From where he was sitting he could barely recognize Hano. Behind them, Martin could see his plane. A couple of guys were busy loading it up with the packages of heroin . . . the bricks, Hano and Val had called them.

Martin figured that would be it—that now that Hano had turned over the money, he'd walk back to the car, and either get in, or signal for him to get out. But he didn't. Instead he just stood there talking to Ramirez. Jesus, Martin thought.

It was like the time his father had sent him to a shitty summer camp. Some all-boy Catholic thing down the coast, past Santa Cruz. He'd been about thirteen or fourteen, and had gotten into trouble for something, so off he went. It was a boring camp, just Ping-Pong and hanging around. But one evening he and two friends had met two girls who'd snuck away from their family's beach house for the evening. The girls had some wine they'd stolen from one of the girls' parents, and so they all sat around drinking. But eventually his friends had paired off with the girls, and Martin had been left behind. "Keep watch for us," one of his friends had said. And he'd done it—sat there like an asshole, listening to the sounds of making out. And then, worse, he heard about it all week, about how great it had been, how they'd scored with some local chicks, how much cooler they'd been than the girls back home. Martin acted like he was in on it—talked up the whole thing to some of the other kids at camp—but of course he hadn't been. Not really.

Martin decided to get out of the car. Fuck it, he thought. I'm not even the lookout here. I'm just the pathetic American sitting quietly in the car, while the big Hawaiian guy does all the talking and schmoozing. But as he reached for the door handle he saw that one of the Mexicans was standing a few feet away, with a rifle in his hand. He didn't know whether or not the guy was supposed to be keeping watch on him, maybe making sure he didn't get out of the car. It seemed kind of unlikely. But he knew he didn't want to find out the hard way—the rifle barrel in his face, lots of yelling. More humiliation.

And so he just sat there. Five and then ten minutes went by, but it felt like an hour. He would rather have been in a motel room in Ensenada, puking his guts out.

He watched Hano and Ramirez talk and laugh, silhouetted by the runway flames. What were they talking about? His willingness to sit there? It also occurred to him that they were talking about hauling him out of the car and shooting him—shooting him and burying him somewhere out there in the darkness. One less loose end.

He shook his head. He was tired, and wanted to get the fuck out of there.

Finally, the guy with the gun walked away, and Hano came walking over. Huh, Martin thought. The guy didn't leave until Hano came back to the car.

"Okay, Mr. Pilot," Hano said when he opened the door. He was all smiles now. "Sorry it took so long. But the plane's all loaded up now. We can get going."

Walking over to the plane, Martin looked around for Ramirez. He figured he'd at least get to shake his hand. Or give him a nod.

Something, anyway. But he was gone, and pretty soon Martin was starting up the plane.

Up in the air Hano was a chatterbox. He wanted to vacation in Mexico soon, maybe do some sport fishing. He joked again with Martin about not getting to go out to Ensenada and see "Miss Mexico." He talked about some upcoming horse races, and the extra money he was going to have from this job, about how great the setup was. No one seemed to think to look up in the sky to catch drug smugglers.

"They're stopping all the cars and tearing them apart," he said. "But we're up here, and it's like we're invisible. Especially at night." He shook his head. "What a joke," he said.

They shook hands and said good-bye in Santa Barbara. Martin could tell that as far as Hano was concerned, everything was A-okay.

But once he was alone and back in the air, Martin felt an overwhelming sense of sadness. For a while he felt the urge to cry—even hoped that he would, for the relief it might bring. But there weren't any tears, and so he just had to deal with the sudden and fairly intense feeling of desolation that was gripping him, six thousand feet in the air. What was he doing? Yes, he was working—making money—and that was motivation enough. But what was he *doing*? He'd felt like a fucking idiot back there at Ramirez's place. And while that in itself wasn't a big deal, the problem was that he *always* felt that way—and always had. Sure, there were bright spots: the first time Linda told him that she loved him (which wasn't until after their shotgun wedding and Sarah's birth); the time Sarah was three and said she'd missed him, even though he'd only been out of the room for a minute; the time he heard Peter brag to a boy down the street about how his dad had caught a shark with three legs (it was a three-foot shark); the first time a racehorse he owned won a race. But in general his life was made up of moments like the one back in Ramirez's car: looking on while other people did the things that mattered. Just wait here, Martin. Eventually you'll belong, but not right now.

Not for the first time, he thought about cutting the engine and pointing the plane downward . . . He could just let gravity do its work. Plunge through the darkness—he'd be dead in no time. But he didn't want to be found with a load of heroin in his plane. For one thing, he was pretty sure that would void his life insurance policy, and Linda and the kids wouldn't get a dime. They'd be completely screwed. But he also didn't want to give that cop Slater the satisfaction of finding him with a load of drugs. At least not like that. If he was going to catch Martin, he was going to have to work a little harder than that.

He thought about flying past Hayward and the Bay Area, maybe up to Reno. If he knew someone who'd buy the heroin from him, he could use it to start a new life and be a new person. Just disappear. They'd think he'd crashed somewhere—that he'd gotten off course over the low clouds and run out of gas over the ocean. "He probably realized too late where he was," someone, a cop of some sort or maybe Ludwig, would say to Linda. Ludwig wouldn't really believe that he'd made a mistake like that. He might say it to Linda, but he wouldn't believe it. Though Linda probably wouldn't believe it, either. She knew he might just be capable of bailing out—saying fuck it, it's your problem now, not mine. But knowing Linda, she'd hunt him down and then kill him herself. And she'd do it in a sly way: she'd hand him a drink with poison in it, and then, when he was lying there on the ground, choking to death, tell him she'd done it.

"Did you really think you could walk out on me like that, Martin?" she'd ask. "After all the shit I put up with from you? I don't think so."

This last thought made him laugh out loud. The sound of his own voice startled him, but somehow it helped him shift the gears of his mood just a little bit. Fuck it, he thought. I'm sleeping in my own bed tonight, and maybe when I wake up in the morning things will be a little better. I'll be five thousand dollars richer, anyway. He laughed again. Then he started singing a song to himself, just to keep the sound of himself there with him in the cockpit. He realized it was "Country

Roads," the John Denver song he'd sung at the restaurant in Ensenada on his first trip to Mexico, and this made him laugh yet again.

The instrument panel told him he was somewhere over the Santa Cruz mountains. But a few minutes later when he looked out the window he realized that he could actually see the lights of San Jose down below in the distance. The coastal clouds were finally clearing out. He'd be touching down soon. Good. He was really beat, and he needed to get out of the plane and drive home. Something—that frightening feeling of sadness, or maybe emptiness (it was hard to say what it was, exactly)—had tried to follow him back from Mexico. It had slipped into the plane with the drugs, or maybe with Hano, and it had grabbed him from behind for a few minutes, had tussled with him. But he'd managed to slip free, and if he just kept moving, it probably wouldn't catch up with him. Or not for a while, at least. And that was all you could ask for, really. Just a little bit of time and distance between you and the thing that was chasing you.

CHAPTER ELEVEN

Martin was right in the middle of telling Ludwig about his crappy morning, about how he'd decided to surprise Sarah by taking her out to breakfast, letting her be late for school. Or summer school. Her grades had been so bad that she'd been forced to sign up for an extra month of classes, three mornings a week. It was some sort of deal the school had cut so that she and a few other kids could get credit for classes they'd failed and graduate from junior high. She was miserable about it—beaten down and humiliated. So Martin thought he'd do something nice for her, a special little breakfast with dad, maybe a chance to talk, figure things out.

But, he explained, she'd been pissy. First she said she wasn't hungry, and then that the food wasn't any good, even though the little diner in Walnut Station had always been her favorite place. Martin was just about to tell Ludwig how she'd said he was boring and wanted to leave, which ended up with him yelling at her right there in the diner. But before he could get the last part of the story out (the dramatic part, which was actually kind of funny, he knew)—he saw the black Camaro pull into the parking area out in front of the office.

"What's wrong?" Ludwig said, following his gaze. "Who is that?"

"Nothing," Martin said. He stood up from his desk and put his hands on his hips. "Or nothing's wrong, I mean. This is the guy I told you about. The drug detective. The one who came by here before—from the plane that crashed up in Humboldt County." He stood there looking out the window, waiting for Slater to emerge from his car.

"Really?" Ludwig said. He swung his legs off of his desk and leaned forward, peering out through the plate glass window. "What's he doing here now?"

Martin looked at Ludwig, then back out at Slater's car. "How the fuck do I know what he's doing here?" he asked. "He wants to crawl up my ass again, I guess. Or up our asses. See if we've sold any more drug planes."

Ludwig sat there, looking out the window at Slater. "But we haven't sold *any* planes," he said. "Tell him that. Tell him to send some drug smugglers our way and we'll sell them some planes—and then we'll turn them in to him. How about telling him that?"

Martin watched as Slater got out of his car and took a long, patient look around the lot. He had the same basic outfit as the last two times he'd seen him—jeans, T-shirt—but he was also wearing sunglasses—aviators—which Martin found both irritating and intimidating.

It was just over a week since his second trip to Mexico. Had the drugs hit the market already? Had there been a sudden wave of heroin overdoses caused by an extra-potent shipment of Mexican brown (or a bad shipment, one laced with rat poison or some other horrible substance)? That was the kind of thing that would happen on TV: the shipment trickles down to the streets, and the dedicated cop starts sniffing around, following leads, turning up the heat.

Fuck, Martin thought. He stood there watching Slater look around.

"Jesus," Ludwig said. He stood up now, too. "Look at him. He really does look like a narco guy, doesn't he?"

THEY SAT ON THE vinyl-cushioned couches in the waiting area by the big front window. Linda had picked them out—the couches and the round coffee table (she had also picked out the big plastic plants between the two couches). She said the couches had a nice modern look that went with the building, and that the off-white color would brighten the place. Plus, the vinyl was easy to clean. Martin agreed they looked good, but they weren't very comfortable. The cushions were thin, and if you sat there for more than a couple of minutes you could feel the wooden frames jabbing at you. And the truth was that the white vinyl didn't clean off very well; there were coffee stains all over the cushions.

Slater had spread a couple of sheets of mug shots on the coffee table, and Martin and Ludwig were looking through them. That was why Slater had shown up: there was another guy they were looking at in connection with the Humboldt case, and he wanted Martin (and now Ludwig) to look at some more people, see if they recognized anyone.

"But the guy who bought that plane came in alone," Martin said.

"I know," Slater said. "But now we think that this might be a wider circle of people, and it looks like they might have another plane they're using. We tracked down some information about a series of flight plans someone filed up at the airport in Redding. And we think it might be this guy, the one connected to the Humboldt thing—you know, your guy. The guy who crashed."

"And you want to know if one of these other guys bought a plane here, too," Martin said.

Slater looked at Ludwig and pointed at Martin.

"Your boss is pretty sharp," he said, smiling. "Nothing gets past him."

Ludwig laughed, and he and Slater exchanged a look.

Jesus, Martin thought. Don't tell me these two are going to end up being pals.

It wouldn't surprise him. They were actually kind of similar. Both were somewhere in their mid- to late thirties, and both were kind of good-looking in that rough and tumble way women tended to like. But most of all, they both had that working-class thing going on—or that up-from-working-class thing. The whole "Sure, I'm white collar, but I'm not pretending to be anything I'm not" thing.

Martin decided to ignore them. He was tired of Jim Slater and his penchant for just showing up, uninvited. "What was the make of the plane?" he asked.

"Uh, hold on," Slater said. He stood up and dug around in his front pocket, and then pulled out a folded-up piece of pink paper. Martin remembered that Slater had done something like this when he was at his house out in Walnut Station. Hadn't he pulled out a crinkled-up piece of paper with information scribbled on it? It occurred to him that this seeming lack of organization was actually just a show—a pretend messiness, one that was intended to get guys like Martin to let their guard down.

"Okay," Slater said. "It's a Piper Cherokee PA 32-300. That's what it says in the flight plan, anyway."

"We've sold a couple of those in the past few years," Ludwig said. "What year is it?"

Slater sat down and looked again at his little piece of pink paper.

"Nineteen sixty-seven," he said.

Ludwig looked over at Martin. "Have we ever sold a sixty-seven three hundred?" he asked, a thoughtful look on his face. "That doesn't sound familiar." He looked back at Slater. "I don't think so, but I'm not positive. Let me take a look."

Martin watched as Ludwig jumped up and walked over to the three file cabinets by the coffee machine. He could tell that Ludwig was hoping to find out that the guy had actually bought the plane from Anderson Aircrafts. It was the same way Martin had felt at his house, just before identifying the guy in the mug shots. He'd wanted to be part of something exciting like that. An arrest, or a bust, or whatever.

But, he knew, he'd also wanted to please Slater. It was more than a little ridiculous. A guy shows up out of nowhere, flashes his badge, and the next thing you know you're doing everything you can to make him happy (or almost everything—Martin wasn't going to turn himself in just to score points with Slater, that was for sure). But there was something about Slater that made you feel that way. He was an alpha dog, the kind the other dogs in the pack gave over to: moved out of the way, averted their eyes, let him have first shot at the females in heat.

Martin looked at Slater and saw that he was looking back at him. He had that cocky half smile on his face, and Martin had the feeling he wouldn't mind sitting in the waiting area of Anderson Aircrafts all day long. Chatting and just generally being a nuisance.

Fucking hell, Martin thought. He didn't know what to say. Go away. I hate you.

He glanced over and saw that Ludwig had his head buried in the open drawer of a file cabinet. He was mumbling something, but Martin couldn't quite hear what.

"So where is this plane now?" Martin asked, mainly for the sake of having something to say. He knew Slater didn't know where the plane was. Moreover, he, Martin, didn't care where the plane was.

"Well," Slater said. "If you'd asked me that question last week, I'd have told you that I didn't have a clue. But we just found out that David Little, the one who bought the plane from you guys here, actually owns a bunch of land out in Livermore. And we're thinking that it might be stashed out there somewhere."

He looked at Martin and adjusted his sunglasses where they were perched on his head. They were tucked into his hair, and Martin felt a quick stab of jealousy as he thought about how careful he had to be when he did something like that—more than once, he'd pushed his toupee off balance doing that kind of thing.

Huh, Martin thought. Livermore wasn't that far from Walnut Station. You drove south to Pleasanton, where Val lived, and then east fifteen or twenty minutes. It wasn't as nice as Walnut Station or Pleasanton. Yes, the Rolling Stones had played out there, at the speedway, but it was mostly a bunch of hick ranchers who thought it was still 1950. So what was going on? Was everyone in the East Bay turning to drug smuggling?

"So why don't you just go out there and look around?" Martin asked. "You can do that if you want, right?"

Slater laughed. "Oh, we can do it, all right," he said. "We're the police—we can pretty much do whatever we want. But the problem is that we're talking about a lot of land out there. He's got twenty-five hundred acres, or something crazy like that. And it's really hilly, or a lot of it is, anyway. Canyons and a lot of oak trees. We drove around for a while but it's just me and one other guy. There's only so much ground we can cover. Plus, we don't have the right kind of car. My Camaro isn't exactly the kind of car you take up into the hills, you know."

Martin was about to respond when Ludwig came back over from the file cabinets.

"Okay," he said to Martin and Slater. He was holding a couple of file folders. Jesus, Martin thought. When I ask him to grab some files it takes at least half an hour.

"These are for the Piper Cherokees we've sold the past few years," Ludwig said. "But I don't think we've sold a 'sixty-seven."

He tossed the files onto the coffee table. Martin looked at the plain manila exteriors of the files and thought about the sheets of paper inside. Contracts. Personal-information forms. Bank statements. Loan applications. Tax returns. All the paper that made the wheels turn, and that left a clearly marked trail back to wherever it was that you were trying to hide. Maybe in a place like Mexico you could just sort of disappear into the ether, hop in your plane and vanish. Here, though, there was always a way to find you. Basically, once a guy like Slater started in after you, it was only a matter of time before he tracked you down.

"Thanks," Slater said. But he didn't reach out to grab the files. Instead he just sat there, looking down at them. Martin felt as if he understood. Who wanted to go rooting through a bunch of old files? Plus, he had a feeling a guy like Slater was more interested in the action part of things, the rundowns and the shootouts. Sure, he'd been shot a couple of times, and he was semiretired out here in the suburbs. But Martin was willing to bet he still got off on that rush of adrenaline that came with the hot pursuit of the bad guy.

"Listen," Slater said. "I have a question for you guys. This is gonna sound a little nutty, but just hear me out."

He looked up at Ludwig, who was still standing there next to the couch, and then over at Martin.

"Okay," Ludwig said.

Martin nodded. "Yeah," he said. "Okay. Let's hear it."

"Well," Slater said. He folded his arms and leaned back on the couch. "What would you guys think about flying me out there? You know, out to this guy's property in Livermore. Or out over this guy's property, I mean. So I could see what's going on. I mean, it's not very far, right? And maybe that way I can see something. You know, from up above."

Martin stared at Slater. Had he really just asked to be taken up in one of Martin's planes? Why not just ask if he could join Martin for his next trip down to Mexico? It was almost as if Slater were yanking Martin's chain, trying to scare the shit out of him. Martin felt a panicked urge to jump up and flee—just jump in his car and start driving.

"Holy shit," Ludwig said. "Do you really want to do that? That would be fantastic." He looked at Martin, then back at Slater. He was smiling. "When could we do it? You'd be amazed what you can see from up above. If there's a landing strip in that area, you'll definitely see it."

"Jeez," Slater said. "I don't know. How about today? We can do it right now, as far as I'm concerned."

Ludwig looked down at Martin.

"We don't have anything else going on, right, Martin? And you're right," he said to Slater. "It's not very far at all. It's just over the hills, basically. I'll bet it's not even fifty miles."

They both looked at Martin as he sat there. He knew he hadn't responded yet, and that he should say something. But he was speechless—tongue-tied. He was thinking of various delay tactics, and it was interfering with his ability to respond. We don't have any gas. Our insurance won't cover it. But he knew it was useless. And if he said he didn't want to do it at all, then Ludwig would say he could do it without him. Plus, the whole point was that he couldn't look unwilling.

And why should he be? They were looking for some clown who was moving marijuana from Humboldt County down to Livermore, not the two shadowy figures who were flying heroin up to Hayward from a small ranch located not far outside Ensenada, Mexico. Still, the notion that he'd go up in one of his planes with Jim Slater to look for a drug smuggler was a little absurd. More than a little absurd, in fact.

"What do you say, Martin?" Ludwig asked. "Are you up for it?"

Martin felt the energy start to drain out of him. It was like someone had unscrewed a tiny little cap, and now his energy, his ability to keep moving through each day, hoping that things would get better, was flowing out onto the ground. He didn't know how he was going to get through the next couple of hours.

"Hey," he said, looking at Slater and then at Ludwig. He gave them a weak smile—knew it was weak, but it was the best he could do. "You know me. I say let's go get those motherfuckers."

Slater laughed and then gave a little whoop. "All *right*," he said. He had a big wide smile on his face. "Let's go catch some bad guys."

He must have been in a daze, because he started walking Slater directly over to the Cessna Skylane he'd flown down to Mexico. Jesus, he thought when they were about two hundred feet away from it. What the hell am I thinking? Do I *want* to get busted by this guy? It was practically a given that Slater was like one of those drug-sniffing dogs, that he could detect the slight traces of heroin that were sure to be in the plane. So he muttered something about a problem with the Skylane, and steered them instead over to the Cessna Cardinal, the plane Martin had used a few weeks ago to fly around with Mr. 240Z and his girlfriend. It was nice and roomy inside, and like he'd told the guy, it was good for survey-style work—exactly what Slater now wanted to do.

The second they were in the plane, Ludwig was jabbering like an excited kid on a school field trip. Martin had tried to get him to stay behind, but Ludwig had insisted. "No way," he said. "I'm coming with you guys." And with Slater standing right there, Martin hadn't wanted to make an issue of it.

Slater was next to Martin, in the front passenger seat. Ludwig was in back, between the two seats, leaning forward and pointing and explaining. Martin hadn't seen him act like this in a long time. He was giddy, like a kid who has suddenly and unexpectedly gotten permission to do the thing he'd never been allowed to do.

Slater asked question after question about the instrument panel and about what the plane could do, and Ludwig gave him eager responses. They had to shout a little bit to be heard over the drone of the engine, which made their back-and-forth that much more irritating. How low can you fly? How much room do you need to land? What do you need to land at night? What's the load capacity of one of these things? The conversation reminded Martin of his question-and-answer sessions with Val Desmond. Val, of course, had been trying to figure out how to sneak the drugs into the country, whereas Slater was trying to keep them out—or to catch the guys who were smuggling them in. But as far as Martin could tell, there wasn't much difference. They were both trying to figure out how to get a little edge in the game of cat and mouse between the good guys and the bad guys. Now, though, Martin had the distinct feeling that Slater was making a move of some sort. It was a shot across the bow, a warning, one that involved making a fool of Martin (in fact, Martin realized, maybe it was the latter goal that was the real object of this little scavenger hunt after all).

Soon they were flying over the coastal hills separating Hayward and the other bayside towns from the inland suburbs. And then, before he knew it, they were flying over Walnut Station. It was an old habit, something he did on his own but also with the kids every now and then. They loved it. And who could blame them? There was just something fascinating about looking down at your own school or your own house from a couple thousand feet up in the air.

He didn't say anything about it to Slater or Ludwig, but within a minute or two he was looking down at his little postage stamp of property. Or he thought it was his house—it was hard to tell, because for the most part all the houses looked the same. But as they flew directly over his block he was pretty sure that he could make out the gray L of his roof and the kidney-shaped pool of 1186 Miwok Drive. And—unless he was mistaken—he'd gotten a glimpse of Sarah and a couple of her girlfriends lying out next to the pool. He had to smile—talk about surveillance. He wished he had a camera with one of those powerful telephoto lenses, so that he could snap a few shots of them, see if they were smoking pot. He wouldn't have cared all that much, but he would have liked to catch her in a lie.

"Well," he'd say. "The problem is, honey, I've got a photo I took of you from one of my planes. And as you can see, it's pretty obvious that you *were* cutting your summer-school classes, and you *were* smoking a joint. Don't you think it's time to cut the bullshit, Sarah?"

He'd love to see her expression after that. Especially given her performance in the diner this morning, and then her performance *outside* the diner. She'd stormed out after he yelled at her, and then started down the street. So he'd followed her in his Caddy, yelling to her from the car, across the passenger seat and through the open window. "Get in the fucking car, Sarah! Right now!" That kind of thing. It was awful, like a bad TV drama. And it was worse because she'd ignored him. She'd walked all the way through town and to school, with him following alongside, yelling. He'd known people were looking at them, and he'd known what they were thinking: That guy's not in control of his family. But he hadn't been able to help himself.

He was about to say this to Ludwig—tell him the silly little fantasy about busting her with the dope—but then he remembered that Slater was in the plane, and so he just kept it to himself. It was a little bit odd, anyway, he realized after thinking about it. Maybe Ludwig wouldn't get it.

"Okay," Martin said, after they'd been in the air about half an hour. "We're coming up on Livermore. Help me figure out what we're looking for. Tell me again how far this place is from the highway, and where that water tower is that you were talking about."

They spent the next half hour making passes over the big empty-looking stretch of land this guy David Little owned—or was supposed to own. Slater was right. It was rough terrain, rougher than Martin expected. Lots of hills, creeks, and ravines. He was a little surprised.

He'd assumed that Livermore was a bunch of flat pasture land. They still had rodeos out in Livermore, for Christ's sake. But from the air everything is different. That was one of Martin's maxims. He used it on potential buyers, but he also believed it. Because from two thousand or maybe four thousand feet in the air and looking down, what you had was perspective—the very thing that you didn't have when you were on the ground and surrounded by all the things that were out there every day, trying to confuse you and make you feel lost and overwhelmed.

And that's why he wasn't surprised when they spotted a stretch of ground that looked like a makeshift airstrip. Or when Ludwig spotted it.

"Breaker, breaker," Ludwig said in a mock aviator's voice, one he followed with fake static sound, as if he were talking into the microphone of the plane's two-way radio. He was looking out the right window of the back seat. "I've got an airstrip sighting at two o'clock. Repeat: I'm looking at an illegal airstrip at two o'clock. Request advice on how to proceed."

Martin thought he was just joking—and making an idiot of himself—but when he glanced back he saw that Ludwig was actually serious. And then when he tilted the plane slightly for a better view, he saw that Ludwig was right—airstrip at two o'clock. Or *maybe* it was an airstrip. It was hard to tell. There was a small open field, and in the middle of it was a long rutted-out stretch where sets of wheels had obviously made a deep impression in the ground. Even from where they were up in the air, you could see where the earth was bare and pale next to what was otherwise undisturbed green grass. This went on for about two hundred yards or so—about the length of ground that it would take for a small plane to take off, or to land. But, Martin realized, it could also just be a stretch where someone—this David Little guy or someone else—had run a truck or maybe a tractor back and forth.

"Holy shit," Slater said as he looked out the side window of the Cardinal. "What do you know. That does look like an airstrip, doesn't it? Or does it? What do you think, Martin?"

He looked over at Martin, and then back out the window.

"I don't know," Martin said. "I mean, it could be for a plane, but it could also just be a stretch of road. You know, where a truck or something has driven a lot. A tractor, maybe."

"No," Ludwig said, shaking his head. "That's an airstrip. Look how isolated it is down there. There's nothing out here. Why would you drive around out here? Plus, Martin, if it were a road, wouldn't it look like that for a longer stretch? Check it out: there's just this one spot that's worn away. That's the kind of wear and tear you get with a plane taking off and landing."

"That's a good point," Slater said. He was looking now through the binoculars that Ludwig had given him when they first climbed into the plane.

And it *was* a good point. The two parallel tracks were out in the middle of nowhere, in a flat open area tucked behind some hills and a big stretch of old oak trees that ran along a creek bed. Maybe it really was an airstrip for some local drug guys. On the other hand, Martin thought, maybe it was actually like one of those things from that stupid book Sarah had been reading, the one about UFOs and ancient landing strips and the rest of that crap. He could picture the big red letters on the cover: *Chariots of the Gods?* It had sat in the bathroom for months, and he'd flipped though it at least a dozen times. There were lots of aerial photos of spots from all over the world where aliens had supposedly landed their spacecraft, or moved huge rocks or left signals for their buddies in other space ships. And some of the photos looked pretty much exactly like what they were looking at right now. So yeah, maybe they needed to look at this from a different angle—maybe an advanced people had left these marks a thousand years ago, and he and Ludwig and Slater were the first humans to really notice it. Compared to that, what did it matter if they tracked down a couple of guys flying pot in from Humboldt County?

Slater had Martin do another pass over the airstrip (or supposed airstrip), but there wasn't anything new to see: no plane hidden in the trees, covered with camouflage netting, no secret bunkers, no other signs of illicit activity. Martin watched Slater as he looked through the binoculars and mumbled to himself. He knew that it was time to head back to Hayward.

"I'm gonna nail that motherfucker," Slater said as they headed back westward. "Just you watch."

"Hey," Ludwig said. "Why wait? Why don't we just land right now? Why not have a look around? You never know—you might be able to surprise someone down there."

For a long, worried second Martin thought Slater might think this was a good idea, and that he was going to have to land his plane down there on what might actually be some sort of low-level drug set-up— probably only a step or two up from a hillbilly moonshine operation. He could just picture it. They'd land, and then someone would start blasting away at them from the bushes with shotguns and rifles. Slater would get picked off, and then he and Ludwig would be tortured and eventually killed by drug dealers out in Livermore, California—out in the boonies, in other words. And all because Michael Ludwig had thought it would be cool to fly around with fucking Jim Slater in a plane and look for bad guys. Or rather ... all because Martin Anderson was involved in his *own* drug-smuggling scheme, and thus too scared and too freaked out to say no to this crazy jaunt out over some god-forsaken property on the far edges of the East Bay.

Fortunately, though, Slater wasn't interested in some sort of macho parachute raid on this guy's shitty property.

"Listen," Slater said, looking at Ludwig. "I'd love to do it—believe me. But I don't think it's a good idea. We could crash, for one thing. But we might also run into trouble out there. You never know—drugs and guns tend to go together. And like I've told Martin, I'm done being a fucking cowboy. I do things the safe way now. And that means heading home and getting a bunch of backup before I go out there. Plus, what if one of you guys got hurt? I'd lose my badge in a goddamn heartbeat. And for what? Some guys flying pot down from Humboldt County? It's not worth it. So listen, even if they had all the money down there from their last deal—had it right now, a quarter of a million dollars or whatever—and we were going to fly in there and steal it, it still wouldn't be worth it."

Martin saw out of the corner of his eye that Ludwig looked a little startled at Slater's mention of guns and getting hurt. In fact, he had the feeling that Ludwig was remembering, suddenly, that Slater was the guy who'd been popped two different times in drug raids out in Oakland. Whatever the case, he wasn't surprised when Ludwig didn't have much to say on the short flight back to Hayward. He just sat back, looking out the window, and thinking whatever it was that guys like Ludwig thought about at moments like this.

But Martin didn't say much, either. Instead, he was thinking about the makeshift airstrip he'd been on recently with his own crew of drug dealers, down in Mexico. They definitely had guns, and Martin had the feeling they wouldn't hesitate to use them, not even for a second, if they ran into a problem. What would Slater have to say about that? Would he think it was worth it to confront them? Martin wasn't sure, but he hoped he wouldn't have to find out.

CHAPTER TWELVE

It was Linda who came up with the idea.

"I think we need to get away," she'd said. "Escape. You, me, all of us."

Martin was in the kitchen, making a sandwich, and for a quick second he thought she was referring to Slater—the whole drug thing—and he froze up. He stood there, not moving, knife and mayonnaise poised over his stack of bread, salami, American cheese, and onion slice. But then he realized that she was referring to a family trip, and he relaxed. A quick run up to Tahoe, she said. She'd take half a day off from work on Friday, and Martin could do the same.

"You can have Michael take care of things," she'd said. "Isn't that what he's for?"

Martin explained that Ludwig had his own plans. He was taking off with Jenny somewhere. Carmel, or something like that. Or maybe it was Mendocino. Martin couldn't remember.

"Just close up for the day," she said. "It's not that big a deal, is it? If someone really wants to buy a plane they'll come back, right? Give yourself a break."

Martin cringed. Her theory about a potential buyer coming back was debatable—was wrong, in fact. But she was definitely right about getting away. He needed to get out of the Bay Area for a couple of days, put some distance between himself and Anderson Aircrafts, not to mention his secret life as a drug smuggler. And though he didn't want to admit it to Linda, he could probably close for weeks and no one would even notice. Business was that bad.

So they loaded up the car Friday afternoon. It was warm, really pleasant late-June weather. Somewhere in the mid-eighties.

"Look at that," Martin said as they pulled out of the driveway. "Alan

Guthrie's working on his train set. That's a big surprise. I'll bet he's got a busy weekend ahead."

"Yeah," Peter said. "He's putting a new tunnel in this weekend. He's got a lot of work to do."

Martin looked at Peter in the rearview mirror, trying to figure out if he was being sarcastic—if he was echoing Martin's own sarcasm, in other words. He couldn't tell. This had been happening more and more with Peter. He and Linda hadn't talked about it yet, but he was planning on it. "Is he actually just fucking with us?" he wanted to ask. It was a little unsettling.

They stopped for an early dinner just before Sacramento, at The Nut Tree. It had wacky theme rooms the kids liked, and a big candy and souvenir shop. But Martin particularly liked it because they had a little airstrip out back. People flew in and out all day long, and Martin liked to check out the planes. He'd actually flown the family up a couple of times for dinner. "*This* is what you call jet-setting" he'd say, and even Linda would smile. Now, though, those little dinner flights seemed like ancient history—somehow flying had lost its glamour for Martin.

They got up to the cabin around sunset, and everyone was in bed by nine-thirty. Careful to be quiet, Martin and Linda had sex. As he was drifting off to sleep, Martin thought that Linda had been right, that a getaway was just the thing.

THE RANCH WAS ABOUT a half hour from the cabin, just over the Nevada state line, in Incline Village. Peter had seen a commercial about it on a local TV station first thing in the morning, and he was desperate to go.

"Dad, *please*," he said. They were sitting in the kitchen, Martin sipping coffee and only half listening. "It's where they film the show. They've got the whole ranch right there, with their house and horses and everything. And they've got souvenirs you can get. Tin cups and stuff. Maybe we'll even see them making one of the episodes."

Martin nodded. He knew where it was—he'd driven past the signs a million times, and he'd always been a little curious. He'd heard that some of the episodes were filmed at Tahoe, but he knew production of *Bonanza* had stopped over a year ago. Not that the show wasn't still on TV. Peter watched the reruns all the time—especially now that it was summer, and he didn't have anything to do in the afternoon, because he didn't seem to have any friends. Martin watched it with him once in a while, if he was home early. It was always the same thing. Little Joe and Hoss and their other brother would ride their horses around, trying to keep their dad from getting upset about something. Usually it was someone rustling cattle, or a plot to steal part of their giant ranch (which was supposedly huge, half a million acres or a thousand square miles or something like that).

From what Martin had heard, some crazy guy had noticed that the pretend Ponderosa Ranch was located right where he owned a bunch of property on the lake, and so he'd started building a replica of the set you saw on TV, the one down in Hollywood. Eventually, the studio heard about it, figured it was a good idea, and cut a deal with him. Or maybe he'd approached them. Either way, money had changed hands. And so now there was a real Ponderosa Ranch at Tahoe, plus a pretty exact version of Virginia City, the nearby town where the characters would go sometimes to see the sheriff or buy dry goods or do whatever you did in town a hundred years ago.

"The Ponderosa Ranch?" Sarah asked, coming into the room. She was just out of bed—she looked tired and sleepy. "Like in *Bonanza*?"

"Yeah," Peter said. "It's right up here in Lake Tahoe. They have tours and everything. We're going there today."

"We are?" Sarah said, looking at Martin. "*I'm* not going."

"Oh, come on, Sarah," Martin said. He gave her his best version of a big smile, knowing as he did that it looked forced and unconvincing, maybe even off-putting. "It'll be fun. I promise. Maybe we'll see Little Joe. Did you know that the guy who plays him is the dad on that *Little House on the Prairie* movie we saw on TV a few months ago?"

She snorted. "Oh my God," she said, folding her tanned arms. "No way. Count me out."

"Hey," Peter said. "How can he be on *Bonanza* at the same time as *Little House on the Prairie*? Aren't those two places a really long way apart from each other?"

Martin looked at Sarah, then over at Peter. Again he wasn't sure if Peter was just yanking his chain.

"Are you serious?" Sarah asked, looking at Peter. "Are you really that stupid?"

"All right," Martin said, his voice more serious now. "That's enough. And listen, Sarah. You're going with us or no beach today. I mean it."

THEY LEFT THE CABIN at about ten-thirty. Martin had promised that they'd be back by one-thirty, so that Sarah could get some time lying out in the sun. She was obsessed about her tan, and insisted that the thin mountain air gave you a darker look, especially if you used baby oil. He doubted they'd make it by then—two-thirty or three seemed more likely—but at least he'd gotten her into the car. And she wasn't being sullen, which was nice. Peter was jabbering about episodes of *Bonanza,* and she was tolerating him. She'd watched the show plenty of times, too, and Martin could tell that she was getting curious about seeing the place.

"So is there horseback riding?" she asked at one point. "And what about the actors? Are they really going to be there?"

Martin was pretty sure that the answer to both questions was no, and in fact he was willing to bet money she'd find it boring. But he didn't care, because the truth was that he was glad to have something like this to do. It was a break from their usual routine at Tahoe, which he'd secretly begun to hate: get up, haul their crap down to the beach, and try to mix with all the other families who were doing the same thing. In some ways, of course, it was exactly the thing they'd paid for when they bought the cabin. The lake, the pine trees, the huge granite boulders (that looked as if they'd been placed by a landscaping crew, Martin often thought). What more could you ask for? He knew plenty of people who wouldn't have complained, including himself six or seven years ago.

The problem was that it felt obligatory . . . or forced. It was as if they'd all been given a script and told to enact a family vacation and the bonding that went along with it. Worse, they weren't very good actors. They read their lines properly, but they were too stiff, there was no flow, no texture of deeply felt or genuine, in-the-moment emotion. If there were a director present (which Martin sometimes longed for, someone to be on hand and instruct him on how to have a family, be happy), he would have yelled "Cut!" and told them to try it again. "Memory-Making in Tahoe, take nine!"

What really bothered him, though, was that it all seemed to come naturally to the other families. Part of it, he knew, was that they were doing fine and had plenty of money. These were doctors and lawyers, or executives at big firms like Boeing or Wells Fargo (they were the bosses of the guys who'd turned down his recent loan request, in other words). Sure, the energy crisis was an issue, but it wasn't going to hurt them, not really. Plus, they'd inherited tons of money, anyway. They could float along for years, even without a job. They were born knowing how to inhabit the rarefied space of a resort like Lake Tahoe. When he watched Gordon Harmon's twelve-year-old daughter swim to that big raft, he could tell that she was using the long, efficient strokes and even kick of someone who'd been on a swim team for years, just as he knew that her life was filled with piano lessons, ballet, and maybe a little horseback riding.

The same went for that kid with the Sunfish sailboat. He was tall and muscular and tan, and when Martin saw him standing with his dad (getting patient and insightful instruction on tacking into the wind, no doubt), he knew that his future was secure. Someday that kid would have *his* kids up at the family cabin in Tahoe. And that kid's future family would laugh and joke and bond just like his own family did as they sat on their beach towels or big Pendleton blankets. And he wasn't going to choose a girl like Sarah Anderson for his wife. No, it was going to be someone like the Harmon girl—a person who had never for a moment questioned her place in the world.

They pulled into the parking lot at about eleven, and right away Martin felt as if he'd made the right decision.

"Jeez," he said, as they walked along the main street of the replica Virginia City. "This is pretty cool."

"Yeah," Peter said, looking around. "It looks really real!"

And he was right. There was a whole series of wooden buildings that had the look and feel of the Old West. They had swinging saloon doors, balconies with wooden railings, and nicely painted signs that said things like SILVER CUP SALOON, LIBERTY BANK, TAXIDERMIST, and ANGIE'S HOUSE OF PLEASURE. There was a church on one corner, and a little farther on, a big waterwheel that was connected to what looked like sluice boxes. There were old wooden wagons and buggies parked here and there along the street, and even a few horses tied to the railings outside the businesses (one or two were real horses, but most of them were made of hard plastic—though the saddles were real).

The best part was that mixed in with the still fairly light crowd were men and women in period costumes. The men were mostly gunslinger types in cowboy hats, with handkerchiefs around their necks. The women either had fluffy, brightly colored taffeta dresses and parasols, or red and black corsets and shorter skirts that showed their ankles. A couple of them were pretty cute—maybe college girls off for the summer, Martin thought.

"Hey," Martin said to Linda. "They must be from Angie's House of Pleasure."

"Uh-huh," she said, giving him a sidelong glance. "Maybe you could go find out."

Martin was about to offer a jokey response when he saw Peter wander into the *Sierra News,* and so they followed him inside. It wasn't very well lit, and it smelled like ink. There were only a few people milling around inside. After his eyes adjusted to the dim lighting, he saw that there were newspapers taped up on all the walls.

"Hey, Dad," Peter said from across the room. "Check this out. They make newspapers in here for you. We can get our own paper made with our own headline."

"Yeah, Dad," Sarah said. "Listen to this: 'Bigfoot Found Near Lake Tahoe.'"

"That's right, sir," said a guy behind the counter. "Any headline you want, right here. Special Edition. Five dollars." He was wearing a straw hat with a colorful band around it, and he had tiny glasses and two little black bands around his arms to hold his sleeves up—like an old-time news guy, Martin realized.

"Okay," Martin said. "So what sort of headline should we get?"

"How about 'Anderson Family Resorts to Cannibalism'?" Peter said.

"Or how about 'Anderson Family Ditches Annoying Boy in Sierras'?" Sarah said.

"All right," Linda said. "Be nice."

They debated for a while, and finally Martin said that both kids could get their own headline, but that they had to wait a bit. "We've got plenty of time," he said. "Figure out what you want, first. Make sure it's one you'll like."

They were back out on the street, talking about possible headlines, when the swinging doors of the Silver Cup Saloon banged open, and one of the gunfighter-cowboy types came stumbling out into the street area. He was so close to Peter that he almost ran into him. Someone yelled at him from inside the saloon—"Hold it right there, Sampson! Hands in the air!" But then all of a sudden the guy drew his pistol, spun around, and fired a couple of shots into the saloon (or a couple of fake shots, Martin realized after a second or two). Someone inside (probably the guy who'd yelled at him) shot back, and a few seconds later two guys ran outside, blasting away at Sampson. But he'd taken cover behind a barrel, so the two guys from the saloon ducked for cover as well. Suddenly it was a full-scale shootout. *Blam, blam. Blam, blam, blam.*

It was kind of goofy, but also kind of exciting. One of the two guys chasing Sampson took a bullet and did a slow roll out into the street. Then a guy came out on the balcony of the building next door and starting yelling that he was the sheriff, and then he started shooting, too. Finally, two guys with handkerchiefs over their faces came riding up on horseback, guns blazing. Sampson (whom Martin was starting to like more and more) jumped onto the back of one of the horses, and the three of them rode away, whooping and firing their guns into the air.

It was quiet for a second, with Martin and Linda and everyone else standing there, not sure how to react. Finally someone, a fat, older man with white hair, started clapping. And then everyone seemed to realize that that was the thing to do.

"That was so cool!" Peter yelled. He was standing in front of Martin all of a sudden, looking up at him with wide, shining eyes. "Did you see that guy get shot? They totally got away!"

"Well," Linda said. "It was really loud, anyway."

"But weren't you surprised?" Peter asked Linda. "Didn't you think they were really shooting each other, at least at first?"

Martin laughed, and looked at Linda.

"Okay," she said. "Yes, they surprised me. But are they going to keep doing that kind of thing?"

Martin shrugged. "I don't know," he said. "We'll just have to find out."

About ten minutes later, after they'd wandered through the jailhouse, they watched the sheriff have it out with the town drunk. They were hamming it up, going for corny slapstick, and people were laughing on cue.

All of it reminded Martin of his conversation a while back with Ludwig—the one about *Westworld,* and about a fantasy camp based on bank robberies. But now that he'd actually had guns pointed at him, and had actually carried large caches of money around (and over the Mexican border, no less), the whole idea had lost its appeal. In fact, what he really wanted now was some sort of fantasy camp in which he was a rich guy out in the suburbs with nothing to worry about. And with lots of friends. That was it—in his camp, he and Linda would be debt free, and they'd host a regular neighborhood cocktail party. Sometimes they'd invite Sal Bando and his family, but sometimes they wouldn't. But the Weavers would always be there . . . well, or Miriam would be. Sometimes Hal would be out of town, and on those nights

Miriam and Martin would exchange meaningful looks, maybe even sit, feet dangling in the pool, chatting and flirting. It would be obvious they wanted each other, but Linda would just roll her eyes. Because she'd understand it was something she had to put up with to keep her rich and charming husband happy.

Martin sighed, and looked back along the main street of the imitation Virginia City. That wasn't too much to ask, was it?

PETER READ OUT LOUD from the sign that was affixed to the back of the wagon. It was handwritten, printed in neat capital leters.

THIS CONESTOGA WAGON WAS ABANDONED ON THE EDGE OF DONNER LAKE, LOCATION OF THE UNSUCCESSFUL CROSSING OF THE DONNER PARTY IN 1846. IT WAS REMOVED IN THE EARLY 30s WHEN THE LAKE WAS AT ITS LOWEST LEVEL, AND IS ONE OF FEW SUCH WAGONS TO HAVE SURVIVED.

"Huh," Martin said when he finished.

"Wow," Linda said. "Just think."

"So did some of the people that got eaten ride on this wagon?" Peter asked. "Or did they eat people right here, right on top of it?"

"I don't know," Martin said. He shrugged. "Maybe."

Sarah shook her head. It occurred to Martin that Peter was saying all this stuff about the Donner Party to get under Sarah's skin.

They'd made their way past the big waterwheel, over to the Ponderosa Ranch area of the park. The guy who built this place was a real nut, Martin thought. But you had to admit that he knew what he was doing. There were now lots of people milling around, and they'd all paid their entrance fees, just like Martin had. This place was probably worth a fortune.

"So do you think we'll see any of the actors?" Peter asked.

"Probably not, honey," Linda said. "But keep your eyes peeled. You never know."

Martin and Linda walked ahead into the big ranch house. It was where a lot of scenes took place in the show, and it was all there: the big stone hearth, the kitchen table, the map of the property that they showed at the start of the show. There was even a life-size wax figure of Ben Cartwright (or Lorne Green, Martin thought, remembering the actor's name). He was sitting at a table in front of the fireplace. He was wearing his usual ranch outfit, and he was smiling, his eyes fixed on a spot somewhere near the back of the room.

"He looks pretty pleased with himself," Linda said.

"Wouldn't you be?" Martin asked. "He's got this nice house, and he owns a million acres of land up next to Lake Tahoe."

"And all three of his wives are dead," Linda said. "Isn't that part of the show? That he has one son from each dead wife? That's why they've got those three tombstones out in front of this place, right?"

Martin shrugged. "I guess so," he said. "I don't know. I didn't see them."

"Oh, they're there, all right," she said, and then she laughed and shook her head. "And so now he gets to be Mr. Bachelor, and have everyone feel sorry for him. I'll bet he rides into Virginia City every weekend to see the ladies at Angie's House of Pleasure."

"You might be right," Martin said. "But that's never on the show. Or I don't think it is, anyway."

"He actually looks a little creepy," Linda said.

"Do you think so?" Martin asked. He looked at the wax figure. "My wife thinks you're creepy, Mr. Cartwright . . . or Lorne. What do you have to say to that?"

He stood there waiting, but there was no answer, just a frozen, waxy silence.

BACK OVER IN VIRGINIA City, they bought some Hoss Burgers. "That's why they're so big," Peter said, pointing to the sign. "They're the kind of burgers a guy like Hoss would eat."

They sat down at a picnic table and relaxed for a while. It was a beautiful day. They watched a woman do a bunch of tricks with a big lasso and then with a whip. After that, the same woman picked Peter and Sarah out of the crowd to be in a line of people that played "Home, Home on the Range" with cow bells.

"I can't believe I don't have a camera," Linda said. "Oh my God. Look at Sarah smiling."

A few minutes later there was another shootout in the street, this time between a bank robber and the sheriff. It was a different sheriff, and this time he captured the bad guy. "Looks like we're gonna have ourselves a little hangin' later on," he said as he led the outlaw away in handcuffs. Martin expected the outlaw's pals to come riding up and save him, but he was on his own, apparently.

They were just getting ready to leave when Peter remembered the newspapers. Martin and Linda sat down on a big granite boulder and waited while he and Sarah ran back to the *Sierra News*.

"Well, Martin," Linda said. "You know I hate places like this, but I have to admit this was fun. I think even Sarah liked it."

"I know," he said. "I thought she was going to kick and scream the whole time."

"She's still got a tiny bit of little girl left in her," Linda said.

They were sitting there like that when Peter came running up a few minutes later and slapped a fresh newspaper down on Martin's lap. He could see that the ink of the headline was still shiny and a little bit wet. It even smelled like fresh ink.

"Check it out, Dad," Peter said. He was beaming.

Martin read the headline. It was printed in two rows of big bold letters.

WANTED DEAD OR ALIVE:
MARTIN ANDERSON, OUTLAW

Martin read it through a couple of times, and then looked up at Peter. He was still standing there, smiling and waiting for a response.

"Well, what do you think?" Peter asked. "Isn't it great?"

"Yeah, Martin," Linda said. "Come on, say something."

Martin nodded, and forced a quick smile.

"Yeah," he said. "It's great, Peter. Thank you. I'll put it up in my office."

CHAPTER THIRTEEN

Finding them had been pure luck. Martin had been saying yeah, yeah, it's all set, I just have to pick them up. But in fact he'd been worried. Since the announcement that Gaylord Perry was pitching on July eighth, the game had been completely sold out, and it was impossible to find tickets. It was a big deal: that's all there was to it. Everyone wanted to go, especially now that Perry might tie the American League record for consecutive wins. The record (according to Peter, who'd been reading the green sports page of the *Chronicle* every day and reporting to Martin about it) was sixteen.

"Are you sure?" Peter kept saying. "I mean, it's all set up, right?"

Martin suspected that Linda had planted a seed of doubt in Peter's ear—some indirect version of "Your dad's a screw-up, don't forget that." But whatever it was, he'd known he was running out of time.

And then, out of nowhere, Ludwig said he had a guy—scribbled a name on a piece of paper, said he knew him from somewhere and that he was looking to unload some tickets. It was a huge relief.

So now it was the day before the Fourth of July, and Martin was in Berkeley with Peter. They were on their way to fetch the tickets.

Driving along Shattuck Avenue, he saw that the gas lines were really big. They were longer, even, than the ones in Walnut Station. People must be filling up for the Fourth, he thought.

He glanced down at the piece of paper Ludwig had given him, and that he was holding in his hand.

He knew the guy lived near Spenger's. The slip of paper said Eighth Street, just north of University.

"Okay," he said to Peter. "We'll be there in a minute."

"Are you lost?" Peter asked.

Martin glanced over at him. He was sitting in the front passenger seat. "No," he said. "I'm not lost. I come over here all the time. And I grew up around here, remember?"

"Okay," Peter said. "If you say so."

Martin turned from Shattuck to University. The UC campus was right there, at the end of University. There were lots of students walking along the sidewalks, and it occurred to him that they must be holding summer classes.

He had to brake for a traffic backup, and leaning out the window he saw that it was because a crowd of thirty or forty people had waded out into the street. It was a bunch of hippie types—long-haired and scruffy-looking. They were waving signs around and yelling. He and Peter were at least ten cars back from the action, but they had a good view of what was going on. Jesus, Martin thought. Didn't they have anything better to do? Didn't you have to study at a school like Berkeley?

"Who are *those* people?" Peter asked. "What're they doing?"

"They're protesting," Martin said.

"Protesting?" Peter said.

"Yeah," Martin said. "You know, demonstrating."

Peter looked at Martin, then back at the crowd. "About what?" he asked.

"Who knows?" Martin responded. "The war in Vietnam. President Nixon. Everything. Nothing. I don't know."

"Oh," Peter said. He paused, and Martin could tell that he was thinking, trying to connect the dots. "So Nixon's a bad president, right?"

Martin thought for a second. "I don't know. I guess. Or he got caught doing some stuff he shouldn't have done, anyway. And then he got caught lying about it. So yeah, he screwed up. He's a screwup, I guess you could say."

Traffic started moving, but slowly. Martin thought about how his father would respond to Peter's question, about how he'd tell Peter that Nixon was a corrupt asshole, and that he was going to grow up in a world where everyone knew you couldn't trust politicians. And he'd tell him that it would be better that way, that people would take responsibility for things, and not just blindly trust their leaders anymore.

Martin closed his eyes for a long second and wondered if he had a headache coming on. When he opened them, he saw that the protestors had made their way to the other side of the street. They were doing the same thing they'd been doing on the campus side—yelling and carrying on. From what Martin could tell, no one was paying much attention to them.

"But Nixon's going to get fired, right?" Peter asked. "That's what Mrs. Bishop said."

"Huh," Martin said. "I don't know about that. I think he might quit. Or resign, that is. I'm not sure."

He tried to picture Mrs. Bishop out on the street with these protestors, yelling at cars and waving a sign that said RESIGN NOW! She'd be wearing the jeans she'd sported for her visit to his house. Or no— maybe it would be one of the short dresses she wore on school days. Either way, he knew, she wouldn't fit in very well.

"Can the President get arrested?" Peter asked. "Or can they chop off his head, like they did to the King of France?"

Martin looked over at Peter. "No," he said. He let out a laugh. "They won't chop off his head. That's definitely not going to happen."

Jesus, he thought. This fucking kid.

But as he drove past the campus it occurred to Martin that Nixon's day of reckoning might coincide with his own. Nixon would get taken away in cuffs the same day Martin was hauled out of his house, hands cuffed and shackled behind his back just like the President (or the soon-to-be ex-President). The lights would be flashing on the cruiser sitting in his driveway (his circular driveway), and Alan Guthrie would be standing halfway up the drive, drinking it in. Maybe Miriam Weaver would see the commotion and come wandering up the street. She'd put a worried hand to her mouth, and she and Martin would make eye contact through the back-door window of the police cruiser. It would be the last time he saw her for a long time—but maybe the look on her face (not just worried but heartbroken) would sustain him through his time in prison.

Martin drove down University to Eighth Street. The house was five or six blocks off University. Number 1640. Not a great neighborhood, but not as bad as he thought it might be. Lots of junky-looking cars on the street and in driveways, but the tiny front yards had plants and flowers (big clumps of rosemary, bright perennials, that kind of thing). And the little stucco houses were painted various colors. Yellow, blue. You could see that people had made an effort. Which was nice, because in general, the streets in that area between San Pablo Avenue and the bay were a little sketchy. A couple of people from Spenger's said it had gotten worse back there. More and more black and Mexican families had been moving into rental places, and there was more crime. Lots of break-ins, drugs, a few muggings.

"Okay," Martin said, slowing down in front of a house with the number 1640 on the wall by the front stairway. "I think this is it."

There wasn't any room to park along the street, and so he pulled his Cadillac up into the little driveway—or part of the way up the drive. There was a big Ford pickup blocking most of the space, and there were a couple of kids' bicycles lying on the ground by the open garage door. The garage was a mess. A table saw, ladders, boxes, a wheelbarrow with a green lawn hose sticking out of it. There were a couple of motorcycles taking up a lot of space (which made sense; Ludwig had said something about this guy and motorcycles). One of them was a dirt bike of some sort. It was up on milk crates and almost completely taken apart. The other one was a big street bike, a Norton or a Triumph.

"How about if you wait here," Martin said. "I'll just be a minute. You can read your magazine." He pointed down at the issue of *Sports Illustrated* Peter had brought along, and that was sitting on the seat next to him. It had just come in the mail a week or so before, and Peter was excited because it had a picture of Reggie Jackson on the cover. He was at the end of one of his trademark swings, legs and torso twisted with effort, and above him in big yellow letters it said SUPERDUPERSTAR.

No one else had a swing like that, Martin had told Peter. And it was true—the guy really was one of a kind.

"Why can't I come with you?" Peter said. "I'll be quiet."

"Just wait here," Martin said. He opened the door and got out of the car.

The house was just a box, basically, but with a little wing up above the garage, on the right. It was a small place. Martin could picture it—a tiny living room and kitchen, a couple of bedrooms, and a bathroom. And that was it.

The door opened before Martin was halfway up the drive, and a big white guy stepped outside. Or not so much big as wide—thick arms and shoulders, big thighs. He had short dark hair, boots, and a black T-shirt with the words *Lynyrd Skynyrd* on it. Martin knew this was a rock band. Ludwig had mentioned them, said they were good. Maybe the two of them got together and listened to Lynyrd Skynyrd records. Maybe they lay on the floor and looked at the album covers and sang the lyrics.

"Can I help you?" The guy stepped over one of the kids' bikes and stopped at the top of the driveway.

"Hi," Martin said. He gave a little wave, but he stopped where he was, halfway up the driveway. "I'm Martin . . . Michael Ludwig's friend. I'm here for the A's tickets. For the game on the eighth."

Martin expected his mention of Ludwig's name to break the ice. Okay, yeah, sure—no problem. Come on in, let me get them. But the guy just stood there. No look of recognition or acknowledgment.

"The A's tickets," he said. Flat—a statement. Not a question.

Martin looked at him. He was pretty sure he had the right place. But maybe not, which would explain why this guy was acting kind of strangely.

"You know," Martin said, taking a step backward. "I think I might have the wrong house. I'm looking for a guy named George Maddox. Do you maybe know if he lives somewhere along this street?" He looked over at the house next door, to the right, and then back at the house on the left. Then he glanced back at Peter in the Cadillac. He was still sitting in the front seat, looking out at them.

The guy watched Martin for a second, not really doing anything. Thick arms and hands still hanging at his sides.

"You've got the right place," the guy said, finally. He had bushy eyebrows (to go with his thick body), and he raised them just a little bit and nodded. "I'm George."

"Oh," Martin said. He'd been about to take another step backward and then turn around and walk away. "Okay, well—"

"You were going to come by a few days ago, right?" the guy asked. He cocked his head just a little bit, and folded them across his big chest, covering up the Lynyrd Skynyrd insignia.

"Uh, yeah . . . I guess so," Martin said. "But I've just been really busy. This is actually the first chance I've had to come by. And I would have called, you know, but I didn't have a number and so . . . I don't know." He gave the guy what he hoped was a friendly expression of helplessness, hands out and hands palms upward. But then he had a flash of anxiety.

"Do you still have them?" he asked. "The tickets? You haven't sold them, have you?"

The guy raised his eyebrows again. "Oh, I still have them," he said. "In fact, I've actually got them right here."

He unfolded his arms, reached back, and pulled out his wallet. Martin noticed that it was connected to a belt loop by one of those little chain things. Jesus, he thought. How does Ludwig know this guy?

But even as he thought this, he was distracted by the green, gold, and white of the tickets as they emerged from the guy's wallet. Yes, he thought. Jackpot. Touchdown. Something had actually worked out.

"Hey," Martin said, pointing at the tickets and taking a couple of steps forward. "Look at that. There they are. Great." He looked at the guy and smiled. The guy nodded. Then he smiled—a real smile—and Martin saw to his surprise that he had beautiful teeth, and a handsome smile.

"July eighth, at seven-thirty-five," the guy said, reading the heading of the ticket out loud to Martin. "Oakland A's versus Cleveland Indians." He held the tickets in his left hand and put his wallet back into his back pocket with his right. Martin watched as the chain swung around with the wallet. Then he held the tickets up so that Martin could see them clearly, and waved them a tiny bit. He was still smiling.

Martin took a quick glance over his shoulder, back at Peter in the Cadillac. He'd seen the tickets, too—he was bouncing up and down in the front seat, and when he saw Martin look at him, he gave him a thumbs-up sign. It was something Martin told him pilots started doing in World War II, and Peter had picked up on it, did it all the time. Martin was tempted to return the gesture but resisted, in case it distracted Maddox somehow.

Martin reached back for his own wallet. He'd put $120 in there for this specific transaction—six crisp new $20 bills.

"Okay," he said. "So Ludwig said that you said eighty dollars, right? For the two? I've gotta admit that I think that's pretty steep, but okay. So—"

"Well," the guy said, interrupting him again. "That's right. That's what I told Michael last week." The guy glanced over at Peter, in the Cadillac, and then at Martin. His gaze drifted down to Martin's shiny alligator shoes. Then he folded his arms again, so that the tickets were tucked away under his left armpit and behind his shoulder.

"That's what you told him last week?" Martin asked. He didn't like where this was going. He stood there with his wallet in his hand, ready to open it, but waiting.

The guy nodded. "Yeah," he said. "But, like I said, I thought you were going to come by here over the weekend. That was the plan, Ludwig said. So in fact, I waited all day for you on Saturday." He shrugged. "I had some stuff to do over in Oakland, but I didn't want to miss you, and so I sat here in my garage, working on my bike all day long, waiting for you to show up. My wife was pretty pissed off, actually," he said, gesturing toward his house with a thumb-over-the-shoulder movement.

Martin followed the trajectory of Maddox's thumb toward the

house. He half expected to see the guy's wife standing there in the window, scowling at him. She wasn't there. But—worse, almost—Martin saw that one of Maddox's kids *was* standing in the living room window, watching him. It was a little girl. She looked like she was about six, and he was pretty sure that she belonged to one of the bikes lying on the ground next to Maddox. She'd pushed the curtains aside, and there she was, watching. He didn't know how long she'd been there. Like her dad, she had dark hair, and—at least from his angle—she looked a little creepy. Someone had cut a straight line of bangs across her forehead, and she was wearing a white nightgown even though it was the middle of the day.

Martin looked back at Maddox. Okay, he thought. I get it. He wants a little extra cash for the hassle.

"All right," he said. "Look, I'm sorry I made you wait around for me. I didn't know you were going to be stuck here. I mean, I wish I'd just gotten your phone number from Ludwig—from Michael. But yeah, I'm sorry." (Though by the way, he thought, have you ever heard of leaving a note? If you leave a note, then you don't need to wait around. People know you're coming back, because you told them so in your note.)

He paused, looking at the guy, waiting for him to respond. But nothing happened. Just more standing there. This guy is a weirdo, Martin thought—then wondered for a brief, scared second if he'd actually said it out loud. It wouldn't have been the first time recently that he'd spoken the thing he'd been thinking. It was as if his private, inside-my-head voice was getting cocky and starting to assert itself by leaping out into public conversation. But he saw from the guy's blank expression that this wasn't one of those times.

"So," Martin said. "It sounds like you're saying that they cost more now, or something. But I gotta say, eighty dollars is a lot of money as it is."

Now the guy nodded, did the whole raised-eyebrows thing again.

"Well," the guy said. "I mean, I'm not a big baseball fan, necessarily. I actually got these tickets from my father-in-law. He got them from someone who didn't want them, and . . . whatever . . . now I've got them." Martin wasn't sure what he was supposed to say. He was pretty sure the guy wasn't done talking, though.

"But, well, yeah, I've been reading about the game," the guy said. He raised himself up on the balls of his feet and then let himself down again. Martin could tell that it was a nervous gesture, probably one he wasn't aware of, and one he'd been falling back on his whole life. "I've also been listening about it on the radio," he said. "The whole Gaylord Perry thing. You know. And I'm pretty sure I could have sold these tickets a couple of days ago for the price I quoted to Michael. But now . . . I mean, people have been going kind of crazy. There just aren't any tickets. Every single seat is gonna be filled. And, you know, usually, hardly anyone goes to A's games—which is kind of fucked up, if you think about it, because they're so good. I mean, they're the world champs, right? But they'll play the Royals or the White Sox, and it's a big deal if they get ten thousand people."

He paused and looked at Martin like he was expecting some sort of response. But Martin didn't know how to respond.

"Okay," Martin said. "So I guess you're saying that you want to raise the price a little bit." He was starting to feel like this guy was more than just weird. He actually seemed like he was a bit of a nut job. Maybe Ludwig liked this quality in people, the whole I'm-a-nut-job-from-Berkeley thing. He was dating Jenny, after all.

The guy rose up on his toes again, let himself back down.

"Well," he said. "After you didn't show up over the weekend, I thought that an extra hundred dollars was fair. You know, for me waiting around and everything." He gave Martin a look suggesting that this was the most reasonable thing in the world.

Martin was mesmerized. Was this guy for real?

The guy cleared his throat. "But then you didn't come on Monday, either. I mean, I thought that when you didn't make it by Sunday, that you'd try to get here on Monday. So I waited again on Monday. And then again on Tuesday. I was in and out, but yeah, a lot of waiting."

Martin was about to say something, but then he realized that Peter was standing there next to him. It was like he'd just materialized out of thin air. One minute he was sitting in the Caddy, the next he was standing there next to Martin, a worried look on his face. Jesus Christ, Martin thought.

"So," Maddox said, glancing down at Peter and hurrying a little bit now. "I'm thinking the original eighty, plus a hundred for the weekend, plus fifty for Monday and fifty for Tuesday. So fifty bucks for each extra day. That makes two eighty. That's what I want—two hundred and eighty dollars."

Martin looked at the guy, then looked over at the window. The little girl was still there, but she'd been joined now by her sister, or a little girl who must have been her sister. She had the same weirdly haunted appearance, though instead of bangs she had two long pigtails, one draped over each shoulder. She was a little taller, probably a year or so older than her sister. She was obviously the owner of the other bicycle lying at Maddox's feet. He looked down at Peter: he was eyeing Maddox, but he'd noticed the girls, too. Martin wondered what Peter thought of them—if he was going to have nightmares about the strange, pale girls he'd seen staring out the window at him in Berkeley.

Martin zoomed outward in his mind's eye, trying to take in the whole picture. Some shit-bird working-class white guy living below San Pablo in Berkeley, trying to get by. Kind of an ass, but maybe not such a bad guy. Ludwig seemed to like him, at least. Probably a carpenter of some sort. No, a machine-shop guy. A welder, maybe. Whatever he was, he obviously needed the money. His house was probably a stretch for him, even though it was a shoebox. And with two kids . . . forget it, he'd never get ahead. But he figured a guy like Martin had money to burn. Why else would he show up ready to pay eighty bucks for a single baseball game?

But come on. Seriously—who out there was going to pay $280 for two tickets to this game? Martin knew he could put an ad out on both KCBS and KNBR for the tickets, and at that price no one in the whole

Bay Area would take him up on it. Not even Gaylord Perry's parents. Martin figured he could prowl around the Coliseum for half an hour and get tickets for a lot less. One fifty, tops. It was a risk, but come on. Fucking $280?

"Listen," he said finally. "Two hundred and eighty dollars is a lot of money for a baseball game. I mean, even for a playoff game or a World Series game, that would be some serious cash. But I know I put you out over the weekend. So here's my offer. I'll give you a hundred and twenty for the tickets. Sixty each. Right now. Take it or leave it."

Martin glanced at Peter again, saw the panic in his eyes, then looked at Maddox—locked eyes with him for a second. Then he pulled out his wallet, and took out six twenties. When he looked back up he saw that Maddox's eyes had lit up at the sight of the money. And then Maddox stepped toward him, and handed him the tickets. Martin took them with his left hand, and gave him his $120 with his right.

And that was it. Maddox was heading back into his house before Martin could even say thanks. But he saw over Maddox's shoulder that he was holding the money up and showing it to someone. At first Martin thought he was showing it to his daughters, which struck him as a little strange ("Look what Daddy got, kids!"). But then he saw that he was showing the money to his wife. She was peeking out the window over the top of the girls. It was hard to see, but Martin could see that she was smiling and holding her fists up in a kind of cheering posture. She was excited—they'd taken that guy for a ride, she was thinking. And, Martin thought, she was pretty much right. But she was in for a surprise, because her husband wasn't going to show her the $280 she'd been hoping for. He'd caved in at the sight of the money and gotten less than half of that. She was going to be pissed off. He could just hear it. Why did you give in so fast? You should have bargained harder. He would've paid. Did you see that guy? Isn't he your friend's boss? Isn't he rich? Jesus, George.

Martin was smiling as he got into his car. Where did Ludwig find these guys? Honestly. He glanced at the tickets—made sure they were real, for the right game, all that—then looked over at Peter as he climbed in.

"Well," he said. "What do you think? We got our tickets."

"I know," Peter said. "Can I see them?"

Martin handed the tickets over, and watched for a second as Peter sat there gazing at them. He remembered the feeling of awe at the sight of something like that—the Willie Mays autograph a friend of his had gotten after a Giants game in the late fifties, not long after the Giants had moved to San Francisco, the ticket stub his dad had from the 1938 fight between Joe Louis and Max Schmeling in Yankee Stadium. (His dad kept it in a little box in his desk drawer, and only let Martin and his brothers see it once in a while. They'd all gather around and hold their breath, looking and wondering.) Martin wanted Peter to have a few things like that—little pieces of evidence that showed he'd been on hand for significant events. He wanted him to soak up the atmosphere that came with a game like that, and—even more—he wanted him to be able to remember that feeling later on. He could look at his ticket stub and know he'd been there and had been a part of it.

"Wow," Peter said. "I'm pretty sure these are in the first deck somewhere. And they're not very far back. We'll be able to see Gaylord Perry really well."

Martin nodded, and backed out of Maddox's driveway. "Great," he said. "Maybe we'll be able to tell when he's doctoring the ball. I'll bring the binoculars."

As they made their way back to University and then onto the freeway, Peter started jabbering about Gaylord Perry's spitball, and about top of the A's lineup: Billy North, Campy Campaneris, Joe Rudi, and of course Reggie Jackson. That was the key, he explained. They had to get Perry to throw a lot of pitches, wear him out. But Martin's mind drifted. The encounter with George Maddox had left him feeling a bit unsettled. The guy had been a nut—no doubt about that. But Martin also felt a little sorry for him. Standing there haggling with Martin, trying to impress his ghost family, he'd been acting like he knew how to drive a bargain—like he had his shit together. But probably when the lights went out at night, and George was staring up into the darkness of his bedroom, he was overwhelmed with fear and confusion. Will I lose my job? Can I keep my house? Can I feed my kids? And, Martin knew, Maddox's worries were linked to things over which he had absolutely no control: the price of oil, interest rates, tariffs, all the stuff Radkovitch had studied in college, and that he babbled about when he and Martin got together to talk about why Anderson Aircrafts was in the tank.

And that was the thing: Martin could relate to George Maddox's secret, nighttime worries because he was fighting a similar battle most nights. For a while he'd thought he had it figured out. He'd pick up the business section of the paper, look through the financial reports, and pretend he had a clear sense of how it all went down. I'm not one of the super rich, but I'm doing all right. I'm getting there. That's what he used to tell himself. But he'd been wrong. Now the financial world was kicking his ass, big time, and according to Radkovitch, at least, it was due largely to events taking place thousands of miles away, and that he'd never even know about: a conversation in a bank in New York or London, the slight turn of an oil spigot in the Middle East.

The question, though, was whether *anyone* knew what the fuck was going on—with money, the stock market, the oil market, and the rest of it. Martin's general feeling these days was that even the people who studied the financial markets—Radkovitch and the other so-called experts—knew about as much about what was going to happen a week from now (and why) as the local weatherman did about the weather. If you lived in L.A., that was okay, because it was always sunny in L.A. (or almost always). You didn't even pay attention to the weather report. But what if you lived somewhere else, a place where the weather was shitty and unpredictable? In Boston, say. Or Buffalo. Or even up in Tahoe. Then a weatherman with his head up his ass was a problem. Not that you wanted to hear a full confession, right there on the air. "I don't know what the weather is going to be like three days from now, okay? Do I look like a wizard? But it's crappy out right now, so maybe it'll be a little better in a few days. Or maybe it'll be more of the same. I don't know, okay?"

So, yeah. The weatherman pretended to know what was going on, and so did the big shot money guys. The Chairman of the Federal Reserve, Nixon, Kissinger. All of them. They were all full of shit.

He drove, checked his rearview mirror, changed lanes. Peter was still babbling about Gaylord Perry. "Maybe the umpires will make him change his uniform," he said. "They've done that before, in case he has Vaseline on it somewhere."

Yep, Martin thought. It was scary. No one was in control. It was all just guesswork, with plenty of mistakes made every day—every minute—and plenty of fallout from those mistakes (broken lives, dashed dreams, the works). But it was also exciting, even a little bit liberating. Because if no one was in control, then there really weren't any rules. And though this was a problem, it also meant that if you were smart, ballsy, and a little bit lucky, you might be able to work the system and come out ahead in the end. And that's what everyone was shooting for, right? To finish further ahead than when they started? Wasn't that what this was all about?

CHAPTER FOURTEEN

By the time Martin got out to the fairgrounds in Pleasanton it was almost two o'clock, and by then it was hot. Ninety degrees, probably higher. It was also crowded and loud and smelly. There were big families with swarms of kids, everything smelled like cotton candy, and you could hear the mechanical carnival music of the merry-go-round and the other rides they carted in for the two or three weeks the fair was up and running.

It had been a long morning—brutally long, in fact—because Linda had insisted that they all go to the parade in Walnut Station.

"We're going," she said. "It's the Fourth, and that's what you do. We always went to the Fourth of July parade when I was a kid. I loved it."

Martin wanted to remind her that she'd grown up in Boston, where they had real descendants of the Pilgrims, and where the Fourth actually meant something, but he didn't bother. They'd had that argument before.

It was just as bad as he'd thought it would be. Usually they were up at Tahoe for the Fourth. This year, though, Temperature's Rising was racing, and so they were staying put. But it was at a cost, Martin thought more than once as he stood in the center of town with all the other local jerks. It was unbearable, watching them whoop it up for their smug kids as they chugged by on their holiday floats or stomped past in their marching bands, banging out John Philips Souza songs. Sarah had wandered away with a friend almost immediately, which had pissed Linda off; and Peter had gotten sulky because he was hot and thirsty and they hadn't thought to bring chairs or umbrellas or water.

"Why didn't you guys bring anything?" he'd asked, looking at the coolers and lawn chairs lining the sidewalks. "Everyone else has that stuff."

Mercifully, the parade was over by noon, and so after weaving through the crowds and the traffic they were back at the house by about one. But both Linda and the kids had lost all interest in the horse race, Peter in particular after Martin told him there wouldn't be time for rides or game booths over at the fair—it was just the horse races today.

"It's too hot," Linda said. "I'm exhausted. And plus that crowd—Michael and Jenny and whoever else is going to be there. They're just going to get really drunk, and yell and scream, and it will be loud, and... Look, I just don't want to do it. Especially with the kids, and especially on the Fourth. We'll shoot off some fireworks when you get home and show us your trophy."

At first he was disappointed. He'd been looking forward to having the whole family see Temperature's Rising at his best—show Sarah that her dad wasn't a complete loser, spend time with Peter, all of that.

But he was also immediately aware of how this might be a good thing. He could drink a little more, be a little looser.

"Okay," he said. "I understand. Fine."

HE PARKED THE CAR and within a few minutes he was moving quickly through the crowd of fairgoers and toward the race track. It was the kind of pace you could set when you were by yourself, not worrying about straggling kids getting distracted or lost. Soon he could hear an announcer on a loudspeaker announcing a race, and he could feel—or thought he could feel—a general buzz of excitement just on the other side of the fence. He paid the guy at the turnstile his two bucks, and then he was through to the other side.

Almost immediately he ran into Ted Reasoner. "Hey there, Martin," Ted said. They shook hands and smiled at each other. Martin and Ted had been friends since Berkeley High. Now Ted was a jewelry guy. He'd taken over his father's shop in Oakland, then he'd expanded and had a second one in San Francisco. Ted loved the horses more than Martin, even, but he didn't own one. Too much trouble, he'd always said. And not enough money.

"Hiya, Ted," Martin said. "Where're you headed?"

Reasoner was wearing plaid pants and a gold-colored short-sleeved shirt, one with a little breast pocket. He was also wearing glasses that had thick black frames. If Martin wore that sort of outfit, he'd look like an idiot. But Ted was tall and thin, probably six-four, but only about 175 or 180 pounds. So somehow it looked right on him. He just had the look—the whole jazz-guy thing.

Reasoner pointed toward the ticket windows. "I'm gonna throw down some money here in a second." He held up a sheet of paper he'd been holding. It was folded over, but Martin could see that it was a Past Performance Sheet. It had Reasoner's crazy scribbling all over it.

Martin nodded. "What race is it right now?"

"This is for the fifth," Reasoner said. "Did you just get here?" He looked surprised.

"Yeah," Martin said. "I was with Linda and the kids over at the parade. You know, it's the Fourth and everything."

Reasoner nodded. He didn't seem interested. "So how does the horse look?" he asked. "What do you think? Should I put some money on him?"

Martin shrugged, going for understated. "Well, Val says he's looking really good," Martin said. "But I don't want to steer you wrong. I mean, the race isn't fixed or anything. Or not that I know of, anyway."

Reasoner let out a quick burst of laughter. "Ha," he said. "You don't want to fix the races, do you? It would take all the fun out of it."

Martin nodded. "I know. No fixes for me. Or at least not in the races that my horse is running. But I gotta say," he added, "I wouldn't mind knowing when there's an occasional fix on."

"Hey, here's a question for you," Reasoner said. He took a step toward Martin. "What if someone said they'd pay you big bucks to make sure your own horse doesn't win? What about that? What would you say if I gave you a check for that right now? How does a thousand dollars sound?"

Martin shook his head. "No," he said. "No way."

"Atta boy," Reasoner said, giving Martin a slap on the shoulder. "That's when you know you're a real owner." He moved toward the betting windows. "Good luck today," he said.

"Thanks, Ted," Martin said. He turned and started walking away, but he stopped short and turned back toward Reasoner.

"Hey, Ted," he shouted.

Reasoner turned around and looked at Martin, waiting with an expectant look.

"The reason I wouldn't take a check from you is that I know it would bounce. Cash, Ted. Cash only."

Reasoner laughed and gave a quick wave.

Down in the paddock area he found Val and Temperature's Rising. It was cooler there than out on the fairground, and filled with the familiar smell of hay and manure. He wasn't sure, but he thought Temperature's Rising recognized him and was glad to see him. When Martin reached out to stroke him between the ears, he pushed his nose forward and gummed his hand.

"See?" Val said. "He wants to know if you have an apple for him. He remembers. I'm telling you, Martin, this is a smart horse. And he's a winner. He's gonna win today, aren't you TR?" He patted the horse on the side of his long neck. The horse neighed at Martin, and pushed at his hand again.

"Okay, okay," Martin said, laughing nervously and stepping back. "I don't have anything to give you. Do you have an apple or something, Val?"

Val shook his head. "No," he said. "Not an apple, not before a race. But give him a handful of that grain."

Martin paused, then reached into a plastic five-gallon bucket that was sitting on the ground outside Temperature's Rising's stall. He grabbed a handful of the grain, and then held his hand out flat so that the horse could take the offering. He felt a wave of nausea as Temperature's Rising's wet lips closed around the little snack, but he stood his ground and didn't let on that he was disgusted.

Val watched as Martin looked around for something to wipe his hand on—these were nice pants, and he wasn't going to ruin them with horse spit.

"Listen," he said to Martin, throwing him a towel and smiling. "All you have to do is sit up in the stands and watch. I just talked to Sanchez, and he guarantees a win. He said Temperature's Rising is absolutely peaking. He said he's running smooth and fast. He's gonna hang back through the first half, but don't worry. The horse'll do the work. You'll see. The only other real horse in the race is Champagne Taste. He's a lot like Temperature's Rising, actually. He'll be making a late move, too. But it won't be enough. Maybe a few months ago, but not today."

Martin nodded. He was thrilled to hear Val sound so confident, and doubly thrilled to hear that Sanchez was feeling good. But he had a feeling Val wasn't done talking just yet.

"One more thing, though," Val said, confirming Martin's hunch. "After we count up our money from this race—and we're gonna win, Martin, I just know it—after that, let's talk. Because I'm hoping to make another run down to Ramirez's place pretty soon. Within a few days, in fact. The stuff is already in, waiting for us."

Martin looked at him in surprise.

"I know you were just down there, but that's how it works, I guess," Val said. He held his hands up, as if to say, What can I tell you?

"The shipments just come in when they come in," he continued. "And it's a big one, so more money for us. Ramirez said he'd hold it for a few days, but if we're not down there soon, he's got someone else who'll take it off his hands. And I don't know about you, but I'd like the extra money."

He patted Martin on the shoulder. It was a friendly gesture, but it made him nervous just the same.

"Plus," Val said. "I want to stay on Ramirez's A list, if you know what I mean. I don't want him thinking we're not really interested, or that he should start sending business to other people." He looked at Martin now, in that Val Desmond way of his, making sure that he was really listening.

"It's not a problem, Val," Martin said. "Tomorrow is a stretch, but after that, fine, not a problem."

Val nodded. "Good," he said. "I knew I was making the right decision with you, Martin. And Ramirez says you're doing a good job, by the way. Touching down on the landing strip, chilling out in Ensenada. All of it."

Martin thought about how nervous he'd been on his first trip, and then how drunk he'd been in Ensenada. The girl at the bar, and then waking up sick in the motel room. And her looking at him in the mirror. He was a little bit haunted by that last moment, by how inscrutable she'd seemed. That was the word all right—inscrutable.

"This is all pretty easy, isn't it?" Val said. "Fly in, fly out, make some money. Why mess with a good thing, right?"

"Val," Martin said. "I'm on board, okay? I said I'm on it."

Val reached out and patted Temperature's Rising. When he looked up and started talking, he seemed more serious, somehow.

"Look," he said, "I'm a little worried about Hano. Have you seen him yet today?"

"Here?" Martin asked. "No, I haven't."

"Well, he's around," Val said. "The Barker people have some horses on the card in the later races. And I've heard Hano's been sort of running off at the mouth down there. Acting like a big shot, saying that I'm taking too much of a cut, that sort of thing."

"Really?" Martin asked. But he wasn't surprised. Hano had a big ego—a huge ego, in fact. Of course he was talking. It was exactly the kind of thing Hano would do.

"Listen," Val said. He pointed at Martin, and narrowed his eyes just a little bit. He looked scary all of a sudden. "Let's get something straight, okay? *I'm* the guy that knows Ramirez. And *I'm* the guy with the up-front money. This is *my* fucking operation—not Derek Hano's."

Jesus, Martin thought. Did Val actually think he needed to get something straight here? That there was something he didn't understand about who was in charge, or who he was supposed to be siding with? And besides, the race was in an hour or so. Was this really the time to talk about a feud between drug dealers—or drug runners, or whatever they were?

"Okay, okay," Martin said. He was about to say something else to try and placate Val, but Val cut him off before he could get it out.

"Just do me a favor," he said. "Just keep an eye on him when you're down there. You know what I mean? Just let me know if you see him wander off with any of Ramirez's guys for a little chat. Or if he says anything to you about me. Or—and this is the most important thing—if he says anything to you about wanting to work out a side deal with Ramirez's people."

Val looked over at Temperature's Rising, and then reached out and stroked his mane. Martin watched him, remembering the way Hano had stood talking with Ramirez while he sat in the car, waiting. They'd talked for a long time. What had they been talking about? Should he mention this to Val right now?

"Because look," Val said. He looked up at Martin again, making sure to hold his gaze. "Ramirez and I go back a long way. He's not gonna work out any side crap with Derek Hano. The only thing that will happen to Hano if he tries to get cute is that he won't be coming back from Mexico. You'll be flying all by yourself. Okay, Martin? You get it?"

Martin nodded yet again, but more slowly than before. He swallowed, and then licked his lips, which were dry. "Yes," he said, making sure to speak clearly and precisely, and making sure not to look away from Val's gaze. "I get it. I definitely get it."

"Good," Val said. "Excellent." His expression relaxed, and he gave

Martin one of his signature smiles. Then he reached over and put a big meaty arm around Martin's neck. He used the crook of his elbow to pull Martin's face close to his.

"Your horse is going to win this afternoon," he said to Martin. "I guarantee it. Seriously—I fucking guarantee it. I've never seen Sanchez so confident." His face was right up against Martin's, and Martin could smell his lunch. It smelled like fried food. Maybe something from the fair. Maybe a corn dog. Yes, Martin thought in his discomfort—his breath smells like corn dog.

Val let go of Martin, and Martin found himself wondering suddenly if there really was a fix on—the sort of thing he'd been talking about earlier with Ted Reasoner. Maybe there was an agreement with the others that this was Val's race (or Temperature's Rising's race). Maybe, Martin thought, that's how things worked at these big races.

But he knew this was ridiculous. In a little while Temperature's Rising was going to run, and he'd either win or not win on the merits of his own talents. And yes, Martin was going to plunk down some money on the race. It was bad luck not to bet confidently on your own horse. Right now Temperature's Rising was a five-to-two favorite. Not great odds, but certainly good enough to make some money. Bet a hundred bucks and come away with two fifty. And so on. Plus, the purse on the race was about two thousand dollars, so even if he didn't bet a dime, he'd be into some serious money if Temperature's Rising won. Some would go to Val, some to the jockey. But still, he'd be driving home with a lot of money.

Martin forced himself to look Val in the eye one more time. "I'll see you in the winner's circle," he said to Val, smiling.

But it was a forced smile. He was trying to be confident, but Val had thrown him off, both with the talk about Hano and with his unusually forthright talk about the race being a sure thing. Maybe it was simple; maybe this was just the first time Martin had been in a position of real strength with a horse. Maybe this was just the confident Val, as opposed to the guardedly optimistic Val that Martin had come to know over the years. But Martin couldn't help but feel that Val was a little rattled, that he was off his game a little bit. This was surprising, because if someone had asked Martin an hour ago to name the one person least likely to be rattled by anything, he'd have said Val Desmond—for sure.

HE MET UP WITH Ludwig and Jenny and a few other friends in the owner's box, and then he and Ludwig peeled off from the group to place a few bets on the eighth race. Martin didn't know much about the horses that were running, but he wanted to get the juices flowing. It was a long line, one of several in front of the five or six betting windows that were open. The ground around them was littered with torn-up tickets. Peter would have had a field day, crawling around and picking them up. He wished for a second that he'd brought him, but he knew it would have been more trouble than it was worth. He'd want something to drink, and then something to eat, and then he'd have to use the bathroom. And Martin would have to do all this with him, because he couldn't send him wandering off alone in this crowd. No, Martin thought, this is my day.

"Hey," Ludwig said, slapping him on the shoulder with the back of his hand. "Isn't that your neighbor? You know, the good-looking one? Marilynne, or something like that?"

Martin looked at Ludwig for a second, trying to figure out how he could have come up with a joke like that. But then he looked over to where Ludwig was pointing and he saw that he was right. It was Miriam—down-the-street Miriam. She was in the betting line just opposite them, with Hal. They were standing there looking at one of the betting sheets you could buy when you walked in, and Hal had a *Daily Racing Form* tucked under his arm.

Holy crap, he thought. They're here to bet on the horses. How about that?

"That *is* her," he said to Ludwig. "What the fuck are they doing here?"

"I don't know," Ludwig said as they stood there, looking over at them. "But look at her. Jesus Christ, how can you stand it? Do you ever peek in their window when you're walking the dog at night?"

Martin thought for a second about having rifled through Miriam's underwear drawer, and how he lay there on her bedroom floor, terri-fied, listening to her pee. What would Ludwig say to that?

He was about to answer Ludwig—something witty about Miriam at a pool party—when Hal saw Martin. He broke into a wide grin and came walking right over.

"Hey there, Martin!" he said. He reached out and shook Martin's hand—a big up-and-down, I'm-a-steel-magnate handshake. "I *thought* we might see you here. We were just talking about you, in fact. You own some race horses, don't you? Hey, Miriam," he said, looking over his shoulder. "Look who it is. It's Martin, from down the street!"

Miriam waved, and then walked over, coming to a stop next to Hal.

"Hi, Martin!" she said. She was smiling—a wide, friendly smile that showed off her big, incredible mouth and her beautiful white teeth. Oh my God, Martin thought. He took in her blue eyes, her thick black hair, and her porcelain skin (that was how Linda had described it, por-celain). And he took in her white slacks, her black sleeveless shirt, and her bare shoulders. He willed himself to avoid looking at her breasts, but he had the feeling that he'd already glanced at them. Had he? He wasn't sure.

"Well, well," Martin said. "What have we here? Sneaking off for an afternoon at the track? Do your parents know you're here?" He was going to go for confident and jocular. He hadn't planned it—he hadn't had time to plan anything, obviously—but it seemed like the right tone to strike.

"That's right," Hal said. "You caught us. The kids are down at my brother's place in Carmel for the Fourth, so we decided to sneak over here and give it a whirl. We're gonna hit the fair later on. You know, what the hell, right? But if you'd been watching us for the past hour, you'd see that we're really out of our league here, I think. It's kind of embarrassing, actually."

"Well," Martin said. "There's a lot to consider. The favorite doesn't always win, you know. He usually doesn't, in fact." He shrugged, look-ing at Hal and trying to convey sympathy. In fact, of course, he was

pleased to hear that Hal wasn't hitting any winners—though his ad-
mission about being inept was itself a little irritating. Martin knew
the shtick: you offered a posture of self-effacement, but your real goal
was to show that you were confident enough to own up to your short-
comings, or your limitations. It's true that I can't do this thing very
well, you were saying. But I do so many other things really well that I
don't really care. Enough already, Martin thought.

"What about you, Martin?" Miriam asked. "Are you here with Linda
and the kids?"

Martin shook his head. "No," he said. "That was the plan, but they
were too hot and tired after the parade this morning, and so they
backed out."

Hal and Miriam both nodded, but Martin had the feeling that they
didn't believe him—which was ironic, of course, in that he was telling
the truth.

"So, Martin," Hal said. "I was just saying to Miriam here that you
have a horse running later on today. In the main event, in fact. Is that
true?"

"Oh, it's true all right," Ludwig said, chiming in finally (Martin
was surprised it had taken him so long). He gave Martin a big pat on
the back. "Martin's horse is running in the big championship race in a
little while. He's a big-shot racing guy around here. Didn't you know
that? He's like a local celebrity, at least at the track. Isn't that right,
Martin?"

Martin shook his head and laughed, aiming now for sheepish. "No,"
he said, looking at Hal and then at Miriam (and making eye contact
with Miriam for an extra fraction of a second). "Don't listen to him. I
mean, yeah, my horse is running today. But the rest of what he's saying
is a bunch of baloney."

But at that moment Martin could have hugged Ludwig. Yes,
Ludwig was just being an asshole, teasing him. But it was exactly the
way Martin wanted to be represented to the Weavers. Our neighbor
is a big shot with the ponies? Wow. That's actually pretty interesting.

Maybe we *should* have them over for one of our cocktail parties again. Maybe there's more going on there than we realized.

"Well, look," Hal said. "I'm sure you're busy getting ready for your race and everything. But if you've got two minutes to spare, how's about giving us a few pointers here about which horses to choose, and what to look for? I mean, I've got to leave with at least a shred of dignity, you know?"

Within a few minutes they were all back in the owner's box. Martin was beside himself. It was the first time he'd seen Miriam since he'd broken into her house. But more significant was that he was actually at the race track with her—and on his big day, no less. It was almost too much. He couldn't have come up with a better fantasy. (Well, okay— Hal could have been off at a steel conference in Pittsburgh, leaving him here alone with Miriam. And after Temperature's Rising's win, Miriam and Martin could head off to a hotel for a few hours. *That* was a better fantasy.)

"So what should I be looking for?" Miriam asked.

Martin had placed his bets, bought some beers, and now he was sitting next to her in one of the green fold-down stadium seats. His first thought had been to avoid her, sit a few seats away, and generally play it cool. Direct his comments to Hal, maybe. But she'd called him over, patted the seat next to her, and asked him for help with her *Racing Form*. So now she was holding it out in front of her, and she was leaning in toward him a little bit. The tip of her knee touched his leg. He gave a quick glance sideways, and saw that she was squinting, studying the columns of numbers and the description of the races.

Huh, he thought. She really did seem interested in the betting thing. And was the physical contact intentional? Probably not . . . or probably not in the way he hoped. It was always intentional when he did it, anyway. Maybe she was just the sort of person who didn't think much about a little bit of physical contact. He tried to remember whether or not he'd ever noticed that she was the type who put a quick, light hand on your shoulder when talking to you, or anything like that. Like at the cocktail party. He didn't think so.

He resisted the urge to look at her again, to see her mouth and eyes and even her nose so close up. Maybe get a glimpse at the texture of her hair as some stray strands fell down across her face. Or see the moisture on her lips. As it was, he could smell the beer on her breath. It was a little stale, but he loved it—it made him feel as if the moment was more intimate, somehow. He couldn't believe they were sitting so close together like this, hunched over a *Racing Form,* with him actually doling out advice. It was like a miraculous, divine form of intervention.

He took a deep breath. "Okay," he said. "Well, the first thing you want to do, especially if you're just coming to a race and you don't know the horses, is see what the odds are, and then maybe see what the odds-maker's picks are at the bottom of the page. Sometimes they're way off the mark, but they're usually in the ballpark."

Miriam nodded. "Okay," she said, glancing at him.

"So, for example," he went on, "in the Eighth Race, which is in about ten minutes, Lucky Charm is listed as having five-to-one odds. That's not bad—it might be a good bet. And let's see, Back Alley is listed as three-to-one, and, Cosmic Reality is five-to-two. So Back Alley is the favorite. And then if you look down here at the bottom of the page," he said, pointing, "you can see that there are three horses listed as 'Expert's Picks.' For this race, they've picked Back Alley, Cosmic Reality, and Go-Getter. So Lucky Charm isn't one of their top three, even though he's got better odds than Go-Getter, who is listed as nine-to-one. But that might be good," he said, "because you can make more money betting on nine-to-one odds than on five-to-one odds."

He looked up and made eye contact with her, but he looked back down at the sheet almost right away. It wasn't as if he had never looked her in the eye before, but this was different, somehow. For one thing, her eyes really were an intense blue.

The key issue here, though, was that she was so close up. She was

more real, somehow, than she'd been before. Yes, that was it. True, he'd
lain on her bedroom floor and listened to her while she was alone in her
bathroom—one could argue that that was pretty real. But in some ways
she hadn't been real at all that day. For one thing, she hadn't known
he was there.

Miriam gave him a playful jab in the side with her elbow. "Listen,"
she said. "I get it about the odds, but I want to know about all the rest
of this stuff here. You know, the expert stuff. There's an awful lot of
information here. How will it help me decide which horse to pick?"

He looked up at her, not hiding his mild surprise. She was a lot more
interested than most women he knew (Linda didn't give two shits about
horseracing). Plus, he realized, his leg was still touching hers. Or he
thought it was. His whole body was numb. He looked down. Yes, there
it was, his knee, up against her knee. They looked happy, he thought.
Our knees are happy together, and we could be happy together, too.

"You're right," he said. "There's a lot of stuff here." He took another
deep breath. It was hot, and he felt a little light-headed. He took a big
swig of beer, and she drank, too.

"Let me just show you a couple of things," he said to her. He pointed
at the far left column, and looked at her to see if she was listening,
which she was. She looked up at him, nodded, then looked down at
the sheet again.

"First," he said, "I want to know how a horse has done over the course
of the past few races. So for example, I can look here and see that this
horse last raced in April. That's this column here. Then I see how he
finished. That's in this column here. Okay, it's a three. That means he
finished third. And the little half number next to that three tells you
how far back he was. This says 'one,' so he was only back by one length.
That's not so bad, actually. And in fact, if you look way over here to the
right, you can get a couple of words describing how he finished. This
says 'wide, hung'—meaning that he swung around too wide at the turn,
but he hung in there until the end. He didn't give up."

He looked at her and watched as she pushed the hair back out of her face. Her neck was a little bit sweaty, and he saw that some small bits of her dark hair were sticking there. He wanted to reach out and stroke her hair there, move it away from her neck.

"Go on," she said. "I'm listening. I'm following you."

He nodded and smiled. "Okay," he said. "Well, let's see. There's one other thing that's good to know."

He paused for a second, thinking about how much to say. He wanted to impress her, show her how much he knew, but he didn't want to overdo it, either. He took a quick glance over at Hal, and saw that he was talking to Ludwig and Jenny—boring the shit out of them, most likely. But that was their problem, not his.

"Okay," he said, pointing to another part of the sheet. "If you look at this column, you can see how long his previous races have been. This might be useful. If he's done well in short races, but not in longer ones, you need to know that, right? Maybe he's a sprinter, so you might hesitate before betting on him for a longer race. My horse, for example, Temperature's Rising, isn't a great sprinter. I don't put him in shorter races, and if I did, he probably wouldn't do well."

At the mention of Temperature's Rising, Miriam looked at Martin and smiled. She crossed her arms across her chest and gave him a sort of sidelong glance—it was a little playful, Martin thought.

"Did you come up with that name, or did someone else?"

Martin laughed, and realized as he did that he was blushing. He didn't know why, though. Why would a question like that make him blush? He let go of the sheet, finally, dropped it on her lap, and sat up a little straighter in his seat.

"No," he said, "I didn't name him. I got him when he was almost two years old, and he'd already been named." He wanted to say something more, be witty, but he was a little tongue-tied.

"Well, it's a great name," she said. "And he's a really good horse, right? I mean, that's why he's in the championship race. What are his odds for today? Should I be betting on him?" She was still smiling. Despite himself, he started to calm down.

Martin shrugged, trying to adopt the same posture of indifference he'd had with Ted Reasoner a little while ago. "He's listed in the book at five-to-two," he said. "We'll see what happens as it gets closer to race time. The odds on the board out there are keyed to bets placed. So if a lot of people bet against him, the odds go up."

"But that would be good, right?" she said.

"That's right," Martin said, more comfortable now. "It would actually be really good . . . because he's going to win."

He hadn't planned to say that, had just blurted it out. But when he saw her momentary surprise—she started back just a bit, opening her eyes a little wide and grinning—he felt as if he'd said the right thing.

He took a quick glance around at the others in their group. Ludwig was hurrying off toward the betting windows—maybe to escape from Hal. Jenny and Hal were sitting together now, talking, but Martin saw Hal give a quick glance over toward him and Miriam. Or he thought he did, anyway. It was a look that said he was bored talking to Jenny. No surprise there—she was probably yakking at him about some film she'd seen recently, or maybe about her intention to apply to graduate school at Stanford (good luck). But it was also, Martin felt, a wary sort of look, one that suggested he wanted to keep an eye on things.

Huh, Martin thought. You can't be jealous unless you think you've got a reason to be jealous.

A few seconds later Ludwig grabbed Martin and pulled him out of his seat to talk with him about something, and then before he knew it an hour had gone by. By then they'd all had too much to drink, especially in the heat of the late afternoon. They'd finished off the gin Ludwig had brought in his cooler, but they were still drinking draft beers. And it wasn't just Ludwig and Jenny. They were all starting to slur a little, talk too loud, Hal and Miriam included. Some of the people in the seats around them were giving them the look, but he didn't care. They were all moving around, talking, laughing, running up to place a couple of bets, running back to the seats. No one seemed to win anything. Miriam teased him when she placed a bet and lost—punched him in the arm, even.

Some time went by, and he looked over and saw Miriam and Hal sitting together, laughing, his arm draped around her shoulders, across the back of the seat she was in. They were sharing some sort of joke. Or that's what it looked like. For a panicked second Martin thought they might have been talking about him.

"Is this guy a knucklehead, or what?" she'd ask. "I can't believe we live near him. He really does think he's something special. You should've heard him with that stupid *Racing Form*. He was acting like it was rocket science, for Christ's sake."

"You don't know the half of it," Hal would say in response. "The guy's a total loser—really just a big sham. He's fucking broke, you know. I heard it from a friend of mine at Wells Fargo. He came begging for a loan, and they told him to take a hike. All of this with the horses is just made-up money—credit. He's a walking house of cards."

Martin took a deep breath and counseled himself to calm down. Who knew what they were talking about? Maybe something to do with one of their kids. It was impossible to say (though he was tempted to march over there and find out. What the fuck are you two talking about? he'd ask. This is my day, you know).

One thing was certain, though, and that was that they were actually pretty close. They were friends, even. He thought for a moment about Linda. Sure, they were married, and yes, they loved each other. But were they close? Good friends? On some days his answer to that question would be an automatic yes. But on other days, and especially in the past year or two, he wasn't so sure. In fact, he wasn't sure that he was friends—close friends, that is—with anyone anymore. He suddenly wished she were here to watch the race with him, and share this moment. Jesus, he thought. It wasn't too late for them, was it? He wasn't sure.

Finally, Martin heard the announcement for the eleventh race—the one he'd been waiting for. "The horses are on the track."

He watched through his binoculars as the horses walked out onto the raked dirt of the track for the post parade. The horses were actually right down in front of them, pretty easy to see, but he liked to use the binoculars anyway. He could tell they were excited; their heads bobbed up and down, straining at their bits. The jockeys were perched on top of them, guiding them, but mainly just working to keep them calm. Martin saw Temperature's Rising right away: his number and eyeshades were sky blue, and Sanchez was wearing a checkered shirt in matching blue. That was one of Val's touches. He hated it, he said, when the jockey and the horse didn't match (which was ironic, in that Val's own clothes routinely clashed).

Martin felt a hand on his shoulder—a woman's hand—and he thought for an ecstatic second that it was Miriam's. But when he brought his binoculars down from his eyes, he saw that Miriam was standing in the row in front of him and that it was Jenny who was standing next to him. A second ago he had seen her over with Ludwig, two rows down. But now she was next to him, her hand on his shoulder.

"Which one is Temperature's Rising?" she asked.

"Right there," Martin said. "In the light blue. The sky blue. Number six." She was leaning against him a little bit, her left breast pressing into his side, and he resisted the urge to take a half step away from her.

In front of him, Miriam was shading her eyes with her right hand and looking out at the horses. "Oh, wow," she said, with a quick half glance back at Martin. "Look at that. He's really something. He's taller than the other horses, isn't he?"

Martin felt a quick jolt of pleasure run through him. As far as he was concerned, the horse had just paid for himself.

He thought about moving away from Jenny entirely, getting her hand off his shoulder and making it clear he didn't like it when she touched him. But instead he slipped the leather strap of his binoculars from around his neck and handed them to her.

"You can see better with these," he said. "I need them for the race, but go ahead and check him out."

"Okay, wow, great," she said. "Thanks."

He put his right arm around her shoulders, and guided the binoculars with his left hand.

"See that horse in the red right there?" he asked her, pointing out toward the track with his left hand. "Number eight? That's the horse we've gotta worry about. Champagne Taste. He's a lot like Temperature's Rising: a late breaker. He'll be hanging back until the last turn. It's gonna be the two of them coming down the stretch."

Jenny nodded, and Martin could tell that she was pleased to be on the receiving end of these details. But he really wasn't talking to Jenny at all. It was the old trick of pretending to talk to one person while in fact directing your words to someone else—the person you actually cared about and were interested in. He wanted Miriam to see how comfortable he was with women, and to be impressed by his ability to plan the race down to the last detail (though of course he hadn't planned anything—it was all Val's doing).

Ludwig came up to Martin on his left and patted him on the back. "So what do you think?" he asked.

"We'll see in a minute," Martin said.

They watched the horses being guided into the starting gates. Champagne Taste reared up, and the handlers had to walk him around in a quick circle to try to calm him down. Martin took this as a good sign. Let him get rattled, burn up some energy. He could see Alex Cordero— a good jockey—patting his neck, trying to calm him down.

Then the bell sounded and the horses exploded out of the gates in a flash of colors and dust. Right away a group of five horses surged to the lead, with several others, including Temperature's Rising and Champagne Taste, sliding off of the main group and locking in behind them. They looked relaxed, as if they were just out for a morning gallop. They moved through the first turn, the clubhouse turn, at cruising speed, letting the lead pack do the work.

Overhead the announcer narrated the progress of the race, and the crowd began to come alive.

"Go, you fucking horse," he heard someone yell. "Run! Run!"

"Come on, now!" Ludwig shouted. "Time to kick it in gear! Make your move!"

He heard Miriam and Jenny yelling as well—yelling and screaming and jumping up and down.

Martin knew that Ludwig was wrong, that it wasn't time yet to make a move. Not quite. And as he followed the horses around the track through his binoculars, he could tell that both Sanchez and Cordero knew this as well. Temperature's Rising and Champagne Taste were basically side by side, each running three or maybe even four lengths behind the lead pack of five horses, and each gliding along, still looking relaxed. But that front group was starting to stretch out, with two horses falling off the pace just a bit.

Temperature's Rising was maintaining a nice long stride, which was exactly what Val had wanted. He looked like he could do that all day long. Champagne Taste looked good, too. Comfortable. It was going to be close.

As they came around the final turn, both Temperature's Rising and Champagne Taste started to move up on the horses in front of them. They picked off the two fading horses right away, moving around them on the outside. Temperature's Rising was on the inside of Champagne Taste. They were still side by side, and it was as if the other two horses were standing still, all of a sudden. Five seconds later they were past another horse that had begun to fade. The two lead horses put up a fight for another hundred yards or so, but with about three hundred yards to go it was only Temperature's Rising and Champagne Taste. They were neck and neck. Both jockeys were working their whips on the horses' flanks, and both horses were running flat-out now. No more gliding. You could tell that each horse really wanted to win.

The din of the crowd was really something—much louder than during the earlier races. Martin himself wasn't yelling. He might shout at the horses in a race he'd bet on, especially if it wasn't anything very serious. But it was different when it was his own horse. Then, he tended to keep it all in, holding his body tight and clenching his fists and grinding his teeth. And that's what he was doing now as he watched Temperature's Rising lean into the final stretch.

"Come on, baby. Come on," he muttered through his clenched teeth. It was almost like he was whispering to himself. "Push, push," he said. Pleaded. He really wanted this.

Their seats were right in front of the big black-and-white checkered pole that marked the finish line, and so he had a near-perfect view of Temperature's Rising as he surged forward at the last second, stretching his long neck and bobbing his head—it was just enough, Martin thought. I think it was just enough. I think he did it.

And that's how the announcer called it. "Temperature's Rising, by a nose," he said.

And then everyone was pounding him on the back, and Ludwig barreled into him for a big hug. Jenny and Miriam hugged him in turn (Miriam's hug an awkward, over-the-seat hug), and Hal shook his hand (another steel-guy handshake) and slapped him on the shoulder with his other hand. They were all shouting and whooping and laughing.

A minute later they were hustling down the steps toward the winner's circle. It was all bodies and noise, and as Martin looked around he saw people looking at them—at *him*—as they moved along. He felt for a precious minute or two like a celebrity. Or not like a celebrity so much as someone you envied, and who made you wonder what it would be like to be that person. He'd always been on the other side of that feeling, the one looking on as someone managed the big win, dated the best-looking woman, made the most money. But now—today—it was him, Martin Anderson, and he allowed himself to give over to the moment, to feel the intense pleasure of winning.

He met Val at the gate just outside the winner's circle. He was all smiles, flashing his bad teeth. He crushed Martin's hand in his big trainer's paw. "I told you so!" he yelled, over and over again.

Martin's plan had been to have his whole group join him in the winner's circle for the photo. It would be fun. Plus, this way, Miriam would be in the photo. But when he saw Val he knew he needed to stick to the basic etiquette of owners, trainers, and jockeys only (and maybe the owner's family). It was obnoxious to bring a big group into the little area where they took the picture. People did it, but it was considered crass, and he knew it would piss off Val (though maybe if he got a look at Miriam he'd understand).

Standing there waiting for the photographer to arrange them in front of the horse and jockey, Martin felt a little dazed. He was giddy, but the drinking and the excitement and the heat had worn him out. He was holding a silver championship cup someone had handed to him. Later, he'd get a check for the purse in the race, probably about two thousand dollars.

He scanned the crowd outside the gated area, looking for his little group, and as he did he made eye contact with Miriam. She must have been thirty or forty feet away, but her eyes were so intense that it was like she was standing right in front of him. She was standing between Ludwig and Jenny, and she was looking right at Martin, smiling. Her expression was hard to read.

Then the flash went off, and he realized that he hadn't been looking at the camera. At first he was irritated—why was the guy in such a rush? But then he realized that later, when he looked at the developed and then framed photo up on his living room wall, he would know that he'd been looking at Miriam when the camera clicked, and that she'd been looking back at him. And that, he knew, would make the picture special in a secret sort of way.

|||||||||||||||||||||

THREE

|||||||||||||||||||||

CHAPTER FIFTEEN

He sensed that something was wrong the minute he walked through the door. It was about 9:00 P.M., maybe a little later. He'd gone out for drinks and dinner (in that order) after the race with Val, Ludwig, Jenny, and a couple of others from Val's stable. Some Italian place out in Pleasanton that Val went to pretty regularly. It wasn't bad, but it was no Vanessi's. Hal and Miriam had begged off, but Martin was so excited he didn't even mind. In fact, he was glad to have a break. Being around her for so long had worn him out.

So it was pretty early when he got home, all things considered. And he was eager to show the big silver cup to Linda and the kids, have them ooh and aah.

He pushed the door open and announced "I'm home!"

"Hello?" he yelled. "Is anyone here?"

He walked into the kitchen and saw a note on the counter top. He saw right away that it was written by Sarah, rather than Linda. What the hell? Standing there reading it, he realized that he hadn't seen the car in the carport. Were they out buying champagne for him?

"We went to spend the night with Aunt Sharon," it said. Below that, it said, "We took Arrow with us." Below that, it said, "Hope you won!"

And then, further down, scrawled in purple felt-tip pen, Peter had written, "Go Temperature's Risin'!"

Martin smiled to himself. He pictured Peter standing there writing the note: insisting on a quick addition to what Sarah had written, and knowing (probably) that it was "Rising" and not "Risin'," and that his dad would get the little joke.

But he was confused. Why hadn't Linda written anything? And

then he was a little pissed off. Or a lot pissed off. What the hell? A guy gets home from a big day—a really big day, actually—and no one's home? And there's no note from his wife?

He knew something was up, that Linda was angry at him. Yes, she sometimes took the kids to see her friend Sharon and her kids out in Oakland. Sharon's kids were about the same age as Sarah and Peter, and they got along pretty well (though Peter made it difficult sometimes). Sharon wasn't a real aunt, they just called her that. "Hi, Aunt Sharon," Martin would say, enjoying the irony.

So okay, an overnight at Sharon's wasn't so unusual. But this was too sudden. Something had happened. Maybe Linda had gotten a bill that scared her (though there was no mail on the Fourth). Or a phone call from someone about money. Or maybe Slater had come by and scared her somehow. No, he thought, she wouldn't bolt out of the house and not write a note because of that. And that was the term—she'd bolted. Write the note, Sarah, we're in a hurry. Make it fast, Peter, just say good-bye.

Martin muttered his way down the hallway. He suddenly felt a little drunker than he'd realized.

When he walked into his bedroom he saw it almost right away. A quick scan of the room—something wasn't right, he felt more than thought—and then it caught his eye. It was perched right there on his bureau, where he always put his wallet and change and whatever else he might have in his pockets. It was Miriam's jewelry box. In his confusion, Martin thought for a second that he saw it blink, as if it had fallen asleep while waiting for him, but was awake now and eager to see what he was going to do, or say.

"You had me in the closet," it seemed to say, "but now I'm out here."

Martin reached out to pick it up, but then he stopped short. He sat on the bed—looked at it, looked at his reflection in the bathroom mirror, which he could just see from his sitting position on the bed, and then looked at it again.

Fuck, he thought. Fuck, fuck, fuck.

He lay back and looked at the ceiling. He felt a little like he had while lying on Miriam's bedroom floor. Like he was trapped, and like he wanted to disappear, and not be there. Or be invisible, anyway. Here, of course, there was no one to hide from (except himself). But that's how he felt.

What he really wanted, and what he was really concentrating on, was how to make this moment go away. He wanted to rewind the film— that's what it was. He wanted someone (the one who was in charge) to reach down and grab the two big reels that were playing out the film of his life and wind them backward. Not super far—he wasn't greedy. Not back to a point at which he wasn't yet in debt and desperate (though that would be nice). Just back to the moment after the parade when he'd said okay to Linda about skipping the horse race. Why hadn't he made her come with him, told her he really wanted her there with him to see the race, be a part of it all? He watched the moment play out on the ceiling, and tried to get it to adjust to this different version of events. Because then, of course, she wouldn't have been snooping. And if she hadn't been snooping, she wouldn't have found the jewelry box. And if that hadn't happened, then she wouldn't have driven out to Sharon's and left him here to shit his pants and try to figure out how to get himself out of this jam. He'd even trade in Temperature's Rising's win—anything to make her discovery of the jewelry box go away.

But the film kept playing out in the same exact way. He watched four or five times as he gave Linda a quick peck on the cheek, said so long to the kids, and then scurried off toward the track. He watched himself pay his money at the little booth and then disappear into the crowd. He didn't watch long enough to see himself run into Ted Reasoner, or walk up to his little crew in the owner's box, or run into Hal and Miriam, but he didn't need to—didn't want to, at this point.

He sat up, finally, took a big breath, and stood up. The jewelry box was still there, waiting patiently for him to acknowledge it. "I'm still here," it was saying. "Aren't you going to open me up?"

Martin stepped toward it and opened it. Everything was still there. The rings, the locket. The earrings. The coins. He reached in and touched the locket. Jesus, he thought. He was glad he hadn't followed through on his impulse—one he'd thought of as a kind of joke with himself—to place a picture of himself in the locket. *That*, he knew, would have been utter disaster.

He closed the box (though he sensed that it wanted to stay open, maybe to show itself off to him) and sat down again.

He thought for a second that he could maybe blame it on Peter.

"He stole it while he was over there playing with the Weaver kids one day," he'd tell Linda. "And then I found it. I didn't know what to do, so I just hid it. It's horrible, I know. The kid is a little screwed up. First with the notes, and now this. Let me handle it, though, okay?"

He thought this over, but knew it wouldn't fly. Peter might be willing to lie for him, but it was too complex, too intense. Plus, Linda would be relentless: she'd circle around Peter, probing his story, looking for contradictions, weaknesses. Not a chance. She was too smart and too skeptical—he'd cave in immediately.

But, Martin thought. How about a version of the truth?

He ran it through, trying it out for himself. Yes, he'd say. I took it. I know—I'm an asshole, you don't have to tell me. But it's not like it seems.

Martin rehearsed the story for himself, went through it again and again. He watched himself do it in the bathroom mirror, adjusting his expression at key moments. Emotional, but not overly so. Just embarrassed—abashed. That was it. Abashed. He did this for ten minutes. Maybe fifteen. And finally he pretty much believed it—which, he knew, was the key to lying, to getting someone to believe you. It didn't matter if you were talking to the cops, your teachers, your parents, your priest, or your wife. The important thing was that you believe what you were saying.

He picked up the phone and called Sharon's and asked for Linda. He could tell from the way Sharon sounded that she knew what was going on. Good for you, Sharon. Just put her on the phone. Then Linda came on the line.

"Martin," she said. It wasn't a greeting, and she wasn't using his name as the start of a sentence. It was just a word—flat, toneless.

He thought about hanging up right there. Why bother? But he knew he couldn't deal with the consequences of hanging up once he put the receiver back down. He'd be cut off from her, and he didn't want that. He had to get her to believe him.

And so he started in. He watched himself in the bathroom mirror as he talked to her. He found it more useful than he would have thought—it helped him feel and sound the way he wanted.

"Look, Linda," he said. "Just let me talk, okay? Just listen, and when I'm done talking, you can decide what to do. Or what to think. Okay?"

He heard her breathing on the other end of the line.

"Martin . . ." she said, and he could hear her trailing off, trying to figure out what to say next. But this time his name sounded a little different when she said it, as if it had some actual texture. As if he existed again.

But she didn't let him talk, or not at first. At first she really wasn't listening at all. Instead she ripped into him, called him a freak, cried.

"Why do you have that thing, Martin?" she asked, first plaintively, but pretty quickly with a sharp, biting tone—tearing into him. "Are you obsessed with her? Are you in love with her? I mean, Jesus, Martin, did you really break into their fucking house, for Christ's sake?"

He waited out this first assault, counseling himself to be patient—to be quiet. Then, when he sensed she was running out of steam, he plunged in.

"We were at a party at their house," he said. "You know, one of those patio things. The things they don't invite us to anymore. I don't know what that's about. I mean, what did we do wrong? I—"

"Jesus Christ, Martin—"

"Okay, okay," he said. "I know." He paused, and pinched the bridge of his nose, watched himself do it in the mirror. He felt a headache coming on.

"Okay," he said again. "So we were there, and I went back to use the bathroom."

"You know, Martin," Linda said, interrupting him. "I really don't think I'm ready for this. If you want to go off and be a freak in someone else's house, that's your business. How about if—"

"And so, *yes*, I was snooping," Martin said. He said it quickly, emphasizing the "yes," making sure to cut her off. He had the feeling that if he just kept talking, she'd listen.

"Okay?" he said. "So I admit it. I was there, I admit. I did it. But listen, okay?"

He paused for a half second or so, and when she didn't jump in or hang up, he knew he had a chance. She was listening.

"So I was standing there, looking at the pictures in the hallway—you know, the stuff on the walls, the pictures of them and the kids." He pictured her picturing this, and he knew that, so far at least, everything he was saying sounded plausible. Just keep going, he thought.

"And then before I knew it," he said, "I was peeking into their bedroom. You know . . . just to see." He paused again. For effect. Again he had the feeling that she was seeing it as he was describing it—that she was a little bit curious, even. What *does* that bedroom look like, anyway?

"And I saw the jewelry box sitting there," he said. "The one you found. But it was open. And, I don't know, I saw that there were some gold coins inside it, and I picked it up. I was just checking them out. They're old . . . But then someone came back into the house, toward the bathroom or maybe the bedroom, and I freaked out. I mean there I was, looking at shit in their bedroom. What the fuck was I doing? It was like I'd been drugged or something, and I'd just woken up and found myself there."

He paused again, looking at himself in the mirror. What would Linda say if she could see him standing there, looking at himself and

talking? Did he look believable? Not really. He looked wiped out—
wiped out and desperate. Fortunately, he still had his toupee on. Lately
he disliked seeing himself without it, even in the privacy of his own
bathroom.

"Jesus, Martin," Linda said. He could hear her shaking her head—or
he could tell that her tone was the one she used when she shook her
head. Not the tone she used with the kids. No, this was the one she
used with him—the one that said I don't really believe you, and I don't
really like you. It was particularly awful, because most of the time her
tone was the exact opposite; it was one that conveyed her love for him.
She didn't have to tell him she loved him, because he could hear it in
her voice—even when she wasn't talking to him or about him. But then
there was this tone, the one that said that it wasn't quite possible for
her love to be absolute or unconditional. Because he'd disappointed her
too many times. This was the tone that popped up every so often, in
moments like this. Like when he'd bought the Viking. Or when he told
her he'd fired Ron Beaton and hired Radkovitch. Or (of course) when
he'd told her twenty years ago that he didn't really live in that fancy
house in the nicer part of Berkeley, and that the guy who'd gotten her
pregnant wasn't quite who she'd thought he was.

And now . . . now was one of the times when he heard that tone.

"Linda," he said. "Please. Just let me finish, okay? Please. Just listen.
Just for another minute or two. Okay? Please."

He heard her breathe, and then sigh. "Oh my God," she said—
muttered. He could tell that she was talking more to herself than to
him. He wasn't sure, but he thought he heard her laugh. Not at him, he
knew. At herself. This was bad, but he saw the opening: She was going
to let him finish. Or she was going to listen a little more, anyway.

"So I hurried back into the hallway," he said. "And it was *Miriam*
who was coming down the hallway, for Christ's sake. And then it was
too late—I had the box in my hand. What was I supposed to do? I
couldn't exactly say, 'Oh, here, this is yours. I grabbed it off your bureau
when I was snooping around in your room.'"

He heard her chuckle again. And though he knew it wasn't an ap-
preciative laugh, it was a step in that direction. No, she didn't see him
as a victim (his overall goal). But she was starting to see how crazy his
situation had been (or his version of his situation, that is).

"And so then I stuck the case in my jacket pocket," he said. "I mean,
thank God I was wearing a sports coat. You were right about that—
about what to wear and everything. Anyway, and then the next thing
I knew we were at home, and I was shitting my pants. Seriously. Really.
I didn't know how to get it back to them. I mean, what should I have
done, break into their house when no one was around so that I could
give it back to them?"

He let out a little tiny laugh—allowed himself the risk, and saw in
the mirror that it was a good laugh. He was smiling as he laughed. And
he heard her chuckle again, too.

"To tell you the truth," he said, "I actually thought about it, about
breaking in, I mean. But what if I got caught? I mean, imagine *that*.
Talk about fucked! So I just stuck it up in the closet. And then when
you said that Miriam had come by the house and was talking about a
break-in, I knew it was too late. Too late to tell you, I mean. Or to do
anything, actually." He sighed. "Maybe I should have just thrown the
thing away. Or put it in the mail, sent it to them. Jesus, Linda, I don't
know. I don't know what the fuck I'm talking about, in fact."

He was quiet for a second—for ten or fifteen seconds, and she was
quiet on the other end, listening.

"I don't know what else to say," he said, finally. "I feel terrible. I feel
like an idiot, actually. I know you think this is really weird—and it is,
I guess. But I just did something stupid, that's all."

They talked for a while after that—half an hour, at least. But by
the end of the call (he kept at it, was persistent—calm and persistent),
he was pretty sure she believed him. Probably not because she found
the story so convincing (though it was pretty good, Martin thought,
especially given the tight spot he was in). No, she believed him because

she really didn't have a choice. What was she supposed to do, admit to herself that her husband was the type of person who broke into people's houses, stole little keepsakes, and then stashed them away in his closet? That behind his husband mask was some other person? Or (worse and far more disturbing) that behind the mask of almost normalcy was a person with a variety of faces, no single one of which was the real one, the one that matched up with the actual, authentic Martin Anderson?

No, he knew she wasn't going to do this. And so although he knew he was in the doghouse for a long time, he also knew he was going to make it. In fact, as the conversation wound down he could tell that her feelings had shifted, and that instead of being mad at him, what she actually felt was pity. She didn't say so, of course, but Martin knew that she felt a little bit sorry for him. It was, he thought, kind of the way they'd both felt for Peter when he wrote those notes to the other kids at school. (And he *had* written them—Martin had no doubt about that. In fact, he realized with a sudden and uncomfortable mixture of alarm and pride, Peter had probably gotten his skills as a liar from *him*. Either the genes Martin had handed down to him were coded for lying, or he'd simply spent enough weeks and months and years around Martin, listening to him bullshit and prevaricate and just generally treat the truth like a problem to be avoided, that he'd begun to operate the same way. Jesus, Martin thought; it was so obvious it hadn't even occurred to him.)

Finally, Linda asked about the horse race. He knew this was a concession, a bone tossed his way—and he appreciated it.

"It was amazing," he told her, genuine in his response. "I really wish you could have seen it."

Then she wrapped up the call. "I don't know when we'll be home," she said. "Maybe in a day or two. I haven't been over here in a while, in Oakland. We might take the kids over to the City. Maybe we'll even go up to the cabin. I don't know. I just don't feel like being at home right now."

"Okay," Martin said. "Fine. Whatever you want." But he was pretty sure that she'd be home tomorrow. And if not tomorrow, then the next day. For sure.

By the time he hung up it was late, and he was exhausted. He was actually glad to have the house to himself. He got into bed with all his clothes on—kicked off his shoes, but that was it. Sweat, dust, alcohol. He didn't care. He'd had a narrow escape—narrower, if possible, than his escape from Miriam's bedroom. But in the moments before fading off to sleep, he thought about the big purse that Temperature's Rising had won, and about the money that would be coming in from the run he was going to do for Val in a few days.

Maybe, he thought, I'm turning the corner. Maybe things are going to work out, after all.

CHAPTER SIXTEEN

When Martin finally found the guy, he was sitting in the first place he'd looked. At the café in Ensenada, the aqua-colored one with the big open window—the place where he and Hano had sat and drunk and met the two girls. Lucille and Maria. He'd given the cab driver bad directions in his halting, broken Spanish, and gotten lost for a while. For some reason he thought he'd see the guy and his metal teeth the minute he got out of the cab, but of course that didn't happen. Why had he thought he'd be standing around at just the moment he needed him?

So when he wasn't there, standing around with some girl (it was about nine or ten, the time when they'd be out, he'd thought), Martin had started walking. It all looked pretty much the same—cantinas, brightly painted buildings, lights strung up, lots of cars in the street— and pretty soon he was lost. Although since he was looking for a person rather than a place, it wasn't necessarily true that he was lost, exactly. He was just wandering. He tried to ask some people if they had seen the man with the metal teeth, but he didn't know how to say it properly. "The man with the dentistas?" he said, pointing to his teeth and giving a grimacing smile. "Hombre?" "Dentistas?"

It wasn't working. He didn't know how to say "metal" in Spanish, and that was the key. People mostly ignored him, but finally someone— a short Mexican guy who was much stronger than he looked—got angry and pushed him away.

He was just getting ready to give up and hail a cab ("*Vamos* to America—*pronto*") when he realized that he was in front of the familiar cantina. And then he saw him—recognized that metallic smile right away. It was as if he'd been there all along.

Martin waded across the crowded street as quickly as he could, weaving through the slowly moving traffic, and walked right up to the guy. He was sure for some reason that the guy would know who he was—would recognize him from the first trip he'd taken to Mexico. In fact, he was pretty sure that the guy would be glad to see him.

"Hey there," he said. "*Hola.* Do you remember me? I'm looking for Lucille. You know, the one I was with before."

But instead of greeting him with recognition—even pretend recognition (because, of course, there was no reason the guy should know who he was)—the guy ignored him. Just sat there, smiling, but looking off into space, across the street. He was so transfixed that Martin turned around to see what he was looking at. But Martin couldn't see anything terribly interesting—certainly not as interesting as a paying American customer, right? What did he have to do, wave a handful of dollars under his nose? They were still worth more than the fucking peso, right?

When he turned back around, the guy still hadn't looked up at him. No acknowledgment. For a second Martin thought that the guy *did* actually remember him, and that he was fucking with him, maybe because he was mad at him. For the puking and all that. But he'd paid his money, right?

So he tapped the guy on the shoulder. But still, nothing. And then, in a fit of exasperation, he leaned down and yelled into the guy's face.

"Hey!" he yelled. "Remember me?"

No response.

So finally, though he knew it was a risk, he grabbed the guy by both shoulders and started shaking him.

And then he woke up, bolting upright in bed with a start. Light was streaming through the sliding glass door, and when he looked at the clock, he saw that it was late—after nine already. He listened for a second for household sounds, but then remembered that Linda was off at Sharon's with the kids, and that he was alone.

• • •

WHEN LINDA AND THE kids weren't home by noon (no, he wasn't going to call again; once was enough), he got into his car. Val had told him to stop by. He wanted to talk about the horse, but he also wanted to give Martin the money for the next trip to Mexico. Val was leaving town early Saturday morning, the sixth, and he wanted to do it today.

It was a problem. Not the money handoff. Martin could handle that. In fact, it would give him extra time to go through it, touch it, look at it (though he'd have to hide it where Linda couldn't find it, obviously—she was now a proven snoop). No, the problem was that Val wanted him to leave for Mexico July 8. That was the night of the A's game. The whole Gaylord Perry thing. Jesus Christ.

Worse still, Linda told him that she'd found a letter Peter had written to Sal Bando. Not a "Jesus hates you" letter (thank God). Instead, it was a letter explaining to Bando about how to bat against a spitball pitcher like Gaylord Perry. Linda had shown it to Martin. It was written in Peter's chicken-scratch cursive, and it explained how Perry probably got the Vaseline from the bill of his cap: "So when you see him adjust his cap, you will know it's going to be a spitball." It went on to explain that the ball would dive downward at the last second, and that he (Bando) should aim lower than usual. "You should tell everyone else on the team about this, and then you guys will beat his winning streak, and go on to win the World Series again. Go A's." It was signed "A Secret Fan. Peter Anderson (You're Neighbor)."

Peter's plan, according to Linda, was to put it in Bando's mailbox on the Fourth of July, when he figured the Bandos would be home. Martin wondered if Linda had swung by their house on the way out to Sharon's. He hoped so. He also hoped Linda had corrected his spelling.

Martin sighed. Had there ever been anything cuter? Probably not. Now, though, Val had him flying down to Mexico the very day of the game. Martin was hoping to persuade Val to wait a day for the trip, but he was pretty sure it wouldn't go over so well. Val didn't strike Martin as the sentimental type, especially when it came to money.

As he pulled into Val's drive, it occurred to Martin that if he were truly desperate, he could get Linda to take Peter to the game. That wouldn't be so bad, he thought as he drove up the steep hill. It was already warm, and with the windows down he could smell the sweet scent of the eucalyptus trees. She'd do it, but it would give her yet another reason to be pissed off at him. But maybe it would be useful: she'd see how good the tickets were, and how hard he'd worked to set this up for Peter. And it wasn't like he was heading off on some sort of pleasure trip to Mexico (though his hangover after the first trip was going to make that hard to believe).

He parked next to Val's Caddy. Next to that was the red Mercedes that Angela drove: a '72 Benz 350, one of those with the removable hard top. It was a nice car, but it didn't have those curved wells coming off of the headlights that Martin liked in the earlier models, especially the ones from the late sixties. Still, he'd take it if someone offered it to him.

Sitting there with the window down, Martin could hear Rex barking. He cut the engine and listened. He knew that if Val yelled at the dog, that would be it—total silence. But apparently Val was inside, or maybe down by the stables. Because the dog was going at it. *Woof, woof, woof.* In spite of himself, Martin was afraid to get out of the car, and so he sat there for another minute, listening. *Woof, woof—woof-woof-woof.*

Jeez, Martin thought. He's really barking. But as he listened he also realized the dog wasn't by the gate. The barking was a ways off, which meant that Rex was probably down in his kennel. Maybe that's why Val wasn't doing anything to shut him up. Martin wondered for a second if Val was actually home, but he reminded himself that both his car and Angela's were sitting right next to him. They didn't have another car, only Val's big horse trailer. Plus, Val had said he'd be around, and he was never wrong about meeting times.

Martin opened his door and got out of his car. Standing up, he could see further into Val's yard: the big acacia tree on the right, next to the house, and to the left the edge of the pool. And then past that, down the slight hill, the top of the dog's kennel. But the yard was empty.

Martin walked over to the thick metal gate and shouted out a greeting.

"Hello?" he yelled. "Val? Angela? Is the dog locked up? It's me, Martin."

There was no response, only Rex's continued barking. If anything, he started barking more frantically.

"Val!" Martin yelled. "Hello?"

More barking.

Okay, Martin thought. The dog is obviously locked up. Val probably walked down to the lower field where the horses are. I can walk down and find him, and if I see the dog, I'll dash inside and wait in the kitchen.

And so, trying to be quick and quiet, he lifted the latch and slipped through the gate. When he pushed it shut behind him, Rex literally began to howl. Martin jumped, and then scooted at a quick half-jog toward the door. Jesus, he thought. This is ridiculous.

He saw that the sliding glass door was open about six inches. He was still nervous about the dog, but he didn't want to blunder inside unannounced, even into the kitchen.

"Hello?" he yelled into the narrow opening. It was dark inside, and he couldn't see anything. "Angela? Val?"

There was no answer, and so he had to decide what to do. Option A was to walk into the kitchen, then out into the beautiful living room, with its high ceiling and big windows, and then maybe down the long hallway that led to the rear of the house. Option B was to just stand there in the doorway, yelling like an asshole.

Maybe, he thought, they're having sex, and I'm going to ruin things for them. He wouldn't be surprised—Val seemed like a pretty randy guy, and he had a feeling that Angela liked that about him.

Or maybe she's in the shower, he thought, and Val's somewhere else. He listened for the sound of water running, or something like that, a vacuum, maybe, but he didn't hear anything.

He changed his mind. *I'm not going in there and making an ass of myself. I'm gonna go find Val.*

Rex kept barking, but he'd been at it long enough that Martin was pretty positive that he couldn't get out of his kennel. And as Martin went down the path toward the stables, he saw that the dog really was locked up. He was in his kennel, and the door was secured. Though when the dog saw Martin, he jumped up and planted both his huge paws on the chain-link fence and shifted into a ferocious series of quick, guttural barks.

"Rex," Martin shouted, trying to sound friendly. He was hoping that, combined with a familiar tone, the sound of his own name would calm him down a little bit. "It's okay, Rex. Good boy, Rex."

But this only made him angrier. *Woof-woof-woof.* Fucking hell, Martin thought. *That dog really would kill me if it had the chance. What kind of pet is that?*

He shouted Val's name again, and then, willing himself to ignore the dog, he walked the hundred yards or so down the long, paved path that led to the stables. Again he thought about how this would be a great setting for a slow, thoughtful walk with Temperature's Rising, Jim McKay, and a camera crew. And with that he remembered that someone, maybe Val at dinner, had mentioned that a reporter from the local paper, *The Tri-Valley Herald,* had said he was going to run a short article about Temperature's Rising's win. He was going to have to get his hands on one of those. It wasn't *Wide World of Sports,* but it would be kind of cool just the same.

But even as he mused about Jim McKay, he was feeling irritated. *Why am I running around like this on the morning after the Fourth?* His fantasy about a spot on national television was spoiled. Instead, by the time he got to the stables and pushed the door open, he was working out a comment to Val about his shitty hospitality.

The sun was brighter than Martin had realized, and so the darkness of the stable was disorienting. He stood in the doorway, waiting for his eyes to adjust. And then, up ahead of him, just past the four horse stalls, he thought he saw Val sitting on a bale of hay out in the larger barn area.

"Val?" he said. He took a few steps forward, shading his eyes even though he was now out of the sun. "Is that you?" he asked, walking forward now. "What the fuck, Val. Didn't you hear me calling you?"

His eyes had adjusted to the semidarkness of the barn. He could see now that it was definitely Val, and that he was sitting there in the shadows, looking right at him. He was wide-eyed, and his mouth was open, as if he was about to say something. But it was still hard to make him out clearly.

"Val?" Martin said again. "Are you all right?" He walked toward him, feeling the crunch of hay and dirt under his hard-soled alligator shoes. He noticed that the stalls were empty—Temperature's Rising and the other horses were probably in the lower field.

Val was sitting semiupright on a hay bale, leaning back against one of the big eight-by-eight support posts. He was wearing a yellow short-sleeved shirt and whitish khaki pants. But even in the half-light of the barn, Martin could see that he had a rope of some sort gathered loosely around his shoulders and waist and even his neck. It was one of those nice nylon ropes Val used with the horses, and as he looked closer Martin could see that it was actually wrapped around the support post. Like he'd been tied up, Martin realized. But even as he thought this, he noticed as well that Val's shirt was soaked with something dark. And, he realized suddenly, it was the same on the pants. The crotch and thighs were soaked.

Martin took a small step forward, then another one. Then he saw (and heard) a bunch of flies buzz away from Val's stomach, and he jumped back with a yelp.

Holy shit, he thought. That's blood.

"Val?" he said. He took another step forward, then stopped, transfixed by Val's stare. He was looking right at Martin. But Martin realized that although Val's eyes were open, he was dead. Or he was probably dead.

He kneeled about three feet away from Val, peering. It didn't look like he was breathing. Then, slowly, Martin leaned forward on all fours, and then he crawled toward him—a careful, I-don't-want-to-get-dirty cat crawl. The ground was surprisingly cool, he noticed.

He stopped when he was about a foot away and started to stand up, reaching toward Val's neck. Check for a pulse, he told himself.

But as he reached forward he found he was leaning a little too far, and he tipped, hand outward, into Val's right shoulder. He caught himself, but it was enough to knock Val sideways. He slid over slowly, and then his body made a muffled thump as it slid off the hay bale and onto the ground.

Martin jumped back with a yelp and landed on his ass. A couple more flies buzzed away from Val in a noisy, skittering zigzag.

Martin sat there and looked at Val. He definitely looked like he was dead. Yes, his eyes were open, but they were staring blankly ahead, at a spot just in front of him on the barn floor. It didn't matter what Martin did—shout or whistle or clap his hands—Val wasn't going to look up at him.

He let his gaze travel over Val's body. He noticed that in addition to the rope around his upper body and neck, there was some sort of thick wire wrapped around his right hand. And, he realized, the hand and the wire were covered with blood. He stared at the wire, and as he did he saw that it, too, was attached to the big post behind Val. The wire had been wrapped around the post a bunch of times, and then it stretched down to Val, and was wrapped a bunch of times around his hand and wrist. Jesus, Martin thought. What the fuck happened here?

Something on the ground caught his eye. It was a pair of wire cutters. The kind you used for cutting baling wire. Martin had seen Val use them to open a new bale of hay for the horses. They were lying a few feet away from Val. When he looked closer he saw that they were wet. They were glistening a little bit in the dim light. And then, not far from the wire cutters, Martin saw what looked like a finger. It had some dirt caked on it, but it was lying on a little clump of straw . . . almost as if someone had set it there to keep it from getting dirty. Martin looked back at Val's bloody wire-wrapped hand, and saw that one of his fingers—his pinky—was cut off at the second knuckle.

Martin did a scrambling crab-crawl backward, then leaned on his side and retched. He threw up quite a bit—his breakfast cereal, maybe the big dinner at Val's Italian place (veal parmesan), maybe even the crap he'd eaten at the track. Three or four big heaves and it was all out of him, spewed onto the hay-strewn ground in front of him.

He lay there for few seconds, panting, wiping his mouth with the back of his hand, and then wiping his hand on the ground. He was trying to get his mind working.

Val is dead. But it wasn't an accident. I was looking for Val, but I didn't know that he'd be dead. Someone cut off his finger, and then killed him. And I found him. I didn't know this was going to happen today.

He sat up and looked at Val. Someone killed Val because Val is involved in drugs, he thought. That's what they do to you—they cut your fingers off before they kill you. And then they kill you. They probably look right at you as you're writhing on the ground, and then shoot you.

Jesus Fucking Christ, he thought.

He stood up, thought he might have heard himself groan as he did. Or was that Val? He looked down at Val as he lay there, and knew it hadn't been Val. He didn't have anything more to say. Martin thought about that for a second. If you hadn't said everything you wanted to say before you were dead—hadn't gotten it all out, or in the way that you wanted—it was too late. And now it was too late for Val. Because he hadn't known when he woke up in the morning that someone was going to come to his house and kill him, and so he probably hadn't said everything he would have liked to say. Martin wondered what he and Angela had talked about in the morning, maybe over coffee. Because that was probably the last real conversation he had had before the drug guys came and killed him . . . cut his finger off and then killed him.

Angela. The red Mercedes was in the driveway. Val's car was in the driveway, and Val was down here, dead. Where was Angela?

He looked down at Val one last time, and then headed back past the stalls and out the door. It was bright, and he had to shield his eyes. The dog was still barking. Now I know why he's barking like that, Martin thought.

As he hurried back up the path toward the house, several things occurred to him. The first was that whoever had done this was long gone, and that he wasn't in any real danger. But that thought led him to wonder if he actually *was* in danger. Because he realized that Hano had probably done this. Just yesterday Val had seemed skittish about Hano—had warned him, in fact, that Hano might be up to something. And the problem was that Hano knew Martin—knew he was involved, knew he knew enough to finger Hano, if it came to that. But Hano also knew that Martin was only the pilot, the delivery boy. And what was Martin going to do, call the police and say, hey, the guy I smuggled dope with for Val might have killed Val? The problem was that Hano might not see things that way. From Hano's perspective, Martin was probably a big fat liability, one he needed to take care of—eliminate—as soon as possible.

Martin paused for a second when he made it to the house. He was out of breath, not just from the short jog but because he was so overwhelmed—scared.

He didn't bother shouting hello this time. He just reached his left hand into the six-inch gap in the doorway, and pushed slowly on the sliding glass door. When it was about a foot open he stuck his head in a little ways, but, as in the barn, it was hard to see. He slid the door open another foot or so, then stepped inside and shut the door behind him.

It was quiet inside—or at least quieter than it had been outside, because with the door shut Rex's barking was muffled into near-silence. But it didn't look quiet, at least not in the kitchen, where Martin was standing. It looked loud—chaotically loud. Or rather, it was loud but with the sound turned off. Drawers and cabinets had been yanked open, the contents dumped on the floor. Papers, silverware, pots and

pans, dishes, even food from the refrigerator. The place had been ransacked. Or whatever they called it in cop shows on TV, or in movies.
"Tossed." That sounded right. Whatever the term, it was exactly like
you'd see in a movie when the bad guys had been to a house and torn
it apart, looking for the secret papers or the drugs or whatever it was
(although sometimes it was the good guys who did this—the FBI or
the CIA or whatever).

He took a few steps forward, but stopped in front of a big, deep
drawer that had been yanked out of the desk to the right of the door.
It was lying upside down, and as he stood there Martin could see that
every door and drawer in the kitchen had been opened, and the contents dumped onto the floor. It looked like a tiny tornado had hit the
kitchen section of Macy's or Capwell's. Plates, pots, pans, silverware, a
blender, a toaster—there was hardly a place to step without stumbling
or tripping.

Martin stepped through the doorway that led to the living room. He
didn't need to go much further, though, because even standing at the
edge of the big living room he could see that this room had also been
ransacked ("tossed"). He could also see that whoever had killed Val had
also killed Angela. She was lying on her stomach, with both hands out
in front of her. It looked as if she'd thrown her arms out as she fell, and
as her hands hit they had skidded forward. Her face was turned away
from him, to the right, but he knew it was her. For one thing, he recognized her thick, dark hair. It was her best feature, Martin had thought
more than once—had even said so to Linda. She was wearing the light
blue bathrobe she often wore around the house in the morning, and the
matching slippers—but one of them had come off. The bathrobe was
hiked up so that Martin could see the backs of her knees; he could see
the blue lines of some spider veins running down toward her calves.

Martin was no expert, but he could tell she'd probably been shot as
she was running away from whoever came storming into the house.
This was because of the position of her body, but also because there
were two big dark circles in the center of her back, each of which had

a small, dime-size hole in the center. Even from where he was, Martin knew that the circles were made by the blood that had seeped out of bullet holes. About five feet in front of her was a sliding glass door that led out onto the big balcony fronting the house, and from which you could see the Livermore valley as it stretched east. She'd probably stood there thousands of times, looking out and having her morning coffee, or an evening drink. Today, though, she hadn't made it to the door, or onto the balcony.

Martin stood there in the living room, trying to think. The living room had been torn apart just like the kitchen, and he felt certain that if he went down the hall he'd see that the same thing was true throughout the house.

He looked down at Angela. He felt frozen. What was he supposed to do right now? He needed to call the police. That's what they're for, right? Someone's dead, you call the police. He was in over his head—they would take care of it. Maybe, he thought, I'll just call, and then leave. At least someone will know about this.

Outside, he could hear the dog, still barking.

"Fuck," he said in a whisper, as if he were worried he might be overheard.

He shook himself out of his daze and walked back into the kitchen, stepping over all the crap on the floor. He wasn't being careful now. He looked around for a phone and saw one sitting on a side table, to the right of the sliding glass door. He took a deep breath, reached down and picked up the receiver. He told himself to just dial, and then someone would be on the other end—someone who knew what to do, and who could help him. But his hand was shaking, and so it was hard to get his fingers into the little hole. After a couple of tries he managed it, then waited, listening to the faint sound of the dog's barking and looking out through the sliding glass door, at the pool. It was covered with acacia flowers, floating in the quiet of the breezeless morning.

"Operator," a voice said. It was a woman's voice, and he found this vaguely comforting.

"Yes," he said. "Get me the police." He knew that it was exactly the line he'd heard dozens of times on TV, but he didn't care.

"Is this an emergency, sir?" the woman asked.

He nodded. "Yes," he said. "It is. Please hurry." He looked around at the kitchen, and then back out into the living room. From where he was standing he could see only Angela's feet, but it was enough. It was definitely an emergency.

He listened to the buzzing silence on the other end, and then he heard someone pick up the phone.

"Police Department," someone—a man—said.

Jesus, he thought. What am I doing? He hung up the phone with a bang.

He took a deep breath. I need to get the fuck out of here, he said to himself.

MARTIN STARTED HIS CAR, but he didn't pull out immediately. He was still trying to clear his head. Someone—probably Derek Hano—had come to the house and killed Val and Angela. Maybe Val and Derek had an argument, and Hano had gotten pissed off, had gone berserk. Maybe he'd killed Val, and then realized he had to kill Angela, too, to cover his tracks.

But what about the ropes, the wire on Val's hand, and the finger? Why had Hano cut off Val's finger? And what about the house? Why was it torn apart like that?

Martin listened to the sound of the dog barking. He was still at it, though Martin thought he might be getting tired. His bark was starting to sound a little scratchy. His mind drifted to the day he'd watched Val walk into the kennel, and then come out with the trash bag full of money. And then it all clicked into place. Of course. Whoever had killed Val had been after his money—the cash he was sure to have on hand for the upcoming drug buy. Val had even said it was going to be a bigger deal than usual, right? Hano would have known all about that, wouldn't he? People had killed for less, that's for sure.

And so Hano had tried to get Val to tell him where the money was. That would explain why he'd tied him up and cut off his finger. But why had it gotten that far? Wouldn't Val have just told him where to find it? Who would suffer like that for a few hundred thousand dollars?

It was an open question, because, Martin knew, Hano hadn't found the money. And he knew this, of course, because Rex was still in his kennel, barking away, and the money was in the kennel. Martin was almost certain of that fact. And he was equally certain that no one—not Hano, not anyone—could get in there without bloodshed. Either the dog would have to die or the person trying to get into the kennel would have to die.

Something had happened. For one thing, only one finger had been cut off of Val's hand. This meant that before Hano cut off more of Val's fingers, really put him through the wringer, he had decided to shoot him. But he'd killed him without finding the money. Again, Martin was positive about this. He'd obviously looked for a while—the house was torn to shreds—but probably only after Val was dead.

Maybe, Martin thought, Hano hadn't realized Angela was there, and she'd interrupted them. Martin could see it; Val is screaming, she runs down the path, shouting to him, wondering what's wrong, and he yells to her to run. And so Hano shoots Val, chases Angela up the path and into the house, and shoots her. Or maybe he chases Angela and kills her, and then comes back for Val. But by then, Val has gotten himself free from whatever situation he was in. (Because there was that, too: Val had obviously been tied up when his finger had been cut off, but he was untied when Martin found him.) So yes, maybe Val gets free somehow, before Hano can really butcher him. Unfortunately for him, though, Hano comes back and shoots him. But maybe that wasn't right. Maybe it had been some other series of events. Whatever had happened, Val and Angela were dead, Hano was gone, and the money was in Rex's shed.

He sat there, thinking. He knew he should drive away. He'd been there for at least twenty minutes, probably longer. With each passing minute, the odds of someone showing up increased—maybe one of Val's stable boys, for example.

But Martin also knew that he was now officially out of a lucrative side job. No more Val, no more paid courier flights to Mexico. And that meant the odds of his going broke had risen fairly dramatically (though his debt to Val had just been erased—that was something, anyway).

On the other hand, if he got out of the car, walked down the path, and killed the dog, he could have the money. In five minutes, he could drive away a rich man.

Martin turned off the engine. He could hear Rex barking. It occurred to him that Rex probably knew that Val was dead. He'd probably heard Val screaming when Hano cut off his finger, and he could probably smell his blood—or even his dead body (his corpse). It was probably driving him crazy, making him more ferocious than ever. It was a bad time, in other words, to break into his kennel. But he had to do it. It would be like the fairy tale (he didn't know which one—they were all pretty much the same) in which the knight has to slay the dragon to get to the hoard of treasure. But it's an angry dragon, one that has been grievously wronged, and one that is therefore exceptionally pissed off.

He sat there trying to figure out a way to kill the dog. Stab him through the fence with a pitchfork from the barn (he wasn't sure, but he thought he might be able to do this through the chain-link fencing). Whack him over the head with a sledge hammer (though he wouldn't be able to do this without opening the gate, he knew). He wondered if Val had a gun anywhere on the property. Probably. But where?

Then he remembered that he had his own gun, the .22 he'd stolen from Miriam's bedroom (or from Hal's bedroom, if you wanted to put it that way—it was Hal's gun; he was pretty sure of that).

He got out of the car and opened the trunk. He pulled back the square of carpet that covered the spare tire, and then reached in and pulled out the pistol. It felt heavy in his hand, heavier than he remembered, especially for such a small gun. But maybe that was because he was so nervous—so scared. Whatever the case—whether or not it was actually a heavy gun—Martin had the distinct impression that it was happy to be out of its hiding place. Maybe, like Miriam's jewelry box, it preferred the light of day, and even resented being hidden away, kept out of sight. Maybe it hadn't been happy under Miriam's bed, either. Maybe it had been thrilled when a mysterious stranger (Martin) came in and rescued it from its cramped life with the other guns under the Weavers' bed, and had then been confused and disappointed when Martin stashed it away in the darkness of his trunk. I deserve better than this, it might have thought.

Martin took the clip out of the handle, or the butt, or whatever it was called, and saw that it was loaded (and again he felt anger at Hal Weaver for leaving a loaded gun lying around his house—talk about irresponsible). Then, moving carefully, he reinserted the clip and lowered the gun to his side. It was almost like a derringer, and he felt a little foolish. But it was the only gun he had, and overall, he felt all right—less nervous than he would have thought. It was just a dog, right? And an asshole dog at that. If you had to pick a dog to kill, this would be the one, at least in Martin's opinion.

He slipped through the gate, trying to be quiet even though he knew it didn't matter. The dog was barking, regardless. *Woof, woof, woof.* It had gotten to the point where Martin hardly even heard it. He walked straight to the kennel. He didn't look to his right as he passed the entryway to the kitchen, and in fact he willed himself not to think about the fact that Angela was lying dead inside the house. He also willed himself not to think about how, if the police showed up at this very instant, they'd peg him for the killer. He might eventually be able to prove his innocence—different guns and so on—but it would be the beginning of the end for him. At the very least, they'd get him for breaking and entering (into the Weavers' house), and it wasn't all that unlikely that they'd be able to connect him to Val's drug operation (though he wasn't sure how, exactly).

As he walked up to the kennel, Rex exploded into the chain-link fence, barking and snarling. Spit was flying everywhere. You killed my master, his bark said. I'll tear your fucking face off. Martin wanted to explain that he wasn't the one who'd killed Val, that it had been someone else. Derek Hano, the cocky asshole from Southern, California, the one with the bullshit story about his dad and Pearl Harbor (yeah, Martin thought, and my dad helped launch *Apollo 11* to the moon).

Martin took a deep breath. He gripped the gun with both hands, raised it in front of him, and aimed it at the dog. He squeezed his eyes shut and pulled the trigger. The gun went off with a bang (not a boom, but his hands did jerk upward with the recoil). It had more kick than he'd expected.

He opened his eyes to the sound of continued barking—a furious torrent of dog words. I hate you. I'll kill you. I'll rip your throat out. Stuff like that. Because he wasn't dead. Not because he was impervious to the gun's small bullets (Martin's initial fear). No, it was because Martin had missed him, even though he was standing about four feet away from him.

Jesus Christ, Martin said under his breath. He was shaking. But he took another deep breath, raised the gun—and then lowered it. He knew that even though Val's house was isolated, it wasn't unlikely that someone on the hill would hear the sound of gunfire, even the pop-gun sound of the .22. This had to be the last shot, and after the dog was dead he needed to find the money and take off. Time was passing.

Martin took one long stride forward, until he was practically nose-to-nose with the dog. Rex lunged at the fence, smashing his nose into it, trying to get his teeth through the mesh and into Martin. Dog spit flew onto his shoes, and he took an involuntary step backward. He was worried that the dog might burst through the fencing, but as he watched him struggle he felt slightly reassured. This wasn't a sliding glass door, and he wasn't the landscaper guy who'd had his arm ripped up like a leg of lamb ("like a leg of lamb"). He really wasn't in danger.

He put the barrel of the gun through the actual mesh of the fence and was about to squeeze the trigger, but he saw that Rex had pivoted to the left and that he was going to miss again. Fuck, he said. He stepped to the right, trying to aim directly at the dog through the fence. But it didn't work, because Rex leapt up at him, right at his face, and Martin was so startled that he dropped the gun. For a panicked second he thought it had fallen into the kennel, and that he was going to have to try to retrieve it from there (or not—in which case the police would find it, and eventually trace his fingerprints).

God*damn*it! he said—shouted. He leaned down and fumbled for the gun. Instantly, the dog was low down with him, biting at the bottom of the fencing, trying, it seemed, to get his teeth onto the gun. Maybe he knew what was going on—though if that were the case, his strategy of all-out aggression was probably less effective than hiding in the shed would have been. That would have forced Martin to go in after him, something he wouldn't have done even for a million dollars.

Martin was having a hard time picking up the gun. It kept eluding his hand, as if it had decided suddenly that it didn't want to be involved in the slaughter of a helpless animal, however much of an asshole it might be. Yes, it was happy to be out of the trunk, but enough was enough. And so finally Martin just dropped down to his knees and grabbed the gun. He put both hands on it, pinning it down for a second, and then raised it and pointed into Rex's chest. He was only about eight or ten inches away, the spit and (now) the foul odor of his breath shooting out onto Martin's face. Martin scooted back a little bit, trying to get room to aim. He lifted the gun and pointed—and then dropped his hands into his lap.

He couldn't do it.

Yes, he'd already fired a shot at Rex; had narrowly missed, in fact. But it occurred to him that he'd actually missed on purpose. Not consciously, of course. Consciously he'd wanted the dog dead. Out of the way. He still did. But unconsciously . . . ? Martin wasn't so sure. He was suddenly exhausted.

I can't do this, he thought.

He looked down at his hands lying in his lap, clutching the gun.

Pick up the gun and shoot the dog, he said to them. But they didn't respond, and for some reason he wasn't quite able—or willing—to send the executive order down to his hands to get to fucking work, rise up, pull the trigger, kill the dog. Worse, the gun seemed to be in on the mutiny. It seemed to be telling his hands to rebel, to ignore Martin and do the right thing—which in this case, at least according to them (and according to the gun), was to let the dog live.

Shit, he thought.

The dog was unmoved by Martin's change of heart. It was as desperate as ever to tear into him. In fact, he thought, it seemed to have sensed his weakness. It was lunging at him, then backing up and lunging again. If ever a dog deserved to die, Martin thought, this is the dog. He's a wild animal.

Martin stood up slowly. He felt like the big-game hunter who'd finally gotten his trophy animal in his sights—the lion or the bear or whatever—only to chicken out at the last second. He'd hiked for days into the wilderness, and though he hadn't really been scared, when push had came to shove he'd looked the animal in the eye . . . and blinked. Here, Martin knew, the big-game-hunter analogy only went so far: the dog was in a cage and couldn't get at him. In fact, it was more like shooting ducks in a barrel than hunting a lion or a bear. But whatever analogy you came up with, Martin had failed. Worse, Rex seemed to know it, and he was taunting Martin now, daring him to put a bullet into him.

Woof, woof, woof. Martin sighed, and looked down at his little .22 revolver. Would it have stopped him, anyway? Maybe not, he thought.

He stood there, staring, fantasizing about ways to get past the dog and into the kennel. Dig a tunnel (too time consuming). Get some tranquilizers (maybe Angela had some in her bathroom), hide them in some hamburger from Val's fridge, and wait for the dog to pass out (not realistic, not right now). He shook his head. I'm really fucking this up, he thought.

But then something occurred to him. The shed door was closed.

Not the exterior, chain-link-fencing gate that opened into the kennel area. No, the door to the shed itself. And, he noticed, there wasn't the kind of doggie door thing he'd assumed would be there, inserted into the door. Maybe they didn't make them that big. Martin had one at his house for Arrow—it opened out into the backyard, and he'd go in and out all day long. *Flap, flap, flap.*

Okay, Martin thought, so the door is closed. He could picture it. Hano comes to the house—just a friendly visit—and so Val puts the dog in the kennel area. But he forgets to make sure the door is open so that the dog can get in and out. And his food and water are outside, in their huge dishes, and so it's not a big deal, really, not the sort of thing Val would think about if he was in a hurry, dealing with a surprise visit from Hano. But the thing is, now the dog can't get into the shed, where the money is. Or that's how it seems. But—and this was the key question, the one that came racing forward in Martin's mind—wasn't there at least one window on the other side of the shed? Hadn't Martin noticed this once, when he and Val were talking about all the little out-buildings scattered around the sprawling property? Hadn't he noticed that the window had made the shed look like a cute little house—a servant's quarters or something like that?

The possibility of a rear entrance to the shed sent a bolt of excitement surging through Martin. He half walked, half ran around to the rear of the shed. And sure enough, there it was: a little plate-glass window right in the center of the rear wall. Four little panes, with the caulking now gray and peeling and weak-looking. Huh. How about that? All he had to do was bust out the glass and climb through the window. Jesus, he thought. Why slay the dragon when you can go in through the back door? He listened now to Rex's frantic barking with a new attitude. Maybe, he thought, the dog had known about this all along, and had been trying to distract him with his ferocious, nonstop barking.

He had to get up on his tiptoes to look in through the window. It was really dirty—caked with dust and grime—and so he had to spit on his hand and then swirl it around on the window in order to look inside. And when he did peer in, there wasn't much to see. It was dark, and he mostly only saw shapes. But the question was simple: was the door fully shut, fully secured? He wasn't positive, but it looked safe. Or pretty safe, anyway. Safe enough to give it a shot.

His calves were starting to tighten up, so he lowered himself and backed away from the window. He looked around for something he could use to break it. He had his gun, but it was too small—he was pretty sure he'd cut his hand if he used it. No sense in leaving his blood for the police to find. One of his shoes? Maybe, but again, that would be too close to his hand and arm. How about the nozzle of that garden hose? No—again, too small, too close to his hand.

He walked back around to the front of the shed. Rex threw himself against the fencing again, but Martin found it easier to ignore him now.

"Fuck you," Martin said. His voice was drowned out by the continued barking, but he didn't care. He felt victorious already.

Then he saw a decent-size branch lying on the ground, not far from the kennel gate. It looked like it had fallen from one of the eucalyptus trees that towered overhead.

Perfect.

He walked back to the rear of the shed. He looked at the window for a second, took a big breath, and whacked it with the branch. It smashed easily. He took a minute to poke at the remaining shards of glass with the branch, then took off his shirt, folded it a couple times, and laid it across the window sill to protect himself from any leftover glass. He wondered where he might have gotten this idea. A movie, a TV show? He didn't know. He felt pretty clever about it, though.

He took one last look inside the shed. The dog had stopped barking, suddenly, and the quiet took him by surprise. It was a little eerie, in fact. He listened, poised just outside the window, but he didn't hear anything—no cars, voices, or anything like that.

He hoisted himself up into the broken-out space of the window. He tried to keep his hands underneath him to keep his stomach from scraping against the bottom of the windowsill. His body felt heavy and awkward as he struggled through the smallish space. But then, suddenly, he was sliding downward, about to fall onto his face. He threw his hands out toward the floor and caught himself before smashing his face, and then tumbled awkwardly to the ground. As he did, he knocked over a metal garbage can. It was empty, and the loud clang scared him for a second.

The dog went berserk. He was just outside the door. *Scratch-scratch-scratch, snuffle, snuffle.* Martin hopped up and checked the door handle. It was secure, but not locked, and so he locked it. Rex had figured out what had happened, and he was enraged. Martin heard his huge paws scratching frantically at the door, and from inside it sounded as if he was a boxer throwing a flurry of hard, fast punches at the door.

Holy shit, Martin thought. Was it actually possible that the dog might break down the door? It was one of those flimsy, hollow things, and Rex was that big and that furious.

The shed was dark inside and smelled of dog. It really was like entering the lair of a wild animal (or a dragon). He felt around along the side of the doorway, found a light switch, and flicked it. A little bare bulb overhead came on. Aside from the big mattress pad that Val had put down for Rex, there was a lawn mower and a bunch of hand tools. Rakes, shovels, brooms—the kind of crap Martin had yet to accumulate, and hoped he wouldn't, at least as long as he could afford a gardener. Martin thought about the fact that Val wasn't going to be using those tools anymore and wondered how long they'd sit around, unused.

He picked up his shirt from the windowsill, shook it out, and put it back on. Then he looked around, trying to ignore the dog's insistent pounding. There were some big plastic bags of soil (the forty-pound kind), but they were unopened, so he didn't bother tearing them open and looking inside, just moved them out of the way. He looked inside the other metal trash can, but it was empty. He dumped out a plastic five-gallon container that was filled with the dog's kibble (just a lot of food). He didn't see any money, or any containers that looked like they had money in them. A gas can? Probably not.

Shit. Was the trip that Val took to grab the money for Martin that day just a one-time thing? Or, more interestingly, was it something Val had staged to fool Martin? As in "Oh, just a second, watch while I grab thousands of dollars from this secret place—which isn't actually the place where I hide my money." Martin didn't know—doubted it, in fact—but he felt the energy draining out of him. Finding a rear entrance to the shed had given him a surge of energy, but it was fading away. He felt tired.

And then he felt desperate. He really needed that money. Rex was still whining and growling and scratching at the door—worrying it, a term Martin had heard once in a description of a wolf chewing through something. (He couldn't remember what . . . Maybe his own foot in a trap. Did that make sense?) Martin was pretty sure he was safe—the door wasn't coming off the hinges or anything—but it was unnerving just the same.

He dug through a stack of clay pots, separating each one and looking inside. Most of them had the residue of soil in them, and he guessed that Angela used them for flowers, or maybe to start vegetables. When he didn't find anything, he smashed a few of them onto the ground. Fuck you, he thought. He unfolded a couple of tarps that were lying on a foot stool—nothing. He turned over the lawn mower—just old grass and that big, fanlike blade. He looked overhead and saw, to his surprise, that there was a ladder and a metal canoe. The canoe was upside down, so he could see inside it, but there were some pockets at the ends. Maybe the money was there, in the canoe. He got the footstool, climbed up and felt around. Empty. Just metal and spider webs.

Damnit! he said to himself, out loud. His voice sounded strange in the nearly empty shed—and in the intense isolation of the house and its large spread of property—post–double murder. He stomped his foot, swore, and started muttering. He understood how Hano must have felt as he tore apart Val's house. He probably started out feeling pretty confident. Yes, I killed two people, but when I find the money, it will all have been worth it. But as time passed, he must have gotten more and more frantic, angrier and angrier. In fact, Martin thought, maybe after

Hano had cut off Val's finger, Val had sent Hano on a kind of wild goose chase, one that enraged Hano so much that he had marched back and shot Val without even bothering to push him for more information. Or, Martin thought, pursuing a different line of reasoning, maybe Hano actually did find the money. Maybe it took a while, but maybe he did find it, finally. And maybe that was when he had killed Val. Thanks for telling me where the money is, Val, but I'm still going to kill you (and your wife is dead, by the way). So maybe Martin was wasting his time here in Rex's smelly storage shed of a dog house. Maybe he should go back out through the window and shoot the dog after all.

Martin swore again, and then started to lash out in a frantic temper tantrum. He kicked the lawnmower and the garbage cans, threw the gas can against the wall, swore some more. He felt like walking down to the barn and kicking Val—forcing him to wake up and tell him where to find the money. He took a step forward and kicked at the dog's mattress. It was big and didn't move very much. This made Martin even more pissed off, and he kicked at it again. "Fucking piece of shit!" he yelled. The mattress flipped up and stood on one end for a second. Then it flopped back against the shed wall and slid down again, but with the bottom side facing up now. It had done a somersault.

But in the time it took for it to flip over, Martin had seen a big square of sheet metal below it, a rusty square of corrugated iron. It looked strange sitting there on the cement floor. Why was Rex's mattress on a sheet of corrugated metal?

Martin leaned over and lifted up the mattress. (It was heavier than he'd thought it would be. Why did everything seem heavy all of a sudden?) Yes, he thought, there's a sheet of metal there, and it's right under the dog's mattress.

He threw the mattress to the side, grunting with the effort. Then he dropped to his knees, and wedged his fingers under the metal. It moved easily—it wasn't secured, it was just sitting there. But it wasn't just sitting there doing nothing, because Martin could tell right away—the second he put his fingers under the metal—that there was empty space underneath it. So in fact the metal was covering something. It was covering a hole. And, he thought as he raised the metal sheet and looked downward to the hollowed-out recess under the metal, it's the hole where Val keeps his money. Or it's where he *kept* his money, that is, because I just found it and now it's mine.

It was just like before. He could see the outline of the blocks of money through the green plastic garbage bag. But even at a glance he could tell that there was more money in the bag than there had been for the first two trips. That seemed like a long time ago.

He squatted down, untied the little plastic strip that had been used to seal up the bag, and glanced inside at the money. It was a lot of money. Bill after bill after bill, all stacked together, and (or so it seemed to Martin) all eager to be spent out in the world—eager to move in and out of cash registers and bank vaults, and just generally enter into circulation. Enough time in the dragon's lair. Time to become capital. Better, time to become legitimate capital. No more drug deals—just the kind that involved banks and stores and car lots and (yes) airplane dealers.

Martin lifted the bag out of the hole. He held it up in front of him, assessing its weight the way he would with a big salmon. Heavy. Or, he thought, smiling now, a keeper. With a big salmon, you whacked it over the head with a nightstick or anything else you had handy, and threw it in the big cooler and high-fived whomever you were with. Martin didn't have a cooler, and he was alone (except for Rex, who hadn't let up in his barking and scratching). But he did a little dance, right there in the dog's kennel. Still clutching the green plastic garbage bag, he held his arms up over his head and did a little silent jig. Because this was definitely over the weight limit.

CHAPTER SEVENTEEN

Several things ran through Martin's mind on the drive home. The first was that it was a good thing Linda and the kids were staying at Sharon's. Hano was out there somewhere, and for all Martin knew, he might show up at Martin's house at any time; might be there right now, for that matter. Maybe the house had already been ransacked. He pictured Angela lying there on her living room floor, two bullet holes in her back, and felt the sudden need to move his bowels. The fact that Hano had killed Val was one thing—that's what drug dealers did to each other, right? But the fact that he'd killed Angela as well was terrifying. It meant that there really weren't any rules to the game at all.

Plus, even if there actually were a few rules, there wasn't anyone to enforce them. Sure, Jim Slater was sniffing around, trying to figure out what was what. And pretty soon someone would find Val and Angela and call the cops, and then they'd run around, trying to do something. But in point of fact, as soon as Martin had signed on with Val's drug operation—and certainly the minute his plane touched down on Mexican soil—he'd stepped over the boundary, into a world where the police didn't really have much say in things. It was like a science-fiction movie, when you passed over from one dimension into the other. Or like when Dorothy tells her dog they're not in Kansas anymore. That was it—like he'd just stepped over into the Technicolor world of Oz, and there was no way back to the secure black-and-white world of his old life. Sure, he was driving along on a nice summer day out in the suburbs, but really he was off the radar now and on his own. Because what was he supposed to do, call the cops? Call Jim Slater and explain what was going on? That he'd gotten caught up in some silly drug-smuggling thing that had gone sour and now he wanted out? He could see Slater smiling that weird, sardonic smile of his, nodding, maybe laughing at him. Oh yeah, Martin, I'll help you, he'd say. But you're going to jail for a long fucking time.

The second thing was that he needed to stash the money somewhere. His own house was out (even if Hano weren't lurking out there, Linda had proven herself a genuine nuisance with her snooping and poking around—and how *had* she found the jewelry box, anyway? He'd been too scared and busy to wonder). He thought about his office, but that wasn't much better. His boat would probably be all right, but only short term. He didn't think Hano knew about his Viking; he didn't remember mentioning it to him, and even if he had, Hano wouldn't know where it was docked. Come to think of it, that was probably the place Martin should spend the night. As for the money, though, the boat wasn't good—especially if the cops started looking around. No, he needed a place no one would think of. He thought for an amused second about sneaking back into Miriam's house and stashing the money under her bed. How ironic would *that* be? Thanks for the old coins— here's a bag full of money. I think we're about even.

But wait a second. The image of walking into Miriam's house conjured up the previous frames in the film, the part where he parked the car in the orchard. How about there? Not in one of the tree houses that were out there (if only things were that easy). No, how about driving in there with a big fucking shovel and burying the money? It wasn't a bad idea. Get a metal box of some sort, dig a hole, and bury it. It would be a treasure chest. Of course, if some kid found it, it would be the most exciting day of his life, and Martin would be screwed. But what were the odds of that? It was just an orchard, for Christ's sake. And the beauty of it was, the ground was already turned over. It would be impossible to tell that someone had been digging there. Or pretty hard to tell, anyway. Plus, it was just for a little while, until he could get Radkovitch to help him figure out what to do with it. How to get it into a bank without attracting suspicion. That's what he'd hired him for, right? He knew how to work the system.

Okay then. That was the plan. Drive to the orchard behind his neighborhood and bury the money. But he was going to need to wait until dark to do it. And he was going to need a metal box, one of those things that sealed up and kept moisture out. He could get one at a hardware store, he was pretty sure.

He drove along, thinking. He'd drive to the marina and hang out on his boat until nightfall. Then he'd drive back to Walnut Station, park the car way back in the orchard, and bury the money. How hard could that be?

He was just passing Walnut Station, and wondered if he could get away with zipping over to his house for a change of clothes (and to take a dump—he really needed to go). It would probably be all right. And it would be great to be in his own bathroom. But it was also a bit risky . . . maybe a little too risky.

Where was the closest hardware store? He was wondering if that sort of place would be open the day after the Fourth when he glanced down and saw that he was just about out of gas. The little line on the fuel gauge was on EMPTY. Was below EMPTY, in fact. What the fuck? He said it out loud in the car. Unbelievable. Where had his gas gone? True, he hadn't filled up in a while, hadn't even been out to his pump in Hayward for a couple of days. But had he driven all that much? Not really. Out to Pleasanton and back a couple of times. And out to Oakland for a *Racing Form*. Not enough to drink up a whole tank.

What the hell? Linda never drove his car—ever. She hated it, said it was too big, that it was embarrassing, even. And she'd driven off in her Mustang with the kids, so clearly she'd had gas. Could Sarah have snuck out for a joyride, maybe with some older boy? Pretty unlikely, even for her. Then he remembered Ludwig saying recently that he'd been caught out with no gas a couple of times, and that he had begun to suspect the kids in his neighborhood: there were some teenagers that hung around together at the end of the block, listening to music and smoking dope, and he had a feeling they'd been siphoning it. "I'd have done it, too, when I was that age," Ludwig said. "But I'll still knock the shit out of them if I catch them." And then Martin thought about all the teenage assholes hanging around in the parking lot at the fair. Jesus, he thought. Someone siphoned my gas.

He looked again at the gauge. He was going to have to stop for gas before getting out to Oakland. Right away, in fact. Right here in town—in Walnut Station. He could try and make it to the next town up, to Alamo, but he had a feeling he wouldn't make it. He groaned. It would be his first visit to an actual gas station since the start of the gas crisis, and his first stint in a gas line . . . and there was sure to be a line. He pictured himself sitting in a long line of cars as Hano drove past, on the lookout for Martin Anderson. Why not just put a target on the passenger door of his car, make it easy for him? He imagined the lead-in on the local TV station: "Next up, a bizarre set of murders rocks the suburban East Bay. In the first incident, a Pleasanton man and wife were brutally murdered in their luxurious hillside home. In the second, a Walnut Station man was gunned down in his car while waiting to fill up at a gas station. Police suspect that the murders are connected, and that narcotics trafficking is involved. More after this break."

At least I can use the bathroom at the gas station, he thought. Can I leave the car in line while I go, or do I have to park, go to the bathroom, and then get into line?

He pulled into the Standard station, the one at the far end of town, past the junior high school. There actually wasn't much in the way of a line, only five or six cars in front of him. A lot of people were probably out of town for the holiday. Plus, it was still early afternoon. The next real crunch would be around five or six, as people got off work. He stared at the cars in front of him. There were a couple of pickup trucks with construction or landscape guys, and a couple of moms. One was in a station wagon, and the other one was in a newish-looking Volvo.

It took about ten minutes for him to work his way up to the front of the line. He kept turning the engine off to save what little gas he had left, and then restarting it to pull forward (though it occurred to him that this might be a bad strategy—that he might be wasting gas rather than saving it). He knew he should be relieved, that it could be worse: half an hour, forty-five minutes. Imagine having to deal with this every day—and in the morning, when you were trying to get the kids off to school and get to work. What a fucking nightmare that would be. He'd be sneaking out at night and siphoning gas, too.

Martin pulled up to the pump and the gas station attendant came over to his window. He was an older guy, kind of crusty. Probably about fifty-five, maybe even sixty. Martin had seen him before, thought he might be the owner, or at least the manager. But he'd never seen him this close up. He had a really weathered face—lots of deep lines down his cheeks and along his forehead. In fact, he looked a little too salty to be wearing the jackass gas station uniform. There was a name tag sewn into the upper left breast of the shirt, but Martin couldn't quite make out the name.

The guy leaned over a little bit, and motioned for Martin to roll down his window, using a quick, circular motion with his hand. Martin nodded, and hit the DOWN button on the door panel. He loved that feature—no more hand cranks for him. He didn't know if he was in a full-service lane; a lot of stations didn't even have them anymore. But it would make it less likely that he'd be spotted if he stayed in the car.

"Hi there," the guy said, leaning down and putting a hand on the door. His arm was hairy and tanned, and strong-looking.

Martin nodded, smiled. "Hi," he said. "Could you fill it up with regular, please?"

The guy nodded, but didn't move. "Listen," he said to Martin, peering in at him now, a little bit intent. "I'm sorry to have to tell you this, but today is an odd-numbered day." He looked toward the back of Martin's Caddy, as if he could actually see his license plate from where he was standing, then back at Martin. "You've got an even-numbered plate," he said. "I can't give you any gas. Sorry about that."

Martin stared at him for a second. He was shocked—couldn't have been more surprised. He was more surprised than when he found Val sitting dead in his barn, flies buzzing around his bloody bullet wounds.

He looked out the windshield, put his hands on the top of the steering wheel, and put his head back against the seat. "Oh my God," he said. Then he leaned forward, so that his face broke the plane of the window and looked at the guy again.

"Look," he said. "I had no idea it was the wrong day for me to get gas. I usually don't do this . . . I mean, I actually have a gas pump out in Hayward. I've got a business out there. I sell used aircrafts, and so I can pump my own gas. So I don't—I'm not really up on which day is which. For gas, I mean. But I've gotta tell you," he said, "I really need to get some gas right now. I mean, it's kind of an emergency, actually."

The guy didn't move from his leaning position, and still had his hand on the door. He hadn't changed expression, either, but Martin could tell that he was processing what Martin had just told him. He could see now that the name tag sewn into the left breast of the shirt said Arnie. Martin wondered if really his name or if it was just the shirt that had been available when he showed up for work.

Now Arnie nodded, and put both hands on the door, arms straight out. "Okay," he said, nodding just slightly and looking Martin right in the eye. "What's the emergency? Is it a medical emergency, I mean? Are you headed out to a hospital or something?"

Martin shook his head. "No," he said. "It's not a medical emergency. I just—it's a work thing. You know? I've gotta meet someone out at my office in Hayward."

The minute he spoke he knew he'd made a mistake. He should've lied to the guy: stepped through the opening, said that yes, his wife was in the hospital or something like that. Maybe one of the kids. The guy had practically asked him to lie.

Arnie shook his head. "Sorry," he said. "Can't do it." He looked back at the cars behind Martin, as if to indicate that it was time for him to move along. Martin did the same, leaning out the window a little farther to see what was going on behind him. There were five or six cars sitting there. They looked like prehistoric creatures waiting their turn at the water hole.

"So unless there's something else . . ."

Martin looked back at Arnie, at his uniform, his name tag, his tanned, weathered face. And then he leaned back into his seat, stretching his legs out as straight as possible, and reached into his front pocket. He took out the packet of bills he'd stuffed in there—one he'd grabbed off the top of Val's money just before throwing it into his trunk. He was glad now he'd done it. He peeled off five twenties. One, two, three, four, five. Then he leaned over and, using his right hand, held them out toward Arnie.

"Listen," he said. He wanted his voice to sound matter-of-fact and authoritative at the same time. "Here's a hundred dollars. For the gas. And for the hassle. You can keep the change." He looked up at Arnie, who was still standing, arms straight and resting on his door. He could have done a few push-ups off Martin's door if he'd wanted to.

But then Arnie stood up straight, and folded his arms across his chest. He was squinting down at Martin, and shaking his head.

"No, you listen, buddy," he said. "I don't want your fucking money." He leaned forward a little bit, unfolding his arms and pointing at the line of cars behind Martin's car. "That's not what this is about," he said. "I'm not selling gas to the highest bidder, you know." He looked disgusted. Incredulous. Then he stood up straight again.

"Look," Martin said. He looked at the five bills in his suspended hand. "I didn't mean—"

"Do you really think I need your hundred dollars?" Arnie asked, cutting him off. "Do you know what the fine is for letting people fill up on the wrong day? Do you? Huh? Who the hell do you think you are, anyway?"

Looking down at Martin, he took a step forward, and then kicked the underside of the Caddy, near the bottom of the door but probably not the door itself. *Clang.*

"Get the fuck out of here!" he yelled.

Martin jumped at the noise and at the aggression of his kick. He pulled his hand back inside the car, but as he did, he dropped the bills out of his hands.

Arnie leaned down, muttering and swearing, and picked up each of the twenty-dollar bills. They barely had time to hit the ground. Pluck, pluck, pluck, pluck, pluck. He moved like a cat—how could a guy his age move so quickly? Then he stood, wadded them up into a loose money ball and threw it at Martin. The bunched-up bills flew apart as they left his hand. One hit him in the face, another in the shoulder. The others fell back onto the pavement. Martin scrambled to start up his car, but interrupted himself to hit the window control on the panel of his armrest. He was afraid the guy was going to lean in and punch him.

"I said get the fuck out of here!" Arnie yelled—roared—through the closing window. He stepped again toward the car, this time with his fist cocked.

Martin got the car started, threw it into gear, and lurched away from the gas pump and Arnie. He wanted to flip him off—let him know he wasn't entirely defeated. But he was afraid that he'd get cut off before he could pull into the street, and Arnie the Gas Rationing Hero would haul him out of his car and beat the shit out of him. Jesus. He was probably some nut-job military guy, a sergeant, maybe, who'd done a few tours in Vietnam, had retired (with a Purple Heart and some other shit), and now was kicking around in the suburbs, missing the life.

He drove down the street, feeling rattled. More than rattled. There were bad days, and then there were bad days.

He headed back toward the center of town. He thought about Hano, but he was too distracted to give over to worrying that he might be spotted by him.

He drove up to the Gulf station and pulled in. There was another line, of course, another half dozen cars or so. Fuck, he said. But this time he knew what to do.

"Hey there," he said when the attendant walked up to his window.

He was some young guy in his early twenties. Blond, kind of good-looking, and fit—like a guy who'd been on the track team a year or two earlier, and who hadn't gone to seed just yet.

"Hi," the guy said. "Can I help you, sir?"

Martin pulled out the wad of money from his pants pocket again, peeled off another five twenties—no, make it six.

"Listen," he said to the kid. "I know I'm not supposed to get gas today. I know all about it. But I've got a problem, and I'm hoping you can help me out." Martin looked him in the eye, but made sure his money was visible, too. And it seemed to be working—the kid was listening.

"Okay," the kid said. "Sure."

"Well," Martin said. "It's like this. I've gotta get out to Alta Bates Hospital in Berkeley. My son—he broke his arm. He was at his aunt's house. I mean, she's not his aunt, she's just a good friend of the family, but you get the point. He's out there at her house, and she just called me. He fell out of a tree house, and broke his arm. So I've gotta get out there right away. I mean, he's all right and everything—she's got him at the hospital, after all. But you know what I mean. He's only eight, and I just really want to be with him. But the problem is that I don't have any gas. I'm not gonna get across town, much less out to Berkeley."

Martin paused, trying to gauge how the kid was receiving his story. And from what he could tell, he wasn't buying it. The kid was leaning forward, open-mouthed, but his eyes were starting to lose their focus.

"So what do you say?" Martin said. "And listen," he said, holding out the six twenties. "Here's a few extra bucks for the trouble. It's all I've got, but seriously—please—take it."

At the sight of the money, the kid's eyes lit up like a Christmas tree.

"Okay, mister," the kid said as he reached out to take the money from Martin. "I understand. No problem. I can help you out."

Martin sighed. Thank goodness, he thought. He watched as the kid turned toward the gas pump, his eyes still on the bills. Martin could almost hear him calculating how much partying he could get out of the money. It was going to be a good night for that guy. Maybe a good few nights, if he didn't get sloppy with his money and start buying for everyone else.

THE FIRST THING MARTIN did when he got to the marina was stop at the pay phone by the bait shop and phone Linda. He knew he couldn't say anything to her about Val and Angela—he had to wait until it hit the news, so that it seemed like he was getting his information at the same time as everyone else. But he wanted to make sure they were staying out in Oakland. He didn't think Hano would actually show up at his house, but he didn't want to find out the hard way.

"Yes," she said. "We're staying the night. I think we're going to the beach tomorrow, in fact. Peter really wants to go down to Santa Cruz, to the boardwalk, and Sarah said she wanted to go, too. And Sharon's kids are up for it, so it'll be fun. Or fun for them, that is. I don't really like it there. The beach is all right, but the boardwalk is seedy."

There was a pause, and as Martin tried to decide whether he should offer to go down to Santa Cruz with them (which didn't sound so bad, actually—he suddenly felt intensely lonely), he noticed that someone had written a message into the face of the pay phone. "Satan Lives," it said. He wasn't sure what it meant, exactly, but it was easy to imagine some disaffected teenager standing there, maybe talking to his equally disaffected girlfriend, and scratching the words into place with his pocketknife. (It was definitely a boy, Martin thought.)

Then Linda was asking if he was still planning to take Peter to the A's game, and he realized he'd missed the first part of what she'd been saying.

"And so now I know what a spitball is," she said. "He's driving me crazy." There was another pause, but it was short, and pointed. "You'd better be planning to take him," she said. "You're going, right?"

He turned around and looked back toward the wharf. There were dozens of boats bobbing in their berths, waiting for their owners to come take them out for a cruise around the bay. He looked for *By a Nose,* but it was hidden behind a couple of really big yachts.

"Yep," he said. "It's all set." He realized suddenly that, with Val dead, there wasn't going to be a trip to Mexico on the eighth—they really could go to the game. And he realized as well that money wasn't going to be an issue. If he wanted, he could buy a new set of better, more expensive scalper's tickets. In fact, if he wanted, he could buy a new car on the way over to the game, just so they could go in style. Huh, he thought.

The only problem now was Hano.

"Listen," he said. "I think I'm gonna stay on the boat tonight. Maybe for a couple of days. Just to get out of the house—away from Walnut Station, in fact. Maybe that's what we both need to do. Just get away for a little bit."

She was quiet on the other end, listening. He knew she was trying to figure out his angle.

"Well," she said. "You can stay wherever you want, I guess. We're here at Sharon's place. And like I said, we're going to the beach tomorrow. And after that, I don't know. But the kids are having a good time with Sharon's kids, and Sharon and I are having a good time, so I think we'll be another few days. So maybe it's like you said—it's a little bit of a break for us."

He threw in an "I love you" as the call wound down, and she said she loved him, too—but only after a pause. He could tell that she was still pissed off, still wary. And who could blame her?

He hung up and hurried down the dock to his boat, lugging the bag of money and the big metal box he'd bought at a nearby hardware store (he'd also bought a shovel, but he'd left it in the trunk). When he got to *By a Nose,* he jumped on board, unlocked the door to the lower cabin, and ran to the bathroom to take the dump he'd been holding in since halfway between Pleasanton and Walnut Station.

Then, finally, after grabbing a beer from the half-refrigerator that was tucked under the main counter, he locked himself behind the folding door of the little bedroom, kneeled down, and emptied the bag onto the left-hand bunk. The bunks came together in a V, which was convenient. He could count the money from a pile on his left, and then transfer it to the bunk on the right.

As before, the money seemed to be in packets of a thousand dollars each. After a minute or two of counting, Martin realized that there were a lot more bundles than the last two times. He counted out ten bundles, then swiveled and deposited the bundles to the right bunk, then swung back and counted up another ten. At some point, though, he got confused, because he was at 179 bundles and there was still a pretty good-size pile on the left-hand bunk. He must have miscounted, or he must have been wrong about all the bundles being exactly one thousand dollars in value.

He went ahead and finished his count, and he came up with 448 bundles. But that wasn't possible, was it? He shook his head and did it again—moved the bundles from the right back to the left, and started over. This time he got 447 bundles. Pretty close. Holy shit. So then he started counting the amount in each bundle. He wanted to make sure that there was actually a thousand bucks in each of them. He did this for about ten or fifteen, and then realized he was wasting his time. Yes, there was the same amount of money in each bundle. And yes, it was a thousand. And that meant that he, Martin Anderson, was now in possession of a small fortune. Close to half a million dollars.

Martin thought about a lot of things as he sat on the floor of his boat. Linda, the kids. Val and Angela. Radkovitch. Miriam. But he also thought about the way this was all starting to feel like a fairy tale, one in which he was playing the central role. Or it had the vague outlines of one, anyway. Like Jack, he'd climbed up the beanstalk and outsmarted Rex the Giant, and then he'd taken back the money that had been stolen from him. Okay, it wasn't a perfect parallel—from what he could remember, the giant killed Jack's father or stole his family's money or something like that. But it was pretty close to what had happened to Martin. Hadn't the Arabs stolen his money? And wasn't Mexican drug money pretty much the same as Arab oil money?

He knew this comparison was pretty far off base, but the point was a good one—the bad guys had gotten ahold of all the money. But Martin had gotten it back, and now he was a new person. Or he was about to become one, anyway. Like Jack, he could live happily ever after. He could pay his debts, save his business, even show up Radkovitch—show him that his brilliant plan to sell Anderson Aircrafts to the assholes at the Buick dealership had been stupid. Or premature. Or just dickish, when you came right down to it. Because weren't there factors to consider along with the pluses and minuses in a ledger book? Couldn't he have just looked at Martin—at his business, his horse, his boat—and been able to see that things were going to work out somehow?

Martin picked up a bundle of bills and flicked it with his thumb, listening to the slapping sound it made. Sure, he'd keep Radkovitch around for a while—he could help Martin clean up the books, and make a few investments with his new infusion of money (not that he'd let Radkovitch see all of it, of course—Martin wasn't stupid). But pretty soon, Martin would cut him loose. It would be good to get rid of him. And who knew, maybe there'd be some other changes. He wasn't sure what those changes might be, exactly, but they were all going to be for the better. Because that's what money could do. It might not buy you happiness, but it could definitely grease the wheels. If nothing else, it could ward off misery and worry and everything else that came with a mountain of unpaid bills (to say nothing of a career in crime—if, like Martin, you were desperate and stupid enough to go down that road).

He set the bundle down, still thinking. He looked at the big stack of money scattered onto the pale yellow of the bunk mattresses. The problem with the Jack and the Beanstalk comparison was that Hano was still out there somewhere. Wasn't it after Jack had stolen various things from the giant's house—the bag of money, the goose with the golden eggs, and something else—that the giant got wise to what was going on and chased Jack back down the beanstalk? He was going to fucking kill him, in fact, until Jack caught a break and the giant fell down the beanstalk and broke his neck. But as Martin sat there, listening to the sounds of the marina, the water slapping against the side of the boat, voices carrying across the water, engines running, the occasional horn tooting, he found himself wondering if Hano would be willing to make it quite so easy for him. Would he really just fall and break his neck so that Martin could live his happy, debt-free life? Probably not.

Martin shook himself, tried to clear his head. He stood up, stretched his sore knees, and realized he was pretty hungry. He wanted to jump in his car and drive over to the Sea Wolf for something to eat, but he didn't want to leave the money behind—and he certainly wasn't going to take it with him to a restaurant.

He unhooked the sliding door and stepped into the kitchenette. There was plenty of food in the cupboard—a couple of cans of chili, a can of tomato soup, a can of chicken soup, some tuna and some SpaghettiO's. There was also a bag of hamburger buns in the fridge and a few more beers. Good enough, he thought. This is what you do when you're hiding out. You rough it a little bit—dig in, disappear.

He turned on the electric stove, opened the chili with the crappy handheld can opener that he was always planning to replace, and put it in a pot. When it was hot, he poured it out onto the hamburger buns. Then he opened a beer, sat down on the couch in the living area that was just beyond the kitchenette, and turned on the little black-and-white TV to KPIX.

If there was news about the murders, it would be on this channel. Probably on the five o'clock news. In the meantime, the A's were playing at home. It was the first game of a home stand. Catfish Hunter was finishing a shutout against the Orioles. Jesus, that guy could pitch. He was better than Vida Blue. Martin shook his head, thinking about Peter and the game against Gaylord Perry and the Indians. It was only a couple of days away, but it seemed like something way off in the future.

CHAPTER EIGHTEEN

When he woke up, it was almost dark. The TV was still on, murmuring, its dim, flickering images casting a bluish glow in the living room area of the cabin. He'd fallen asleep sitting up, with his head back against the top of the little couch. His neck was sore.

He couldn't remember his dreams—which, given the way things had been going, was probably a good thing. Did he really need to know what his sleeping, unconscious self had to say to him right about now? Wasn't it obvious? He didn't need to remember one of his horrific pursuit dreams to know that he was scared and on the run—that he was confused and unhappy. Sure, finding Val's money had been a lot like a fairy tale. But lying on his bunk and trying to wake up, it suddenly occurred to Martin that his situation was also a lot like one of those nightmares he was always having, in which he was in enemy territory, and hiding, but the enemy had tracked him down, surrounded him, and was just waiting for the right moment to move in and finish him off.

He looked blankly at the TV. It was a sitcom—*The Mary Tyler Moore Show*. Probably a summer rerun. Mary was yapping at her boss, Mr. Grant, about some newsroom crisis. Ugh.

So he'd definitely missed the five o'clock news. And the seven o'clock news. He looked at his watch, and saw that it was just about 8:35. He'd been more tired than he'd realized. He never took long naps like that. On the other hand, he didn't usually stumble onto the scene of a double murder and then find $450,000, either.

He wanted to have a beer, but thought better of it. Instead, he had a glass of water, splashed some water onto his face, and then went forward to load the money into the metal box he'd bought. The dimensions were printed on the side: 18" × 10" × 12". Pretty much the size of a bread box. Or a big bread box, maybe. It was some sort of ammo box, apparently, but you could use it for anything (like burying money). It was painted army green, and the metal was nice and thick. The best part was that it was designed to stay dry inside. It had a rubber gasket around the opening, so it really sealed up when you pushed the side handle down. It would definitely keep moisture out; the guy at the store had been clear on this point.

He counted the bundles one more time as he loaded them in. This time he got 451. Okay, then—it was probably $450,000, and he was just miscounting. The box was pretty full when he finished packing it. He was about to close the lid and seal it when he realized that he should keep some of the money (no sense burying *all* of it). He took five bundles of bills off the top. He paused, and then took another five. Then he gave in and took five more. Then he thought about the fact that he might need to leave the box buried for a long time, and that he wanted to be able to give Radkovitch some of the money: to pay off some bills . . . and to impress him. But it couldn't be too much, of course. Okay. So finally he took out twenty-five more. That made forty—or forty-one, including the one he'd grabbed back at Val's house and used at the gas station. He'd give thirty to Radkovitch and keep the other ten for himself.

He sealed up the box, walked back into the kitchen, and set it on the counter. He looked around for a minute, then stooped and opened the little cabinet under the sink. There was an old red tool box in there; he squatted down, lifted out the top tray, and put the forty bundles in there. It wasn't a great hiding place, but sometimes the obvious places were the best. Look at Val's hiding place for his money—it had fooled Hano. And it would have fooled Martin, too, if Val hadn't been so nonchalant about walking in there and grabbing the money.

Val had obviously trusted him, Martin thought. Maybe Val thought he was too weak to be taken seriously. Or maybe it was because he thought of Martin as a friend—someone he could trust. They'd known each other for a long time, and they'd had some good times together, especially at the track. It was possible that, had someone asked Val to list his ten best friends, Martin might have been one of them. Maybe somewhere around seven or eight, maybe nine. But now Val was dead.

He closed up the toolbox and fit it back inside the cabinet. Then he tucked the metal box under his arm and headed up to the deck. It wasn't quite dark, but it would be by the time he got out to Walnut Station and the orchard behind his neighborhood—behind Miriam's house.

He rehearsed things as he drove. If some nosy neighbor came out and asked him what he was doing out there in the dark, he'd say that his son had left something, and that his wife had sent him out to look for it. "It's not like I was gonna say no to her," he'd say, playing the role of beleaguered suburban husband and father. There was no way it wouldn't work. Even a cop would buy it. But he only rehearsed it once or twice, because it wasn't going to happen. No one was going to stop him, because no one was going to see him. He'd be invisible. He'd bury his box, slip away, and wait.

Walnut Station looked sleepy as he pulled into town. There were some older teenagers driving around, looking for something to do post–Fourth of July, but for the most part it was dead. Perfect. He drove to the spot where he'd pulled into the orchard before, when he'd broken into Miriam's house. He turned off his headlights and then inched along, making sure he didn't plow into a walnut tree. He drove for about fifty or sixty yards, until he was right in the center of the orchard. He rolled down the window, turned off the engine, and listened. Some crickets, some frogs, a few doors opening and closing in the distance, a voice or two (was that Hal Weaver, yelling at one of his kids?). A car drove past on the frontage road, but the headlights didn't come close to penetrating this deep into the orchard. He'd been right—he was invisible.

He was about to open his door when he paused and thought better of it. Gotta take care of the interior light, he thought. It didn't have an on-off switch—it just came on no matter what. He leaned forward, felt around under the seat, and pulled the .22 pistol out from its hiding place. (Did it know it was always being stashed away?) Then he grabbed it by the barrel, and, closing his eyes, smashed the butt hard against the light on the ceiling. It was an awkward angle, and he had to do it three times. Whack, whack, whack. The first time nothing happened, and the second time he only cracked the fixture cover. But when he hit it a third time, the whole thing exploded, pieces of plastic and glass falling down onto his head and shoulders.

He climbed out of the car, pleased that he'd been so clever about the light. He must have seen someone do it once in a movie, but he wasn't sure, couldn't remember which one. But it made sense. You didn't want a cop (or Derek Hano, for that matter) driving by and thinking, "Hey, why is someone sitting in his car out in the middle of that orchard?" The obvious assumption would be that it was kids smoking pot or drinking beer, and so a cop would be sure to pull in, check it out. And even with his planned excuse, Martin didn't want to risk it.

He shut the door and walked back to the trunk. He was stumbling a little on the uneven clods of dirt, and realized that he shouldn't have kept his alligator shoes on. They'd given him trouble the last time he'd been out here—why hadn't he changed into his boat shoes?

He opened the trunk. Peering into the darkness, he spotted the shovel, and set it against the bumper of the car. Then he lifted out the metal box. It felt heavy—substantial.

It was dark, but the backyard lights from the Weavers' house and the people who lived next to them, to Martin's left (the Hermans), gave off just enough of a glow to allow him to see what he was doing. He walked about twenty feet, and then he picked a tree that was directly behind Miriam's house, three rows back. He measured out from the tree the length of two shovels, aiming directly away from Miriam's house; due east, he was pretty sure. Then he started digging.

Soon he was panting and sweating with the effort of pushing the shovel into the ground and moving spade after spade of dirt. The top layer was awkward because of the big chunks of hard dirt left from the most recent plow job. But once he was past this, it wasn't too bad. It was good soil, not too dry or hard.

As he dug, he thought about pirates—Captain Kidd, Long John Silver, and the rest of them, burying their treasure along the Atlantic coast or in the Caribbean somewhere. He had a dim memory of reading *Treasure Island* at some point. Had he read it with Peter? Maybe an abridged version? He wasn't sure. Anyway, he knew that he was too far inland for any self-respecting pirate. The ocean was forty or fifty miles away. But maybe he was a new kind of pirate. A suburban pirate. Yes, that was it—he was a new brand of outlaw, one who lived on the other side of the coastal hills. He stole from either the rich or other criminals—it didn't matter to him. But like the pirates of old, he didn't put his money into banks or other places where it might be traced. Because he was off the radar. He buried his money, and kept it safe from recessions, depressions, and all the other financial crises lurking out there. It would just be there in the ground, waiting for him, and whenever he needed some, he could go dig up his metal box—his treasure chest—and inside would be the solution to his troubles.

He dug for about fifteen minutes. He could've stopped sooner, but he wanted to make sure that he buried the box deep enough to really hide it. He didn't want the blades of some plow to rip into it, open it, and let the moisture in. And he sure as hell didn't want Hal Weaver's kids to find it. Imagine that. First the guy inherits a steel mill, then he manages to land Miriam as his wife. And then, out of nowhere, one of his kids wanders into the house with a treasure chest full of money. "Guess I'm just lucky," he'd say to Martin at one of their cocktail parties (if Martin ever managed to get himself invited to one of these again, that is).

When he was finished digging—or thought he was finished—he stepped into the hole. It came up to his thighs, almost. This will work, he thought. He set the box into the hole, climbed out, and worked quickly to fill it back up. When it was full, he very carefully picked up a bunch of large dirt clods like those covering the top layer of the or-chard, and set them on top of the area he'd disturbed. This took longer than digging the hole itself, but that was okay. It's all in the details, he thought.

The whole thing had taken less than an hour, probably only forty-five minutes. But he was exhausted. Sitting in his car, sweating, dirty, Martin took in the view from behind his street—from the east side of Miwok Drive. Most of the houses had lights on in the backyards, and in several of the yards people were outside, talking, laughing, listen-ing to music. In two of the ones he could see, people were swimming in their pools. You could hear the kids splashing and yelling. At one house they were playing Marco Polo. It was all very pleasant and dreamy. Isn't that what they'd paid for when they'd moved to the suburbs?

Actually, though, Martin thought, with the exception of the Weavers, he didn't know anything about his neighbors. And certainly Martin's family had never been invited over for any of these little back-yard activities. No late-evening phone call with an offer to bring the kids over for a swim, we'll have a drink. No, this was as close as he'd ever come to knowing any of them. And while, yes, they'd been invited to the Weavers a couple of times, they'd barely scratched the surface of any kind of real interaction.

Martin had a sudden urge to be in his own house. The one sitting just a few hundred yards away, down the street on Miwok Drive. He was dirty, his clothes were soiled and smelly, and he just wanted to feel the feel of his own house, even if only for a few minutes. Yes, Derek Hano might be sitting in the living room, waiting silently and patiently for Martin to come blundering in, but Martin didn't care. Or at least he didn't care enough to not want to take the chance. He really wanted to go home.

Plus, he did have a gun. It was only a .22, but he might be able to sur-prise Hano, and put a couple of slugs in him before he had a chance to react—before he had a chance to realize that Martin Anderson wasn't fucking around, at least not when it came to some cocksucker breaking into his house and messing with his stuff, his furniture, his life. (He had a sudden, excruciating vision of Hano walking into his bedroom and discovering his Styrofoam heads and their fake hair. What would Hano think of that? Martin pictured him standing in the bedroom, pissed off. He's searched the room, searched the whole house, but no money. He doesn't lose his cool, though. Instead, he picks up one of Linda's eyeliner things and draws a frowning face on one of Martin's Styrofoam heads. That would be his warning to Martin. I'm not done, it would say.)

He started the car and, with his eyes fully adjusted to the darkness, negotiated his way back out of the orchard. He pulled out onto the frontage road, careful lest a cop was lurking. But all was quiet in Walnut Station, and he drove quickly back around to his street—took a left onto Muwekma Way, stopped at the four-way intersection of Muwekma and Miwok, and then drove toward his house, which was about a dozen houses up, on the right. He kept driving, barely glancing at it. Everything looked quiet enough. But of course he wasn't sure. When he was well past his house, he turned around, pulled over, and parked.

He took a deep breath, made sure he had his gun securely in hand, and hopped out of the car. At least there wouldn't be any glow from the interior light. He started to walk, realizing that no one actually walked around in this neighborhood, especially after dark. People didn't even walk their dogs—and if they did they seemed odd. So he wondered if he was a bit conspicuous as he moved along. The street was pretty dark, and it was likely that no one could even see him (and that no one would have cared if they did). But he had a feeling that his effort to affect an ambling gate—just a guy out walking in his neighborhood— was transparent. Which was absurd, because he really was in his own neighborhood, just outside his own house. Had a cop stopped him, his story would have been pretty hard to challenge—better, even, than his planned alibi for being out in the orchard: "I live right there. See? That's my house. What's the problem?"

Martin walked quickly up the left side of his circular driveway (he liked the fact that he had this setup, thought that it set him apart from all the people with the boring, perpendicular driveways). Then, quietly (he remembered with relief that Arrow wasn't around to bark), he undid the latch on the gate and slipped into the backyard. The house was dark, except for the light in the kitchen. It cast a dim glow out into the backyard, and reflected quietly off the water in the pool. It looked peaceful. Another peaceful aquatic setting out in Walnut Station.

He made his way toward the back door, which opened into the laundry room, stopping every step or two to listen. No sound. He leaned down, found the spare key under the potted plant that was sitting by the door, and inserted it into the doorknob. Click. It unlocked. He opened the door and walked into the laundry room. It occurred to him that someone (Hano) might shoot him right there, right in the laundry room ("Walnut Station Man Gunned Down in Laundry Room by Prowler"). But nothing happened. And so he stood there for a minute, trying to decide how to proceed. (Move stealthily forward? Turn the light on and charge down the hall? Call out to Hano? . . . Taunt him?)

Then he heard the phone ringing. *Ring-ring. Ring-ring.* It was the last thing he expected, and it threw him off his game plan.

Ring-ring.

He knew he should sit tight, not move, wait it out; it would stop ringing in a minute. But he couldn't. He really needed to answer it. So without thinking—almost instinctively, really—he walked out of the laundry room and toward his bedroom, where there was a phone by his bedside. He didn't hit the light switch, just walked forward, feeling his way in the familiar environment of his house (it immediately felt good to be in his own house).

He sat down on the edge of the bed. Outside he could see light reflecting off the pool.

Ring-ring.

He reached out and picked up the phone.

"Hello?" he said.

There was a pause on the other end. He knew someone was there, but there was no response.

"Hello?" he said again, more forcefully this time.

"Martin?" a voice said. "Is this Martin? Martin Anderson?"

Martin was quiet for a second, listening, thinking. He knew who it was, but he needed to think for just a second.

"Yeah," he said. "This is Martin. Who is this?"

"Martin, it's me, Derek. Derek Hano. Listen, I just got a call from someone up in the Bay Area. In Oakland. He said he was just watching the news, and he heard . . . he saw a story that said that Val is dead. That someone broke into his house and killed him and his wife. Have you heard about this?"

Martin nodded, sitting there in the dark. Yes, he thought. I do know about that. But he was also thinking, suddenly, that this call meant that Hano wasn't sitting in another part of his house, waiting for him. This was a relief.

"Yeah," he said. "I know. I mean, yeah, I heard about it. I've been getting calls all evening."

He heard Hano let out a big sigh. He sounded very upset.

"Jesus Christ, Martin," he said. "What the fuck? Do you know what this means? This is about Ramirez—you know, the job. The thing." He paused for a second. "Fuck," he said. "I can't believe this. I can't fucking believe this."

Martin didn't say anything—didn't know what to say, how to respond. The guy was a great fucking liar, that was for sure.

"Where are you?" Martin asked.

There was a pause—Martin could hear the line buzzing faintly. "I'm in fucking Santa Barbara," Hano said. He sounded impatient. "At home. I'm at home. For now, at least. I just got back a few hours ago. Jesus. I can't believe this. I wasn't sure you'd be around—or if you were all right. You should get out of there, you know. I mean, if they came after Val, you never know. . . . Do you think anyone would connect you to Val? About the drugs, I mean?"

Still holding onto the phone, Martin stood up. The cord connected to the receiver bobbed as he moved. He could see the faint outline of himself in a wall mirror that was to the left of the king-size bed. He stood in front of it and looked at his shadowy image—more like a silhouette—in the darkness of his room.

"How did you get my number?" he asked.

Another pause on Hano's end.

"How did I get your number?" Hano asked. "I called Directory Assistance. I picked up the phone, dialed four-one-one, and asked for your number. What do you think I did? Are you all right?"

Martin was confused. What sort of game was Hano playing? Was this a subtle message that he wasn't planning to kill Martin or his family—as long as he left town? Or just so long as he kept quiet? Or was this just the classic move of the guilty one being the first to come forward? Like toward the end of *The Godfather,* when Marlon Brando tells Michael to watch out for the double-cross. Martin had memorized the line—mostly after hearing Ludwig say it over and over in his rasping Marlon-Brando-as-the-Godfather voice.

"Listen," Don Corleone says to Michael, "whoever comes to you with this Barzini meeting, he's the traitor. Don't forget that."

"Hano, I need to go," Martin said.

"Okay, but wait," Hano said. "Hold on. We need to talk, okay? How about if we meet up? I mean, shit, we've got a few things to work out—get our story straight. Also, Martin—I'm getting the fuck out of my house. Tonight—right now. And I think you should do the same. Get out of there, and get your fucking family out of there."

Martin nodded.

"So is there a way I can reach you?" Hano asked. "I'm coming up there in a few days. Or I'm supposed to, anyway. Let's meet up, and we can figure this out."

Martin looked at his shadow reflection, and then leaned over and hung up the phone. He could see all right in the dark now, but he still struggled to get the receiver in the cradle. It clattered before it settled into place.

He stood up straight again, listening. Then the house was completely quiet. He wondered if the phone was going to begin ringing again. He hoped it wouldn't. He waited, but nothing happened. He turned and looked back again at the mirror next to his bed. But he couldn't really see anything—just a dim shape. Hardly a reflection at all.

He looked out through the sliding glass door of the bedroom, out at the shimmering light on his pool. He felt a sudden urge to take off his clothes and take a swim. He felt dirty and tired. He knew he wasn't going to do it (he was too tired, for one thing), but he thought that it would be just the thing. And as he stood there, considering the possibility, he thought that if he turned on the backyard lights and made some noise, splashed around, maybe shouted a little, the neighbors might think that the Andersons were finally getting into the swing of things, figuring out how to spend a summer evening in Walnut Station.

CHAPTER NINETEEN

Martin fell asleep the second he put his head down on the cool plastic mattress of the bunk. No sheets, no sleeping bag, no nothing. He didn't even have the energy to pull a pillow out from the drawer underneath the bottom bunk. When he woke up the sun was streaming in through the two little portal windows of the boat's V-shaped bedroom. The curtains were drawn, but the sun was insistent: Wake up, get out of bed. He looked at his watch. It was 6:20, maybe 6:21. Late for the marina.

He lay there on his bunk and tried to sort things out. I'm in my boat, in Jack London Square Marina. Linda and the kids are at Sharon's house, in Oakland. Val and Angela are dead—someone killed them. Probably Hano. Yesterday I went to Val's house, saw what happened, then found Val's money. I counted it, buried it, and then went to my house. Then Hano fucking called me, claimed he didn't know what was going on, that he was worried, scared, and the rest of it. Now I'm here.

Martin sat up, rubbed his eyes, stretched, yawned. Sometimes—like today—he noticed himself doing these waking-up things and felt silly, as if he'd been taught at some point how to properly rouse himself from a resting state, and now did it mindlessly, thinking it was natural.

Hano. In some respects, the phone call had seemed genuine. "You should get out of there." That wasn't the sort of thing someone said when they were trying to hunt you down and kill you. But wasn't that just the posture he was assuming in order to convince Martin that he hadn't committed the murders? That he was freaked out, didn't know who'd done it?

But was that really Hano's goal? No, what he really wanted was the money, and maybe he was thinking that the best way to get to Martin was to put him at ease, make him think they were on the same side. Us versus Ramirez. Ramirez and the rest of those jerk-off drug guys. Jesus. They're fucking crazy, Martin. Tell me what's going on—where the money is—and we can figure this out together. Two is better than one, right? Let's meet up. We can figure this out. That was the sort of thing someone said when he was trying to pull a double cross, wasn't it?

Martin groaned, stumbled into the bathroom, sat down to pee (yes, a recent habit, especially in the morning, one he'd been hiding from Linda). He cleaned himself up a little bit. He had to hunt around to find toothpaste, but he eventually found a mostly squeezed-out tube of Crest, brushed, then washed his face. He needed to shave, but he didn't have a razor . . . or shaving cream. His toupee looked crazy, so he peeled it off his head. Ouch. But it felt better, less itchy. Okay, he thought, I'm bald, and today I don't really care (though he knew he needed a trim to clean up the ring of hair that was left. He was starting to look like Ben Franklin on a hundred-dollar bill).

He flicked on the TV, but the news wasn't on, just some exercise thing with Jack LaLanne. Jesus, he thought, look at that clown, with his tight clothes, prancing around. Sure, he was strong, but come on.

He needed to call the police. He needed to act like he'd just heard, and was horrified—not to mention worried about his horse (and it was true: who was taking care of him now?). But he was nervous about talking to anyone connected with the police. Would he reveal, somehow, that he knew more than he was letting on? He'd have to get into the mindset of someone who'd just heard that his friends had been murdered, and forget that he'd actually been there, seen the bodies (and stolen the money).

Even if he didn't call, the police were going to come around at some point, probably with a bunch of questions about him and Val. It would be much better to seem forthright and act like a guy with nothing to hide. But would they know anything about Val's connection to the whole drug thing in Mexico? Hard to say . . . though a chopped-off finger and a ransacked house (a swanky house) were probably give-aways, especially to the discerning eye of a narcotics detective.

Martin thought about Jim Slater. Of course, Slater's investigation into the plane that went down in Humboldt County was unrelated, but how long would it be before he put two and two together? He could just hear it, Slater going through the paperwork and talking to his part-ner, or some other detective sitting at the desk next to him: "Hey, wait a second—it says here that Val Desmond was the horse trainer for that Martin Anderson guy. You know, the one I talked to out in Walnut Station. The airplane guy. He sold the plane to the guys who went down up in Humboldt Country, and then I flew around with him, looking for that landing strip in Livermore. That's quite a coincidence, don't you think? I think we need to do some digging."

Really, though, how much was there to find, regardless of how much digging Slater did? That was the question. Martin's trips to Mexico were pretty much invisible. Sure, he'd logged out of the Hayward Air-port, but he'd listed Reno as the location—a day at the casinos. And they never checked you out up there. Too many people coming and going. It was like parking your car; there was no way to know if you'd actually been there or not. As for Santa Barbara, he'd used fake infor-mation there, and he hadn't talked face-to-face with anyone. The guy on the radio had just asked for the serial number on his plane, and Martin had given him a fake one. It was like he'd never been there. Sure, if someone had taken pictures of him there with Hano, he'd have some explaining to do. But that wasn't going to happen, because this wasn't some sort of movie where the police were really fucking smart and two steps ahead of the the bad guys. No, here the bad guy (Martin) was going to disappear into the ether, because with Val dead, there just weren't any strings attached to who he was or what he'd done. At least for the police—Hano was a different story.

He'd call the police after breakfast. He needed to wake up, get some coffee, eat. He was starving. He thought about calling Linda, but he knew it was too early. Had she heard about Val and Angela yet? It was possible. Would she think he was involved? Unlikely. But she'd have a vague feeling that there were links. She wouldn't be able to see these links, of course, but she was likely to suspect something. It would be an intuition, one that set off little internal alarm bells. And her radar would be especially sensitive after having found Miriam's jewelry box (though Martin again congratulated himself on his fantastic cover story about that). She just wouldn't know what it was she suspected.

He hopped into his car and drove over to Nelda's in Hayward. Yes, this was going against his pledge to himself to stay in the boat, no exceptions, for forty-eight hours. But enough with the roughing it on canned food—was he supposed to have SpaghettiO's for breakfast? Plus, Hano wasn't going to be able to trace him to Nelda's. He listened to the radio as he drove—KCBS. Nothing about Val and Angela.

Nelda's was quiet. It was always dead early on the weekends. He didn't recognize anyone, except one or two of the employees and a couple of older Mexican guys who were always at the same booth in the corner. He downed some coffee, and then had two fried eggs, sunny-side up, a big slice of ham, hash browns, and toast. He was really hungry, and he wolfed his food down; he thought he saw his waitress (blue hair, grumpy) give him a disapproving look at one point. There wasn't anything about the murders in the Saturday *Tribune* or *Chronicle*. That figured; the weekend papers were mostly prepped in advance, and didn't really try to keep up with the news. Sure, if somebody had popped Ronald Reagan, for example, or captured Patty Hearst, they'd stop the presses and get it in there (especially at the *Chronicle,* which was the morning version of the *Examiner*). But no one held up production of a newspaper for some random horse trainer out in Pleasanton.

After breakfast he went back to the marina, walked around. It was a nice day, but Martin didn't have plans to take the boat out. Not a chance. He walked along the docks, looking at boats, watching the seagulls and checking out the schools of fish darting around in the gray-green water. He saw lots of other guys who reminded him of himself. Late forties, into their fifties. Maybe early sixties. Hanging out, either avoiding the wife and family or out-and-out divorced. Everyone looked happy enough, but people also kept to themselves—quick hellos: how are you, how's it going. No chats, no effort to connect. It was an unwritten rule, one Martin had always followed.

Okay, he thought. Time to make the calls. He walked up to the pay phone, put in a couple of quarters, and dialed Sharon's number. They were still there—hadn't left yet for Santa Cruz.

"Help your brother find his trunks, Sarah!" Linda yelled before she even said hello.

He told her about Val. He said he'd just heard it on the news, and then listened to her freak out. It was the first time he'd talked about it with anyone (unless you counted Hano's phone call), and it was both good and bad. Good because he could actually say the words: someone had killed Val and Angela. But bad in that her reaction was so straightforward and honest. It had the effect of cutting through the layer of protective emotional covering that Martin had immediately applied to his memory of the scene.

"What?" she said. Screeched. "Someone what? Are you sure? How horrible! This is awful! Oh my God! Martin! I can't . . . I can't believe it! Poor Val—and oh my God! Angela!"

They talked for a long time, with Martin feeding quarters into the marina phone over and over. Eventually Linda got around to asking if he was all right, but by then the answer was no. Her horror had gotten through to him, and made him realize how badly things had gone. He pictured Val sitting there in his barn, the blank expression on his face, the flies buzzing around him, landing on his belly. The image of Angela was just as bad. Worse. Martin was pretty sure that she hadn't known the first thing about Val's drug-world deals. So she wouldn't have had the faintest idea what was going on. At least Val had known why he was going to die. Angela had just seen a guy with a gun marching toward her, run, and then felt the bullets tear into her. Jesus. Thank God her head had been turned away, and he hadn't seen her face. He was pretty sure she'd have a surprised expression—surprised and terrified.

Eventually—finally—they ended the call, and Martin hung up. He needed to pee, then he'd call the police station. He headed back to the boat and flicked on the radio. Just the general blathering you got on KCBS, but as he was coming out of the bathroom he finally heard a spot about the murders.

"In the East Bay, police are searching for clues to the murder of a Pleasanton couple that was slain in their hillside home early Friday morning. Horse trainer Val Desmond and his wife Angela were found dead of gunshot wounds Friday morning. Police are not yet speculating as to a motive. Desmond was the trainer for several horses that had been racing at the Pleasanton County Fair in the days leading up to the murders. Anyone with information is asked to please contact the Alameda County Sheriff's Department."

It felt strange hearing an official description of what he'd already seen. It also felt strange knowing how much they were leaving out (or—maybe—how much they didn't know). But the mention of the horse races at the fair sent a shock wave of fear through his body. The guy may as well have said, "By the way, he was hanging around with Martin Anderson all day—and if you don't believe me, check out the photo they took together in the winner's circle. They're right next to each other!"

He headed back out of the cabin, and walk-ran up the dock to the manager's office. He took out a five, got some change, and hustled over to the phone again. He dialed 0 for the operator, and waited while she connected him to the sheriff's department.

"Sheriff's Department," a voice said. Was it the same guy he'd gotten yesterday when he called from Val's house? He couldn't tell, but he had exactly the sort of deep, gruff voice you'd expect.

"Hi, yeah," Martin began. "I'm calling about the thing out in Pleasanton. Val Desmond and his wife. The murder, I mean. Uh, I was with him yesterday, at the track. And, well, my horse is actually at his house. And so I thought I ought to, you know . . ."

"Okay, sir, hold on a second. Can I get your name, please?"

Martin paused, didn't respond right away. He knew it was a normal question—pretty much the first thing they'd ask anyone who'd called about anything. ("My dog is missing." "Can I get your name, please?") But he felt suddenly that by giving his name he'd be confessing to everything—the flights to Mexico, stealing Val's money, and anything else he'd ever done wrong in his life (like fake his tax returns—something he hadn't thought about recently).

"Sir? Are you still there, sir?"

"Uh, yep, I'm still here. It's just that . . ."

"Is there a problem, sir?"

"No, sorry. No problem. Just . . . okay. My name is, uh, Martin Anderson. And like I said, I was with Val yesterday, at the track. In Pleasanton. And I don't know, I—"

"I understand, sir. I'm going to connect you to someone in a second. But can I get a phone number, Mister Anderson?"

Martin gave the guy his phone number out in Walnut Station, and then a minute later he was talking to a detective. Leon Grabowski. He stumbled a little bit, but overall he thought he did pretty well, all things considered (such as the fact that he was scared shitless). He said he'd just heard the news on KCBS, and that he'd picked up the phone right away—had run to a pay phone, in fact. It was horrible—terrible. He couldn't believe it, he didn't know how something like this could happen. "I was just with him. We had dinner at Antonio's, in Pleasanton." He also said he was worried about his horse, which was at Val's house—because Val was his trainer. But mostly he just wanted to try to help out.

They went back and forth for a few minutes, with the guy apparently jotting some stuff down, asking a question or two, but basically sounding bored. Uh-huh, he'd say. Okay.

"Look," the guy said after a few minutes. "Someone else has the lead on this, and I need to pass it along. But I think we've got most of this already. I mean, yeah, you should definitely plan to stay in the area for the time being. We'll want to send someone out to talk to you in a day or two. But just sit tight for now."

And that was it. By the time Martin hung up, he had the distinct impression that the guy hadn't been really interested in what he had to say. He certainly hadn't been all that hot to do any sort of follow-up with him, anyway. Or at least not right away. In fact, it was so easy that Martin's first assumption was that the guy was just trying to throw him off the scent—make him think he was in the clear when in fact the noose was tightening even as they sat on the phone yakking. (Maybe, he thought, they'd been tracing the call, keeping him on the line just so that they could figure out that he was at the Jack London Square Marina. Send over a few cars—let's nail this guy right now, before he gets away.)

Martin wasn't sure how to feel after the call with Mr. Incurious over at the Alameda County Sheriff's Department. It was reassuring to hear such disinterest, but he knew he wasn't in the clear yet. He wondered if the detective he'd spoken to had been referring to Slater when he said that someone else had the lead on the case. What would Slater think when he saw Martin's name? It could go either way. He might say "I was wondering if he was going to call in—and since he did, he must be innocent." Conversely, he might say something like "Oh yeah, I forgot about that guy. He's obviously calling as a preemptive strike, hoping to convince us he doesn't know anything. Let's go arrest him."

He sighed, wondering how long he was going to have to wonder about this sort of thing. Probably a long time. He went back to his boat and tried to relax. He read a magazine, then watched a fishing show on TV (it was freshwater fishing, which didn't interest him at all). Eventually he dozed off. He slept for about two hours. When he woke up, he thought about taking the boat out. But he knew he really didn't have the energy. He just wasn't motivated. Plus, that was something you did when your mind was clear and you were able to concentrate. He was too anxious right now.

He laughed at himself. He'd never last if he had to really hole up and lie low. It was too boring, and he couldn't handle the anxiety.

He thought about things he could do, places he could be where

Hano wouldn't think to look for him. The track was out, of course. He could jump into a plane and go somewhere, maybe up to Reno to gamble, but he was afraid to even go to the airport in Hayward.

Hayward—he needed to get ahold of Ludwig. Fortunately, it was a Saturday, and a holiday weekend at that, so there was no way he'd be at the office. But Martin didn't have a plan for Monday. How could he open up the office if he was hiding? Shit.

He thought about just climbing into the car and heading up to Sharon's house. He'd surprise Linda and the kids, and go with them down to Santa Cruz. Now that she knew about Val and Angela, she'd forget she was mad at him. But that was the problem: he didn't think he could handle talking about what had happened. And even if she didn't say anything, she'd look at him in a way that would communicate her horror and sadness. No, it was too much. He couldn't face her just yet.

Eventually, it occurred to him that he could go to a movie. That's what people did when they were just kicking around, right? He used to go to the movies by himself all the time. Before the kids, or when they were really young, to get out of the house, take a break on a Saturday or Sunday. (Linda would get furious, but he could only take so much.) He'd loved it, sitting there in the dark, no one to bother you, no one knowing where you were. You didn't even tell anyone you were going to a movie. Someone might ask you later on where you'd been, but you'd just shrug. And while you were there, you could get completely absorbed in the story. It didn't matter what the movie was. *Lawrence of Arabia, Doctor Zhivago, The Great Escape*. Even something older, like *Gone with the Wind* or *Casablanca* when they were playing somewhere. He'd really enter into that world, feel the emotions of those people. He'd fallen in love with Julie Christie while watching *Doctor Zhivago*—that's all there was to it. He'd walked around in a cloud for days.

So okay. He got a paper out, and saw two films he was interested in. The first one was *The Taking of Pelham One Two Three*. The other one was that new Coppola film, *The Conversation*. *The Conversation* was playing in town, at the Grand Lake Theater. Ludwig had seen it . . . had raved about it, in fact. This was either good or bad, but Martin decided to give it a shot. He'd loved *The Godfather,* so this seemed like the better bet.

He drove across town. At least he'd have a couple of hours in which he didn't have to think. Just sit there in the dark, eat some popcorn, be someone else.

It was a great building—one of the old-time theaters. There was a big tall neon sign on the top of the building. It was basically an over-size billboard. You could see it for blocks when they lit it up at night. But the sign fit the building, because the whole place was huge. The main auditorium seated something like two thousand people; it had a giant balcony, and an organ they'd play before films. It had origi-nally been used for vaudeville acts and silent films—his dad still talked about that sometimes. He loved it: the plush carpeting, the fancy gilt patterns on the walls, even the heavy-looking curtains in front of the screen that would part when the film started. They just didn't do it like that anymore.

He and Linda used to come here all the time. He remembered when they'd gone to a Hitchcock double feature a long time ago. They'd seen *Psycho* and *The Birds,* back-to-back. Linda had been completely terri-fied. So had Martin. The whole crowd had been scared—over a thou-sand people, probably, everyone screaming and yelling. They'd all been really into it: Linda, Martin, everyone.

He walked inside, paid the girl in the glass booth. She gave him his ticket, and he walked it around to the kid who tore it in half and gave his half back to him. He got some popcorn and a Coke. He made his way to his seat—dug in as he watched the curtain rise.

He lasted about forty-five minutes. Less, in fact. First of all, the film was slow and boring. Leave it to Ludwig and that nitwit Jenny to rec-ommend something like this. Maybe this was Coppola trying to appeal to an arty, college crowd after *The Godfather* (though both of them had raved about that one, too, so it was hard to say).

But this film . . . Jesus. It was about a professional surveillance guy—a wire-tapping, microphone-planting expert. It was Gene Hackman, and he wasn't bad (better than in *The French Connection*). And it was set in San Francisco, which he liked. But it was the last thing Martin needed to see right now. By the time he'd decided to leave (something he'd hardly ever done before; he always stayed to the end of films), he was convinced that the police had been tapping his phone for months. Or wait, he thought as he was walking out (excuse me, sorry, excuse me). Not his phone. Why bother with that? *Val's* phone was the one they'd have tapped. And they had heard him talking to Val. He tried to remember the specifics of his calls. Val was usually at home. That he knew. There hadn't been very many calls, probably only about half a dozen, but he was pretty sure that they'd been fairly explicit. Come get the money. When you deliver the drugs in Mexico. And it was a given that Val had talked to Hano and that he and Hano had talked about Martin. Probably more than once. How could he have been so stupid?

By the time he was in his car, he was certain that his boat was bugged. He knew that this was silly, that he was being paranoid. But he couldn't help it.

He drove, trying to clear his head. Maybe he'd catch an early dinner at the Sea Wolf. He'd get one of the tables at the long, slanted window that looked out over the water, and not think about anything. Maybe just get drunk—plastered, even. He knew he wasn't going to do this, but it sounded good. Anything to numb himself against the feelings of fear and confusion that were making their way into his head. On the one hand, he felt as if he'd survived a genuine ordeal. Making it out of Val's house in one piece (and with the money, no less) felt nothing short of miraculous. On the other hand, he had the nagging feeling that this wasn't over yet—that in fact his ordeal had just begun.

CHAPTER TWENTY

Martin left the Sea Wolf at about 5:30. He'd sat at a table that overlooked the water, had a few drinks, eaten the filet of sole. The place had been almost empty, which was a relief—he was able to just sit and blank out. When he emerged from the restaurant, the fog was starting to roll in, and it was really cooling off.

He stood in the parking lot, trying to decide what to do. He wanted to go get some groceries, but he knew he was dirty. He put his nose to his right armpit and sniffed. He smelled sour—the smell of stress, of anxiety. He'd go down to *By a Nose* for a quick shower, then go to the market. He didn't like the little shower in the boat—it was a tight fit, and the water really only trickled out—but he was really stinky . . . rank, actually . . . and the thought of cleaning off sounded pretty good.

Okay. He walked over to his car, leaned in, grabbed the little .22 from under the seat again, and put it into his front pocket. It was probably a good idea to keep it with him, just in case. He was pretty sure that a shootout with Hano at the marina was unlikely, but it couldn't hurt to be careful. Not that he thought he'd have what it took to use it, necessarily—to point it at someone and actually pull the trigger. He hadn't even been able to kill a dog, for Christ's sake. Was he really going to pop a few slugs into Hano's big Hawaiian muscles? Probably not. But he put it into his pocket anyway.

He was almost to the boat and thinking about a warm shower when he looked up and saw the guy standing on the deck. For a second he thought he had the wrong boat. Then he realized no, it's my boat, and someone is standing on it, looking at me. And then he realized, it's Jim Slater . . . the drug detective.

"Ahoy there, Matey!" Slater shouted, waving his hand and smiling. "Ahoy!"

He was using the exaggerated accent of a salty old sailor, or a pirate, maybe, flashing his big Cheshire grin, laughing, and basically hamming it up. It was a big joke, and Martin could see that he was enjoying the opportunity to yank Martin's chain, throw him off balance.

And it was working—had worked. Martin had been hustling along, but now he slowed to a stop just short of the boat. He felt like someone who'd run a long race and had been raising his arms at the finish line, ready to signal victory, only to see his opponent dash past him at the last second and break the tape. But it was more than that. It was as if the whole notion of victory, of winning the race, had been an elaborate hoax. He'd believed he was competing, but in fact he'd never had a chance to win, because the other guy was always going to be faster, stronger, smarter, more determined. It was as if it had all been rigged from the start.

"Don't look so surprised, Martin!" Slater said as Martin got closer, then stopped again, right in front of the Viking. His voice was charged with enthusiasm, but Martin could hear the sarcasm. ("Don't look so surprised, you fucking idiot." That's what he was really saying. "Did you really think I wouldn't find you here?")

Still smiling, Slater leaned forward, both hands against the side of the boat, and looked down at Martin as he stood there on the dock. He was wearing what Martin had come to realize was his uniform, basically: blue jeans and T-shirt. This time it was just a plain navy blue T-shirt, with a little pocket on the left breast. Again Martin was struck by how lean he was, and how athletic he looked. Sinewy muscles, big fat veins down the biceps and into the forearms. He looked strong. Martin wouldn't have been surprised if he'd done a quick, somersaulting hand vault over the side of the boat and landed behind him. It certainly wouldn't have left him any more surprised than he already was.

"Aren't you glad to see me?" Slater asked. "I've been waiting here for at least an hour. Maybe closer to two. The old guy a couple of boats down said that this was definitely your boat, and that you'd been here, but I was beginning to worry. I mean, first you clear out of your house in Walnut Station, and then you aren't here . . . What's a narcotics detective to think?"

As with the early moments of Slater's visit to his house (how long ago had that been—years?), Martin knew that this was the time to act indignant, or at the very least, put out. What's this all about? Why are you standing on my boat? Do you know you're trespassing? Do I need a lawyer? That kind of thing. But again he didn't have what it took. And, of course, Slater knew this, which was why he could stand there on Martin's boat and fuck with him: because he knew that deep down Martin was just a big pussy. Even Gary Roberts would have been able to muster the courage to call Slater out right now (of course, Slater would probably kick the shit out of him for it, but that wasn't the point—or it wasn't the exact point, anyway).

But instead of pretending outrage, Martin just sighed.

"Okay," he said, still standing on the dock. "Slater. What can I do for you? Is this about Val Desmond and his wife? I called the station, you know. I called them and told them I didn't know anything about what happened out there at Val's house."

"It's Detective Slater," Slater said. But he was still smiling, and so Martin didn't know if he was serious or not. Or he didn't know if he was completely serious, that is.

"Okay," Martin said. "Sorry. Detective Slater."

Slater nodded. "That's all right," he said. He smiled at Martin again, and Martin nodded back, trying to think. He was too scared and confused to figure out what was going on, exactly. Here he was, standing on the dock, while this motherfucker was standing on his own boat, taunting him.

Slater put his hands in the front pockets of his jeans. Then he looked around—at the control panel and the steering wheel, up at the bridge, and then back at the rear of the big deck. He nodded to himself. "This is one nice boat," he said. More nodding. "What is it, about fifty feet? You can go way out in the ocean with this, can't you? Do you go out deep-sea fishing in this?"

"Uh, yeah," Martin said after a pause. "We go pretty far out. For salmon. Mostly salmon."

Slater gave a slow back-and-forth shake of his head and whistled.

"Man," he said. "That must be pretty cool. Do you go out there with your kids? What's your boy's name? Peter? He must love it." He shook his head again, looking around—even reached out and ran his hand along the polished teak framing that ran along the control panel.

Martin felt tired. He felt like he was a mouse that had been cornered by a big cat, the kind that played with you for hours, never really going in for the kill, just wearing you down until you were dead.

"Look, Detective Slater," he said. "I can tell you everything I know about Val, but it isn't much. I mean about Val and Angela. How about if I just step up there—"

"Oh, right," Slater said. "Of course." He looked at Martin and smiled, then gave himself a whack on the side of his head with the palm of his right hand. "What am I thinking?"

Then he reached his hand out for Martin, to help him climb on board. "Permission to come aboard, Anderson," he said. Martin looked at Slater's big hand and sinewy forearm for a second, and then reached out and accepted the offer. A second later he was on the boat—his boat. He felt the slight roll of the water beneath him as he landed on the deck.

"So," Martin said, looking at Slater—or looking up at him, because he really was kind of tall. Six-two or six-three, even. A lot taller than Martin. "Do you mind if I ask why you're here?"

Slater shrugged. "Not at all," he said. He crossed his arms over his chest, put his hands under his armpits, and gave a little shiver. "But to tell you the truth, I'm actually a little chilly. Do you think we could go inside and talk? Or go downstairs, I mean? I'll be honest—I peeked in there while you were gone, and it looks pretty cozy. And the second I saw you I thought, good, now we can go down into the cabin and warm up." He looked at Martin, not really smiling now.

Martin looked at him for a second, assessing. It wasn't as if he had much of a choice, of course. If Slater said he wanted to talk inside, then they were going to talk inside. But he was still trying to gauge things. Was this situation out of control, or was it salvageable, somehow? Was Slater here to arrest him? Or was he just someone who enjoyed keeping people off balance even if he wasn't planning to arrest them? He'd referred to himself as a narcotics detective, and he'd said something about Martin clearing out of his house. So, clearly he was on to Martin. But how much did he really know?

Martin shrugged. "Sure," he said. He held his left arm out for Slater to go in ahead of him. "After you," he said.

But Slater smiled, stood his ground, and then extended his right arm and gave a slight, almost indiscernible mock bow.

"After *you*," he said to Martin—more sarcasm.

Martin reached out to open the little doors that led down into the cabin. They weren't strong, just louvered panels, but they were made of the same teak that was on the rest of the paneling. They were nice doors.

Martin pushed the doors open and started down the short staircase to the cabin. It was darker down there, especially when first stepping in out of the late-afternoon sun. Plus, there weren't any lights on, and the curtains were drawn on the narrow windows that were about chest high on both sides of the room. But he knew his way around, and so he moved easily down the four steps, and then stepped across the room to the wall switch that turned on the overhead light. He reached out, flicked it, and turned around as the light buzzed into full wattage.

He saw right away that the cabin was in disarray. Cabinets opened, pillows overturned, kitchen drawers dumped onto the floor. Shit everywhere. What the fuck? The first thing he thought of was Val's house. It wasn't as bad as at Val's house, but it was the same general feeling.

It was the feel of silent loudness—as if the noise of everything falling and crashing had only stopped the second that Martin opened up the louvered cabin doors, and all the scattered objects agreed to hit the floor and stop moving and clattering. And Martin was about to say something to this effect—say a sentence that contained the word *ransacked*—when Slater stepped forward and punched him in the stomach. Hard. Incredibly hard. So hard that Martin felt in his confusion as if he'd run full tilt into a protruding pole of some sort, one that someone had mistakenly inserted into a wall at a dangerous perpendicular angle. And it was the twin notion of a "mistake" and of "someone" that floated somewhere in the front of his consciousness as he fell to the floor and gasped for breath . . . retched, saw green and red and yellow. Someone made a mistake and hurt me. Someone needs to help me.

He wasn't sure how long he lay there on the cabin floor, balled up and panting, his hands opening and closing in some kind of embarrassing, primal effort to control—or to at least deal with—his pain. He had no idea it could hurt so much to be hit in the stomach. Fucking hell. He didn't feel nauseous, though, and even lying there he was thankful for that. But he was definitely lying down, and so he knew that there had been an accident of some sort, and that he'd been hurt. As his vision started to focus (and as he opened his eyes, finally—he must have had them closed for a minute), he saw the orange shag of the boat's rug, and he saw Slater's feet and shins. He was wearing his black high tops.

Martin rolled over a little bit, felt a surge of pain, and laid back, resting on one elbow. He had thought Slater was standing and looking down at him, but he was actually squatting. He was up on the balls of his feet, and his elbows were on his knees. Had Slater punched him? He'd been about to tell Slater that he'd had a break-in, and that he was glad that a cop was on hand to see it. But then Slater had punched him . . . right?

"Martin," he said, with the same edge of sarcasm. "Are you okay?"

Martin looked up at Slater. He was still confused, but he was glad to hear the question. "Yeah," he said. "I think so. I don't know what happened. Did you just punch me?"

Slater was quiet for a long second. He looked down at Martin and shook his head, still smiling his mysterious little smile.

"Martin," Slater said. "You've been a naughty boy, and we need to talk."

There was something in the quality of Slater's voice that made Martin snap back into fuller awareness: awareness of what Slater had just said (that he was a naughty boy) and that yes, Slater had just punched him in the stomach. Laid him out—boom, just like that. And then Martin saw that Slater was holding a small stack of bills in his hand. Or rather, a stack of bundles of bills. Bundles that looked a lot— exactly—like the bundles that Martin had put into his tool box. When he saw that Martin had finally spotted them, he started to flick the end of them with his thumb.

Jesus Christ, Martin thought. The money. He's got it, and he's flicking it with his thumb just like I did.

Martin sat up a little more—pulled himself up onto his ass, pulled his knees up toward his chest, and wrapped his arms around his shins. He put his head down onto his knees, then looked up at Slater. Fuck, he thought. I'm going to jail.

"Okay," he said to Slater. He could tell that his voice was a little bit hoarse. "Fine. Let's talk. Jesus. You didn't have to hit me like that. That's fucking police brutality, you know." He looked up at Slater as he said this, and made eye contact with him.

Slater nodded, but didn't move. Just sat there, squatting and smirking at Martin.

"I'm going to ask you a question, Martin," he said. He was looking right back at Martin, his green cat eyes a lot more serious than Martin had seen them before. "Okay? And just so you know, I'm going to use it as a gauge for how much I can trust you right now. Okay? All right? How does that sound?"

Martin nodded. He moved his head slowly, and didn't look away.

Didn't blink, even. He knew that a lot was hanging in the balance right now. Was he going to jail?

"Good," Slater said. "Good. All right. So tell me—where did you get this money?"

Martin paused, trying to think quickly.

"Where did I get it?" he asked. He was stalling. It was the sort of question he'd asked in high school, when the teacher called on him and he didn't know the answer. Maybe someone will pass me a note with the correct answer. Or maybe the bell will ring. There was always a chance. Here, though, Martin actually did know the answer—he just didn't want to tell Slater. Slater had obviously found the money that he'd stashed in his tool box, under the sink. But the question was whether or not Slater knew that it was part of Val's larger stash. At this point, Martin wasn't thinking about hanging onto the money so much as avoiding any connection to Val—or to Val and Angela's murder, for that matter. If he told Slater he had Val's money, what would stop Slater from assuming that he'd killed Val and Angela?

"That's right, Martin," Slater said, nodding his head and smiling just a little bit. "Where did you get it? Did you rob a bank? Did you buy it at a store? Are you a male prostitute? Do you turn tricks for perverted rich guys down here in the fucking cabin of your boat? Where did you get it?" By the time Slater got to his last question, his voice had risen to a near shout. And it was a scary kind of almost-shout—sudden and frightening, with an edge. One minute he was smiling and calm, the next his voice was cutting into Martin, angry and threatening.

Martin took a deep breath. He was going to go for it. He didn't want to go to jail—didn't want to take a chance on trusting Slater.

"That money?" he asked. "That's just—that's money from a plane sale. I—we. Well, we didn't want to declare the money on the books, because we didn't want to pay taxes on it. So . . . you know . . . it's money I'm hiding from the IRS."

Slater cocked his head to the side a little bit. He didn't look pleased—he looked like he was wincing, in fact. "The IRS?" he asked.

"Yeah," Martin said. "Actually, it's from a couple of planes we've sold this year. But, yeah, it's money from my business. Why? What do you think it is?"

Instead of answering, Slater stood up, yawned, stretched, then put his hands on his hips.

"Martin," he said, rubbing his eyes. "You're wearing me out. I think I need a nap. Waiting around for you out here made me tired, and now you're testing my patience with your answers to my questions."

He started to walk around to the side of Martin. Martin started to adjust himself to try to keep him in his line of vision, but just as he did he felt a blow to his side, just under his ribs. He fell over with a half-yell, half-groan, knowing even as he did that Slater must have kicked him. And hard—just as hard as the punch in the stomach. Harder, maybe.

And so again he lay there panting and writhing on the ugly orange carpet, trying to control the pain. Now he did feel nauseous. He remembered a blow like this once when he was playing football as a kid with some friends, and someone had plowed into his side—into his kidney. He'd puked right there on the grass. He felt the same urge to throw up now, but he wanted to preserve at least a little dignity. He found himself thinking about his kids. There weren't any cogent thoughts, just images. Their faces, the sound of laughter and crying. The sound of fear—times he'd told them not to worry, that there was nothing to be afraid of. Climbing into bed with them after they'd woken from a bad nightmare.

EVENTUALLY HE PULLED HIMSELF up onto his knees. He was hunched over, elbows on the rug. He looked sideways at Slater, who was sitting now on the little coffee table that was anchored to the floor in front of the couch. He was hunched over, elbows on his knees, just like when he'd been squatting in front of him. Martin wasn't quite sure how much time had passed. Probably not much, two or three minutes, maybe.

"How're you feeling, Martin?" Slater asked. "Are you all right?"

Forehead on the floor, Martin turned his head to look at him. Slater looked distorted from the upside-down angle—distorted and more frightening. But in spite of himself, Martin felt a little bit reassured to hear Slater ask if he was all right. It must mean that he didn't really want to hurt me—that he won't do that again.

"I'm all right," Martin said.

"Good," Slater said. He paused, looking down at Martin. "Are you ready to have a real discussion now? Yes? Okay? Ready?" He nodded, acting like he was talking to a little kid, or a dog, maybe. That was how Linda talked to Arrow sometimes.

Martin pushed himself off the floor and sat up, butt on his ankles. He sighed and looked at Slater. His side was killing him. Jesus. Then he shifted over onto his ass again, put his feet out in front of him and pulled his knees up.

"Sure," he said to Slater. "Yeah. Let's keep talking."

Okay, he thought. Here it comes. Have you been flying drugs up from Mexico for Val Desmond? You have? Okay then. Martin Anderson, you're under arrest. You have the right to remain silent, and anything you do say can be used against you in a court of law. And so on. He knew the lines from watching *Dragnet*—where Slater would never get a part. And rightly so—Joe Friday never punched and kicked his suspects. Neither did Serpico, for that matter. Apparently, Slater was more of a Popeye Doyle type—the rogue cop. Broke some rules, pushed the envelope. But unlike Gene Hackman, who seemed neither strong nor scary, Jim Slater was the real thing.

"Okay," Slater said. "Excellent." He leaned forward and patted Martin on the shoulder. "I knew you were all right when I first came to your house with the thing about the plane up in Humboldt. Oh, and we nailed that guy, by the way. Did I ever tell you that? That guy was a real clown. Really stupid. And I should tell you, we had a good laugh at the station over what you said about his mustache and how he looked like a porn star. One of my buddies even told him about it when we busted him. Not about you saying that, I mean. But he told him that we were referring to him as the porn-star drug dealer."

He shook his head, chuckling to himself. Martin tried to picture the
guy, but couldn't. He was too confused. And what was his name? Or
what had he said his name was? He couldn't remember.

"Huh," Martin said, not sure if he was actually supposed to respond.
"No. I don't think you did call me about that. But good. I'm glad you
got him."

"Well," Slater said, raising his hands and then bringing them down
hard onto his thighs, slapping himself. It was a kind of punctuation to
his comment. "I should have called you. You were a big help. Flying me
out over Livermore and everything. And yeah, I don't know, I just had
the feeling that you were an all-right guy. You were honest about your
daughter's drug bust. And you brought her to that class, which shows
something. Or I think it does, anyway. And your son with the baseball
thing. Really cute."

He nodded, looked at Martin, raised his eyebrows. I approve, his
expression said. Which was baffling to Martin, because the guy had just
punched him in the stomach and kicked him in the kidney.

"So listen, Martin," Slater said. "You're not stupid, are you? I mean,
like that guy up in Humboldt? Look at you—this boat, your nice
house, your business. Please tell me you're not stupid."

"No," Martin said, shaking his head. "I'm not stupid." (Yes, he
thought, I'm stupid. I'm a fucking idiot—I'm the very definition of a
stupid person.)

"No," Slater said. "It doesn't seem like it. And that's why I was so surprised to see all those pictures of you and Val Desmond together. You
know, up on the wall in your living room—the horses and everything. I
mean, Val Desmond is—or was, I should say—a pretty nasty guy. We've
been looking at him for a while now. I'll bet you didn't know that, did
you? But anyway, when I saw the pictures of you guys together . . . well, I
was surprised. You know? I just think a smart person would steer pretty
wide of a guy like that."

Martin looked at him for a second, not sure what he meant about
the pictures. But then he remembered. When he'd been sitting there at

the counter in his living room, looking at the mug shots that Slater had brought for him to look at, Slater had walked around the room, looking at pictures, books, and so on. And, Martin remembered now, he'd even muttered to himself a couple of times as he looked at the pictures of Martin and Val and various other people standing in the Winner's Circle after some races. "Huh," he'd said. And, "Mmm."

"Well," Martin said, trying again to think, to maintain his composure (even if his dignity was gone—look at me, sitting on the fucking floor of my own boat). "I don't know, he's just my horse trainer. Or he was, I mean. That's not exactly illegal, is it?"

Slater shook his head, and then raised his hand and wagged his forefinger at Martin. It was an admonishing gesture, one Martin had always found incredibly irritating, but one that here was very unsettling.

"Don't bullshit me, Martin," he said. His voice had become sharp again. "I hate it when people do that. The last person that bullshitted with me was Val Desmond. And look what happened to him."

There was a silence in the room after Slater said that. Martin could hear it—it was the sound of a menacing quiet right there in the cabin of *By a Nose*. It blocked out the sounds of the marina outside, on the docks and in the water. Boat engines, horns, the occasional voice. Here in the cabin, there was only the empty vacuum of nonsound that followed in the wake of what Jim Slater had just said.

And then the thoughts started to flood in. The fact that the boat had been ransacked, just like Val's house was torn apart. The fact that Slater seemed to know a lot about Val. The fact that Slater's questions seemed to have less to do with Val's murder, or with drugs, than with Val's money.

And then he was hit by the realization that it might not have been Hano who'd broken into Val's house after all. No, in fact, it might have been—probably had been—Slater. Just as it had probably been—must have been—Slater who'd killed Val and Angela. And cut off Val's finger.

But that didn't seem possible. He felt a wave of nausea. He pulled his knees up to his chest again and took a couple of deep breaths.

"Martin," Slater said. His voice was flat. No more irony. Just flat words. "Where's the rest of the money?"

Martin had to pull himself back into the now of the moment. He'd been starting to fade. He took one more deep breath, then raised his head and looked at Slater.

"The money?" he asked. He wasn't trying to be evasive. The problem was that he was having trouble with words, suddenly. They were like spoken blobs, and he had to concentrate to make them cohere into meaning.

"Listen, Martin," Slater said. He sounded patient now, like he didn't mind being expansive for a minute. "When I came back to Val's house—the second time, after I got the call from the precinct and drove out there again, to the murder scene, acting like I didn't know what the fuck had happened—I saw that you'd broken into the dog's shed. I couldn't fucking believe it. The broken window, the hole in the ground. I almost said it right out loud. I mean, I tore that whole fucking house apart looking for the money, and it was in the dog's kennel the whole time."

He shook his head, and then he pointed at Martin, smiling his cat smile. "That was smart," he said, looking at Martin and nodding. "Though maybe you knew that that was where Val kept it, so it wasn't really so brilliant. I don't know and it doesn't matter. But it was still ballsy—that dog is fucking scary. I would have just shot it. But that doesn't matter, because you got the money, and I didn't."

Slater sighed and rubbed his eyes with the palms of his hands. Then he stood up, a move that made Martin fold up and cringe. He was certain he was about to get another kick in the side.

"It's all right, Martin," Slater said. More baby talk. "I'm not gonna kick you again. Because I don't need to, right?" He reached over and patted Martin on the head.

"But," Slater said, "if you don't mind, what I *am* gonna do is get something to drink out of your fridge here. I saw that you've got some beer stashed in there, and I'm dying for one. In fact, I can get one for you, too, if you want."

Slater walked over to the mini-fridge, crouched, opened it, and took out three cans of Coors. Then he stood up, set them down on the counter, and opened them. First one, and then the other, and the other. *Fizz, pop. Fizz, pop. Fizz, pop.* He looked at Martin, smiled, and flashed him the two-fingered V sign—the peace sign. Jesus, Martin thought. Talk about inappropriate. Or off the mark. Or just brutally sarcastic—which was the point, he realized.

Slater took a big gulp of his beer and burped. He picked up the three beers by the tops of the cans, walked around the counter, and handed one to Martin where he was still sitting on the floor in the middle of the room.

"'Ere you go, mate," he said. "Cheers." He was affecting what Martin thought might be an Australian accent. Or maybe a British accent of some sort. He wasn't sure. But it was unsettling, whatever it was.

Slater stepped over the coffee table, set his beers down, and sat down on the couch with a grunt. He grabbed a beer, took another big swig, and then looked at Martin. Martin took a sip of his beer, and found to his surprise that he was really thirsty—or that he really needed a drink of beer. He took another long swallow, and then another. Then he burped, too.

"Okay, then," Slater said. "So this is the part where you tell me where the rest of Val's money is. Because I know that you guys were planning a buy in Mexico in a few days, and that Val had the money for it at his house."

He took another long gulp of beer, and Martin watched his big Adam's apple bob as he swallowed.

"That's right," Slater said, looking at Martin and smiling. "I know all about that. And do you want to know how I know? Because I had a bug on Val's phone line. Pretty good, huh? I set it up myself. Climbed up the telephone pole, did the whole fucking thing. No one else in the department knows about it. I'm the expert from Oakland, you know? The big-time drug guy. I'm like . . . I don't know, the Reggie Jackson of narcotics detectives out there. Which means that these suburban narco clowns, they let me do whatever the fuck I want." He laughed and held his hands out in a can-you-believe-that? kind of gesture.

Then he sat forward, took a long swig, and looked down at Martin. "Not that it matters," he said. "But I'll tell you that this whole bad cop thing is actually pretty new for me. It's only since I switched out to the suburbs. I mean, I'm running all these wire taps, on Val Desmond's house and a few other places, and basically I'm spending my time listening to guys like you talk to guys like Val. And I'm thinking, are you fucking kidding me? I'm used to dealing with real criminals, the fucking blacks and the Mexicans and the Asians out in Oakland and Richmond and those places. Or the Hells Angels. Those guys are bad news. Scary. And gangs? You don't want to know." He shook his head. He emptied his beer and threw it toward the kitchen, where it landed with a tinny, bouncy clatter. Then he burped again.

"But you guys," he said. "I mean, Jesus Christ. Race horses and boats and planes and on and on. And I thought, this is different. This is the suburbs. No one gets hurt out here. It's just rich kids in daddy's car. So I began thinking, what if I can tap into a little of that? I mean, enough is enough. I live out in fucking Martinez, you know? 'Tinez. My wife is a waitress, I'm a cop, and we live with two kids in a shitty little three-room ranchhouse. And in a smelly neighborhood. Because of the fucking refineries. It's terrible. Who knows what the cancer rate is out there. And the schools, they suck, because what teachers want to live out there?"

He picked up his second beer, took another long draw from it, and sat back again on the couch. He looked like a guy digging in for a Sunday of football watching. Maybe the Raiders and the Steelers. Ken Stabler and Franco Harris. What the hell.

"And the kicker is that I've been shot not once but twice," Slater said. He was talking to Martin, but he was looking across the room, over Martin's shoulder and toward the door. Martin was tempted to turn and see what he was looking at, but he was afraid to distract him.

"And what do I have to show for it?" he asked. "For two bullets in the line of duty? Nothing. Some big ugly scars that I can show off to other cops. Or at drug classes like the one your daughter took. And then I see guys like you, skimming off the top, working the system—all of you. You all want a free ride, no questions asked. And from what I can tell, you're all getting it. So I thought, fuck it, I'm gonna get a little for me, too."

Now, finally, Slater was quiet for a minute or two. He seemed suddenly like an overwound clock that had run down. Martin was quiet, too. Thinking. Slater's rant had given him time to think, and the beer was helping him sort things out, feel less confused. Not less scared—he was more scared every second, in fact. Because he was fully aware now that Slater was really, genuinely dangerous. Crazy dangerous. This guy is nuts, he thought, and unless I figure something out pretty quick, I'm dead. He's gonna get me to tell him where the money is, and then he's gonna kill me, just like he killed Val and Angela. Why wouldn't he? He shot Angela right in the back, for Christ's sake. And he'll make it look like I was killed by the same guy who gunned down Val and Angela.

In fact, Martin thought, he might even frame Hano for it. Because if he'd been bugging Val's phones, he knew who Hano was. (And how ironic was that, by the way? Coppola had been right.) Why *not* frame Hano?

But then it occurred to Martin that there were probably plenty of Hanos out there for Slater to choose from. Including Martin himself. That's right—maybe Slater would frame *Martin* for killing Val and Angela. He'd kill him, and then set it up so that he looked like the guy. What would Linda and the kids make of that? Would Linda refuse to believe that her husband was capable of such a thing, even in the face of overwhelming evidence? Probably not. She'd be horrified, but she'd think it was simply part of whatever had started a year or so ago, and that had included his theft of a jewelry box from his neighbor's house. He'd simply unraveled, until she really didn't even know who he was anymore.

The thought of his family suddenly overwhelmed him, and he was pretty sure he was going to start crying. His stomach and his side were incredibly sore, and he was running out of energy. But, he knew, this wasn't the time to give in. He needed to think clearly, come up with a plan of some sort.

"All right, Slater," Martin said. His voice croaked when he spoke; even though he'd finished his beer, his mouth was dry. "I'll tell you where the money is. No problem. We can go there right now. I don't give a shit. Really."

And it was true. He didn't care about the money. But still, if he could have pulled it out of his pocket right now and given it to Slater, he wouldn't have done it. Because Slater would kill him right there, no question about it. And Martin wanted to live.

Slater nodded, a slow up and down movement, definitive. "Good," he said. "That's the answer I wanted to hear. You're not so stupid after all, Martin. I knew it. I knew I could count on you. Fucking Val Desmond. He gave me all kinds of attitude. He was a real prick. Unbelievable. But you're gonna make this easy, right?"

"That's right," Martin said. "All we have to do is run the boat out to Suisun Bay. It's out there. We've got plenty of time if we leave right now."

Slater looked confused. "Suisun Bay? What the fuck are you talking about? Do you mean up by Benicia and Martinez?"

Martin gave an exaggerated shrug. "Yeah," he said. "That's where I hid it. I didn't want it anywhere near me. I didn't want to be tempted to go and get it, at least not for a while."

"Suisun Bay," Slater said again. "Okay, whatever." He shook his head. "But we'll just drive. I don't have all night to play around on your boat, Martin. I'm supposed to be tracking down the ruthless drug dealer that gunned down Val Desmond and his wife. I've got a job, you know."

He chuckled at his own joke, but Martin held his gaze. He had to hang in there. He was making this up as he went along, but he thought he'd come up with something. It was kind of ridiculous, but he was hoping that it was so odd and wacky that Slater would buy it. It was worth a try. If they just drove out to the orchard behind Miriam's house, he didn't have a chance. He could see it. First, Slater makes him dig up the money—his buried treasure. Then he makes Martin keep digging, so that the hole is big enough for Martin to lie down in. Then he puts a bullet in his brain. Sorry, Martin. That's what he'd say as he shoveled big clods of dirt onto him, hiding him until the stench of his corpse eventually led someone to look for the source. (Is this Martin Anderson, the guy who went missing? I think so. It must be. Wow! He must have gotten mixed up in something really nasty for this to happen.)

Martin coughed, and his side seized up with pain. "No," he said. "We can't drive. We have to take the boat. Because the money is out in the bay—on the water. I hid it on the water."

Slater was quiet for a second. "What do you mean, you hid it on the water?" he asked. "Is it on a buoy or something? I mean, is it safe? Did you fuck this up, Martin? Did you lose the fucking money?"

"No," Martin said. He made an effort to sound irritated. He knew he needed to sound confident. "It's not on a buoy. And yeah, it's safe. It's on a boat. On one of the mothball fleet ships. You know, out in the bay. In Suisun Bay, like I said. My son and I go out there to fish sometimes, and . . . I don't know, I just thought it was a good spot. To hide it away for a while. I mean, who would ever look there? So, yeah, I took the boat out there, climbed up the ladder on the side of one of the ships, and hid the money in a little storeroom. But don't worry, because it's in an ammo box. It's watertight, airtight, and all that. I even locked up the door of the shed it's in with a big padlock. It's fine."

Slater was quiet for a second, processing. "Jesus Christ, Martin," he said, finally. "That's the craziest thing I've ever heard. Those boats are pretty fucking huge, aren't they? What the hell?"

Martin smiled. It was a forced smile, a fake smile, but it wasn't hard to produce, for some reason. He could do this. He'd get Slater out there, and then he'd at least have a chance. He knew Slater was afraid of the water; hadn't he said he couldn't swim very well, and that this was one reason he hadn't gotten a swimming pool for his kids? It was while he was watching Sarah and Peter play in the pool out at Martin's house, when he'd said he was thinking about an above-ground pool for his own house. So, yeah, he was hoping that he'd have an opportunity to knock him overboard, somehow. Either that, or use his pistol. Because, yes, he'd remembered a couple of minutes ago that he had his .22 right in his pocket. He couldn't get it out now; Slater would pounce on him in a flash. He knew that. Pounce on him and beat the life out of him. Literally. But if he could put some space between himself and Slater at some point . . . well, it might work.

"Look," Martin said. Again he went for slightly irritated. "It's a better hiding place than the one Val used, right? A lot better. And I'm telling you, it's just a big graveyard out there. That's what they call it, in fact—a ship graveyard. No one ever goes on them. They're just sitting there because no one wants to admit that they're useless now. The next time someone gets on that boat, it'll be because they're getting ready to scrap it. And that won't happen for a long time, believe me. Because even scrapping it costs lots of money, and no one has any money anymore. Right? Except the drug dealers, that is."

Slater liked this, he could tell. "You're right about that," he said. He shook his head.

"Okay," Martin said. He wanted to keep the momentum going, didn't want to get sidetracked. "So, what do you say? Can I get up and get us ready, get things going?"

Slater looked at him for a second, and Martin could see the wheels turning in his head. His cat eyes narrowed a little.

"Just tell me one thing," he said. "If you can do that, then we'll go."

Martin shrugged. "Okay," he said. "Fine. What do you want to know?"

"What's the name of the boat that you put the money on? What's it called?"

Martin didn't even pause. "The SS *O'Brien*," he said. "You'll see. There's a big ladder right on the side."

CHAPTER TWENTY-ONE

It was about seven by the time they got through the Oakland estuary, where they had to putt along at a slow speed, and then out into the San Francisco Bay proper. It was now downright chilly. The fog had waited like a barbarian horde just beyond the Golden Gate Bridge, but now it was pouring into the bay, big time. It would cool things off for a while, especially the bay side of the foothills. There was a layer of gray clouds close overhead, and Martin could see a wall of gray-white fog not far off, around Alcatraz. Half of San Francisco was already enveloped in it. Martin wondered what it would be like by the time they got out to Suisun Bay.

Martin stood at the lower helm, adjusting the speed every now and then, and Slater sat on a seat a few feet back, watching him. The bay sped past underneath them, and the boat rocked up and down with the steady *slap, slap* of the hull hitting the water as they cut northward.

Fortunately, the water was pretty calm, almost no chop at all. That was good. Martin was able to cruise along at a nice clip, about twenty knots. They'd be out to the mothball fleet in an hour or so. There was plenty of light left. Sunset wasn't until almost 9:00 P.M. As long as the fog didn't block everything out, they'd be fine.

They came up on the Bay Bridge. The sun was too low in the sky to create the kind of dramatic shadow you'd see earlier in the day as you moved under the bridge (Peter always liked that, for some reason; he would point at it and make a big deal about it). But as they passed under the bridge, Slater slapped Martin on the shoulder, pointed upward, and yelled, "Commuters." Martin nodded. Slater wasn't referring just to the cars themselves, but to the whole lifestyle of commuting—which was, of course, the lifeblood of the suburbs. Hop in your car, drive, take the bridge in to work. Then get back in your car, cross over the bridge again, and go home. And of course it was a given that there would be a backup on the bridge. Traffic would grind to a halt, and you'd sit there like an asshole, swearing and fiddling with the radio and asking yourself why you were doing this.

He looked back at the bridge as they moved north, the boat slapping and sending spray out to the sides. Through the steel girders he could see that the cars were moving along in what seemed, at least from his perspective down on the water, to be a slow, antlike progression. He wondered which of them were headed back out to Walnut Station.

He turned back to watch the water, feeling nervous. He didn't actually have a plan—wasn't at all sure how this was going to work out. He did know he didn't want to be climbing up into the *O'Brien,* pretending something was there when it wasn't. But what to do? Ask Slater to steer and then pop him in the back of the head with the .22? Not likely. The minute they'd left the dock, Martin had begun to see that Slater really was afraid of all things water. He wasn't going to steer the boat. Plus, he wasn't stupid—it wasn't going to be easy to get the drop on him. He was sitting right there behind Martin, patient and concentrating.

One option was to act like the boat had died out—that it had run out of gas. Maybe then he could figure out a way to separate himself from Slater. Tell him he had to go below and fix something, then sneak up on him and whack him over the head with the big pipe wrench he had in his tool box? Or (again) just shoot him? No. Too far-fetched. Slater wouldn't buy it. Plus, Martin knew for sure that there was no way to sneak up on Jim Slater.

He didn't know what do. He'd had a brief moment in which he thought that if they could just get out onto the water, and maybe to Suisun Bay, that things would work out. But why would they? He was in as much of a jam now, speeding across the bay, as he'd been sitting in his slip at the marina.

The engine was pretty loud, and with the wind whipping through their hair, it was hard to talk. And there really wasn't anything to talk about, anyway. They'd done their talking, Martin thought. In fact, any more talk and it would be weird. And so at least half an hour went by without either of them saying anything. Martin wondered what Slater was thinking about. Killing Val and Angela? Probably not. He didn't seem fazed by this in the slightest (which was terrifying). No, he was most likely thinking about how he'd spend his money once he had it. A gift for his wife. Buy that pool—or no, move out of Martinez altogether. Maybe move into Martin Anderson's house, after his widow put it up for sale; that house had a nice in-ground pool (and the high school was supposed to be wonderful). Or he was thinking about how to cover his tracks. Martin knew Slater wouldn't try to kill him out on the water; he needed Martin to get him back to the dock—to land. But after that . . . well, maybe he was thinking about that right now, too.

Once they were past the central part of the San Francisco Bay and into San Pablo Bay, the fog was closer. The bulk of it wasn't on them yet, but there were patches of it here and there as they motored along. There was a good chance they'd be enveloped in it as they pulled close to the ships out there—that area was notoriously foggy. Martin knew this would be really bad, because he didn't know his way around the fleet very well. Not well enough to do it blind, that's for sure.

As if reading Martin's mind, Slater pointed toward the fog. "Can we get lost out here?" he yelled over the sound of the boat's engine. "Do you know how to navigate in the fog—or at night? You've got some sort of radar, right?"

Martin nodded. "Don't worry!" he shouted.

Half an hour later they were passing under the Martinez Bridge, heading east now as the upper bay pushed inland, into Suisun Bay proper. Martin could see the mothball fleet in the distance. The ships were still about half a mile or so away, and they looked small—like a bunch of cabin cruisers, similar to the Viking. But with every minute or two that passed, the ships appeared larger, until soon they were looming up out of the water and towering above them.

"Wow," Slater yelled. "They look pretty cool from this perspective. I've only seen them from the bridge. They're really big!"

Martin nodded again.

Soon they were between the rows of ships. It was like being in a large valley, one sided by steel cliffs. You couldn't get out by climbing up the valley sides; you had to go forward. But it wasn't just a straight-ahead valley. There were various rows of battleships, and after a turn or two down the long corridors they formed, it was easy to get disoriented. Plus, the ships blocked out much of what was left of the late-evening light, and so as they moved along toward the *O'Brien,* it was increasingly hard to see.

"Are you sure you know where you are?" Slater asked. He was still perched on his seat behind Martin and just off to his left. They were moving more slowly now, so he didn't have to yell like he had when they were traveling up through San Francisco Bay and San Pablo Bay.

Martin looked back at Slater. "Yep," he said. And then, about five minutes later, he pointed.

"Okay," he said. "There it is."

And there it was. The SS *O'Brien.* It was stationed at the end of a long row of ships. It wasn't as huge or as tall as some of the others out there, but from their vantage point it looked big enough. A lower section was painted a darkish gray, and above that it was a lighter, more standard navy gray.

As they pulled nearer, Martin began to feel as if they were stationary on the Viking and the *O'Brien* was moving toward them. In fact, all the ships around them seemed as if they were closing in on his own little boat. The fact that they were surrounded by patches of swirling fog didn't help. It was just like the game he'd played with Peter—like they were a fleet of pirate ships emerging out of some ghost dimension to snatch them up and haul them back to their scary pirate place.

"So you think you know how to bury treasure?" Captain Kidd would say to Martin—a comment that would make Slater spin around and realize suddenly that the whole *O'Brien* thing was just a ruse. "Okay,"

Slater would say. "I know we've been kidnapped by these ghost pirates, but just so I know—where did you really hide the money?"

Martin pulled back on the throttle and brought the boat to a crawl. This made it quieter—quiet enough that Martin was reminded, suddenly, of how little noise there was out there. The ships were rising up above them like big skyscrapers—it was like walking down Market Street in San Francisco, practically—but there wasn't any sound. No cars, no horns, no asshole businessmen. Nothing. Just a few seagulls, and the slap of water against the hulls of the ships.

Closing in on the *O'Brien,* Martin told Slater to run up to the bow and grab the rope that was lying there, coiled up. "I'll glide us in and you can grab hold of one of the ladder rungs," he said. "Just slip the rope through and tie it off. It doesn't have to be a fancy sailor knot. Just make it secure. I'll be able to come check it in a minute, once I get the boat set."

Slater stood up from where he'd been sitting behind Martin, and looked at him. Martin could tell he was trying to decide what to do. And it was in that instant that Martin realized that this might be the opportunity he was hoping for. He hadn't planned it this way—he really did want Slater to be ready with the rope—but he saw now that it might give him just enough space to make some sort of move on him. Or to try, anyway.

"Hurry up," Martin said. "Otherwise I'll have to swing around again."

This time Slater nodded, climbed slowly onto the side of the boat, and started making his way toward the bow. Martin watched him as he inched along, shuffle-stepping, and clinging to the railing that ran along the top of the cabin. He was glancing down at the water every few steps.

Huh, Martin thought. He really is afraid.

They were about twenty yards from the ship when Slater made it out to the bow. He bent down, picked up the rope, and then glanced back at Martin. Martin gave him a thumbs-up gesture, and Slater returned it.

Okay, Martin thought. He reached into his pocket, pulled out the .22, and checked the safety to make sure that it was off. Then he put it into the right pocket of the windbreaker he was wearing.

He slowed the boat even more, and then eased it into reverse, so that the momentum of their forward movement would keep them heading toward the *O'Brien,* but the backward thrust would allow them to avoid slamming too hard into the side of the ship. But then Martin realized that that was exactly what he wanted: to slam into the side of the *O'Brien* and throw Slater off balance. He knew he couldn't do it too hard or he'd fall down, too. He might even hurt himself—or the boat, which would be bad. He didn't want to sink it and be stranded on the *O'Brien,* alone with Jim Slater the dirty narcotics detective. But yes, a hard bang. That was the plan.

And so when they were about five yards from the ship, Martin eased the throttle forward again. There was a low grinding as the engine worked to respond (and tried to figure out why Martin couldn't seem to make up his mind), and then the boat surged ahead. There wasn't enough space to pick up any real speed, but it was enough to make *By a Nose* slam into the *O'Brien* with a loud metallic boom. It was also enough to throw Slater off balance.

"Hey!" he yelled as he stumbled forward and bumped hard against the iron wall of the big ship. Martin was thrown forward, too, but he'd been prepared for it—had both hands on the tiller.

"Sorry!" Martin yelled, as loud as he could.

He cut the throttle, and then he scrambled up the ladder to the bridge of the Viking. It just took a second to get up the ladder, but he saw that Slater had already regained his balance. He was kneeling, one knee up, and just starting to look around. Martin thought that he looked a little uncertain—like he was shaken up.

Good, Martin thought. He took the .22 out of his pocket and leaned over the low plexiglass screen that protected the driver up on the bridge. Then he closed his left eye, aimed the gun with both hands, and pulled the trigger. *Blam.* Nothing. He'd missed.

Fucking hell.

Slater didn't move, just looked around, wary. He looked like he was trying to figure out if he'd actually heard what he thought he'd heard. It took him an extra second to look up toward the bridge, and then fix his gaze on Martin. They made momentary eye contact, and in that split second Martin could see Slater's expression shift from confusion to understanding. He suddenly looked pissed off. Not scared, just angry.

Martin pulled the trigger again. *Blam.* This time Slater yelped— yelped and reached up to grab his left shoulder with his right hand. He didn't fall over, though. Instead, he threw himself forward and then scrambled up, running in a low tuck to Martin's right. He was moving to the starboard side of the boat.

Martin swung the gun around to his right and pulled the trigger again. *Blam.* He saw Slater stumble and grab his right thigh, but then he disappeared out of his line of vision, onto the narrow walkway next to the starboard side railing.

Jesus Christ, Martin thought. It's true—bullets really don't have an effect on this guy. And then he was seized with terror, because he knew Slater would now have his own gun out—one he knew how to use, and one that had a lot more power than the little .22-caliber pistol Martin had stolen from under Miriam's bed.

He needed to get off the bridge. Slater was right below him, sidling along the edge of the boat, and he'd be back on the deck in seconds. Martin considered leaning over the back edge of the bridge, trying to put a shot into him just as he reached the deck, but who was he kidding? It was too risky—crazy, in fact.

Fuck.

He crouched, listening, trying to hear over the sound of his terrified breathing. It was incredibly quiet—utterly silent—and he was afraid that his panting would give him away. He was pretty sure Slater wasn't the type to breathe hard . . . and that he knew enough to listen for exactly the sounds that Martin was making. His lungs wouldn't stop

demanding air. It was his heart. His heart was pounding in his chest—
thump-thump, thump-thump—and it was forcing his lungs to demand
air, and demanding that his mouth follow suit and gulp it in.

He looked back, and saw that *By a Nose* had drifted from the *O'Brien.*
Twenty or thirty yards already. They were just floating now in the
eerily quiet canyon of World War II battleships. Fog was drifting past,
and he realized that visibility was getting bad pretty quickly. In a few
minutes he wouldn't be able to see the *O'Brien,* even though it was
towering right overhead. It would be lost in the fog—and a few minutes
after that, the Viking would be lost as well.

He felt frozen. If I just stay here, I'll be all right. Someone will come
to help. The police. Or what if I yell to Slater, tell him I'm sorry? That
I'll take him to the hospital, make sure he's all right?

He put his face against the plastic seat cushion of the bridge chair,
breathing and thinking. He knew he was on his own—and that a guy
like Jim Slater didn't need medical attention. Not really. He'd pull the
bullets out and keep coming.

He was sitting there, trying to figure out what to do, when first one,
then two, then three shots rang out. *Thwack. Thwack. Thwack.* Slater
was behind him now, on the deck, shooting through the fiberglass floor
of the bridge—trying to pick him off blindly, like the sitting duck he
was.

Martin ran forward and threw himself onto the Plexiglas windscreen
of the bridge and over it, rolling. The edge raked across his stomach,
and then he came clattering down onto the front deck. He turned to
face the lower-deck windshield, but couldn't see anything. He crawled
to his right, to the port side of the boat, and crouched behind the exterior wall of the cabin.

Again he sat, panting, listening to the sound of his own heavy
breathing. He positioned himself so that his gun was pointed down
along the port-side walkway that ran outside the cabin. As he did, he
saw with alarm that the boat was now completely enveloped in a pocket
of fog. One second he was eyeing the sightline to the rear deck, and the

next he was in a pillow of whiteness and only able to see a foot or two ahead. It was, he realized, just like when he was flying: One second you were surrounded by beautiful blue sky, with the world spread out around you down below, and the next you were in the colorless no-time of a cloud. You knew you were moving (the instrument panel was insistent on this point), and you could hear the engines working away—but it was as if you had suddenly stalled, stepping out of the moving world and into . . . something else. No bearings, no nothing. He'd heard of pilots who'd gotten completely lost in huge cloud banks, who didn't even know if they were flying upward or downward. And some died that way. They just lost their bearings, and that was it.

"Hey, Martin!" a voice yelled out, making Martin jump so much that he lost the grip on his gun for a second. He only caught it as it fell into his lap. Another few inches and it would have fallen, *plop,* into the water.

It was Slater, of course, but because it came at him out of the sudden fog, he couldn't tell if he was close up (fifteen feet away, on the bridge?) or way back on the rear of the deck (a safer thirty feet away). His voice carried right out over the water, and echoed back to them off the *O'Brien* and the other ships.

"Martin! Are you all right? I'm sorry I shot at you, but what the fuck are you doing? You shot me, you know! Twice! If that had been a real gun, I'd be dead right now, you know that?"

Martin didn't answer. He strained to hear where the voice was coming from. Slater was probably shouting to cover the sound of his own movements.

"Listen," Slater yelled. "I can't get this fucking boat back by myself. I don't want to hurt you. I need you. Look at this fog. What am I supposed to do if you're dead, Martin? And I don't even know where the money is. What are you doing? You're fucking crazy. Do you want to split the money? Is that it? I'll do that if you want. What the hell. Fine. Fifty–fifty. How about it?"

Martin thought about this for a second. Surviving this situation and a fifty-fifty split. He'd take that deal in a flash. But, of course, it wasn't a real deal, not at all, as the mention of his name in the same sentence as the word *dead* reminded him—that and the image of Angela lying on her living room floor with two bullet holes in her back. He pictured the veins on the backs of her legs, exposed for the whole world to see, and he felt a moment of stark terror.

Martin looked at the forward deck. He was thinking. When he and Peter played pirates out here, his favorite move was to open up the forward hatch, the one right above the sleeping compartment, and slip down into the cabin. He'd move slowly, tiptoeing, and then sneak up on him. It worked like a charm, every time. Boom, boom. Gotcha! You're dead! But Peter was nine going on eight. Would it really work on Jim Slater, trained narco guy? It was pretty unlikely. But what were his options? Wait for Slater to track him down in the fog and shoot him?

"Martin!" Slater yelled again. "Look, this is your last chance. I'm bleeding from your pop gun shots, and it fucking hurts. I'm getting impatient, and angry, Martin . . ."

Slater kept talking, but Martin wasn't listening. He put the gun into his jacket pocket and started a quick, sideways crawl to his left. He was up on his toes and fingertips. The timing was perfect, because Slater kept on talking and threatening him as he moved. He was still at it when Martin located the hatch and lifted it open. It slid up on its hinges, and Martin paused for one more second, listening.

"I don't want to shoot you," he heard Slater say, "but if you don't walk the fuck over to the deck, I'm gonna . . ."

And then he was sliding down through the hatch, setting his feet onto the bed and then onto the floor. He was scared—really scared—but Slater's voice was actually reassuring. If he's yelling at me, he's up on the deck, still trying to see into the fog.

Martin saw with relief that the sliding door to the sleeping bunk was open. He took the .22 out of his pocket (he knew he had two bullets left) and started forward. He was just at the kitchen counter when he heard a shot, and he froze. It took everything he had not to pull the trigger of the .22. But he knew that the shot was outside, aimed out into the thick fog of the encroaching night—a night hastened by the way the battleships blocked out the last of the light from the sunset. Martin could still see in the cabin, but it was a mess from Slater's pillaging, and he had to move carefully.

Soon enough, though, he was at the steps. The louvered doors were closed. He was tempted to charge up the steps and start firing at the first thing that moved, but he knew better. He stood listening. He was pretty sure that if Slater was on the bridge, directly above him, he'd hear his footsteps. But as he stood, wondering, Slater took another shot. This time Martin knew for sure that it was off to his right, to the boat's port side.

Jesus, he thought. That's right where I was. He wondered if he would have been able to detect Slater's movements, or if the bullet would have smacked into him as he sat crouched and hiding.

He heard movement, a *squeak, squeak* of sneakers. He knew that Slater was inching his way along the outside of the cabin. He thought for a second that he could dash to the port-side window and have a decent shot at his legs, but the curtains were drawn, and he needed a better shot. And he needed to hurry. Once Slater made it out to the front deck, he'd see the open hatch and figure out what Martin was up to.

Martin walked carefully up the four cabin steps and eased the doors silently open. He felt the wet of the fog on his face, then he was out on the deck, leaning over the railing and peeking around the side of the cabin, to his right.

And there he was. Slater was about halfway along the walkway, his back to the cabin. He was only half visible in the fog and the quickly dimming light, but he was there all right. And Martin could see that he was moving awkwardly. He was clearly uncomfortable balancing on the side of the boat, but it was more than that. It looked like he was holding his left arm close to his body, and Martin could tell he was favoring his right leg.

Huh, Martin thought. He's actually hurt. I really did shoot him.

And then he looked down at the railing, and saw a couple of dark pools of blood.

Okay, he thought. I can do this.

Martin stepped up onto the walkway as quickly as his shaky legs would let him, and took one side step toward Slater. Then he held the gun out with his right hand—the same posture as Slater's as he stood there in front of him—and pulled the trigger. *Blam.* He heard Slater yell out, and saw a flash as Slater's gun fired toward the front of the boat. Then Martin pulled the trigger one more time. *Blam.* He heard a splash, but he couldn't see anything. The fog was even thicker down there, like it was sitting on the water—or rising up out of it, even. He aimed, and when he heard another splashing sound, he pulled the trigger. But he was out of bullets. *Click,* the gun said. *Click, click, click.*

He stood for a second, not moving, not sure what to think. His head was buzzing with the sound of the gunshots. Then he heard a splash, and another. Right down below him. Martin worried that Slater might shoot at him from the water, but he wasn't sure if this was possible. Were there guns that could shoot when they were wet? He didn't know, and so he jumped back down onto the deck, ducking behind the thick wooden railing and listening as the splashing sounds continued.

Holy shit, he thought. He's not just flailing around. He's swimming. He's heading for the stern—back to the ladder. I thought he couldn't swim very well! What the fuck? Sounds like he swims all right to me.

Martin's first thought was that he'd just lean over the ladder and shoot Slater again (how many bullets could one supercop take before succumbing to mortality?). Then he remembered he was out of ammo.

Jesus Christ, he said. He heard more splashing, and Slater sputtering and making gurgling noises.

But then Martin saw the long metal gaff that he used for grabbing ropes or, sometimes, fishing line. He always liked the feel of it as he did that: I've got this handy tool, and look how nautical I am when I use it. It was snapped into some brackets along the stern, right next to the big fishing net he had secured there (he liked using the net even more).

He pulled the gaff out of the brackets, and turned toward the ladder on the port side of the stern. As he leaned forward, over the railing, he saw Slater. He was a slick-looking shadow in the soupy mass of fog that was clinging to the water. He had just reached the ladder and was hanging on to the bottom rung. He was breathing hard, trying to keep his face out of the surging water. He looked up and made eye contact with Martin.

"Martin," he gasped. He was panting, either from the cold or the gunshot wounds. Or both, maybe.

Martin didn't say anything, just looked down at him. He saw that Slater was struggling to keep his head above the water. He looked pretty bad. He probably couldn't make it up the ladder alone.

Martin took the gaff and lowered it over the railing. Slater sputtered, let go his grip on the ladder with his good arm, and reached up for it. As Slater got ahold of the gaff, Martin pushed down, hard, shoving the gaff into Slater's stomach and forcing him away from the ladder. The move caught Slater by surprise—forced the air out of him, and then pushed him under the water before he could get a breath.

Martin hung on tight with both hands as Slater thrashed around, trying to get clear of the gaff. He could feel the panic on the other end of the pole. But Martin kept the pressure up, leaning on the pole with all his might and following Slater's body as he moved left and then right. Slater's hand broke the water and grabbed the gaff, but there wasn't much strength in his grip.

The gaff bucked in his hands. It was like having a huge fish at the end of his line, but one that had less life in it than you would have thought. Usually this feeling of impending victory was exciting, but here, with Slater under the water, thrashing, it was sickening. But Martin knew he had to do it—knew that if he didn't, Slater would climb up that ladder somehow and kill him. It didn't matter how many bullets he had in him.

He held on and pressed downward as far as he could reach. He leaned into it—put all his weight on top of the pole. He heard himself yelling as he pressed—yelling with fear and horror and maybe a little bit of rage. But mostly fear.

It didn't take much longer. Thirty seconds, maybe a minute. Then there was no movement, just something bulky at the end of the gaff.

A FEW MINUTES LATER he pulled Slater's body to the little wooden platform that jutted out from the stern of the Viking. The gaff had hooked onto a belt loop in his pants (maybe that's why he couldn't get free, Martin thought). He propped Slater's body onto the platform's narrow ledge, then tied him securely to the ladder with a rope he'd grabbed. There was no way Martin could have hauled Slater over the railing and onto the boat. He was literally a dead weight, and with his wet clothes and shoes, forget it.

He went down below, into the cabin, and found what he was looking for: the big five- and six-pound weights that he used for salmon fishing. They were the kind that would take your line way down—forty fathoms, even sixty—to where the big boys were swimming.

It took him over half an hour to attach enough weights to feel confident that Slater would sink and not come up. He had to use sinker wire and fishing line. He threaded the weights onto the wire, and then wrapped the rig around his midsection, and then around his chest, and then his legs. It was hard to do, because he couldn't turn Slater's body over for fear that it would roll off the ledge and into the water. He ended up having to reach way around Slater's torso, and this meant leaning into his body, his face pressing against his stomach and chest.

He tried to work quickly but patiently. He even tied a few weights to Slater's belt loops. But in the end he was shaking with cold and had to settle with what he had. He figured that this would all come undone, eventually, but he hoped that it wouldn't be for a long time. Martin was about to let him go when he remembered Slater's wallet. But he decided to leave it. Maybe when he was finally discovered, it would look like a drug hit of some sort (which it was, at least sort of).

Then, finally, he untied the rope and just pushed him off into the bay. As he watched him disappear into the inky black water, Martin felt a flood of relief. He'd survived. He knew that by all accounts it should have been he who was sinking down into the water tonight. But it wasn't, and for that he was glad—very glad. He'd used his wits, gotten lucky, and survived. There was something to that.

Martin was cold and tired. He knew it was time to start the boat, make his way out of the fog and off the bay. It was time to get home. For starters, he needed to go and see what Slater had done to his house. He had to get it cleaned up so that when he talked Linda into coming home again (and she'd be home eventually, he knew) she wouldn't know what had happened. Maybe he could make a new start now. Not so that they could live happily ever after—he knew better than that. But maybe happily enough, which might just be possible now that he had the money all to himself.

For a confused moment he thought he needed to climb up the ladder of the *O'Brien* to fetch the money. But then he realized that no, his money was tucked safely into the ground out in the orchard behind Miriam Weaver's house. He pictured the orchard—pictured the boys in the neighborhood (minus Peter, of course) running over the top of his little treasure chest during their crazy walnut-war battles. They wouldn't know it was there, but Martin would. He'd have to sneak out there and pull out a lot of it to pay his debts, get the creditors off his back (the forty thousand sitting in the cabin wasn't enough—not even close). But even then there'd be a lot left. A whole lot. He could get rid of Radkovitch once and for all, and wait out the oil embargo—wait out the Saudis and the Iranians and the rest of them. Maybe when Nixon resigned (and he was going to resign; it was just a matter of time) things would change. The big refineries in Martinez and Benicia would still be there, yanking everyone's chains, but maybe the gas lines would disappear and people would start buying airplanes again.

And while he was waiting for the oil to start flowing—for America's lifeblood to start pumping back through its system—he'd just leave the rest of the money where it was. It wouldn't earn any interest out there in the ground, but that wasn't the point. He wouldn't even have to see it, or touch it. Just knowing it was there would be enough.

ACKNOWLEDGMENTS

I would like to thank the following people for their time, patience, and enthusiasm in responding to various drafts of this work: my editor, Kathy Pories; my agent, Michael Strong; and my wife, Erin Anthony.

ERIN ANTHONY

David Anthony grew up in the Bay Area. He is an associate professor of early American literature in the Department of English at SIU-Carbondale. This is his first novel.